Jan Coffey

Triple Threat

Two strangers
race against the
clock to save the
American dream.

Also available from bestselling author

Jan Coffey

and
MIRA® Books

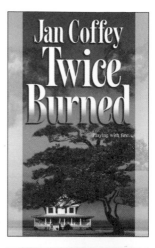

EAN

"What's wrong?" Ellie asked quietly.

"Want to go for a ride?"

Ten minutes ago she would have given Nate a hard time for the suggestion, convinced that he had an ulterior motive. But right now she knew something much more serious was on his mind. "Where are we going?"

He got to his feet and pulled Ellie with him. "We're going to ride by Mr. Teasdale's place."

"He was pretty definite about not wanting to see us until Monday."

"I know. We're not going to drop in for dessert." He gathered up the bottles and the plate from the table. "I'm just going to tell the guys inside we're going off to neck by the lake."

"Don't you dare."

He kissed her and disappeared inside.

Ellie grabbed her sweatshirt off the railing and put it on. She understood how Nate felt. To start with, this job should have been a simple one. No matter how valuable an offered artifact was, whether stolen or legitimately owned, the auctions were generally hyped with more bells and whistles than this one. The secrecy about the whole thing was getting on her nerves. And since they'd started looking for someone to duplicate the flag, there was a feeling of doom hanging over them.

She thought back to when she'd felt this first. It had all started with the SUV heading right for them. In all the years of her life, living in the city, Ellie had never had a car come that close to running her over.

"Are you ready?"

Jan Coffey
Triple Threat

MIRA®

ISBN 1-55166-703-7

TRIPLE THREAT

Copyright © 2003 by Nikoo K. and James A. McGoldrick.

Visit us at www.mirabooks.com

Printed in U.S.A.

To Larry & Gail. You are loved!

One

Fort Ticonderoga, New York
Friday, June 18*

A field trip in the last week of the extended school
year had sounded good when they'd planned it back in
April, but after a full day of loud shrieks, complaints
and tireless bursts of energy, the adults accompanying
the second-graders were now questioning the sanity of
the decision.

Chris Weaver separated himself from the line of
other noisy eight-year-olds and started toward the back
of the waiting area, where his teacher was talking with
one of the museum guides.

"Stay in line," one of the chaperones said wearily,
reaching for him. The boy skipped wide of her and
rushed to Miss Leoni's side.

"And when are they taking the flag?"

"Tomorrow morning, as I understand it. In fact,
we're closing the museum early this afternoon for security reasons. You were lucky to get your class—"

"Miss Leoni?"

"Just a minute, Chris."

The guide glared at Chris when he reached up and
tugged on the teacher's sleeve.

"Wait." She placed a firm hand on his shoulder and returned her attention to the museum worker. "You were saying?"

"You and your class may just be the last group to see the Schuyler flag here. The way things look, we're not even a pit stop on President Kent's Spirit of America celebration tour."

"Have they already told you as much?"

Chris watched the fat guide push his thick glasses up on his nose and glance quickly at the reception desk. "The truth is, we can't get an answer. All we know is that the tour starts next month, and at present we're not on the itinerary."

"But how about when this whole thing is over?"

"You mean after the election?" The man's bushy brows went up meaningfully. "If you ask me..."

Chris crossed his legs and tugged harder on his teacher's sleeve. "Miss Leoni?"

"What is it?" She glared down at him.

"I have to go to the bathroom."

The young teacher bent down until she was at eye level with him. Her voice was reprimanding and low. "Christopher, you were given a chance to go not even fifteen minutes ago. Now we're ready to get on the bus. There is no time. You can wait until we get back to school."

"But I can't wait," he whined.

"Yes, you can. Now, get back to your place in the line," she ordered, straightening up and turning to the museum guide. "Sorry."

"There's one like this in every group."

"Not like this one..."

As he backed away, Chris saw his teacher say something behind her hand to the guy. He didn't have to hang around to know what she was saying. Foster kid. Mother's a drunk. Father's in jail. Living in a car for a month before they found him the last time. He'd heard it all before. The teachers talked about it. The kids and their parents pointed at him like he was a zit ready to pop. But he didn't care what they said. Summer vacation was coming. He could take care of himself.

Right now, though, he had to go to the bathroom.

The waiting area by the glass doors was packed. Kids from one of the other schools were filing onto a bus outside. Glancing toward the doors, Chris figured that their bus would be a while. He looked behind him at the two hallways that came into the waiting area. He tried to remember which one of them led to the small lunchroom. The bathrooms they'd used before were right next to it.

The problem was they'd been in and out of too many darn rooms. After the scavenger hunt in the fort, they'd looked at old newspapers and books and paintings in the museum until he was ready to puke. There'd been some cool swords and guns in one of the rooms, but they wouldn't let him touch anything. And in another one, there was this flag framed inside a glass case. Named after some General Schuyler who used it in the war. Possibly the oldest American flag still around, Chris remembered the fat guide telling them. One of the first ones made by Betsy Ross. Chris had heard about her.

He squirmed and crossed his legs and looked again at the glass doors, hoping it was their turn to go outside. The other school was sending another of their classes ahead of them. He wanted to yell and complain.

But none of the chaperones or Miss Leoni seemed to care.

He didn't want to think about how embarrassing it would be if he wet his pants here. No kid ever dared to make fun of him face-to-face just because nobody wanted to keep him. But peeing in his pants would be something else.

Chris was getting a wicked sharp pain in his side. He knew he wouldn't make it. He decided that the hallway on the left was where they'd seen the room with the flag. Chris thought he'd seen a bathroom near the flag room, and it had to be closer than the lunch area.

He slipped to the back of the waiting area. Miss Leoni was still yapping with the guide. Seeing his chance, Chris turned and ran down the hall. No one called after him, and the voices faded behind him like the end of a TV show.

Halfway down the hall, another corridor joined in on the right. Everything looked the same. Gray flooring, white walls, all kinds of framed pictures and display cases, rooms opening up on either side. Suddenly, he wasn't sure which way it was to where the flag was.

Panic gripped him as he started to go in his pants a little. Chris grabbed himself and ran down another hall. By an emergency exit door at the far end, there was another smaller sign that he couldn't see. The school nurse had given him a note to take home about needing glasses, but Chris had lost it. It might be a bathroom, he thought, running toward it.

Just then, a woman hurried out of a room on the left, and Chris had to let go of his crotch. She looked quickly up and down the hallway before focusing on him. Chris slowed down and glanced over his shoulder at the empty hallway. She wasn't wearing one of those badges that people who worked here wore. As she came toward him, though, Chris told himself he hadn't done anything wrong.

She was young and kind of pretty with short dark hair, but had that uptight look about her that Miss Leoni had a couple minutes ago when she'd been scolding him. Just then, the bag she was carrying over one shoulder started to ring, and she reached in and pulled out her phone.

Chris stuffed his hands in his pants pockets and moved quickly toward the sign, hoping it was a bathroom.

As he approached her, he could hear the woman talking fast.

"Yes…no…three o'clock…can't talk. Bye."

They were right next to each other, and he hugged the wall as he hurried past her.

"Are you lost?"

She was talking to him, but he pretended she wasn't and quickened his steps. His underwear was starting to stick in certain places. If he stopped, he was a goner.

"Where are you going?"

He started to run when she reached out for him. But the stupid stick figure picture on the door to his right came too late. By the time Chris threw himself against it and rushed in, the pee was running down his leg. His face burned with embarrassment, and he rushed into a stall. He didn't want someone coming in seeing him like this at a urinal.

His pants smelled wicked. Even his socks were wet. Pulling down his briefs, Chris sat on the toilet and finished. He felt sick, and his chin started to quiver. He didn't want to cry, though. Only babies cried.

This wasn't his fault. He never waited to the last minute. But there was this astronaut food Allison had bought at the gift shop, and when everyone else was using the bathroom, she'd been showing it to him. Chris didn't know how it tasted, but he'd been thinking how perfect this stuff would have been for his mother and him when they were living in the back seat of the old Dodge Dart. No need to cook it or put it in the fridge, Allison said. It didn't take much space, and you could keep it for a hundred years.

Chris plunked his head of dirty-blond hair on his hands and tried to swallow the knot in his throat. He was eight years old, and he couldn't remember when was the last time he'd peed in his pants. There were no portable johns near the Dodge Dart. He'd learned to do his business from nine in the morning to nine at night in the old railroad station, two streets away from the lot where the car was parked. If he'd had to go anytime after that, then it was tough luck.

His pants were wet now, though, and he knew he was going to have a hard time explaining it to Mrs. Green, his latest foster mother.

The PA speaker on the ceiling crackled to life, startling him. "The museum is now closed. Remaining visitors must exit by way of the..."

Chris jumped to his feet. Taking fistfuls of toilet paper, he wiped his legs. His underwear was a mess. Peeling off his pants and underpants, he tried to flush the briefs down the toilet. When he pushed down the lever a second time, the water backed up in the toilet fast and flowed over.

"Jeez!"

Standing in the running water, he pulled his wet

pants back on, opened the stall door, and carefully tip-toed through the flood.

The kids would laugh at him. No one would want to sit next to him on the bus going back. Chris went to the sink. Using a few sheets of paper towel, he tried to dry the front of his pants the best he could. If he could only get rid of the smell, maybe they'd believe him if he said he got water on himself when he was washing his hands.

He came out of the bathroom feeling beaten. The hallway was quiet, and they'd shut off every other light. The woman was gone. His shoes made funny squishing sounds on the tile floor.

Lies bounced around in Chris's head. He could say he slipped and fell in a puddle in the washroom. Or the sink faucet was busted and soaked the front of his pants when he turned it on. Chris stuck his hands in his pockets, ballooning them out, hoping they'd dry out a little by the time the bus showed up.

As he passed the opening to the room on his right—the one the lady had come out of—he thought he heard a sound from inside. He paused in the doorway. The room with the old flag. He remembered what the guide had been telling Miss Leoni about their class being the last one to see this thing here. He looked at the faded red and white stripes. He stared at the circle of stars and moved closer to count them.

That was when he saw it. A small, funny-looking gadget stuck to the bottom edge of the wooden frame around the flag. He moved closer and stared at it. A little box of some shiny things and a tiny digital watch held together with black tape. The whole thing was stuck to the frame with something that looked like chewed-up gum. Chris was sure it wasn't here the first time they'd come through. He'd been standing in the same place he was standing now. It definitely wasn't there before.

It looked like something from a spy movie, and he reached up to pull it off.

''Don't touch it.''

Two

"The flag is totally destroyed and there's nothing we can do about it. What's important now is to put the rest of this situation in context."

Sanford Hawes planted his mitt-size hands on the conference table of the Fort Ticonderoga Museum. His shoulders were hunched. The FBI assistant director's broken nose—easily the dominant feature of his rugged face—was beet red. Piercing dark eyes peered through bifocal lenses at individual faces around the table. He had their attention.

"This recession has been dogging us all for some time now. The unemployment rate is at a ten-year high. People are out of jobs, and a lot of folks who still have jobs feel disgruntled with their own situation. Added to that, we've got cable and network news shows flashing pictures of ten thousand American flags being burned all over the world this past Tuesday." His heavy frame leaned forward. "As a country, we cannot afford this disaster with the Schuyler flag to get out. That's the bottom line."

A dozen people—firefighters, police officers and Department of the Interior museum employees—sat around the oblong table. The door was closed. The venetian blinds on the long windows were shut.

As Hawes finished talking, Nate Murtaugh leaned over and spread one of the blinds with his fingers. He peered at the news camera crews from Albany waiting on the sidewalk outside. Still here. Instincts like a pack of wolves. Turning his back to the window, Nate tried to settle his six-foot-three frame more comfortably in the swivel chair. He jotted down some notes on a pad of paper he was balancing on his bum knee.

Eric Wilcox, director of artifacts at the Smithsonian Institution National Museum, sat forward in his chair. "Gentlemen and ladies, this could be the straw that breaks the camel's back when it comes to the nation's morale." Wilcox tapped the table nervously with his pen and looked up at Hawes. Receiving a curt nod from the assistant director, he charged on. "The Spirit of America celebration is a huge undertaking, unlike anything ever attempted by any past U.S. president. In the scope of its planning, this far exceeds the bicentennial celebration, in fact. In bringing so many of our country's national artifacts together, President Kent hopes to once again unite this country with a common purpose. He is trying to reinforce that bond that we share as Americans, the sense of purpose that overarches all differences of race, class or ethnic heritage. Regardless of restlessness and hostility elsewhere, he refuses to allow us to become a country divided against ourselves. We are all Americans, and we need to rededicate ourselves to the ideals these artifacts represent."

Nate cursed silently as he banged his knee for a second time against the chair next to him. Downing the last of his coffee, he tossed the foam cup into the nearby wastebasket.

Wilcox continued to quote from the president's speech from last fall. Nate had heard it firsthand on the September 11 anniversary last year in New York, and too often in media clips since then. The government would spend a billion or so and bring things like the Schuyler flag, the Liberty Bell, the Declaration of Independence, George Washington's sword, Abe Lincoln's law book, Martin Luther King Jr.'s Bible, and tons of other stuff together in Philadelphia on July 4 and then send it all on a month-long national tour— with the president leading the parade.

Nice. The concept was darn good. Even the patriotic underpinnings had value. But Nate was too jaded to overlook the coincidence that this was all happening in an election year. He glanced up at the hatchet-faced director of artifacts. Those on the inside knew that Wilcox had been the originator of the idea. But the White House was taking the full credit for it. It was just the responsibility of the bookworm to put the collection together. Nate's feeling was that they should have gotten Steven Spielberg or the guys from Disney to do it. But what did he know? He was just an FBI agent.

The air-conditioning made the conference room feel like about ten above. Still, when Wilcox stopped talking, he took out a handkerchief and wiped the beads of sweat from his bony forehead.

Hawes stood up again. "From our preliminary investigations, it's clear that the fire that occurred here yesterday was a professional job. The remnants of the incendiary device on the flag's case and the disabling of the security cameras in the room both point to this. What we don't know at this point is whether or not the incident was the act of a terrorist organization, though we have notified Homeland Security."

Nate was relieved to have the assistant director take charge again. Thirty-two open cases had been wiped off his New York desk with one quick sweep yesterday, and he was ready to get down to business. In spite of the fact that they had been ready to spring the trap on a high-profile brokerage firm's CEO who was trying to hide income through some foreign art transactions, Nate had left behind the four special agents in his group and flown out of LaGuardia last night on an hour's notice. Sanford Hawes acknowledged the well-groomed man sitting beside him at the head of the table.

"Chief Buckley and your police department are diligently working on the case, and they might even have a witness," Hawes explained. "The decision regarding how to proceed with the press, though, has been issued from the top. That is why we have brought you in here. We cannot afford, at this time, to admit that the Schuyler flag has been burned. We cannot let the perpetrators know that they have succeeded. The world is watching, and if it becomes public that this artifact—a focal item in this Spirit of America celebration—has been damaged, we will be seeing not only the group responsible for this attack, but similar terrorist groups, as well, targeting other items."

Police Chief Buckley leaned forward, stabbing the table with his index finger as he addressed the police officers and firefighters who had been directly involved with the flag-room fire. "This is a presidential gag order. When these reporters ask, you say you put out a fire in a trash can. Some smoke damage to the ceilings, but there was no damage to anything else in the room. Understood? This is the same thing that I said in the press conference last night, and you will simply refer any more questions to my office. That's all.''

Nate looked at the faces of those around the table. None seemed adversely affected by the directive.

The director of the Fort Ticonderoga Museum raised her hand, looking at Wilcox. ''The Schuyler flag was to be the backdrop of the entire ceremony. How are you going to explain it when it's missing?''

''That is a separate matter that we'll remedy before the start of the celebration.''

A heavyset museum guide snorted. ''Since President Kent made the announcement last fall about this patriotic road show, we've had a dozen guys—experts and pseudo experts—coming in here and poring over that flag. You won't be able to stick in some forgery. And if the press got hold of *that*—''

''We have no intention,'' Wilcox sputtered, ''of anything so underhanded as to use a forgery in a celebration of our heritage.''

Hawes held up his hand, cutting off the National Museum director. ''We have nothing of the sort in mind, sir. Do you really think we would try anything so lacking in integrity?''

The museum guide flushed. ''Well, no…I…''

''I am obliged to tell you, however, that the legal consequences of anyone failing to comply with this security directive are severe.'' Hawes smiled, baring tiger's teeth. ''But I know that it's unnecessary to even bring up such matters. Working with such a group as this, I am certain we will prevail in our efforts to comply with the President's wishes. And on behalf of the President, I can say that the nation thanks you all for your loyalty and professionalism.''

Hawes looked around the table before fixing his gaze

on the local museum director. "As far as what the replacement flag will be and where it will come from,
that's something Dr. Wilcox and the FBI are working
on. We have already taken what is left of your flag into
our custody. All you need to tell any reporter who asks
is that the Schuyler flag has been handed over, as
scheduled, to Dr. Wilcox at the Smithsonian in preparation for the celebration on the Fourth of July."

The words and the tone were convincing enough.
Nate watched the portly museum worker laugh self-
consciously at some crack by one of the firefighters
about what they could really say to the reporters.

Nate knew finding another flag was where he came
in. He and Wilcox and Hawes were supposed to meet
after this call-for-solidarity meeting and go over the
specifics. Apparently, the artifacts director had something up his sleeve.

There were no other questions, so the non-law-
enforcement personnel were dismissed. The handful of
police officers stayed behind to discuss the possible
witness. A young officer handed out a fact sheet and a
photo.

Nate leafed through the manila folder beneath his
writing pad and found the additional information he'd
been given before the meeting.

Christopher Weaver. Eight years old. Male Cauca-
sian. Forty-four inches tall. Sixty-five pounds. Light
brown hair. Brown eyes. A second-grader at Washington Elementary School. Reported missing after the
class field trip to the fort and museum yesterday afternoon. The museum security cameras' timed shots of
the hallway outside the flag room were a positive match
with the boy's pictures on file with the Department of
Child Services. Nate thumbed through the attached

pages. Domestic disaster. Foster homes. Runaway. Tons of history.

The report read that after separating from his classmates yesterday, Christopher had vandalized a bathroom. After doing some damage there, he'd walked across the hall to the flag room and then run off by way of a back exit door.

Nate looked closely at the school picture of the boy. A good imitation of a tough look, but there was vulnerability behind the brown eyes.

The officer who'd passed out the fact sheet spoke. "We've already checked all his usual hangouts. We have a cruiser sitting by the trailer park where the mother dropped anchor a couple of weeks ago with a new boyfriend. There's been no sign of him."

"As you requested," Chief Buckley said to Hawes, "publicly we're treating these incidents as separate. There's been no connection made with the fire. As far as the school and the teachers are concerned, he left the museum but never boarded the bus. And he's a chronic runaway. Everyone figures he'll probably show up in a day or two—a week, tops—like he always does."

Nate thumbed through the manila folder and checked Christopher's age again.

"You're dealing with an eight-year-old," he said. Everyone turned around and looked at him, as if noticing his presence for the first time. The chair creaked when Nate shifted his weight in it to face the police chief. "This is still a missing child. The perps responsible for the fire could very well have grabbed the boy. Are we considering the possibility that this Christopher Weaver might be at risk?"

"Of course we are," Buckley answered immediately. "But as you can see for yourself, Agent Murtaugh, his footprints show him leaving the room, and we have his fingerprints on the door where he exited the building. Naturally, we want to know if he saw anything that could shed some light, but there is also the strong possibility that the device was planted much earlier." The chief looked at Hawes for support as he continued. "And you have to remember that this kid has a record of delinquent behavior. He runs away all the time."

"But what if this time is different?" Nate asked, staring at the man's perfectly groomed hair and crisp uniform. Buckley obviously came ready for a press conference. "What if there is foul play involved here? I mentioned the possibility of abduction by the perpetrators, but let's forget about the flag and the fire for a minute. How about parental abduction? Hasn't the state declared both of them unfit? Has anyone checked to see if the father is still in prison? Isn't there a possibility that after he left the building some deviate off the state highway picked him up and—"

"We know the drill, Agent Murtaugh," Chief Buckley snapped. "And yes, we've gone through *all* of it."

Nate was ready to press the police chief for more, but he caught the "let the damn thing go" look Hawes was fixing him with. Clearly, he was stepping on the chief's toes, and the fire and the boy were not specifically part of the task he had been assigned. Nate shrugged, letting the subject drop—for now.

Eleven years ago, Sanford Hawes had been Nate's first special agent in charge when he'd started with the FBI. If there were any good old days that he could recall of his years with the Bureau, those first four years of reporting to Sanford had been it. Tough as reinforced concrete, the big guy also had that touch of humanity and loyalty that you rarely found in the guys on the fast track. As a SAC, Hawes worked his guys to the bone, but he had common sense, too. Nate and the others trusted his judgment and would have followed him to the gates of hell, if he'd asked. It was the memory of those days that shut Nate up now.

A quick summation followed, and Hawes ended the meeting.

Nate remained in his seat while Buckley's people pushed out of the room. From the folder, he jotted down the name and address of Sharon Green, identified as Christopher's current foster mother. As he was writing, the same police officer who'd passed out the fact sheets approached him.

"I'm leaning your way, Agent Murtaugh," he said in a hushed voice. At the head of the conference table, Hawes and Buckley were doing a postmortem on the meeting. "I don't think things are as cut-and-dried as we'd like them to be."

Nate looked at the young man's name tag. "If you could use some help, Officer McGill, just let me know. That's what we're here for."

"Call me Tom." He threw a hesitant glance over his shoulder at his superior. "I'm still fairly new at the job, and I don't want to shoot myself in the foot. If you happen to drop by the station, though, I'd like to show you what I've got on the boy and see if any of it makes any sense."

Nate rose stiffly to his feet and shook the officer's hand. "I'll do that. Hold on a second," he said, scribbling his cell phone number on his pad. He tore the piece off the page and handed it to the young cop. "In case you need to get hold of me."

As McGill left, Nate saw that Hawes was watching him. His left knee was rusty as an old gate hinge, but he refused to let the assistant director see him hobbling around. Making sure he didn't favor his bum leg, Nate turned to the window and looked through the blinds again at the reporters who appeared to be camped out permanently on the sidewalk. They were more like vultures than wolves, and they all clearly smelled something nasty. He glanced over his shoulder at Eric Wilcox. The artifacts director was talking into his cell phone and taking notes furiously in the corner of the room. He sure as hell hoped the man had an ace up his sleeve.

Hawes closed the conference room door behind the police chief. Seeing Wilcox still on the phone, he crossed the room to Nate. "How's the knee?"

"Good as new. Coffee?" Nate walked to the table in the corner to get himself another cup.

"Still looks stiff to me," the older man said, joining him there and pouring a cup for himself.

Nate refused to talk about it. Following two knee surgeries and four months of physical therapy after being shot, he'd ended up with a bum leg and a promotion that had taken him out of the field and shoved him behind a desk.

"How's the new job?"

"Stinks."

"I thought so." Hawes took a sip of the scalding coffee.

"How do you do it, Sanford?" Nate asked. "How do you deal with all the bureaucratic bullshit and ass-kissing that goes along with it?"

"Mouthwash." Hawes flashed his big teeth. "Thought you'd like a break. Are you up for the job?"

"What's to be up for?"

Hawes shot an impatient glance in the direction of the artifacts director. "Dr. Smithsonian over there has identified another flag made about the same time as the one that was burned."

"Private collection?"

"Yeah. And more closely linked to George Washington than this one."

"How's that?"

"There was a guy named Robert Morris who practically financed the whole American Revolution. Signed the Declaration of Independence and everything. Story is that Washington gave this other flag to Morris after the revolution. Wilcox claims this flag may be the first one that Betsy Ross delivered."

"I thought that Betsy Ross stuff was all a myth." Nate cast an incredulous look at the tall thin man with the phone growing out of his ear. "How come nobody knows about this other flag, then?"

"Apparently, quite a few collector types *do* know and *have* known about it for some time." He gestured to the museum director to cut it short. "We can both hear all the particulars as soon as he gets off the goddamn phone."

From the tone of the conversation, it sounded as if Wilcox was wrapping up the call. Nate sat down next to his superior at the conference table. "How about the weave and wear of the two flags? That museum guide had a point. How is Wilcox going to substitute one flag for the other?"

"I don't think there'll be any need. We come up with the original Betsy Ross flag, and nobody will care about this one."

"Do we know who has the flag?"

"No. That's where you come in. Wilcox is supposed to get us some leads on who had it last and where they kept it." Hawes's voice turned low and confidential. "This operation has to be discreet. No publicity. Your job is to find the flag. I don't care if you buy or steal it, but you will bring it back in under fifteen days. This thing's got to be in Philadelphia on the Fourth of July for President Kent's kickoff of this Spirit of America thing."

"So this might be as simple as approaching the present owners and convincing them to loan it to us for the length of the president's tour." Nate swiveled his chair toward Wilcox, who had just joined them. "This doesn't look like a Bureau job. Sounds to me like you'd be much better off using some artsy society diplomat type."

"I'm afraid things aren't as simple as they look, Agent Murtaugh." Wilcox opened his briefcase and took out a file more than three inches thick, held together by a couple of thick rubber bands. "This is only a sampling of the work special agents at the Department of the Interior have done over the past ten years chasing this flag. You've told him the details?"

"As much as I know," Hawes said.

"How do we know this is the real thing?" Nate asked.

"The authenticity of the claim is supported by one entry in a letter from Robert Morris's personal manservant. The letter refers to the flag as George Washington's gift to the financier," Wilcox explained.

"Why has this never made the news?"

"Because the flag immediately disappeared after it was found on one of the Morris descendants' properties back in the late eighties. Apparently, it was sold to a private collector.'' Wilcox slid the file across the width of the conference table to Nate. ''I had just joined the Department of the Interior at the time of the find. We got wind of it then, but the decision was made to keep it out of the news since we had nothing to show for the discovery, anyway.''

Nate opened the file. ''How can you be sure that the whole thing wasn't a hoax? You said there was no verification of its authenticity.''

''We have a report of the flag changing hands six years ago for twenty-five million dollars.'' Wilcox reached across the table and pointed to a tab on the folder. ''Serious collectors don't put that many zeros on their checks for a fake.''

Nate opened up to the marked page and looked at the name. ''Does this guy have it now?''

''Unfortunately, no. What we've found out is that the flag has changed hands at least twice since then, but as to the identity of the buyers or how much they paid for it...'' Wilcox shrugged.

Nate didn't even bother to ask why the ball was dropped. The flag wasn't stolen property, and after the September 11 disaster in 2001, all the federal agencies had gone through some serious overhaul, especially the FBI. In that climate, keeping an eye on something merely for the sake of its potential historical interest definitely took a back seat to tracking down terrorists.

''This flag could be anywhere in the world,'' Hawes snapped at the artifacts director. ''And we have barely two weeks left. How the hell could you promise the President that we'd find the thing when we have no leads?''

''But we do have leads...or I think we do.'' Wilcox took a small pad of paper out of his pocket. ''My con-

tacts in the private sector tell me that there's been a
rumor going around for a week or so about an original
Betsy Ross flag coming up for auction again. Soon.''

''Well, that simplifies things, anyway,'' Hawes
grumbled. ''We're authorized to pay whatever is necessary to get it. When and where is the auction?''

Wilcox pushed the wire-rimmed glasses up the
bridge of his long, thin nose and reached into his
pocket again, this time for the handkerchief. ''This is
the sticky part, I'm afraid. These private auctions are
only attended by invitation. Certainly you know how
the art world works, Agent Murtaugh. Because of
the…ah, shady backgrounds of some of these collectors, a representative of the U.S. government would
definitely be persona non grata.''

Nate leaned back in the chair and listened without
interest to Hawes chewing Wilcox's ass over how the
museum director was going to get Nate on the list of
bidders for this auction. Going undercover had its appeal, but acting like some rich art collector just to buy
a flag wasn't exactly Nate's idea of getting back in the
field. Still, remembering the piles of paperwork and
reports on his desk, he told himself it was a start.

Wilcox was thumbing through his notes and successfully avoiding eye contact with the FBI assistant
director. When Hawes took a breath, Wilcox jumped
in.

''The only way to go about this is to have the right
people recommend him. There is a network of dealers
involved here, and it is not a large community. Everyone knows everyone. The whole business—that is, collecting in the private sector—is about so-and-so knowing so-and-so, who tells their cousin or therapist, who
tells a dealer about some guy with money who is look-

ing for a certain property. There are corporate buyers who occasionally work their way into the network, but they, too, need a reference." Wilcox paused. "Of course, most artifacts of American history with any significant value are bought and sold only by members of the 'good old boys' network."

"We need names, Wilcox," Hawes barked. "Someone we can squeeze. We need a place where Nate can start."

"I know that." Wilcox looked at his notes again. "My people have come up with a name of a former art dealer who served time in prison for her involvement in her late husband's fraudulent operations. She's back on the street again and, as far as we can tell, is very well connected and respected in the community."

"What's the name?" Hawes asked.

"You should know," Wilcox answered quietly. "You were the one who put her behind bars."

Hawes thought for a moment. "Helen Doyle. The last time I saw her, she'd become a nun. She was out of that business."

"She is out of the business, and she's still a nun. But she's still connected. Sister Helen is the only person we have right now who might be able to refer us to the right people."

Three

The grillwork and wrought-iron railings effectively set off the solid facade of redbrick and white trim. The classical doorway, with its graceful arch and fan-shaped glasswork above, added an air of distinction to the colonial look. Like a lot of the houses and shops along Pine Street, the building dated back to around 1770.

Ellie Littlefield had her Early Americana antique shop on the street level. The second floor consisted of an art studio with separate spaces that she rented out to struggling artists and friends. She lived in an apartment on the third level, beneath the sloping eaves. A large balcony, shaded by the top branches of a century-old oak, looked out over the tiny backyard of her building and that of a home being renovated on the next street.

The house had all the quirky annoyances that an eighteenth-century building would normally have—plumbing that could be downright ornery, drafty windows and the occasional rat in the basement—but Ellie worshipped this little gem of a home that she'd been the proud owner of for almost six years. To her, everything about the place was perfect—except for the steep, narrow stairs.

"The bitch is too wide. Go back up a step. Wait, I'm stuck."

"Relax, Victor! Just follow my lead. We're almost at the bottom. Lift this side off the railing," Ellie ordered from five steps up. She put a slim shoulder under the upper end of the mirror's frame and lifted.

"Wait…Christ!" Victor complained when the entire weight of the mahogany-framed monster slid down across his sculpted biceps and muscled chest. "You just scratched the wall."

"Don't worry about the wall, Vic. Lift your end." Ellie gasped, resting the frame partially on top of her head and trying not to collapse under the weight. "I can't hold on to this thing much longer. Come on, back down a step."

Victor inched the frame up onto his chest and went back down a step. "Wait, it's still scratching the wall."

The bell inside the shop door rang.

"Then tilt it. Come on, another step."

"Somebody's at the door."

"We're closed. They'll see the sign and go away."

The bell rang again.

"Maybe they can't read."

"Another step. We're almost there." Ellie felt the sweat trickling down her face and arms as Victor lifted the massive thing and followed her direction. "Great. Don't forget, at the bottom of the stairs turn right."

"It's a he."

Ellie groaned when Vic turned left toward the door instead of right, wedging her painfully between the mirror and the wall with the railing digging sharply into her hip. "I said turn right...right."

"Your right or my right? He's a hunk. A suit hunk!"

"Vic!" she cried painfully. Her fingers couldn't hold on to the weight anymore, and she let the corner of the mirror rest on the hand railing. The fifteen-foot stretch of railing gave only a slight creak before popping out of the wall and crashing down on the steps. The mirror and Ellie crashed right down next to it.

The bell rang again.

"You let it go." Victor complained from around the corner. "It's bad luck breaking a mirror. Did you break it?"

"No, I didn't break it," Ellie snapped, fisting and unfisting her fingers, thankful that none of them had been crushed under the weight of the thing.

"Look at what you've done." Victor's horrified face appeared over the mirror after he put his end down. Despite the exertion, the young man had not broken a sweat, and Ellie wondered how was it that she was covered with dust and dirt, and he looked as if he'd just stepped out of some calendar centerfold. "Now, if you'd listened to me and waited until this afternoon, then I would've had Brian and—"

The sound of persistent knocking tore his attention away. She saw him wave at someone. "Who's there?"

"The same one. The suit. He wants to come in."

"Too bad. We're closed." She stood up in the cramped space and wiped her dirty hands on the butt of her jeans. "Help me get this down, will you?"

"He's motioning to me."

"Victor!" Ellie called louder. "It's nine in the morning on a Sunday. We don't open before noon. Ignore him. He'll go away."

She knew her words were landing on deaf ears when he bit the end of one gloved hand and then the next. Victor put the gloves on the top ledge of the mirror.

"Damn, I broke a nail." He looked from his fingers back toward the door. "He probably got lost on his way to church. I'll be back in a minute."

Ellie let out a deep sigh of frustration. Putting her shoulder to the edge of the mirror, she made a weak attempt to push it down the stairs on her own. It wouldn't move an inch.

She sat back down on the stair. She'd have to wait for Vic. A third-generation Italian with a sculpted face and the body of a model, at five-foot-five Victor Desposito had been told he was too short to make it in the fashion business, but he was a treasured friend and an invaluable employee. In addition to having plenty of brain and brawn, he also did an excellent job of running Ellie's business and even, sometimes, her life.

Victor's only flaw was that he was helpless when it came to tall hunks in suits.

Some motorcycle driver on Pine Street, deciding on that moment to test the decibel level of his or her engine, drowned out the intruder's conversation with Victor. Ellie wiped at a scratch mark on the frame and leaned down to make sure there was no damage to the thick beveled glass.

She'd asked Victor to come over early this morning to help her with some rearranging in the shop. When it came to tourists and spending money, this year's Fourth of July was supposed to see the largest crowds Philadelphia had ever seen. To gear up for it, Ellie had gone farther afield for inventory, and she'd definitely hit more than her share of auctions these past couple of months. The collections in her packed front and rear showrooms were a testimony to her efforts. The problem was, though, that there was no room left to breathe, never mind to walk around the shop. Opening up her back storage room to the customers was the only solution Ellie had been able to come up with. But with no windows, she had to rely on temporary track lights and this monster of a mirror to brighten the space.

The four-by-six mirror had been hanging in the second-floor studio when she'd bought the house. Beveled glass, steel backing, mahogany frame...now she understood why the last owner had been so generous in leaving the pricey item behind. The damn thing weighed a ton.

Ellie caught her reflection in the mirror and cringed. No shower, no makeup. A smudge of dust staining her left cheek. At least she was thankful for the baseball cap covering her short mop of black hair. Taking a second look, she decided that in the sleeveless T and jeans shorts, she could pass for a twelve-year-old at a Philly game, though she'd have a hard time proving she was the same sophisticated antique dealer who had been invited to co-chair—alongside Main Line socialite Augusta Biddle—the Children's Hospital Celebrity Auction next Thursday night. The thought of moving in those circles sent a small tingle of pleasure up her arms, and she let herself bask in the glow of everything that had been going right in her life these past few months.

The ringing of Victor's cell phone jarred Ellie out of her reverie. She remembered him putting it next to his keys on a side table at the bottom of the stairs. A second later, he appeared and snatched it up.

"He wants to talk to *you!*" he whispered, shaking

one hand and mouthing "hot" before going toward the rear of the shop.

"Victor, get me out of here," Ellie called after him. Getting no response, she pushed herself to her feet and made another futile attempt at shoving the mirror out of her way. From what she could hear, Victor had already started another one of his ongoing arguments with his mother. Mrs. Desposito, after a recent trip to Rome, had elevated her denial of her son being gay to wanting to find him a wife.

Ellie remembered the person by the open front door. She pressed her back against the wall and was about to attempt climbing over the mirror when a dark gray suit filled the bottom of the staircase.

As she felt the old-and-familiar sensation of her hackles rising at the back of her neck, she had no doubt about what she was dealing with. If this guy wasn't a cop, then she couldn't tell the pope from a potato. Instinctively Ellie retreated, climbing up a step to where she was at eye level with him.

"Need a hand?"

She stared down at the large hand extended in her direction. She shook her head. "What can I do for you, Officer?"

The hand slowly withdrew. She forced herself to look up past the wide shoulders into his face. Intense blue eyes. Short brown hair, brushed back. A bump on his nose where it must have been broken at one time. A small scar on his cleft chin. The button-down white shirt and a dark tie and suit completed the effect. All in all, a nicely weathered and conservative package. To anyone else, he could have been an insurance salesman or a political lobbyist. For her, his looks only reaffirmed what her instincts had told her right off. She was looking at an intelligent, macho, former athlete turned cop. Taller than the usual flatfoot, though. Definitely Victor's style.

"I'm not a police officer."

"If you say so."

He ignored her, turning a critical eye on the demolition site on the stairs. "Doing a little remodeling here?"

"Looks that way." Her instincts were never wrong, and she wasn't about to make small talk. "Listen, we're running a little behind, so if you aren't here in some *official* capacity, then I'm going to have to ask you to leave. The store is closed. You can come back at noon."

His blue eyes turned hard when he looked into her face. "Are you this friendly with all your potential customers, or is it just me?"

Ellie wasn't going to make this personal. She had good reason to distrust the police—her history was full of good reasons—and this guy was not giving her any cause to be nice to him.

"I'm afraid my charm-school training doesn't kick in until twelve noon. That's when the store will open. You can come back then if you want." She looked over at Vic, who was still talking on his phone. Ellie moved down a step and started to climb over the mirror.

He didn't ask this time, but took hold of her elbow and helped her over. "Are you sure you don't need a hand in moving the mirror?"

"No, thanks. This is exactly where I wanted it." His grip was like steel, and she pulled her arm away, trying not to rely on his help but only managing to stumble against him at the bottom of the stairs.

"It'll be one hell of a show watching you maneuver up and down the stairs a couple times a day."

He was even taller and broader now that she was on his level. And she wasn't about to be taken in by the crooked half smile. Ellie couldn't wait to get rid of him.

"Well, it can only get easier from now on. So if you don't mind?" She motioned toward the door, expecting him to go. He turned and sauntered to one of the glass cases.

"You have an impressive collection here." He bent over and looked at some of her rare Early Americana books.

"They look a lot better with the lights on. We turn them on at noon."

"America's First Conscientious Objectors," he said, reading the tag on one of the books. "Isn't this one about the Philadelphia Quakers who were held in the Mason's Lodge before being exiled to Virginia?"

"First edition, second issue, and the price is five hundred fifty dollars." She crossed her arms, leaning a shoulder against the open door, not wanting to be impressed with the fact that he'd recognized the book.

"Can I see it?"

"Yes, at noon."

"I won't be available then."

"We're open until five."

"That's not good for me, either."

"We have extended hours during the week."

"I'm afraid not." He gave her a cool glance and moved down the glass case. "You know, I'm pretty sure your attitude can't do much good for your business."

"Actually, I have no problem attracting customers. In fact, business is very good," she said arrogantly.

"Then it must be me."

"You said it, not me."

"Okay. Tell me how to do it right."

"I suggest that you call in ahead and make an appointment for a mutually convenient time with my assistant, Victor Desposito, whom you met when you came barging in here." Ellie glanced at Vic, who was standing with his back to them, the phone still attached to his ear. "Victor will be more than happy to spend whatever—"

"I'd like to make that appointment with you."

Ellie bit back her immediate urge to refuse. "Whatever. If there is something that Victor can't help you with, we could always arrange a time when you can meet with me and my attitude. Now, if you don't mind…"

"Is your collection limited to what is in these showrooms, Ms. Littlefield?"

"How is it that you know my name, Officer—pardon me, *Mr.*—by the way, may I see some identification?"

He straightened, but instead of looking at her, he went around another glass display case. "My name is Nate Murtaugh. And I know your name from this." He picked up one of her business cards from the top of the glass case. "And do you ask for an ID from all your customers?"

"Only the ones who insist on coming in when we're closed."

"Fair enough." He reached into his pocket, took out his wallet and opened it. He placed it on the glass case. Even without picking it up, she could see it contained a New York driver's license. "I assume you also want to check the limit on my credit card before we go any further.''

A middle-aged couple walking down the street appeared in the open door and started inside. Ellie made some quick excuses and told them to come back at noon, closing the door and reluctantly trapping herself inside.

''Look, Mr. Murtaugh, I'm very busy,'' she said in as controlled a tone as she could manage. ''Why don't we just cut the nonsense and get down to why you're here and what you want?''

''Do you ever do any consulting work, Ms. Little-field?''

Finally they were getting somewhere. She walked to the other side of the glass case and took a good look at the address on his license. She pushed the wallet toward him.

''What kind of consulting?'' she asked cautiously. ''Appraising?''

''No, what I'm looking for is your expertise *and* your connections. I need to find a specific item that falls within the area of Americana.''

She planted her elbows on the glass and leaned toward him. ''Do you mean 'specific' like a certain edition of some book, or 'specific' like the only copy of it left?''

''The only copy left. But I'm not talking about a book.''

''One-of-a-kind items have a way of finding a home and being perfectly happy in them. And unless the present owner has made known that he or she is willing to part with this specific item, then you're wasting your time.''

"But you will be able to identify the who and where."

That prickly feeling on her neck became more distinct. "I'm afraid not."

Many priceless antiques, including stolen or smuggled artifacts, were held by collectors who preferred to remain nameless and faceless. These people believed that laws against the antiquities trade were designed to be violated rather than enforced. And there were many different government and insurance agencies that existed solely to prove this privileged lot wrong. Ellie considered involvement with either group an occupational hazard she would rather do without.

"Mr. Murtaugh," she said in a low voice, looking up into the man's steely blue eyes. "I'm not an informant, and I am certainly not as connected in the collectors' universe as you seem to think. I'm just a shop owner like the other dozen or so lining this block. I don't break any laws. I don't trade in stolen goods. In terms of expertise, I'm afraid my knowledge is limited to what I regularly buy and sell in the shop. In so many words, what you see is what I've got." She took a breath, told herself to stay calm and sound rational. She could not push him out with force, but maybe reason would work. "I don't know what or who convinced you to come in here, as opposed to any of the other shops on Pine Street, but the fact remains I may be the least qualified to help you with your problems. If you'd like me to refer you to someone else—"

"Ms. Littlefield…"

Ellie held up a hand. "That's the best I can do. I have a lot to do before we open at noon, so you're going to have to leave."

The wallet disappeared inside his pocket. Ellie busied herself straightening the stack of business cards as he came around the display case and headed toward the door. Vic was sitting in a Windsor chair by the window, listening to his mother on the phone. Ellie was very relieved that Murtaugh was leaving. He stopped with his hand on the door and turned around.

"Maybe you would answer one last question." He didn't wait for her to speak. "Don't worry, I wouldn't ask you to give away any of your friends."

Ellie wasn't rising to his bait. She watched him reach inside the pocket of his jacket and take out a picture.

"Would you just tell me if you've seen this boy?"

"What boy?" She approached him and took the small photo he held out to her.

"A missing eight-year-old."

Ellie stared at the picture. "'Missing' as in the system lost him, or 'missing' as in his family is looking for him?"

"The system is all he's got. And he's been reported missing."

She handed him back the picture. "Can't help you."

"You and that boy were two of the last people to leave Fort Ticonderoga Museum on Friday afternoon."

Ellie immediately bristled. "I was also one of the first people in line at Independence Hall yesterday morning, along with a few hundred tourists. Do you expect me to remember all those faces, too, Mr. Murtaugh?"

"You know, Ms. Littlefield, I would have thought you of all people would have a little more empathy for this little boy and the trouble he could be in right now."

"So now we get down to it. What are you, Social Services or FBI? Well, if you're Social Services, think about this. Maybe I—of all people—think that being missing is a blessing for a kid like him. Maybe I think it's better than being a file tab in some state office drawer identifying children who are too much to handle.'' She reached around him and yanked open the door. "Good day to you, Officer."

She was angry enough to shove him out the door, but he saved her the trouble and stepped out himself. She slammed the door and felt great satisfaction at the solid sound of it.

Ellie leaned her back against the door and looked at Victor, who was staring at her openmouthed from the rear of the shop, the phone still in his hand. No matter how many years passed, these authorities never forgot. But Ellie Littlefield had come a long way from the motherless twelve-year-old constantly being shoved from one foster home to the next while her father served his time at Graterford Prison. And she was done going hungry.

Waving off Victor's questioning look, she went to the phone beside the cash register and dialed a number in upstate New York. Her past was part of the person she'd become. The days of lying and stealing, the nights sleeping on cold floors and in stairwells of empty buildings were behind her, but they had also pointed her toward where she was now. It took six rings before the phone was picked up.

"It's Ellie. They're looking for the boy."

Four

Nate Murtaugh drove slowly by an abandoned car, smashed and stripped and sitting on its bare axles. Fifty feet past it, an overflowing Dumpster sat on the cracked sidewalk in front of a brick building that looked as if it had probably been condemned during FDR's first term. Nate glanced at the scribble on the piece of paper in his hand and pulled to the curb before two buildings that could have been used for practice sessions by the Philly fire department.

His destination, across the street, was a marked improvement over the rest of the neighborhood. Nate looked again at the building. It was a well-kept brick place, just one version of a thousand houses like it in Philadelphia. Neat, tidy and austere, it reminded him of a gaunt, bloodless second cousin who once came to dinner on Thanksgiving, sat in a straight chair with her purse in her lap and never took off her coat. Well kept, but scary. Nate cut the engine and glanced at his watch. He was early.

Some kids—no doubt just released from reform school for the summer—were playing in the street, and the bubble-gum-colored ball bounced off the windshield and disappeared somewhere on the sidewalk. It was too hot in the car, and Nate grabbed his jacket off the passenger seat and stepped out.

The kids had stopped their game and were staring at him as if he were from another planet. He locked the car and leaned a hip against it, staring back.

One of the boys sauntered up to recover the ball. Seventy pounds of skin and bone and attitude. Picking it up with a wise-guy look on his face, he tossed the ball back to the pitcher, put his hand in his armpit and made a noise like a fart before trotting back to his spot by the abandoned car they were using for third base.

Nate thought of Chris Weaver and imagined him having the same kind of attitude. Yesterday, after the briefing by Hawes, he'd stopped at the police station to talk to McGill. The young cop had gone out on a call. Nate tried to contact him again before leaving town last night, but they hadn't been able to connect.

After watching the security surveillance tapes from the museum yesterday, Nate was more curious than ever to talk to McGill about Christopher Weaver and what was known about the kid. The video cameras had captured a child moving down the hall in an obvious search for a bathroom. They had also caught Ellie Littlefield coming down the same hall and talking to Chris.

Putting a name to her pretty face had been easy, considering the fact that she'd used her credit card to pay for admission to the museum. Reading her file had felt like winning one of those instant-lottery scratch cards. She had an extensive file on record and was connected with legit and shadier members of the antique collecting world. And the fact that she was at Fort Ticonderoga looking at the Schuyler flag minutes before it was destroyed couldn't be coincidental. Luckily for her, the security cameras in the room had filmed her exit before they were put out of commission some minutes later. Other surveillance equipment in the building had recorded Ellie Littlefield's departure, as well. What confused the hell out of Nate, though, was her denial this morning about seeing the boy. Well, she hadn't exactly denied seeing him, but she hadn't been particularly forthright about it, either.

Nate crossed the street and waited on the sidewalk. Less than a minute later, a second sedan containing a driver and two passengers pulled onto the street and parked in front of the Dumpster. Eric Wilcox stepped out of one side. As Sanford Hawes closed the door on his side, a deep drive to left center banged off the hood of the car. Hawes fired a dirty look over his shoulder at the ball players as he and the museum administrator crossed the street.

"Been waiting long?"

"Just got here," Nate answered, pulling his jacket on. The three men climbed the steps and Wilcox rang the bell. "Is she expecting us?"

"Yes, she is."

"Did you tell her anything?" Nate asked Hawes.

"Enough for her to understand the gravity of the problem."

Nate flexed one shoulder, pulled the sleeve of the jacket tighter down one arm and straightened the knot in his tie. The assistant director cocked an eyebrow at him.

"Catholic school, huh?" Hawes asked with a knowing grin.

"How could you tell?"

Nate noticed that Wilcox was clutching the handle of his briefcase in a death grip. As the artifacts director went to ring the bell again, the door opened. A young Latino-looking woman dressed in a navy-blue habit and wearing a large silver cross on a chain around her neck looked out at them. After Hawes's brief introduction, the nun invited them in, telling them that Sister Helen would join them in a few minutes.

Nate brought up the rear as they were ushered in. He looked into the small, dark sitting room furnished with old mismatched furniture. The only window in the room was open and an ancient oscillating fan creaked back and forth on a table in the corner. Nate shoved a finger inside the neckline of his shirt and adjusted his necktie again. He could feel the sweat running down his back and considered taking off his jacket.

The ridiculousness of his anxiety hit him when Hawes motioned him into the room. The young nun left them alone. Nate shook off the feeling, reminding himself that he was thirty-six years old and one threatening sonovabitch. This broad might be a nun, but she was also an ex-con and he was a special agent with the United States Federal Bureau of Investigation, the most prestigious law-enforcement organization in the world. Period.

Feeling a little more in control, Nate tried to identify the familiar feel of the place. It wasn't just the flashback to fifth grade; it was the fact that the place looked a lot like his grandmother's house in Albany. But the convent was missing the scent of oatmeal cookies she liked to make.

Nate moved to the window. As he looked outside at the noisy ball game still in progress, he kept an eye on the other two men. Wilcox sat stiffly on a straight chair near the door, with his briefcase upright on his lap. Hawes stood staring at old framed pictures on a table. The pope. The Virgin Mary. Men in clerical garb.

Hawes picked up the photo of the pope in his meaty

hands and looked at Wilcox. "Are you sure she still has her *old* connections?"

Eric Wilcox glanced uncomfortably at the door and lowered his voice. "I'm sure. For the past twelve years, since becoming a nun, she's received a generous amount in donations for her charities from dealers she worked with before being sent to jail."

"Art dealers believe in supporting charities, too, Dr. Wilcox," a soft voice responded from the doorway.

Nate and Hawes turned abruptly to the woman dressed in a blue habit. Sister Helen Doyle was standing and watching them in the doorway. Medium height, with a plain but expressive face, she looked to Nate like a woman with tremendous pent-up energy. Like a racehorse waiting for the gates to bang open. Wilcox, in his rush to stand, knocked over the chair he was sitting on.

"And my former colleagues are not the only ones on my list of benefactors, which also includes several U.S. Senators, the governors of three different states and a number of police officials from the city of Philadelphia. And on occasion we've even received donations from a former assistant to the Pennsylvania Attorney General." She cocked one graying eyebrow at Sanford Hawes.

"That would be me," he admitted in a strained voice. "Sister Helen's projects are known to be both effective and, uh, useful."

Sister Helen Doyle entered the room, casting a withering glance at Wilcox and eyeing Nate, who received a nod in response to his own.

"This meeting is off to a wonderful start," she said, crossing the room.

Eight years of parochial school had given Nate a

good understanding of the kind of discipline and dedication it took to become a nun. These women gave up the pursuit of fancy cars, comfortable checking accounts, fashionable town houses, exotic vacations and sex to follow their spiritual beliefs. The fact that Helen Doyle had once been married and had spent eight years in jail for art forgery and swindling before discovering her true calling made no difference. Her file said she'd been a nun for twelve years now, and this made her too damn intimidating for Nate.

Hawes and Wilcox both sat down after Sister Helen seated herself in a well-worn wing chair beneath a wooden cross. Nate held on to his square foot of space near the window.

"Sanford, is this the agent you were telling me about on the phone?"

Nate felt his face growing warm under the nun's critical scrutiny.

"Yes. Sorry, my apologies. We somehow bypassed the introductions." Hawes motioned to the museum director first. "You know Dr. Wilcox."

"We've never been introduced, but I've seen enough of him on television these past few months." With a dismissive nod, she turned her attention to Nate. "Is this the gentleman who will be working on this case?"

"Yes. Sister Helen, this is Special Agent Nate Murtaugh. I think I told you he's been with the Bureau for eleven years. Syracuse, then Columbia for his law degree. He has been one of our top agents in the New York City white-collar-crime division for about four years now. Last year, Agent Murtaugh received a medal from the Attorney General for bravery in the line of duty during the recovery of more than seventy million dollars in stolen art and cultural artifacts. Lives of a half dozen police officers and others were at risk during the operation.''

Nate looked in disbelief at Hawes as he continued to rattle off confidential information. There'd been no mention of Nate's name in the public record of the Rockwell case for the purpose of preserving his anonymity in future cases. Right now, though, short of giving her a copy of his medical records, Sanford sounded as if he was selling him to another Bureau division chief.

''Wait a minute, Sanford.'' Sister Helen raised her hand, silencing Hawes midsentence. ''My understanding was that this would be a simple operation. No wiretaps. No gathering of information for secret files. No hidden agenda. And definitely no gun-slinging hotshot.''

''You are correct in that. I was just trying to give you an idea of Agent Murtaugh's experience and qualifications. In the Bureau's opinion, he's the man for the job.''

Just as Nate was thinking of pulling Hawes aside for a friendly reminder that confessions were made to a priest and not a nun, Sister Helen appeared to read Nate's mind as her gaze narrowed on him.

''Our mission here, Agent Murtaugh,'' she began, ''is to help people from all walks of life.''

Suddenly, he was back in parochial school and nodding his understanding.

''In addition to our traditional role of ministering to the poor, the elderly, the infirm and unwed mothers, we also try to help those who have gotten onto the wrong path in their lives and are trying to correct that. These people have sinned. They have been lawbreakers. But these people have now found in themselves a

desire to serve other people and God. They are already
on the road to reform. We work very hard to help
them…whether the statute of limitations has run out or
not." The nun's piercing glare moved from Hawes to
Wilcox, before coming back to Nate. "We try to help
people like me. Can you trust an ex-criminal, Agent
Murtaugh?"

Nate's knee started aching again. "I respect what
you're trying to do, Sister. Your mission is a necessary
one."

"You didn't answer my question."

"There are different levels of trust. I'm here, so you
can assume that I trust you."

"You're here because your boss told you to get your
butt in here," she challenged him, arching her brow
expressively.

Nate looked at her steadily. "I have an assignment.
My understanding is that you might be the person who
can help me accomplish this task within the time limitations that we have. That's why I'm here."

"Now we're getting someplace." Her nod was pa-
tronizing at best. "Let's discuss this for a moment. You
have sworn to uphold the law. Now, here you are, and
I am agreeing to help you with your assignment. But
because of your instincts as a law-enforcement officer,
you come in contact with people whom you suspect
have not yet paid their debt to society."

"We know what you're getting at, Sister," Hawes
chirped. "You have my word that Agent Murtaugh is
perfectly capable of using his discretion to focus
solely—"

"I am speaking to Agent Murtaugh, Sanford," she
snapped at the FBI assistant director. "He appears perfectly capable of answering for himself."

"The nature of my job requires that I work with people of all kinds, just as you do," Nate explained in what he hoped was a reasonable tone. "I have no intention of getting involved with anything other than the case in question. On the other hand, if I witness the commission of a crime, then I have to take action."

"And that will make two of us." She leaned forward in her chair. "We only try to help *reformed* criminals, those who have sworn to change their lives. We don't sponsor illicit activities, no matter how large or small. Is that clear?"

"I'm glad to hear that, Sister."

"If I agree to help you, you must agree to respect the efforts of these people."

It was impossible to ignore Hawes as he repeatedly rubbed the back of his bull neck. Nate didn't need a signal. He knew he was supposed to agree to everything that was being said here.

"Short of breaking the law myself, Sister, I won't betray any confidence here. But before I add any more length to the rope that is eventually going to hang me, are you telling me you've heard the same thing that Wilcox has been telling us about the existence of an original Betsy Ross flag, and about the rumor of it going on auction soon?"

"Yes, I have. But I should tell you that how I feel about you will not serve as an admission ticket to any auction."

Hawes looked relieved, but Nate knew that had to do with the first part of the nun's answer. "Whatever it is you want Agent Murtaugh to do, he'll do it."

Nate felt the squirmy movements in the can of worms he was putting his hand into.

Sister Helen's attention focused on Hawes. "I trust

you to make whatever arrangements necessary to avoid any unpleasantness if Agent Murtaugh cannot fight the temptation to pursue those he comes in contact with through me.''

''Yes, Sister,'' Hawes offered eagerly. ''There will be no unpleasantness. Our specific task is to acquire that flag and have it available for the Fourth of July celebration.''

She nodded and turned to Nate. ''Except to a handful of people who must know the truth, you'll be introduced with a false identity to everyone else in the art crowd we have access to. What I know of the flag and what your Dr. Wilcox here has told you amounts to nothing more than rumor. Once we get your name and face out there in the right circles as an interested and credible buyer, a real lead might appear.''

''And how do we do that?''

''The place to start is to get you introduced to a friend of mine who happens to be a well-respected dealer here in Philadelphia. She'll be able to put out the word that you're looking for an old flag. She can even take you along to some of the high-end auctions so the other dealers can size you up.'' Sister Helen turned to Wilcox and Hawes. ''Of course, your other option would be for all of you to stay in the background and let my friend act as your agent. As it is, we are putting her at risk if Agent Murtaugh messes up.''

''Either way we play it, there is no guarantee that we'll even get a chance to bid on the flag within the two weeks we have left, is there?'' Nate asked.

''No. There's no guarantee.''

''We want Agent Murtaugh directly involved,'' Hawes stated. ''We need to know that everything that can possibly be done is happening.''

"I can understand that."

The nun turned her gaze back on Nate. He felt as if he were back in second grade and in trouble. He was still standing and this gave her more square footage to be critical of. His knee was aching again, too, and the damn room was too hot. And Wilcox—who'd been silent since Sister Helen entered the room—wasn't helping matters by continuously wiping the sweat off his thin face.

"Time is of the essence here, Sister Helen," Hawes said, interrupting the silent interrogation. "How soon can Murtaugh get started?"

"As soon as I decide if it's wise to reveal Agent Murtaugh's true identity to my friend."

"The fewer people who know of this the better," the assistant director said. "We want fewer explanations necessary when this is all over."

"I agree. Your entire hope for success depends on Elizabeth agreeing to help, but knowing how much she distrusts the authorities…" Sister Helen paused, studying Nate from the toes of his wing-tip shoes to his hair. "Yes, I think it'd be best if she didn't know."

"Elizabeth?" Nate asked, getting a bad taste in his mouth.

"Littlefield. Everyone else calls her Ellie, but she's Elizabeth to me. I'll ask her to come over tonight after dinner, to get her onboard. You and I can meet here again tomorrow morning at seven. Bring your new identity and whatever story you'll be using. Better yet, call me beforehand with the information, so I'm prepared."

"You'll introduce him as another friend?" Hawes questioned.

The nun turned to Hawes. "A friend of a friend or

whatever. He's visiting for a few days. Elizabeth will understand. There are always new faces around. And considering his specific interest, it'd be logical for me to ask for her help.''

"This is great." Hawes showed his big smile. "On behalf of the President and the Justice Department, we can't thank you enough for everything you're doing here, Sister Helen."

Nate interrupted as Wilcox stood up to express his own gratitude. "I believe it'd be best to introduce me to Ms. Littlefield as myself."

Three sets of eyes turned on him as if he'd lost his mind.

"Ms. Littlefield and I have met before."

Sister Helen let out a breath of relief and sank back against the chair. "I'm so glad. Elizabeth is like a daughter to me. It would have been very difficult to hold back any kind of information like that from her for any length of time. This makes everything so much easier."

Five

The ground was wet from the rain shower. Dirt and leaves stuck to Chris's leg where he crouched low in a gully behind the trailer. His dad used to tell him to go play, but not to go past the gully, where the "slime men" lived and waited for little boys. He could hear the noises of things in the woods, but they weren't as scary as the two men going through the trailer.

Chris could see them through the dirty windows, the gleam from their flashlights flitting around the small living space. He'd known it was only a matter of time before they'd come looking for him here. The old tin can of a trailer, with its tires shot out years before he was born, was supposed to be his father's secret hideout in the woods, but just about everybody in town knew about it. Everybody at the Green Lantern bar and poolroom, anyway.

One of the men stepped out of the trailer. The other followed a few seconds later. Chris hugged the box of stale Lucky Charms tighter against his chest. The men were looking out at the woods, and he pulled the stiff square of faded green tarp he'd found outside the trailer over his head. He could hear them talking low, but he couldn't make out the words. It looked like one was giving directions, pointing his light one way, and then the two men started circling the trailer, shining their lights on the ground and into the woods at the edge of the small clearing.

Chris pressed his face against the dirt and held his breath. The image of the uniformed guard's angry face at the museum flashed before his eyes. Chris's shoulder still hurt from the way the man had dug his fingers into him. The guard was holding him the way Peebo, his mom's scumbag ex-friend, used to, then called somebody on his walkie-talkie. Chris wasn't deaf. He'd heard the guard whisper, "Gatz. Problem here. There's a kid." When the man on the other end said, "Hold the fuck on to him," Chris knew they were doing something wrong.

He'd seen enough movies to know the bad guys. He knew museum guards wouldn't use the f-word. And that thing on the flag…it didn't belong there. This guy was a fake, and holding on to a kid meant they'd be getting rid of him. That was when he kicked the guy in the shin as hard as he could and ran out the back exit door by the bathroom.

He thought about running now and peered from under the tarp at the flashlight snaking through the trees to his left. He hated the woods. They were dark, and you didn't know what was in there at night. Maybe there really were "slime men." Besides, he thought, with these two guys so close, they'd see him now for sure if he tried to run for it.

He stared at them. In the reflection of the lights, he saw they were both wearing suits. Like Will Smith and the other guy in *Men in Black*. But these guys were bad guys, too. Social workers didn't dress like this or drive down his dad's dirt road at night with their headlights off.

One of them was looking out in his direction. Chris

ducked his head. He saw the lights shining out over the gully now, and a cold feeling of panic washed through him. He could hear their footsteps. Something was crawling up one leg of his pants, but he didn't dare move. Didn't dare breathe.

He should have stayed with that lady outside the museum. She'd been really nice to him when he'd burst out the exit door and jumped in front of her car. She'd believed him when he babbled about having to go to the bathroom and wetting his pants. She'd seen him in the hallway. She knew.

Chris could see the fake guard standing inside the slowly closing exit door, talking on his walkie-talkie, so when she'd said the bus wouldn't have left without him and offered to give him a ride to the front of the building, Chris had climbed inside of the car. She didn't say anything to him about smelling bad and being all wet.

As soon as she'd started around the building, though, Chris had realized the guard might be there waiting for him. Panicking, he blurted out a sob story about how the other kids would make fun of him on the bus. And his foster mother would get mad at him for coming home like this. He'd begged her to drop him off at his father's trailer, where he could change first before he went home.

There'd been another phone call. She was running late. But Chris didn't feel bad at all about turning on the tears and telling her how horrible his life was and how this would be the only thing the kids remembered about him all summer. He'd done his best to make her feel bad. There were no buses in front of the building, anyway. Chris didn't mention that the bus that was parked next to the road was his. He could see Miss

Leoni inside as they went by. She was counting heads and looking a little upset.

The lady was a softy and had dropped him off at the trailer park on the main road where he'd lied and told her his father's trailer was. He'd promised to walk to Mrs. Green's house, on the next street, from there. She'd even given him a piece of paper with a couple of phone numbers on it. In case people weren't home and all that.

Now Chris was sorry about all the lying. He'd seen something he shouldn't have, and he didn't know how to get out of this kind of trouble. And he didn't think going back to Mrs. Green would help. She had three other kids she looked after, and her favorite saying was that she was in no mood for trouble.

A twig snapped not far from his hiding place, and Chris bit down hard on his bottom lip.

"He has to be here," a deep voice said from the top of the gully. "He sure isn't making it too easy for us with all these woods around."

"He won't go far," the other man answered. "We just have to wait for morning."

Chris shoved one fist into his mouth to quiet his cry. He was dead, for sure.

Nate held the phone out and tugged on his earlobe, certain that there had to be some permanent damage to his eardrum. Holding the cell phone two feet away from his head, he could still hear Sanford Hawes's voice blaring out of it clear as a bell.

"You fix it, Nate. You screwed this thing up. Now you straighten it out. And I don't give a f—"

Nate put the phone down on the passenger seat as the door of the dinner club across the street opened and a well-dressed couple sauntered out. He picked up the phone again.

"You sonovabitch, are you still there?"

"Yes, I'm still here. By the way, since you're done bawling me out—"

"What makes you think I'm done bawling you out?"

"Why don't you start from the beginning and tell me exactly what Sister Helen said to you."

"She called to say it's not going to happen. She said she'd just gotten off the phone with this Ellie Littlefield, and the woman adamantly refuses to have anything to do with you. She said the deal's off. Oh, and she also told me, don't fucking bother to send Agent Murtaugh around tomorrow morning."

"Nice mouth for a nun."

"Don't get cute on me. I was making a point. And here's another point. I could have your job for this. You've put your entire career in jeopardy here."

"That right?"

"There was no reason for you to make contact with that woman beforehand, Nate. No reason to stop at her shop. I know this has to do with that kid, but I made it perfectly clear that you don't have time to f—"

Nate dropped the phone on the seat again as a noisy group of two women and three men came out of the club. A limousine pulled up to pick them up, and the driver jumped out to open the door for them.

One of the women, holding a small take-home bag of food, spoke quietly to the driver, and together they began maneuvering the others into the car. She was polite, classy and obviously the only one not trashed. Nate let his eyes take in Ellie Littlefield. Though he'd thought she was pretty damn cute in her jeans and a baseball hat, she was a knockout in a sleeveless black dress and short pumps. Yes, the woman cleaned up very nicely.

While a woman and two of the men managed to tumble into the car, a young, preppy-looking guy looped an arm around Ellie and drew her toward him. She smiled and wedged her arms between them, turning the eager Romeo toward the limo and pushing him in. Ellie kept her weight against the door and said something to the driver as he hurried around the car.

"Murtaugh!"

Hawes's voice from the cell phone made Nate pick it up again. "Look, Sanford, I'm trying to fix it as we speak."

"Just how are you doing that?"

"I'm trying to get into Ms. Littlefield's good graces." Nate snapped. "But I can't very well do that with you nagging at me. I'll call you when I have something."

"You do tha—"

Nate hung up and pocketed the phone. The limo had already left the curb, and Ellie was striding north along the street.

The club was only four blocks from where she lived. Walking distance. Figuring that was where she was headed, Nate left the car in the no-parking zone near the stop sign and took off after her.

The assistant director's news about Ellie's refusal to work with him had come as no surprise. Although he wasn't sure how he'd gone awry, it took no genius to figure that he'd rubbed her the wrong way this morning. It was just bad luck that he needed her now. Calling her or showing up at her door were not going to get him too far. He knew that. Charming her with his magnetic personality, though, was definitely the only way to go. He didn't want her to think he was stalking her, and he picked up his pace.

Ten steps behind her on the next block, Nate was surprised to see Ellie cross the narrow street and start a conversation with a homeless guy in a wheelchair. Calling him by name, she handed him the bag of food. From what he could hear, she seemed to know this Jack well enough for him to ask about her father. Nate busied himself with putting quarters in someone else's parking meter and saw her hand five bucks to the man before she started down the street again.

Nate figured she was one hundred ten pounds soaking wet, and it would be stretching it to call her height "medium" at five two...maybe three. But she had the stride of someone who knew where she was going and who obviously felt safe on the city streets. In fact, it occurred to him that she carried herself differently now, more confidently, than she had when she'd been with her limo buddies.

Pine Street was quiet, with only a few people sitting on steps and walking dogs and chatting with neighbors. She seemed to know everyone. When she got to the door of her shop, he saw her reach inside her purse and search for keys. Nate thought this was as good a time as any to approach. He crossed over.

She turned to face him before he stepped onto the sidewalk. "Looks like I wasn't too far off this morning, was I?"

Nate looked down at the keys she'd positioned like a weapon between her fingers. "You're not going to use those on me, are you?"

"It depends."

"The current thinking is that you'll hurt your hand more than your attacker."

"Thanks for the professional advice." Her voice dripped with sarcasm, but the keys disappeared into her fist. "Why are you following me, Agent Murtaugh?"

"I was hoping for a few minutes of your time."

"You had that this morning."

"I'd hardly call it that. You practically threw me out of your shop."

"We were closed, and you barged in uninvited."

"Your assistant, Vic, invited me in. This time, though, I'd be much obliged if you'd give me the chance to explain." He stepped closer to her, but she didn't back up. The street lamp cast shadows on her face, but Nate had no trouble appreciating how delicate her features were. "And apologize."

"No dice. I have no interest in hearing anything that you have to say," she responded. There was a huskiness in her tone. "I don't know what kind of story you fed Sister Helen for her to even consider helping you, but you don't fool me. I saw through you this morning, before you even opened your mouth."

"You knew when I offered to help you climb over the mirror?"

"Don't get cute," she snapped.

"Everybody thinks I'm cute these days."

"Well, I don't. What you're pulling here is an old game, Murtaugh. You guys are forever plotting ways of rounding up dealers and collectors. I know as far as you're concerned, we're all crooks."

Two men passing on the far side of the street who obviously knew Ellie paused at her raised voice. She waved at them, and they moved on.

"Can we go inside and talk about this?"

"No." She looked at him as if he'd grown a second head. "I want you to leave me alone. I don't have to talk to you at all."

"But you will."

"Why? You think you can force me to help you?"

"No, you need to talk to me because you're wrong about what you think we want to do."

She snorted.

"All right, then, maybe I can appeal to your sense of civic duty. You have a social responsibility to help your country."

"Yeah, right!"

"Listen." Nate leaned toward her and lowered his voice. "I couldn't say anything about this assignment this morning. Frankly, even now I don't know how much Sister Helen has told you about what we're up against."

"She said enough for me to know that the whole thing doesn't add up to a hill of beans. Besides that, I want nothing to do with it or with you."

"Are you telling me that this country means so little to you? That you can just turn your back while the entire nation is dealt another crushing blow?"

"Just when I thought you could sink no lower." She shook her head and started turning toward the door.

"What did I do, hit too close to home?" Nate taunted her. "An upscale shop, rich friends, private clubs and parties. I'll be honest with you, Ms. Littlefield. I can't believe Sister Helen would even recommend you for this job. You are so far removed from your days as a kid in the system that I don't think you even know—or care—how the rest of America lives."

She whirled on him and pressed a finger into his chest. "Let's get something straight, Agent Eagle

Scout. I don't need *you* to remind me of my roots or my civic responsibilities. But now that you've opened up this little discussion, I'll tell you that the majority of the people in this country don't give a damn about this Spirit of America celebration. They see right through it as the campaign song-and-dance routine that it is.''

''Look, I—''

''People in this country need solid productive action, not some dog-and-pony show. They need jobs. They need a good education for their kids. They need health care that they can afford and that actually covers them when they're sick. If President Kent really wanted to help all the people in this country, and not just his business buddies, then he'd veto that billion-dollar con job they're calling the Water for America project. Everybody with half a brain can see it's meant to help his home state of Oklahoma at the expense of programs for millions of other Americans. How about showing the people of this country that we're united by more than just a few symbols!''

''Look, I'm not here to argue politics with you.''

''Oh, how inconsiderate of me to mention it.'' She let out a frustrated breath and then jammed the key into the latch. ''Why did I even bother? Good night, Agent Murtaugh. Better luck finding a brainless sap someplace else.''

The door slammed in his face before Nate could even think of a comeback.

Ellie had passed a big milestone this year, and it wasn't only because she'd turned thirty.

In just a few years, she'd made a name for herself in antiques. She was trusted by top decorators for her taste and her expertise, and her client list included many of the elite of Philadelphia and the Main Line. Certain highly eligible bachelors were showing interest in her. She had a few very good friends. She and her father were talking again. She was healthy. And for the first time in her life, she had a very nice balance in her checkbook. All and all, life was good.

She wasn't going to let Nate Murtaugh ruin it.

With the agent's face still visible through the glass, Ellie snapped the dead bolt into place and turned her back on him. She didn't bother to turn on any lights. She also didn't wait around to guess at Murtaugh's next move before starting for the stairs.

The handrail was still lying on the steps. Vic's friend Brian, who sometimes helped out in the shop, had come around this afternoon and patched the plaster. He was coming back tomorrow afternoon to paint the hallway wall before putting the railing back on. With Brian's help, Vic and another friend had hung the mirror where she wanted it in the back room. There was some small satisfaction in seeing that having the mirror there worked.

In the hallway at the top of the stairs, Ellie poked her head into the second-floor studio. The lights were off, but she breathed in the pungent odors of paint and turpentine, canvas, wood and clay. Because of her father, an artist himself, they were some of the first smells she could recall. Ellie kicked off her shoes and dangled them from her fingers as she went up to her apartment.

She stopped at the window at the top of the stairs and looked out at the dark street. She wondered momentarily if the annoying man was still outside, planning to stake out her building all night.

It wasn't so much Murtaugh. He wasn't really annoying. He would actually be a very attractive man, if he weren't an FBI agent. That was the most surprising part of it all. Why would Sister Helen assume that she'd agree to have anything to do with some FBI agent? These were the same people who'd used Louis Littlefield—despite his cooperation—and put him in jail, with no thought about the welfare of his motherless, twelve-year-old daughter. Did the FBI care that Ellie had been left to fend for herself on the street and in foster care? No, they didn't.

Entering her apartment, she tried to shake off the old memories and rein in her temper at the same time. Well, no one was perfect. Sister Helen was a great woman, and she did a lot of good. She was just becoming a little detached from reality lately.

Ellie turned on the light next to the bookcase. Out of habit, she adjusted some of the photo frames on the shelves. She picked up an empty coffee mug from the floor next to the love seat and carried it to the kitchen sink. She took a peek inside her refrigerator, immediately grimacing at the smell and at the stack of foam take-home boxes bearing the labels of several restaurants she frequented in the past couple of weeks.

Old habits were tough to break. No matter how sophisticated she tried to look and act, she couldn't tolerate waste. She just had to remind herself not to order fish. Jack hated fish.

The red light on Ellie's answering machine was blinking in the darkness. She dropped her shoes by the door to her bedroom and pressed the button for the messages. The first one was from a local church group about some weekend workshop-antique show that they were putting together as a fund-raiser. They were hoping for her participation. The smell from the fridge still lingered in the air, and Ellie started opening the windows in her living room. The warm air poured into the apartment, and she took a deep breath. The second message drew her to the phone.

"Hi, Ellie. It's John." There was a pause. "Sorry I didn't get back to you sooner, but between the show today and the cleanup after, this is the first chance I've had."

She planted her hands on either side of the answering machine, mentally urging the man to go on. "I went to the address you gave me this morning, but the kid doesn't live there. The woman who answered didn't know of any kid by that name. In fact, I knocked on a couple of doors in the trailer park to make sure, but everyone said the same thing. And as far as a Mrs. Green on the next street, that was bogus, too. I checked in the phone book, but there's a whole column of Greens. So…sorry to hand the ball back to you like this, but I can't find the kid." There was another pause. "You know, I'm thinking it might be best if you just tell the cops what you know. It's not like you did anything wrong. You just gave a kid in trouble a ride. And who knows, that little boy might just be in over his head. Anyway, you know best."

Ellie's head sank, and she closed her eyes. John Dubin, an antique clock dealer and an old friend, had arranged a private sale for her at one of the old estates in the area for three o'clock last Friday. By the time she'd dropped Chris off, she'd been running half an hour late.

Maybe it hadn't been right to tell John everything that had happened. And maybe she shouldn't have called him back this morning to ask him to go and check the address where Chris had said his father lived. Right or wrong, Ellie had felt a little uncertain about the whole situation with the kid. So she'd followed her instincts and called John. Now she felt positively queasy about the whole thing.

The answering machine beeped again, and Ellie realized she'd been listening to an empty message left for her at 10:05. She checked her watch. It was now 10:25.

It was only a hunch, but she searched inside her purse and took out her cell phone. She'd forgotten to turn it on. There was one message. She dialed and listened.

"Hi. This is Chris Weaver. You…you gave me a ride." The voice crackled and started to break up. Ellie went to the window, desperate for better reception. "I…I'm in this…trouble…really scared. I'm hiding in a phone booth near the junkyard." She rushed to get a piece of paper as he went on to say the name of the street where the junkyard and the auto body shop were located. "If you're around…I was wondering if you…if you could come and get me."

Six

"I'm not a goddamn secretary or a parking attendant, Agent Murtaugh." The police officer scowled and tore up the parking ticket she'd left on his windshield earlier.

Nate pocketed his badge and smiled apologetically. "Hey, I understand. I appreciate your—"

He answered his cell phone, only to have Hawes's gruff curses come pouring out. The woman's look turned immediately sympathetic. Nate held the phone against his chest. "It's my boss."

"Nice mouth," she whispered with a grin.

Nate spoke into the phone. "So is my dry cleaning ready to pick up?"

"No, I'm calling with your fu—"

"Thank you, Officer." He smiled again as he slid into the car and shut the door.

"...and I want to know how the hell you did it?"

"Did what?" Nate asked.

"This Littlefield broad wants to see you at her place right away." Nate sat silent, puzzling out what might have happened to change Ellie's mind. "The woman called Sister Helen a couple of minutes ago, insisting that it was urgent for her to meet with you right away. Now, I want to know what the hell you're up to, Nate.

You didn't harass her or do anything that's going to get the Bureau in trouble now, did you?"

"I'll call you back. I'm two minutes from her shop." He cut the connection and pulled away from the curb, sending a salute to the police officer who was just getting into her squad car.

It took less than two minutes to reach her building, and he pulled into a space in front of a hydrant. He could see Ellie through the window of her shop. She had changed into a pair of jeans and a T-shirt, and she looked strikingly young again. She was watching him as he crossed the street, and opened the door before he reached it.

"Come in." She stood back. "You must think I'm fighting PMS."

"No. I figure this must just be your charming personality."

"Well, I hope you don't expect an apology because you're not going to get one." Ellie closed the door and leaned her back against it.

"Okay. What's going on?"

"You showed me a picture of a boy this morning. Chris Weaver."

"I never told you his name."

"Don't play super-sleuth with me, Agent Murtaugh. I didn't ask you to come back here to deny knowing him." She went to the counter and picked up her cell phone, dialing a number. She was a bundle of nerves. "I want you to listen to this message that was left for me tonight." She handed him the phone.

Nate listened to the eight-year-old's nervous stammering. He reached into his pocket for his pad as the boy said where the phone booth was, but Ellie handed him a piece of paper with the information already on it. After listening to it a second time, he disconnected.

"What exactly was your interaction with him?"

"I saw him first in the hall at the Fort Ticonderoga Museum. He was in a rush and looked lost, but he wouldn't talk to me. Then I saw him again when he ran out the back door of the museum. He'd wet his pants and had been crying. The short version is that he asked for a ride to his father's place, which was supposedly a street away from the foster house where he'd been placed. He needed help. I felt bad for him, and I did it." Seeing his frown, she crossed her arms defensively before her. "I already know it was a stupid thing to do, and I've kicked myself a hundred times since you showed up this morning and told me he's missing."

"You must be pretty bruised, then. But why didn't you tell me the truth this morning?"

"You weren't exactly up front yourself. Plus I didn't think there was anything wrong with Chris." She ran a hand impatiently through her short dark hair. "But tonight, after hearing his message, I'm worried. It sounds like he's really scared, and it'll take me six hours to get up there. I dialed the number he called me from, but it keeps ringing. If he's still there, he's not picking up." She'd started pacing. Now she stopped. "Are you going to help him?"

"Of course. Just give me a minute to change into my blue-and-red spandex suit and I'll fly right up there and rescue him for you." He pulled out his notebook and found the number of the Ticonderoga Police Department.

"You don't have to be so sarcastic."

"To keep up with you, yes, I do."

Nate dialed the number and introduced himself to the dispatcher. After being told that Tom McGill was off duty, he asked for his home phone number.

"I could have done that myself," Ellie said as he started dialing McGill's number. "Chris is scared and sounds like he might be in some kind of trouble. He's not going to trust some uniformed cop showing up in a police car to pick him up."

Nate suppressed the urge to tell her exactly how much trouble she could be in herself, but he needed her cooperation in finding the Robert Morris flag, and he was going to be pleasant to her if it killed him.

"Why don't you sit back, Ms. Littlefield, and let me do my job."

She pulled a stool next to him and climbed up, watching his every move. Luckily, McGill was home. Nate briefly explained to the police officer what had happened.

"I'll go pick him up myself," the young officer offered from the other end.

"This little guy's been on the run for two days now, and he sounds pretty scared. Once you get hold of him, is there any way you could take him to his foster mother's place and leave the questioning and paperwork and everything else until tomorrow?"

"Absolutely. I'll call you after I locate him."

Nate went over how he should approach Chris and exactly what to say to the boy. Lastly, he gave McGill his cell phone number again. When he finally hung up, he was surprised to find Ellie sitting quietly, watching him with a peculiar look on her face.

"What's wrong now?"

She shook her head and her silky locks shone beneath Victorian-era chandeliers. "Do you have children of your own, Agent Murtaugh?"

His throat tightened. "Nope. No children."

She climbed off the stool and went around the sales counter. All her energy had been punched out of her. Ellie's hands absently straightened a stack of business cards. "How long do you think it'll be before he calls you back?"

"Not long. He was going right away."

"You don't mind staying until he calls?"

"No, I don't mind."

Actually, he liked it better when she was nipping at his heels. This vulnerable look she was wearing brought out a side of Nate that he liked to keep under lock and key in situations like this. He never mixed the professional with the personal...and he was feeling the personal right now. He turned and studied a Remington bronze of a cowboy on a buffalo hunt. The horse's throat was a whisker away from the buffalo's horn, and the rider was about to fire his rifle. Buffalo, horse and man, connected at a moment of destiny. Nothing impersonal about that business. He turned back to Ellie.

"I've met McGill. He's a good man, and he's in Chris's corner."

"Other than running away, what kind of trouble is he in, anyway?"

Nate didn't know how much she knew. Despite the fact that the loss of the flag was being kept under wraps, Sister Helen had been told most of the details. "Were you briefed about the Schuyler flag?"

"I was told it was destroyed in a fire at the Fort Ticonderoga Museum on Friday. But I told Sister Helen that I didn't believe it." Once again she took a combative stance, one hand on her hip. "I was there that afternoon. I was the last visitor in that room. I told her there's something funny going on and that this is some lame story you people are using as cover for something else you're trying to pull. I don't care what you've got in mind, Murtaugh, but I don't believe that flag was destroyed.''

"Well, it has been. And I can produce the ash and burned scraps to prove it." Nate sat down on the stool she'd vacated. His knee had started aching again. "And your little friend Christopher might have witnessed the crime."

"He disappeared into the bathroom and then came out of the building and jumped in front of my car."

"Not before he made a stop in the room with the flag. His wet footprints were everywhere."

"Even if he did go in there, I was in the same room only minutes before. There was no one else in there, or in the halls. And they were closing the museum." She shook her head and then hesitated, looking at him suspiciously. "Unless you think I started the fire."

"We have a clear picture of you leaving the building."

"Then why do you need Christopher to tell you who else was in there? What about the security cameras? The guards? All the bells and whistles you have protecting America's treasures from the big, bad wolves out there?"

"For someone who has no interest in helping us with the case, you've got an awful lot of questions."

"You cops are all the same. You grill people right and left, and then you're shocked when someone gives your own treatment back to you." She spun on her heel, picked up a stack of books and moved them a couple of feet to another table.

Nate watched the emotions play across her face. He remembered what he'd read in her file. No record of what happened to her mother. Her father jailed when she was twelve for interstate transportation of stolen property, theft of major artwork, five felony counts of grand theft and an assortment of lesser charges. It'd taken social services more than six months to find Ellie and put her in a home. She ran away—was found— ran away again—then was arrested trying to sell stolen goods. Things had gone from bad to worse after that, but then something happened and she apparently turned herself around. Ellie's slate was clean from the time she turned eighteen. She'd smartened up…or had learned how to avoid getting caught. Looking at the attractive and graceful woman before him now, he found it impossible to think that history belonged to her.

"He's only eight, Ellie. He's not old enough to fend for himself. He might have seen something that could put his life in jeopardy."

"If there *was* anything to see," she said stubbornly. "I was in that back parking lot when he came out of the building. No alarms went off while we were on the grounds. And he was only concerned about one thing…and that was his wet pants."

She was still riled up, and Nate was not about to lose her now.

"If the flag is what we're arguing about here, then as I said before, I can arrange to show you the little that is left of it," he said calmly. "Regarding Christopher, though, we're both standing on the same side of the fence. Everyone wants to help the boy, and the question of what he saw—if anything—will be answered as soon as McGill picks him up."

Ellie looked as if she was going to disagree with him again, but then abruptly started toward the back of the shop. "I need some coffee."

Nate watched her go and decided to follow. If he wanted the chance to change her mind about helping him, he had to take his shot now. She turned on the lights as she went along.

The smell of old furniture assaulted his nostrils as he followed Ellie into a dark room to the left. A light switched on, and he found himself looking at the oversize mirror, hanging on the back wall.

"I thought you were going to keep that thing on the stairs."

"I wanted to, but Vic thought it wasn't appropriate, aesthetically."

"Or functionally, blocking the stairs as it was."

"Yeah, well, Vic is more into form than function." She pointed to the coffeemaker and the TV on the counter. A small fridge sat underneath. "These are the exceptions. He thinks there are some twenty-first-century amenities that serve an essential function."

"Aesthetics be damned," Nate finished amiably. "He's an interesting guy."

She picked up the glass pot off the coffeemaker, swished around something in the bottom that looked like 10W40 oil sludge, and brought it to her nose.

"He likes you, too. In fact, he'll be really disappointed to hear that you were here tonight and he didn't know about it."

Nate caught the reflection of her shapely bottom in the mirror when she bent down to get a tray of ice out of the fridge. "Well, he's not my type."

"Want some iced coffee?"

He considered for a moment that women usually

jumped on that line. The question whether or not *they* were his type was routine. Not for this one, obviously, and he realized he was mildly put off that she showed no interest in him whatsoever. Better to keep it strictly business, he decided. "How old is that coffee, anyway?"

"Beggars can't be choosers." She filled two ice-packed plastic cups and handed one to him. "Sorry, looks like we're out of milk and sugar."

Nate took a sip. "Can I have the recipe? My '67 Mustang could use this."

She shot him a "not amused" look and walked out of the room. Nate ended up following her again. "Can we sit and talk for a few minutes?"

"I never sit."

"Okay. Then could I sit and talk and you listen?" His knee was starting to throb.

The coffee sloshed over the edge of the cup when she turned to him. "My answer is still the same, Agent Murtaugh. What's going on with that little boy changes nothing. Even if you convinced me that the Schuyler flag was destroyed, I wouldn't be interested in helping you."

"Will you change your mind if I got another agent involved?" At her incredulous look, he rephrased the question. "I mean, is it me that you don't want to work with?"

"No, and no." She took a long sip of her drink. "Shouldn't your friend have called by now?"

There were half a dozen cars in various states of disrepair parked in the body shop lot. In the chain-link-fenced yard to the back of the cinder-block building, rusting cars and trucks were piled up in tilting stacks.

Graffiti messages of No Trespassing and Dog Will Bite! covered the gate. A single floodlight mounted high on an old telephone pole shone starkly on the immediate area around the gate.

Chris crouched low in the back seat of a windowless station wagon close to the gate. His gaze never wavered more than a few seconds at a time from the phone booth leaning up against a utility pole near the road. The box of Lucky Charms was propped between his knees. He'd made a little game for himself of popping one stale moon or heart or shamrock into his mouth any time a car went by. He wasn't making any dent at all in what was left in the box.

A while ago—he didn't know how long it was, maybe an hour or more—the phone had started ringing. At exactly the same time, Chris had seen a muddy car pull off the road and slowly circle the lot. He'd been scared enough to pee in his pants again. Piling all the garbage in the back seat on top of him, he'd fit himself in the small space behind the passenger's seat.

It had been a miracle that he'd found his way to the body shop and the phone. He'd walked through the woods in the dark forever. But they tracked him down somehow.

The phone kept ringing, and after a while he heard the car drive off down the road. It took a few minutes for Chris to get himself to look up. The lot was empty. All was quiet except for a noisy mosquito buzzing around his ear. He wondered if the person who was calling had been Miss Littlefield. But he was too scared to get out and walk to the booth. Besides, the phone had stopped ringing.

There were no cars coming now. There hadn't been for a while. Chris cheated and popped a fistful into his mouth. His stomach was growling, and his mouth was almost too dry to swallow the cereal. He looked at the tall soda machine next to the dark glass windows of the station and reached into his pocket, counting the change. Fifty-five cents was all that he had left after the phone calls he'd made to Miss Littlefield. And to think he'd felt so rich finding all that change just by scrounging under the seats of the cars in the outer lot.

The coins in his hand dropped onto the floor when a pickup truck pulled into the lot. The truck parked next to the phone booth under the light. Chris slid down in the seat and watched the man behind the wheel look around at the cars. The truck's windows were down, and from this distance Chris couldn't see the man's face too well, but he could tell he wasn't wearing any suit or tie, or anything like that.

He slid down farther and pressed his face against the torn vinyl of the seat when the stranger opened his door and stepped out. Scrambling in the small space, Chris pulled newspapers and other trash on top of him.

"Christopher!"

The loud call made the young boy start shivering. This guy knew his name. He knew he was here.

"Christopher, I'm Officer Tom. I'm here to help you." The voice was getting closer. "You called Miss Littlefield tonight—the lady who gave you a ride on Friday. But she's in Philadelphia and couldn't get up here fast enough. So she called me to come and help you."

Chris heard a car drive by on the road. His mind was getting more confused by the second. She'd trusted this guy. But what if he was lying? Then again, how would he know Chris had called her?

"I'm a friend, Chris," the man said more gently.

"There's no reason for you to hide. You haven't done anything wrong. We just need to ask you a few questions about the fire."

"What fire?" he whispered, then shut his mouth, realizing his mistake. Suddenly, everything had become too quiet. He waited a heartbeat before his curiosity got hold of him and he snaked up to look out the window. Officer Tom was peering inside a mashed-up sports car across the lot from the station wagon Chris was hiding in. Like a big cat's, though, the man's head snapped in his direction. He was caught.

"There you are. Why don't you come out, Chris?" he asked softly, taking a couple of steps and stopping. He was holding out his hand. "You must be starving."

Chris didn't know what to do. This guy didn't sound mean, and he wasn't running over to get him. There was no point in hiding anymore, anyway.

"Everybody has been pretty darn worried about you. Mrs. Green. Your teachers. Your classmates. I stopped yesterday and talked to your mom. She's very worried."

"Right. As if she'd care," Chris mumbled under his breath.

"Miss Littlefield says she'll be up here first thing tomorrow morning to see you at Mrs. Green's." He took another step toward the car. "Come on, kiddo. You're not all alone in this. There are people who care, you know."

Fear, hunger, the feeling that there were bugs crawling all over him—there were a hundred reasons to go with Officer Tom, and none he could think of for not going. Chris slowly pulled the handle and pushed the creaky door open until it scraped the chain-link fence.

He hesitated and reached back into the car for the

box of Lucky Charms. Then, as he was backing out, the sound of a car roaring into the lot reached his ears. Chris barely had time to turn around when the screeching of tires stopped him cold.

Seven

Waiting for the phone call from Murtaugh's upstate New York cop friend, Ellie decided the silent treatment was her best defense. The man was everywhere. She ran a hand up and down her arms. No invisible strings connecting them that she could find. It was impossible, though, to ignore him, and getting worse by the minute.

She'd returned to the back room to reorganize the lighting. He came in, and suddenly there was no air in the place. She moved to the adjacent area and rearranged some of the end tables and chairs. He joined her and, without being asked, gave her a hand. Ellie escaped to the front of the shop and went to work on the displays under the glass showcases. Murtaugh walked in and sat on the high stool, watching her through the glass. Then he had the gall to ruin any chance of ridiculing him by making intelligent comments about the pieces.

If he were anyone else, Ellie thought, she'd probably enjoy his company. Educated, a good sense of humor and certainly easy on the eyes. He'd fit into any circle. She had to remind herself that this was exactly the plan. That was why he was chosen for the job. He would slip without any trouble into the role of a collector.

"Where did these come from?"

She pulled her head from under the glass to see

which items he was pointing at. On the other end of the display case, he was bent over her new collection of snuffboxes. She moved over and brought out the three pieces. "I bought them in a private showing of an estate near Ticonderoga this past Friday."

"Is that why you went up there?"

"Are you interested in them or in me?"

"I guess it would be inappropriate to say 'you.'"

Ellie looked at him steadily, stunned by the odd sensation of butterflies his comment triggered. "Very."

"Okay. How about 'both'?"

"Still wrong, would be my guess. What do the regulations say, Special Agent?"

"Guess I'll have to plead my Fifth Amendment rights on that." His boyish smile made him look downright handsome, even to Ellie. "Mind if I handle the pieces?"

"Go ahead."

He reached for the white-enameled snuffbox. His hand was large, but the gentleness that he used to caress the ribs on the cover and the depictions of blue crowns in the corners was unsettling. Ellie looked up and found herself noticing how long and dark his lashes were. His head came up and for a second she was lost in the depth of his blue eyes. She blushed.

"What's the story with this one?"

"An enameled snuffbox from London. Dates back to the 1750s. Because of the patterns, I believe it was fashioned to celebrate the creation of the future George III as Prince of Wales."

He looked at the small price tag on the thread. "Twenty-four-hundred dollars. How much did you pay for it?"

"Twelve hundred."

Ellie planted her elbows on the glass and met his gaze head-on. "I don't apologize for the markup."

"Nor should you. I wouldn't have been surprised if you told me you paid five bucks for it. As a matter of fact, I think my grandfather had a box like this on his dresser when I was a kid. My mother sold it at a yard sale for a buck."

"I should start going to more yard sales in your neighborhood," she replied. "Where do your parents live?"

"Upstate New York."

The dimple in his tanned cheek was too much. Ellie had to do something with her hands, so she organized the pen collection on the top shelf.

"Why the private showing? I'd have thought an auction could have done better for the previous owner."

"Maybe, but the owner didn't want an auction. In this case, she's a widow, in ill health. For financial reasons, she wanted to liquidate the estate, but for personal reasons she didn't want the public nature of an auction. I was contacted through a mutual friend who is also a dealer but was only interested in her clocks."

"You could have given her less for this, I'm guessing. Why didn't you? You sound pretty generous to me."

"I wasn't being generous. I gave her a fair price. It's what she would have gotten if she'd had time to sell it somewhere on consignment. I'll hold it and hope the value goes up, but that's the risk of being in this business."

"Interesting that she trusted you."

"My business works because of trust and word of mouth."

"She was right to trust you." Nate was openly

studying her face, and she found herself getting flustered. "I'm impressed."

"Well, don't be," she snapped, angry with herself for letting him put her off with just a look. She took a deep breath to calm herself before continuing. "For every purchase like this one, I've stolen at least a hundred in tag sales and church auctions. I've even culled through stuff on the side of the road."

"You mean road kill?"

"Sometimes you get lucky." Ellie stopped and put the boxes back into the display case. She shot him a threatening look. "The funny thing about road kill is that often there are no witnesses around when a person does the killing."

Nate took a pad of paper and a pen from next to the register and started scribbling on it. "Would you care to elaborate on that, Miss Littlefield?"

She leaned over the counter and smiled innocently at him. "No. Not really, Agent Murtaugh."

"You sure know how to pique a man's interest."

"Not a man's," she replied. "A federal agent's."

"I'm afraid I have to correct you on that point, Ms. Littlefield."

His blue eyes were riveted to her face. Ellie ignored the tightening in her stomach and tried to come up with something flippant to say. Luckily, his cell phone began to ring. As it did, the guilt and anxiety she'd had about Christopher rushed back.

The transformation in Nate was immediate. His face became unreadable. He walked into a shadowy corner at the far end of the room. The words he spoke were cryptic, and Ellie had no idea if this call had anything to do with the young boy or not. The suspense was nearly killing her.

"Which hospital?" she heard him ask.

She almost tripped over a stack of Shaker baskets in her rush to get around the counter. Murtaugh, rubbing the back of his neck and with the phone still plugged into his ear, was disappearing into the back room.

The thought of something having happened to Chris washed through her like February rain. It was all her fault. She should have taken the boy to his school, or to the museum office. The world was a different place now than when she was young. And just because Ellie had been able to manage alone, she shouldn't have assumed that Chris could, too.

She had been twelve; he was eight. She had lived in a city with thousands of people around. He was isolated in the country. She'd survived. He was hurt. And it was her fault.

Ellie caught up with Murtaugh. He was still talking on the phone. She went around him, trying to get his attention. He turned his back on her. She moved next to him, playing the part of his shadow.

"Tire tracks...yeah...hold on a minute."

He gave her an irritated glare over his shoulder. "Do you mind?"

"Is it Chris?" she asked.

Nate paused a second, but instead of answering, he went back to his conversation. "You know the procedures. I'll be up there first thing in the morning."

A lump in her throat threatened to choke her. Her feet were locked in concrete.

"Well, I don't care what he says. I'm involved with this now." Nate ended the call, and she was immediately in his face. "Things didn't go as planned."

"What happened to Chris?"

"We don't know. Maybe nothing. As far as we

know, McGill and the boy never connected. Sorry, I have to go." He turned around and started for the front of the store.

Ellie cut in front and blocked him. "And you wonder why is it that normal people don't want to have anything to do with you people? I asked you to come here. I *gave* you the information about Chris. If you had one shred of decency, you would tell me what the heck is going on."

"Officer McGill went down tonight."

Nate's statement knocked the air out of her. "Where? How did it happen?"

"In the lot of the body shop where he was supposed to meet up with Chris. It looks like a hit-and-run. A police cruiser passing by saw McGill's pickup truck and then spotted his body on the ground."

"How bad is he?"

"He's still unconscious. Other than that, it's too early to tell. They airlifted him to Moses-Ludington Hospital in Ticonderoga."

"And Chris? Did anybody even look for him?"

"Tom had called in to the station before he left his house. They looked for Chris, but there was no sign of him."

"I'm going up there with you," Ellie blurted. "I heard you say you were going. Maybe Chris is hanging around. If he sees me, then he might come forward."

"There'll be a police investigation into this. I'd just as soon not get you involved at this point."

"Why?"

"Because you're..." He stopped.

"What?" she pressed. "Because I'm the daughter of an ex-con? Because I have a record myself?"

His cell phone started ringing again. Ellie didn't

back up when Nate answered and half turned away. From where she was standing, she could hear some creative obscenities pour out of the phone.

Nate walked past her toward the front of the store. Ellie followed him. "I don't see what the problem is. I'm only going for the day. But I would've thought Chief Buckley had something better to do than call you with minute-by-minute updates. I just got off the goddamn phone with him."

The voice on the other end was so loud that Ellie saw Nate pull the phone away and tug on his earlobe irritably. When the person on the other end paused, Nate dove in again.

"We don't know what happened. And Buckley can't possibly know if this was a case of drunken driving. He has no one in custody yet. Hey, I was the one who sent McGill out there. The least I could—"

The voice started shouting again. Ellie heard her own name. Sounded like Nate's only something-something job was to get her to help acquire the something-something flag. She had no doubt that the foul mouth belonged to Sanford Hawes, a big gun at the FBI. Sister Helen had warned her about this Hawes, now a supposed friend but the same guy who'd put her behind bars. He had a reputation for being a pit bull who always got the job done, whatever the cost.

Sister Helen had given her a number of bits of advice about Hawes and the FBI this afternoon. Get involved on your own terms before you're forced to help them, and insist on working with a reasonable agent. She watched an increasingly frustrated Murtaugh run a hand through his hair, making the short tufts stand out in every direction. This was a side of him she rather liked seeing right now.

"No. Now you listen to me, Sanford. You're busting a gasket over nothing. I'm not trying to handle everyone else's job at the expense of my own. What...let me finish—"

He switched the phone from one ear to the other and stalked to the front window. For the first time she noticed the slight limp.

"Reassign me, if you think that's called for," Nate yelled back. "You've been on my back ever since you gave me this assignment...I know our asses are on the line. But if you think you can run this thing from your office..."

Ellie shuddered at the very thought of Hawes's direct involvement. She hadn't even met the man, but the idea of being pushed along by someone like him was revolting. Sister Helen had said there were no options. The politics of the election was one hundred percent the motivation behind this, and Helen's and Ellie's names were already mixed up in it. And Ellie knew that she had enough ghosts in her closet. If anyone dug deep, they could put a headlock on her.

"I'm done talking about this, Sanford. You're so full of this political crap that you can't even hear or see straight." He sat down on one of the stools and rubbed his knee. "I'm fed up. Get someone else down here or come yourself. I'm going back to New York."

"Wait!" Ellie cried out. She hurried to his side.

"You won't do that to me. But even if you did, I'm sick and tired of—"

"Wait!" she said louder, touching Nate's shoulder to get his attention.

His tired gaze met hers.

"Let me talk to him." She lowered her voice. "I think I might have a solution to all of this."

He stared at her for a moment, then—with no warning or explanation to Hawes—he handed Ellie the phone.

"You're not stupid enough to throw away eleven years of service over a fu—" Ellie held the phone an arm's length away and gave Murtaugh a sympathetic look. It wasn't the language but the volume of it that was objectionable. "Mr. Hawes!"

He continued to rumble on. Nate held her hand with the phone in it and brought it to his face.

"Listen, goddammit! Ms. Littlefield has something to tell you."

She took back her hand and spoke into the phone again. "Mr. Hawes?"

Silence filled the line.

"Mr. Hawes, I've changed my mind. I've decided to assist Agent Murtaugh in locating the original Betsy Ross flag, if that's what it is that may be out there."

"We have no time for 'maybe I will, maybe I won't,' Miss Littlefield. This is not the way the FBI conducts operations, and we've got only two weeks to accomplish this assignment."

"That's what he's been telling me."

"What are your leads?"

"Before we get too specific here, you need to hear my demands." Ellie returned Nate's narrowed glare.

"What do you want?"

"I want you to stay out of it."

"Come again?" Hawes asked in a higher pitch from the other end.

Ellie leaned her back against the counter and watched a trace of confusion cross the tough expression of the man sitting beside her. "In addition to the guarantees that I understand Sister Helen asked of you, and a financial arrangement allowing me to bill you for my time, I'm demanding that you stop micromanaging us. This is my life and my reputation I'm putting on the line here. Agent Murtaugh appears perfectly qualified to go undercover to do this job, but I can only be effective if you leave us alone and let me make the contacts for him. We have to make his interest in the Robert Morris flag known in the proper circles. To do that, you need to keep your hands off. Wherever we go or whoever we see, we'll be the ones to decide that from here on out. We'll call you when we need you, but other than that, my demand is that you cease to exist.''

From the breathing on the other end of the line, she envisioned a bull pawing the earth and preparing to charge.

''Do we have a deal, Mr. Hawes?''

Eight

The television ad featured split-screen images—on one side, views of prosperous farms, impressive waterfalls and industrial complexes amid the wheat fields of the Midwestern plains; on the other, a dramatic contrast, with stark images of crowded classrooms, the homeless huddled in rags along alley walls and silent factories behind chained and padlocked gates on the eastern seaboard. The pithy comments on the planned expenditure of billions of dollars on the Water for America irrigation project, with its pipelines running from the national parks in the Rockies to the storage facilities in the lower Midwestern states, were just overkill. A picture speaks a thousand words, and the way things were presented here, an idiot could see who was benefiting from this project and who was being left out.

President Ron Kent punched the TV remote as his opponent came on the screen to add his two cents. He leaned back in his leather seat and studied the furnishings of his private sitting room in the west wing of the White House. Four years wasn't enough. He was only beginning to see progress in getting Congress in line on his programs. He looked at the painting of Mount Vernon over the fireplace. In spite of all the security and the formalities of being the country's head of state, he no longer felt this place was just temporary. The White House was just starting to feel like home, and he had no intention of giving it up after only one term.

He stood up abruptly and turned to his chief of staff. "How many points did this cost us?"

"I don't think I have those numbers...." George Street glanced through the folder on his lap, shaking his head. "They started running the ad on the six o'clock news on all the major networks and affiliates, and on CNN, of course. They've been repeating it—"

"How many points?" Kent asked impatiently, snatching up his glass and going to a side table to pour himself another two fingers of Chivas.

"Our 8:00 p.m. poll showed a four-point drop." George cleared his throat and thumbed through the pages again. "We believe there may be a problem with the tabulations of the 10:00 p.m. poll, though."

"How bad was it?"

"Mr. President, it would be counterproductive to pay attention to a temporary dip in these numbers right now. With more than four months left till the election, we have plenty of time to counteract this kind of negative advertising. With the situation in the Middle East and our options regarding escalated action there, the mood of the nation can be—"

"Don't tell me about the mood of the nation, George." Kent banged his glass down on the table, and the drink sloshed out onto the polished mahogany. "Facts and numbers. That's what you're best at. Give them to me, damn it."

"The ratings registered another seven-point drop in the ten o'clock poll."

Kent moved to the fireplace and gazed at the picture of Mount Vernon for a moment. "Get the key players from Congress in here tomorrow morning."

"But you have the Turkish foreign minister scheduled for—"

The President turned to his chief of staff. "Reschedule. I want bipartisan faces behind me for a press conference in the Rose Garden at noon. It's time I made it public. Voters need to know that I'm planning to veto the Water for America program."

"Mr. President—"

Kent began to pace the room, thinking out loud. "I should have done this a month ago."

"Mr. President—"

The subtle change in Street's tone of voice drew Kent's attention. He ceased his pacing and frowned at his chief of staff. The younger man was wearing the look of a man trying to figure a way to get back on a horse that had just thrown him.

"Sir, responding like this will look like a knee-jerk reaction at best." Street laid the folders on the table beside his chair. "Mr. President, I am not your domestic adviser and I'm not the chair of your reelection committee, but there are a few things that I'd like to say about this, if I may."

"Spill it, George. You know I value your opinion."

"Something you need to consider is the fact that there are some very influential people—people who have contributed heavily to your reelection campaign—who will feel that you have strung them along on this for several years now. These people—acting on the basis of your support—have made huge financial investments in that region. Aside from them, however, the negative consequences of what could be construed as a last-minute change of heart—or even worse, as waffling—could be brutal.''

"There's nothing last minute about this, George. I warned Graham Hunt about the way I was leaning more than six months ago. He should have gone back then and asked the coalition of businessmen behind him to rethink their plans.''

"Hunt told me he was not happy you were rethinking the project, but I don't believe he knows that you plan to pull your support of it entirely. Nor do I think our party leaders in Congress know. Hunt and his people aside, we need to consider the impact of a veto on the other investors—the little guys in your home state, as well as the farmers and the construction industry and everyone else who's been banking on this thing for so long. A lot of effort and expense went into the lobbying that it took to push this bill through both Houses.'' Street lowered his voice. "Even the Vice President is supporting this project, and he's from New York. Talking this thing up handed you a landslide victory in those states in the last election, but you'll lose them for sure if you veto this project.''

"We'll have to risk that. I won't give that sonovabitch the high ground four months before the election,'' Kent growled. "The people in this country know that things are different now. We were in a growth pattern four years ago. Now we're struggling to beat back a recession. The economy is in no shape to handle this kind of expenditure on a program that will directly benefit only one region. I'm surprised they're not running ads showing me taking food out of children's mouths and putting it in my business friends' pockets.''

"We don't want to give them any ideas. But nobody—except the radio hosts on the lunatic fringe—is blaming this recession on you. There may be real value in finishing what you started."

Kent looked over his chief of staff. The scion of an old political family, George Street was Ivy League smart, country club polished, and he had a knack for saying the right thing in every situation. He had been a trump card in Kent's hand throughout this presidential term. But he had a strong feeling that he and Street had drifted apart on this project, and Kent now realized that it was critical for him to win the young man over. If he couldn't convince his own man, then he had no chance against the pack of wolves that Hunt ran with. He sat down across from his chief of staff.

"Do you remember what our intentions were at the beginning?"

George nodded. "In your election campaign, we identified the benefits of Water for America to the Midwestern states in terms of jobs and an overall boost to the region's economy. We spoke of the substantial improvement in agriculture. We also argued that the entire nation would benefit in times of drought. We—"

"That was the campaign push. I'm talking about two years before the election, when we were still struggling to jump-start the funding for the campaign. Do you remember sitting down with Graham Hunt and looking for ways to entice some of his investors to join our camp?" There was a blank expression on Street's face. "Cut the shit, George. We were both there together. This whole Water for America thing came about as a means of giving Graham and some of his investors a healthy return on what they were putting in. The program had merit, but the proportions of who benefited most definitely tipped toward those who were buying the land the pipes would run through and those who were investing in the construction outfits."

"I do remember, Mr. President. And don't you think it's important that you follow through with your initial promise?"

The man's eyes were as black as pools of crude oil on a sunless Oklahoma day. Kent got up and retrieved his drink from the table. Returning to his chair, he sat down and finished what was left in the glass.

"No, George. I don't." The President stared at the sharp angles of the cut crystal in his hand. "I have a responsibility to act for the greater good. I have to make the right choices. And I don't need to see the promotional spots of the opposition camp to know that a lot of people will be affected adversely by this program."

"Every decision you make affects people one way or another, sir. Your actions on this will affect you, the election and your place in history."

"Call the press conference. I've made up my mind."

George gave a curt nod, gathered the folders on his lap and stood up. Kent shook off the disappointment that he hadn't swayed the young man. Street would stick with him, in spite of their differences on this issue. He'd grown up in politics. He knew the give-and-take of the business. Kent did, however, need Street to help him handle this whole issue smoothly. He needed him to handle the details, and to see to it that he said the right things to the right people at the right time. Details were crucial, and he needed his chief of staff to see to them.

"If I might offer a suggestion, sir," Street said, stopping at the door.

"Of course."

"I believe it would leave you too open to potshots

if you were to make such a public statement the day
after the airing of these television ads. Your critics will
have a field day, saying your good deed is just a reaction. They won't give you any credit for it. Your
sincerity and credibility will be the next thing they attack.''

"What do you think I should do? Wait a day or
two?''

"I think you should wait and make the announcement in Philadelphia at the opening festivities of the
Spirit of America celebration. We can circulate the rumor now that we've been holding off on a big announcement for several weeks. That event—which the
polls show the country knows is your baby and is
viewed favorably across the board—is devoid of con-
troversy. It will give you the perfect opportunity for
gaining the most credit for this monumental decision.''

"As always, you know these things best. Take care
of it. We'll make the announcement on the Fourth of
July.''

The confrontation on the phone had brought out a
pink shade in Ellie's flawless cheeks. Nate found himself staring. She had long, dark lashes and large, dark
eyes that almost overpowered her straight nose, her
high cheekbones and her wide sensual mouth. Almost.
In this wound-up state, she had a kind of Audrey Hep-
burn look, a classic beauty.

"Very impressive.''

"You mean the way you and Hawes tricked me into
cooperating with you? What do you call that, the 'good
cop, bad cop' routine?''

"I don't call it anything.'' Nate took back his phone.
"No. I mean the way you succeeded in shutting an FBI

assistant director's mouth. Not that it'll last for more than a couple of hours.''

''I could have asked for more. He won't dare back out of our deal when he's really getting his way.''

''You don't know what Sanford Hawes is capable of doing.'' Nate pocketed his phone and looked at the door. ''I'm going up to Ticonderoga first thing in the morning.''

''And I'm coming with you.'' She blocked his path to the door. ''Agent Murtaugh, would you like me to give *you* an ultimatum, as well?''

Nate found her tough talk very amusing, considering her elfish size. But he decided not to go there now.

''As I said before, I don't think it's a good idea for you to show your face up there right now. Besides, don't you think you'd be more effective at looking for that flag if you actually started looking? What do you have to do, make some calls? Talk to people in the business?''

She planted her hands on her hips and refused to back up. ''Don't tell me what I should do. You can be as annoying as your boss.''

''Point taken. But I'll call you tomorrow night to see what you've got.''

''And I won't be here. In fact, I can't see any reason for your involvement at all. You're only an added headache. I can do this perfectly well without you.'' She went around him and reached for her phone. ''I'll call Sister Helen and have her change the arrangement. I can do all the legwork and even arrange for the purchase of the flag. Now, whoever Mr. Hawes decides to send for the final exchange is up to him. But I won't be needing that person until then.''

''You win.'' His hand covered the handset before

she could lift it from its cradle. ''You can be pretty annoying yourself.''

''Thanks.'' She walked to the door and opened it wide. ''What time are we leaving for New York?''

''I'm planning on an early flight.''

''I'll meet you at the airport. You can call me with the time and the gate.''

Nate paused before her by the door. The idea of walking away from all this had sounded very enticing when Sanford had been threatening him with his job over the phone. He'd caught himself thinking—in vague terms—about resigning from the Bureau several times over this past year. He was turning into a miserable middle-aged complainer with a bum knee, he had no personal life to speak of, and he'd been shoved behind a desk. There had to be a better life outside of this.

''I won't get in your way, Agent Murtaugh. And you don't have to worry about me. I know how to become invisible when it comes to the authorities.''

The soft voice was back. Beautiful, vulnerable...nothing like the tough-talking thief-turned-antique dealer who'd been bargaining with Hawes a few minutes ago.

She was looking pretty damn good to him, in spite of her past. His judgment was clearly going to hell. Maybe he did need to make this his last job. Maybe he should walk away from it now.

''I'm not too bad to work with. You might actually like it.''

This was part of the problem. He knew he'd like it.

''I'll call you later,'' Nate said as he went out the door.

Nine

Ray Claiborne was one of the few people Ellie had a difficult time lying to. This was why she was relieved that she was doing this on the phone and not face-to-face.

"Sister Helen introduced us. His name is Nate Moffet. Young, thirty-something, a lot of free time apparently. Bored trust-fund baby, I'm guessing. I think somebody told him it was cool to be a collector. He's into a variety of niche collecting. Strictly Americana stuff, he says."

"Anything like that trophy wife from Newport two years ago? Remember how her interests broadened from Americana to French Empire as soon as I showed her those sex toys?"

"I don't think I ever met her."

"You ought to see what she's collecting this year," Ray said with a laugh.

Ellie didn't want to know. But she knew there was no sense saying it since Ray was already launching into a list of the woman's latest purchases. She realigned the dozen sticky notes bearing instructions for Vic on the counter and looked down at her watch. Ten of seven. Nate was picking her up in ten minutes. For his sake and for her own, she hoped Ray would buy her story and put out the word about her client's interest in the Morris flag. Last week, Ray had been the one who told her of the rumors of a Betsy Ross flag coming on the market.

Dealmaker, collector and former high-rolling fence for Louis Littlefield, Ray Claiborne had been Ellie's mentor and protector for most of the years her father had been in prison. Everything she'd learned about the legal and illegal acquisition of precious artwork and antiques had come from her "uncle" Ray. Even the start-up money for her business had been a present from Ray. Of course, the criminal record she'd acquired as a youngster had been another gift from him.

"Where did you say this guy was from?"

"He says he moves with the sun these days. Has a place in Palm Springs and Maui and skis in Aspen when he feels like it. But I think he said something about being 'born and drug up' in New York State."

"I've never heard of him."

"I'm not surprised. He's not stick-it-in-your-face rich. Kind of old money attitude, you know? And as far as his collecting, I'd bet money he's pretty new in the game."

"Good-looking?"

"Ray!" She drawled out his name and heard him chuckling on the other end.

"Answer the question, babycakes."

"He's too old for the way you like them." She tucked the phone into the crook of her neck and waved at the door, motioning for Nate not to knock. It figured he'd be early. "Actually, I don't think he leans that way at all. Vic tried to hit on him already, with no success.''

''That may just mean that Vic isn't his type.''

''I'd still bet he won't be interested.''

''I haven't met him, so I won't take your money yet.''

As she moved to open the door for Nate, she realized it had been a good thing that she hadn't immediately shared her suspicions with Vic that Nate was a cop. If she'd even told him Nate's last name, they would be doing this all differently.

Ray's tone became businesslike. ''So you want me to start a buzz about this young man?''

''Just get the word out that I have a new client who's a player. Will you do that?'' Ellie waved Nate in. He was wearing a gray suit, a quiet patterned tie and another one of his starched white shirts.

''Now, why does he have to have that specific flag...the Morris flag? If he's a new collector, there are many other—''

''The man's got the money, and he tells me that's what he's looking for right now. He says he's willing to pay big for it and pay me a handsome commission if I find it for him before the Fourth of July. Says he's going cruising on a friend's yacht for a couple of months around the middle of July. Now, do you want me to talk him out of it?''

''No, no. I understand perfectly. In fact, I myself hate it when you walk into the florist shop looking for gardenias and the clerk shoves daisies at you,'' Ray grumbled. ''I suppose my problem is that there is just too much chitchat about this supposedly fabulous flag and no solid word about any auction. Maybe the rumor-mongers are just being coy to stir up interest—bring out money-people like your client—but everything is pretty vague, even for this kind of item. I haven't heard of anyone who knows where this flag is or when they're selling the damn thing. Also, there hasn't been a single word about a starting price. Whoever it is that's handling this is being pretty clever. And I don't think it's anyone from Philly or New York.''

''That's why I thought I should call you right away. I figured if the word went out about a live customer, we'd start hearing more.'' Nate pointed to his watch, and Ellie turned her back on him. ''I've made a few calls myself, but I was hoping you'd do the same thing and see what it gets us.''

''I'll see what I can do, kid,'' Ray told her. ''By the way, I hope you're planning on bringing this guy to the house this Friday for my dinner party. I can't wait to meet him.''

Ellie looked over her shoulder at Nate's stiff shirt and frown. He had *cop* stamped all over him. ''We'll see. I have to work on him.''

He had already picked up her leather overnight bag from the chair and was waiting by the door when Ellie hung up. ''We have less than twenty minutes to make it to the airport.''

''I have faith in you, Agent Murtaugh.'' Ellie grabbed her purse and keys and walked out behind him. The blue sedan, another obvious sign of his profession, was parked illegally on the sidewalk. She climbed in, and he took off while she was still pulling on her seat belt.

''You were talking to Ray Claiborne.''

''Are you guys tapping my phone?''

''No.'' He ran a red light. ''What did you tell him about me?''

"The stuff you gave me last night on the phone. I like the Moffet thing. It's close to Murtaugh—Moffet, Murtaugh. It's easy to explain if I slip."

"Try not to." He cursed at a car that didn't get out of his way fast enough. He glanced over at her. "Not a morning person, are you?"

He stepped on the gas, and she clutched the door handle until he'd run through another red light.

"As a matter of fact, I am. Ray is, too. That's why I called him this morning. He's much better connected out there than I am. In fact, I'm surprised you people didn't go to him for help instead."

"When it comes to cooperating, Ray Claiborne's willingness and expertise ends with incriminating his friends and the child who's been left in his care. I'm surprised you don't know that."

It would have been a loyal gesture to argue on Ray's behalf, but there was no point. The circumstances around Louis Littlefield's arrest and jail sentence were not Ray's fault, and the fact that her father had refused to drag his main contact into the mess was Louis's own decision. And as far as Ellie's own arrest when she was fifteen, it was a matter of him going to jail for years and his operation folding or Ellie taking the rap and having her hand slapped as a juvie. She'd known what she was doing. She'd just stuck to her story. There was no mastermind directing her when she'd been caught stealing a two-million-dollar painting out of a house on the Main Line. There were no buyers waiting. Nobody had given her any lead. It was just a spontaneous thing that she'd grabbed the canvas and not the owner's wallet. She didn't know it was worth that much. She just liked the painting. The family court judge had bought the story. Now it was ancient history.

Ellie looked out her window. At thirty, she could live with her conscience and her decision to stay loyal to Uncle Ray when she'd been a teenager. But she also knew that at sixty-eight, Ray still felt guilty for what he had done to her.

No regrets. She was where she wanted to be in her life. She had a nice apartment. Owned her own business. Drove a fancy sports car. And going shopping no longer consisted of illegally rummaging through a Salvation Army collection box. Ellie turned to the maniac driver next to her. "We have to go shopping when we get back."

"You can discuss your expense account with Hawes." Nate weaved between two cars. "And I hate shopping."

"Well, that's too bad, since it's *your* expense account we'll be dipping into. *You're* the one we'll be buying for."

"Buying what?"

"Cooler clothes. Maybe some silk shirts. A bit of jewelry. A different cut of pants. Definitely better shoes. Clothes that don't say 'I'm a career G-man.' By the way, we also have to do something with your hair."

"Why?"

"To look cooler." Ellie touched the fabric of his jacket with the tip of two fingers. "To hang around with me, you'll have to do a lot better than this, Mr. Murtaugh...Moffet...whatever your name is. I have a reputation to protect."

He parked the sedan illegally in front of a terminal. Before they stepped out of the car, a security guard immediately approached. After a couple of quick exchanges with Nate, the guard called someone over to park the car for him.

"You tell them to jump, and they want to know how high," she commented as they raced through the terminal. "You have it made, don't you, Agent Murtaugh?"

"I did, before I started hanging around with you."

"It's good that you realize there'll be a change, because you won't be the same person after I'm done with you."

"Is that a threat?"

"No, a promise." She smiled at him when they reached a security checkpoint. "You haven't seen anything of my ability to bring out the more stylish side of people. In the case of men, I like to think of it as their feminine side. Now that I think of it, you'd fit much better into this role if you were gay."

He gave her an incredulous look. "I don't think so."

"Oh, I do. I'll just need to get Vic's help, and you'll be in top form in no time."

The newly renovated hospital, with its modern critical-access facility, twenty-four-hour emergency room and helicopter pad, sat on a rise overlooking Ticonderoga, New York.

Nate stared through the glass at the computer monitors, plastic tubes and perpetually moving apparatuses designed to keep the body functioning. The roomful of equipment was keeping Officer Tom McGill alive. His condition was still grave. It hadn't changed since Nate had stopped by this morning.

He'd spent the couple of hours in between visits at the police barracks going over the reports, evidence and photos that they'd taken at the scene.

They were calling it a burglary gone bad. A couple of morons trying to rob the body shop and caught off guard by finding Tom in the lot. They'd hit him hard enough that he'd been thrown twenty feet, till he came to rest against the concrete-block wall of the shop. They'd taken a look, panicked, then left him to die. That was the preliminary report, anyway.

Nate didn't need the itchy feeling at the base of his scalp to tell him something didn't jive. So far, the local and state police had found no sign of the car. The state labs were still analyzing tire tracks and footprints. The only thing they knew for sure was that two people had gotten out of the vehicle after hitting McGill. And of course, there was the possibility of a witness. And once again, it was Christopher Weaver.

The boy had left enough telltale signs behind that the locals had determined where he'd been hiding and how he'd gotten away, slipping through a loosely chained gate at the rear of the junkyard. Beyond that, there were woods for a mile or more and there was no telling whether the perpetrators were on his trail or not. If it went down the way the locals thought, those two jokers were probably shaking in their boots somewhere between here and Ohio right about now. But there was also the possibility that it hadn't happened that way.

"The folks over there are Tom's parents." The officer standing next to him nodded toward a young-looking man and woman, holding hands and sitting on a light blue faux-leather sofa down the hall. They were in their late forties, maybe fifty, tops. Not much older than he was. The realization washed over him like cold water. Nate started toward them.

The father stood up when Nate introduced himself. After he pulled up a chair for himself, he explained that it had been his call that had sent McGill out last night.

"Tom mentioned you," the mother said quietly. "That's where he'd love to end up someday...in the FBI."

"He's got a good head on his shoulders," Mr. Mc-Gill said, "just like his mother." He put an arm around his wife's shoulders.

"I'd be happy to write a recommendation for him when he's ready," Nate whispered hoarsely, relieved that they had not given up hope.

He made some small talk, unable to add anything to what these people already knew, and listened to snatches of stories about Tom growing up. A few minutes later, Nate spotted Ellie sitting on a bench near the elevator, cup of coffee in hand. She darted an anxious glance their way. He said goodbye to the McGills, gave them his card and walked over to her.

She'd had Nate drop her at a little antique store near the center of town when they drove in from the airport this morning. Since his first stop was the police station, Nate had been more or less happy with the arrangement. He hadn't been the only person who had watched the security shots of Ellie talking to Christopher in the museum. And though she was working with the Bureau, the locals didn't know anything about it. As far as Nate was concerned, at this point the less anybody knew the better. When she stood up, he could see there were dark lines under her eyes.

"How long have you been waiting?"

"Just a few minutes."

"Something wrong?"

"I was thinking that if I hadn't given Chris a ride Friday afternoon, then he wouldn't be missing, and there would've been no reason for that cop to go looking for him last night."

"Look, if it wasn't last night, then it would have been another night, another call, another creep," he said grimly. His knuckles brushed gently against the backs of her fingers. "It can happen anytime. It's in the nature of the beast. You join up to help people, but sometimes you end up becoming a target yourself."

He took the cup from her and sloshed around the mud that was left in the bottom before dropping it in a trash can next to the elevator. "Why don't we get out of here. I'll buy you a fresh cup of coffee, and on our way back to the airport you can tell me what you've been up to since this morning."

She got inside the elevator with him. "What time is our return flight?"

Nate glanced at his watch. "Not until five-thirty. Why?"

"I had a call on my cell from Sister Helen. Now that I've agreed to work with you people, she wants the two of us to come by the convent to go over some ideas and possible ways she could hook us up with some other connections. Basically, she wants to get things rolling."

"She's a master planner, isn't she?"

"Absolutely." She stepped out of the elevator in front of him. Aside from a white-haired volunteer standing next to the receptionist's desk, there were only a few people in the lobby. The volunteer was wiping the leaves of a potted plant and smiled at them as they went by. "I think becoming a nun satisfied a spiritual need in her, but it also gave her a means of directing her energy and creativity. The mission she's chosen gives her the opportunity to change things. And yes, she is definitely an organizer. Where to?"

Nate took her elbow and turned her toward a row of

snack machines along a wall. "Sorry, this is the best I can get you here."

"I'm not fussy."

Nate realized that he was allowing his hand to linger on her bare arm, and he let it drop. "Maybe Sister Helen and Hawes would make a good team."

"No." Ellie wrinkled her nose and shook her head. "But I think she would make a good replacement for him. Not that your agency would ever—"

"Are you Miss Littlefield?"

They both looked with surprise at the blond-haired girl who had stepped out of nowhere.

"Yes. That's me," Ellie whispered, shooting a hasty look around the quiet lobby.

"Can I talk to you alone for a minute?"

In those few seconds since the girl had sprung up in their path, Nate had tried to estimate her age and possible connections to Ellie. She was young. Maybe eight or nine years old. He looked around the lobby, too, searching for Chris.

"Of course." Ellie squeezed Nate's hand. "I'll be right back."

He watched her talking quietly to the young girl as they walked away. They went out the front door of the hospital. When he'd dropped Ellie off this morning, Nate knew she was going to talk to her antique-dealer friend. Where she'd gone from there and who she'd talked to, he didn't know yet. But he was certain she'd spent the day looking for the missing boy.

"Can I help you with something?"

Nate shook his head at the elderly volunteer and started toward the front doors. Christopher Weaver was a complication in the assignment, and they had to forget about him; this was what Hawes had been telling

him. Well, that wasn't going to happen, obviously. Ellie was determined to help the kid, and Nate wanted
him safe. But what constituted "safe" for a kid—that
was what he was struggling with.

Despite dealing with some of the toughest sons of
bitches on and off the street since joining the Bureau,
Nate was pretty ignorant when it came to children.
Kids had parents who raised them. Kids had homes that
social services agencies placed them in. But what about
the rest of the ones on the street? Or the ones who got
tossed out of their homes? Or the runaways? What
about all the kids nobody wanted?

Nate had seen them, dealt with them, but he'd never
thought that one of those kids would slap him with his
reality wake-up call. He'd never thought a kid would
make him question life and what the hell he was doing
with his end of it.

Nate hadn't repaid Joey Sullen very well for the gift
the boy had given him.

He waited by the door until a man in a wheelchair
pushed his way in.

On the hot sidewalk outside, he saw Ellie hurrying
across the parking lot and up the grassy hill to him.
She'd shed her jacket and was carrying it on her arm.
She walked a couple of steps, then ran a few, then
walked again. Nate started toward her. He saw her
smile.

"You don't have much of a poker face. Where is he?"

"Give me your keys." She was breathless. Nate saw
the little girl who had approached them sitting on a
bike across the parking lot. Ellie saw her, too, and
waved back at the blond youngster. In a moment the
girl had pedaled off.

"Who was she?"

"Allison, a classmate of Christopher's," she answered, giving up asking for the key and instead taking him by the arm and dragging him toward the visitor's parking lot.

"What's going on?"

"We're driving Chris back to Philly."

He stopped short, causing her to spin around and face him. "Hold on a second. We're not taking a missing child across state lines."

"Yes, we are," she replied firmly. "The boy is terrified. He says there are some bad guys after him. He wants to go someplace safe, and he has trusted me to help him."

"That's how this whole mess started," he snapped. "The boy is here. We put him in the car, notify the local police, then take him to the closest family services office and let them deal with him."

"How can you be so heartless?" Her eyes were huge and filled with hurt. "This little boy has been running scared since Friday. Of all the people he knows, he comes to me. Why?"

"Because you're a soft touch and don't have an ounce of good sense in your head."

Her jaw dropped in disbelief, but he grabbed her by the wrist when she tried to walk away from him.

"I can't believe you."

"Listen to me, Ellie. This kid is wanted for questioning by police because he was a witness to the hit-and-run that put McGill in this hospital—never mind what he might have seen in the museum. We just can't whisk him away and pretend a stork dropped him on your doorstop."

"I know that. We can take him to Sister Helen's.

Once he feels safe there, I know he'll tell whatever he knows to anyone you want to bring in.''

"No. He says what he has to say right here.''

"He won't. He'll run away again.''

"That's not our problem.''

With her free hand, she grabbed the lapel of his jacket. "Listen to me. Do you know what it feels like to be this alone and scared?''

He couldn't answer, taken aback by the raw emotion seething up from just beneath the surface. He envisioned Ellie as a young kid, alone on the street—like the ones he'd been thinking of—having no one who cared. She herself had been where Chris was right now.

"This morning, after you dropped me at John's shop, I used his car and stopped at the foster home where Chris has been staying. That woman, Sharon Green, was doing her best, but she has three other kids—toddlers—living there. She hasn't had time to even worry about Chris. I stopped at the trailer park where his mother is living now. She was so stoned that she could barely even remember that she had a son, never mind that he was missing.''

With his thumb, Nate wiped away the tear that escaped from her eye. Her skin felt like silk. "How did you make the Allison connection?''

She stared at him for a second. "I…I stopped at the school and caught his teacher cleaning out her classroom. After I lied and said I was an aunt who was visiting for a day, Miss Leoni told me that the only student who ever talked to Chris was this little girl. On a hunch, I told her where I would be this afternoon. I think the message got to Allison through her.''

"Has Chris been staying with Allison?''

"He hid in their shed just last night. She found him

there this morning, after her parents were already at work. An older sister watches her during the day, but I don't think Allison told her anything.''

''What happened to the days when kids took their problems—or problems with their friends—to their parents?''

''I wouldn't know. I never had a parent around.''

He reluctantly loosened his grip on her wrist. ''This is a tough one. We'll be up shit creek when Hawes hears about it.''

Tears glistened like jewels in her dark eyes. ''I'll promise to do everything I can. I'll use every contact I have. Whatever needs to be done. I'll find that flag for you. But we have to take Chris to where he'll feel safe. I really believe that the convent will be the best place for him right now.''

''I must be losing my mind.'' He looked around him before starting toward the parking lot. She stayed beside him. ''I just want you to know that what you and I want doesn't matter a damn to the system. We might drive him all the way to Philly, only to have an agent waiting there to drive him all the way back.''

''You *can't* let them do that. You'll see for yourself in a minute. He's scared. He needs time to recover, to get over whatever it is that he's been running from these past few days.'' She shot him a sidelong glance. ''Make me sound like a monster if you have to. But when you talk to Hawes, tell him…tell him I *demand* that Chris stays in Philly for a week or two, maybe more. Tell him the whole thing is my fault.''

''The police have a right to question him immediately about McGill.''

''Let them send someone to Philadelphia. Or you do it. Come on, Nate,'' she said in a gentler tone. ''I'm not asking for the world. Just think of how unimportant moving this one little boy to Philadelphia is compared to the number of laws the FBI bends or breaks to get their jobs done.''

He snorted. ''Well, now that you put it that way!''

There was no one by the car when they reached it. ''Where is he?''

''Just get in. He'll show up.''

He opened Ellie's door and waited for her to climb in. Going around the car, he looked across the lot at a row of daily newspaper machines. He glanced inside the bed of the pickup truck parked next to him. There was no sign of the kid anywhere. He got inside and started the engine, flipping on the air-conditioning to high.

She was sitting on the edge of the seat, looking anxiously in every direction.

''Where did you leave him?''

''Right here. He was crouched down next to the passenger door when I came to get you.''

Looking in the rearview mirror, Nate spotted the unmarked police car entering the visitors lot. ''We might never get the kid out of this parking lot, never mind take him to Philadelphia.''

As she turned around to see what he was talking about, the car pulled into the parking spot next to Ellie's door.

''The chief of police,'' Nate told her under his breath as the man climbed out. ''It doesn't get any better than this.''

Ellie sank back against the seat. Her face had gone pale. One of her feet tapped nervously on the floor. ''Please, Nate. Do something. You can't let them take him. He needs our help.''

He knew Buckley would recognize him, and the police chief didn't disappoint him. Nate gave Ellie's hand a quick squeeze and pressed the power button, opening her window as the chief got out of his car.

"Agent Murtaugh. The boys at the station told me you were back in town." Buckley leaned a forearm on their car. His gaze moved over Ellie and stayed there. She stared out the front windshield, totally ignoring him. "We're not happy about Tom. We don't like our own taken down that way."

"You here to see him?" Nate asked.

"I thought I'd make a quick stop on the way home. We're like family. I hear they're not giving him much of a chance. His condition hasn't improved."

"I wouldn't be too quick to count him out." Nate felt himself getting angry as Buckley continued to ogle Ellie's body. The chief hadn't been part of the group that had gone over Friday's security shots inside the Fort Ticonderoga Museum. He doubted that the other man's interest was strictly professional at this moment, either. "You'd better go up, if you want to get in. I heard today they were cutting back the visiting hours."

"Hey, I'm the chief here. Even small-town cops have a few perks, you know. Have we met before?" Buckley asked Ellie the question directly.

She looked coolly at the chief. "No."

"I didn't think so, but since Agent Murtaugh isn't making any introductions, I thought—"

"We're mixing a little work and pleasure today." Nate put an arm around Ellie's shoulder and pulled her toward him. She reached up and entwined their fingers. It was impossible to ignore the feel of her slender body against his, the scent of her perfume, the crazy things his body was doing. "Now, if you'll excuse us, Chief, we've got a long drive ahead of us."

"Yeah...sure. Good seeing you again." He straightened up, and Nate closed the window as Buckley stepped up on the grass divider. He glanced back briefly over his shoulder and waved.

Ellie waved back. "I think this is when you're supposed to back up the car," she whispered, moving away from him and pulling on her seat belt.

"No, you and I are supposed to kiss passionately while he chuckles to himself and goes the hell inside. Don't you watch any movies?"

"I could never kiss you," she said quietly, sliding away from him on the seat.

Nate's gaze narrowed first on the gentle blush coloring her cheek, then on her mouth. "Why is that?"

Ellie crossed her arms over her chest and stared at Buckley's back while he strolled toward the main entrance to the hospital. "That was never part of the job description."

"And transporting an eight-year-old—a kid who's wanted for questioning as a material witness—back to Philadelphia with us *was?*"

"That's different."

"How?"

"After you see him, you'll agree that Chris needs help." Her face turned to him. "We're forced to work together, for few days or a couple of weeks at the most. We're from totally different backgrounds. We have different tastes in people. It might just be possible that, although we're doing our best to be civil to each other, we don't even like each other. My guess is that the FBI has a few regulations about this, too. Am I wrong?

Considering everything, I believe we should keep our relationship totally professional.''

"You stole the words out of my mouth," Nate said gruffly. "And for your information, I'm not interested in you at all."

"I didn't think so."

"You don't have to have the last word in this." He put the car in Reverse and looked behind him to pull out of the parking spot, angry with himself for sounding like an adolescent.

"But I do."

Before he could respond, the back door of the car opened and a breathless four-foot bundle of muddy clothes and dirty hair climbed in. He smelled as if he'd spent the night curled up around a gas can.

"Christopher?" he asked gently, seeing the child's frightened glance at his jacket and tie.

The boy nodded and took Ellie's hand when she reached over the back of the seat.

"I'm Nate Murtaugh."

He nodded again and slid onto the floor. "Could we please leave now?"

Ten

A state-of-the-art security system, an automatic gate, thirty-six acres, seven bedrooms, five-thousand square feet of floor space, an indoor lap pool, a four-bay garage. And what the hell for?

Hawes kept the car window down and listened to the crunch of gravel under the tires as he drove up the winding driveway. He slowed down and looked up at his house as the headlights caught it. There was a time when just the sight of the house after a long day would buoy his spirits. No more. Three daughters—one still married, two divorced—and six grandchildren who didn't come around but once or twice a year was not reason enough to hold on to this white elephant Martha called home. Sometimes he felt like the Great Gatsby, except that he never threw any of those wild, fantastic parties where everyone came and had a wonderful time.

Sanford took out the souvenir panties Cheri had stuffed into his jacket pocket as he'd left. He could smell her woman's smell. He looked back at the house. None of this was worth what he was missing when he was away from that girl's bed. Cheri was wild and hot and liked to live dangerously. And it seemed as if she couldn't get enough of him. Frankly, he didn't care that at twenty-five, she was younger than his youngest daughter. Neither did he give a damn that as an administrative assistant in his department, technically she worked for him. All that was just bullshit, anyway. Life was too short.

The bay door on his side of the garage opened. Hawes pulled in and cut the engine. Both of Martha's cars were there. He inhaled again, breathing Cheri's smell in deeply. A man needed something to help him get through the night.

She'd been sharing a house with two other girls in downtown D.C. when she started working in his department. That was eight months ago. But once they'd begun to go out, the roommates definitely put a crimp in their style. The best thing Sanford had done was to buy some "investment" property this year and put Cheri in it. This way, he came and went as he pleased, and they weren't paying cash at cheap hotels or pulling onto side roads at night for sex in the car.

Some habits, though, were difficult to break. Like tonight. They'd picked up some Chinese takeout, and on the way back to her house she'd gone down on him in the car while he was driving—with considerable difficulty—along the Rock Creek Parkway.

Thinking about that for a minute, he reached under the seat and found her blouse. She'd used it to clean them up afterward. Driving along that road with her topless and her mouth around him was a fantasy come true. But that had only been the beginning. If there was one thing Cheri liked, it was rough sex and they'd had plenty of that tonight.

"Are you going to sit there all night?"

Sanford was startled at the sound of Martha's voice. He hadn't even realized it, but the timed lights of the garage door opener had already gone off. He hurriedly stuffed Cheri's things under the seat and reached for his tie, jacket and briefcase on the passenger seat. She was standing in the open door to the mudroom.

"What are you doing up this late?" he asked casually, getting out and pressing the remote button for the garage door to close.

"You had a couple of calls tonight. I didn't want to write a note and have you miss it."

Once again, the lights in the garage had come on, and as Sanford approached his wife, he couldn't stop mentally comparing Cheri's D-cup breasts and round, firm ass to Martha's less voluptuous build.

"I didn't know you were working with Nate Murtaugh again. He called tonight. It was nice to hear his voice again."

"That sonovabitch accuses me of calling him too much, so here I leave him alone for a few hours and suddenly he's dying to get me on the horn."

She puckered up her lips when he reached the door. He planted a fleeting kiss on her cheek and went inside. It was impossible to miss the scent of extra perfume she'd put on tonight.

"What was the other call?"

"You also had one from the White House. The chief of staff's office. I wrote down the number. Why didn't they call you at work? Or on your cell phone?"

He ignored her questions. "Did they say anything else?"

"It has to do with the President's press conference tomorrow."

He dropped his jacket and tie on the banister. "Don't wait up for me. I'll be in the library working." Without sparing Martha another glance, he headed to his office on the east wing of the house.

"Sanford?"

"What, Martha?" Hawes snapped without stopping.

She stayed on his heels. "Nate was calling from his car, and we didn't have the best connection, so I couldn't ask him myself. Is he back in Washington again?"

"No."

"But he's working for you." She turned on lights as they walked down the long hall.

"Just temporarily."

The dozen recessed lights in the coffered ceiling of the library came on as Martha flicked a switch. "Talking to him lit up my day. He's a lovely man—always asks the right questions and knows how to make people feel special. He even remembers the minutest details. That's good upbringing, if you ask me." She perched on the corner of his desk. "If he comes to town, could you invite him over for dinner?"

"I will. Now, be on your way. I have work to do."

"But weren't you doing that at the office?"

"Yes, I was." Sanford picked up the day's mail off his desk and started flipping through it.

She leaned over and turned on his desk lamp. "Did you eat any dinner?"

"Yes."

"What did you have?"

"Chinese."

"Takeout?"

He grunted a yes and dropped the pile of letters back on his desk, turning on his computer and printer. "Martha, I have work to do before I call the White House."

"What did you order?"

"Come on," he snapped at her. "It's late. I have a shitload of work to do. Now, be a good girl and go to bed or watch one of your old movies or something."

When she slid off the desk, his eyes caught sight of her bare thighs. He hadn't really looked at her before. She had on a thin silk wrap that he didn't remember ever seeing before. He was fairly certain he hadn't given it to her. His gaze moved upward, and he glimpsed a small, firm breast as she leaned forward. She was wearing nothing underneath the wrap.

She'd cut her hair short recently, maybe even this week. She looked quite fashionable with her bangs caressing her forehead. This was definitely a new look. She seemed younger. Sexier. She also had on makeup and was wearing two diamond studs in each ear.

"Where were *you* tonight?" he asked with more accusation in his tone than he intended.

"Here."

"Did you have company?"

She gave him a curious look over her shoulder. "Does it matter?"

The answer should have been no. He screwed around. Before Cheri, there had been others. When it came to their marriage, his responsibility was to work, earn the money and bring in enough dough to support Martha in the style she'd been accustomed to since childhood. In return, the girls, the grandkids and everything else around here were her problem.

"Yes," he heard himself say. "Who is he?"

"The letter carrier." She came back and leaned her hip on his desk again, this time crossing her tennis-smooth legs so that Hawes had a clear view. "Why, he's twenty-three years old. All muscle and tan, with long, blond hair. He comes around to deliver our mail in the morning…and stops back after lunch. He delivers anytime I need a good fuck."

Hawes was out of the chair in an instant, his hands

gripping her shoulders hard. He bet she'd never said that word before in her life.

"What the hell kind of talk is this?"

"You don't like it?" she asked, obviously trying to sound casual.

"No, I don't. And the last time I checked, there was a woman with a physique similar to Lennox Lewis delivering the mail. Whatever this game is you're playing, Martha, I don't like it."

"Well, I'm only getting started, honey," she said quietly. Her blue eyes were hot, but she was fighting to keep her expression cool. "You and I are stuck together for life, but after thirty-seven years, I've finally realized that you'll never change. So, to keep my sanity for another week or another year or another decade, I've decided to follow your lead."

"If that means you're getting a job, I'm all for it…honey," he replied in mocking tones. He dropped his hands and stood back. This had always been his winning card in arguments. He earned the money, so he was in charge.

"I'm sure you are. But that's the easy part in the changes that are going to take place around here. In fact, I already have something in the works." She stood up. "The new territory for me is in having affairs. You know, the kind where you forget about your marriage vows and your family and go out and screw someone half your age on your *anniversary*."

"Martha…"

She tried to push him out of her path, but he didn't budge. They'd been married on a beautiful June morning thirty-seven years ago today, and for the first time he'd forgotten even to send her some lousy flowers.

"No, I had some tough luck today. Not one deliveryman worth looking at. Even the clerk at the grocery store was a teenage girl.'' Her chin quivered a little, but she held it high and started around him. ''But starting tomorrow, watch out. I'll be ordering Chinese take-out and skipping on wearing underwear and—''

''I'm sorry, Martha.'' He reached for her. ''Happy anniversary, babe.''

She shook loose of him. ''Don't touch me. I don't need your pity. There are men out there who think I have a few things left. Men who are even worth a tumble.''

''I'm sorry,'' he whispered, this time only able to get hold of a piece of her wrap. The flimsy fabric opened in front.

She was indeed naked underneath, and a spontaneous flash of heat shot through him. She still had the ability to stun him with her beauty. She was his wife. She belonged to him. This was the one woman on earth whose body had been touched only by him. He knew every gentle curve, every sensitive spot. His thumb brushed against her nipple and he watched it extend and grow hard.

He gazed into her face. ''Please, Martha. Let me make it up to you.''

''No.'' She pushed his hand away. ''I've made up my mind. I want to be a slut. Just like your latest girlfriend. What's her name? Cher…or Cheri…or Cherry. I want to live like her. Those women have the best of both worlds. Sex when they want it. Men who dote on them. And no…no…need for the appearance of respectability.''

''I'll give you everything. All of that. I can change.'' Sanford pulled her into his arms and crushed his mouth down on her lips, silencing the rest of her complaint.

It took a moment, but he felt her come alive against his body. He wanted her, and suddenly Cheri was not even a blip in his memory bank.

Tearing her mouth from his, Martha backed away, wriggling out of the robe as he peeled it off of her. She took hold of his belt and shoved him back against his own desk. Without a shred of gentleness, she lowered his zipper. He grabbed a fistful of her hair and scraped his teeth against her throat.

After thirty-seven years, she was as sexy and hot as the day he married her. And she still wanted him.

Eleven

"What's with the box of Lucky Charms?"

Ellie looked over her shoulder at Christopher, who was sound asleep on the back seat and cuddled up to the empty box of cereal. He'd been clutching the thing when he first climbed inside the car, and he hadn't let go of it since.

"A security blanket, I guess. Or maybe a good-luck piece," she whispered. "Or maybe his only source of food since last Friday."

Ellie remembered vividly the days when a package of stale cookies had to feed her for three meals. When a doggie bag handed to her by someone leaving a restaurant was Christmas. Her security blanket in those days was an old button-front sweater of Lou's that she'd been able to snatch out of their apartment before she'd been picked up by the social workers that first time. Navy blue, a button missing. Three moth holes on the right sleeve.

Everywhere Ellie went, she took that sweater. The first foster family knew she'd run off when the sweater was gone. The last family took it away from her as punishment. Ellie got it back and then ran away.

She looked over the seat at the innocent face of the sleeping boy. "Do you think he got enough to eat?"

"I'd say so," Nate replied.

Chris had refused to get out of the car at a rest stop for dinner, but picking up food at the drive-through was okay with him.

"Two burgers, a large order of fries and a supersize chocolate shake. I don't know where he put it all."

Ellie looked at the taillights from the lines of traffic stretching along the congested Schuylkill Parkway leading into Philadelphia. "We're almost there and still no phone calls from Hawes." She let out a contented sigh of relief.

"Don't get too comfortable. I left a message for him to call me. He doesn't know what we've done."

"He has the power to do as he pleases," she said confidently. "And after we explain everything to him, he'll be on our side. I just know it."

He mumbled something under his breath that sounded a lot like an obscenity.

"Watch it. There's a minor in the car," she warned. "Take this exit. It's a short cut."

He pulled off where she pointed, making some quick turns along nameless streets and alleys as Ellie navigated them into Center City.

"I noticed how you've strategically avoided telling Chris that he'll be staying with a bunch of nuns."

"What's the difference? He could either camp in the corner of my apartment or sleep in his own room at the convent." She gave him another quick direction for a turn.

"It would make a huge difference to me."

Despite the darkness in the car, Ellie saw him grinning. "But you're an adolescent who will probably never grow up. Chris isn't."

"I say it will still make a difference to him. Nuns

are serious and scary, especially that one. I went to parochial school. I know.''

"Will you stop?" she scolded in a hushed voice, before looking back again and making sure Chris was asleep. "You're supposed to set a good example, not terrify the poor child with your old emotional scars."

"And that comes from a real adult, I suppose. What a great example you set for him since you two met. Lie, run away, don't take responsibility for your actions, don't cooperate. Whine, cry some more, and wait until someone comes along and makes it all better."

"He is only eight years old."

"Was it any different when you were twelve, or fifteen, or seventeen?"

The stony cop look was back, and Ellie looked out her window. Yes, it had been different for her. She had to take responsibility, not only for herself but for her father, too, before they dragged him off to prison. There was never anyone in her life that could make it better. Not even Ray.

And they hadn't let her take Lou's sweater to jail with her.

"Tough one to answer?"

"Have I told you how heartless you can be?"

"Yeah, six hours ago."

"Good. Take a right. We're there."

Louis Littlefield's living arrangements consisted of one fifteen-by-twenty finished room in the basement of the convent. The place had no windows, but it did have a bathroom with a tiny shower stall. He had no complaints, though. The cell at Graterford Prison was smaller, and the company there far less agreeable. The room in the nun's basement was much better.

He only wished that the lighting were a little better. He sat back and looked at the canvas he was working on. He needed more touches of blue on the left side.

Lou ate, slept and spent nearly all of his free time in this room. And he had plenty of time. Being a handyman for four nuns was not a demanding job. He didn't have any friends or social obligations other than his occasional Sunday walk to St. Joe's, two blocks away. He only went because of Sister Helen's threats.

Lou minded his own business, and the nuns minded theirs, for the most part, with the exception of Helen barging in from time to time to rattle on about what Ellie was doing. Reconciling the two of them was the nun's favorite hobby, but as far as Lou was concerned, some storybook ending wasn't about to happen. The fact that he and Ellie were civil to each other and exchanged a word or two here and there would probably be the extent of their relationship as father and daughter.

Ellie had her own lifestyle. She'd earned it. She could have her rich and important friends. She could travel with the dealmakers and the hustlers. Maybe she'd have better luck avoiding all the traps a person could fall into. No, it was a life that he wanted no part of. His years behind bars had cured him of that. Now Lou had his quiet routines. Maybe they seemed boring to her, but they suited him: painting, a little reading, listening to some old scratched-up Sinatra records. He was content with things as they were. He wanted nothing more.

The past couple of days, though, Helen had been whistling a new tune in his ear, and he couldn't put it out of his mind. In confidence, she'd told him about the Schuyler flag and about the agents that showed up looking for help finding this other flag Betsy Ross supposedly made. They called it the Robert Morris flag. Like it or not, Helen was involved and so was Ellie. Lou had been watching the news. He knew how important finding this rag would be. Everyone was expecting it. Both politicians and normal everyday folks were talking up this Spirit of America thing, as if a few relics and some flag waving could show the world that the U.S.A. had a lid on its troubles and was still standing united as a country.

Maybe they were right, but that was no guarantee that the right flag would show up in time. Lou had been thinking about that.

Hearing footsteps on the floor above, Lou laid down his palette and brushes and carefully covered the painting with a piece of canvas. He pushed the easel into a corner, facing the wall.

As if being involved with this flag business wasn't bad enough, Sister Helen told him this afternoon that Ellie was bringing some foster kid here all the way from upstate New York. He glanced at the clock on his bookshelf. This should be them.

Lou cleaned his brushes in the old slate laundry sink in the corner and put them on the drain board. He stretched his shoulder muscles as he put the caps on the containers of turpentine and linseed oil. He wasn't going to get all wound up about it. This was like everything else Ellie did. She was trying to make a statement. Reminding him one more time how bad things were for her when she'd been left alone. He turned up the volume on the record player a notch and told himself for the umpteenth time that he wasn't going to get upset.

"Lou?"

He saw the man standing on the landing halfway down the stairs. White shirt, rolled-up sleeves, loosened tie. Lou figured he must be the agent Helen had been talking about—the one who was working with Ellie. He turned the music back down. "Yeah. Do you need something?"

"A place to hang for a few minutes. I'm Nate Murtaugh." He came down the rest of the way and extended a hand.

"What did the good Sister do, give you the boot?" Lou liked the strong handshake and direct look. Cops didn't generally greet ex-cons like that.

"Yeah, but she didn't want me to go too far. So she said, go visit Lou." He stuffed his hands in his pockets and stood at the bottom of the stairs, looking around the room with interest. "You have quite a place down here."

Lou looked around himself. A patched overstuffed leather recliner, a table and a couple of chairs, tiny fridge and hotplate, an old television set, a twin bed and two bookcases. "It's home. Come in."

Nate walked in, stopping by one of the bookshelves.

"I'm just cleaning up."

"Go ahead."

As Lou capped his tubes of paint, he noticed that the man's head nearly brushed against the low dropped ceiling.

Nate turned to him. "Does she do this kind of thing all the time?"

Surprised by the question, Lou wiped his hands with a rag. "It's part of who she is."

"I'm afraid in this case, what she's doing with this kid is going to drive a few people up the wall."

"She'll deal with that, too. Once she decides to do

something, she does it. Doesn't matter what anyone else thinks."

"I've noticed." Nate started looking at the couple of frames he had on the upper shelves of his bookshelf. They'd been there so long that he'd almost forgotten about them. "She was a real cute kid."

The realization that the agent had been talking about Ellie and not Helen brought a smile to Lou's lips. He threw the rag aside and opened up his small refrigerator. "I could use a beer. How about you?"

"Sounds good." He accepted the cold can. "How do you keep this stuff in the house with four nuns living upstairs?"

"They don't drink much." He pushed one of the battered kitchen chairs at his guest and motioned for Nate to have a seat. Lou sat down in the leather chair. "I know your people are all gung-ho about keeping stuff top secret, but Sister Helen told me about your troubles."

"I figured she would." Nate drank some of the beer. "Having you right here, Mr. Littlefield, convinced me that we had some chance of getting this job done."

"I'd like it a lot better if you called me Lou. But you're off base. I can't make a fart of difference about anything anymore." He pushed up the footrest of the chair and got comfortable.

"Look, I know you've been keeping a low profile since you were released. I'm also aware that you've cut all of your connections with your previous line of work." Nate leaned forward. "What I'm hoping for are some ideas—maybe something that we haven't thought of."

"Something unconventional?"

"Absolutely," Nate stressed. "The way this job is

coming together—or not coming together—is about to drive me nuts. There's nothing for me to do but throw some lines out there and sit pretty and wait for a fish to bite. That's not my way of doing things."

"Because the fish might not bite, is that it?"

"Exactly," Nate replied, getting up from his chair and walking back to the bookcase. "The way things stand now, I have no idea if the information I have is even accurate. And even if this mythical flag is out there, I don't know if this goddamn auction will take place in two weeks or two years."

"That auction could very well be down the road a ways. Standard procedure is to give time for word to circulate. Build interest. Of course, they'll want to offer it at the most opportune moment. Generally, though, the longer the lead time, the larger the pot." Lou took another swig of his beer and stared at the back of the canvas he'd been working on for several weeks now. "How about a duplicate?"

"Do you mean a forgery?" Ellie's question drew Lou's gaze to the staircase. She was sitting with her arms wrapped around her legs on the landing.

"How long have you been here?" Nate asked sharply.

"Long enough." She frowned at him before turning her attention back to Lou. "Do you want them to present a forgery to the American public?"

"I'm suggesting that they should have *something* out there waving on the Fourth of July. Now, if the real McCoy shows up before that day, that's great. And if it shows up after the Fourth, then they can go through whatever song and dance is required and make a big deal out of the 'startling new find' or something."

"What do you make it look like?" Sister Helen

asked, coming down the stairs and standing behind Ellie. "Do you make it look like the Schuyler flag or
what we think the Robert Morris original might have
looked like?"

"This place is getting too damn crowded," Lou
grumbled.

"Watch your mouth, old man, and answer the
blessed question."

"Of course you make it look like the Schuyler flag.
There's documentation about that one, right down to
the restitching they did on it in the 1800s." He levered
the footrest down with a snap. "How the heck would
anyone know what the wear and tear on the other one
would be? We have no idea."

"You've been doing some homework on it, Lou,"
Sister Helen teased. "Admit it."

Lou looked away and said nothing.

"Do you know anyone who could do that type of
work?" Nate asked, looking definitely interested.

"I used to," Lou replied. "I could check around and
see if any of these guys are still breathing."

"How close could they get?" the agent asked. "I
mean, are we talking about fooling television viewers,
or experts?"

"How the hell would I know?" Lou complained.

"Why don't you tell us what you do know, pleasant
one," Helen encouraged in a mocking tone.

Lou growled at her. Ellie had slipped down the stairs
and was now sitting on the bottom step. This was as
far into this room as she'd ever come.

"Some of these people used to be very good," he
said. "But that was years ago. To be honest...I don't
know. But I can make a few calls and find out."

* * *

The two of them sat across from each other at a table in the convent's small kitchen. The hands of the ancient clock on the wall were about to meet at midnight. Sister Helen was still in the basement talking to Ellie's father. The other nuns were upstairs, settled in for the night. Chris had been taken to the small guest room at the top of the stairs, and when Nate had poked his head in a few minutes ago, the boy appeared to be sound asleep.

"Are you going back to your place tonight?" Nate asked, eating the bowl of cereal Ellie had poured for him. She fiddled with her teacup.

"Definitely. I need a shower and a change of clothes. But I want to be back here before Chris wakes up in the morning."

"How did he take it, being in the same house as all these nuns?"

"I think he actually liked it." She shrugged. "He seems a lot more comfortable around women."

"What's he going to do during the day?"

"There are a couple of kids whose mothers drop them off here weekdays. Sister Helen will keep him busy with them."

"You asked me to put it off for today, but I have to question him tomorrow and send the reports up to New York."

Ellie nodded, absently folding and refolding her tea bag's paper tag. "He's already used to you. I think it'd be okay. Did Hawes call you?"

"No. But the more I've got to give him when he calls, the better chance I have of keeping my head. What do you think of your father's suggestion?"

Ellie's eyes were tired when they looked up. "Dealing with forgers used to be part of Lou's work. He knows that business and the people who used to work in it better than anybody else I know.''

Nate finished the cereal and took the bowl and her empty teacup to the sink. ''But it does make sense. I mean, it's a long shot that anyone will call you now and say, bring your client to this auction at a certain place at this hour.''

''Stranger things have happened.'' She leaned back in the chair and looked up. ''But considering the cramped timing of everything, yes, it's tough to think that it could work so fast. And it's always smart to have a backup plan. Just in case.''

''When you talked to Ray, did you tell him I have time constraints?''

''Of course—you're going on some world cruise in two weeks.''

''Am I?'' He leaned against the cabinet. ''What else should I know about myself?''

''Other than your name…?'' Ellie thought back. ''I told Ray you were young, thirty-something. Come from money. You're trying your hand at collecting and you're from upstate New York.''

''What else?''

''That's all. We only talked for a few minutes on the phone. As far as the rest of my contacts, I'm just saying that I have an interested client. No specifics.''

''When do you want to start playing the game?''

Ellie arched a brow questioningly.

''When do I start being Nate Moffet? And, other than the people in this house, who else in your circle knows who I really am?''

''My assistant Vic is the only other person you've met, but he doesn't know. My problem is not when, but *if* you can play the role.''

Nate had a hard time standing still as she began studying him. Her eyes scrutinized him, from his choice of shoes and the belt he was wearing to the way he combed his hair. He waited until she was done with her perusal before making a comment. "What's the verdict?"

"You'll never cut it looking like this."

"I can fix that."

"How? Are you going to wear a sport jacket instead of a suit tomorrow? A striped tie instead of a solid one?"

"I said I'll take care of it." He pushed away from the cabinet.

"Maybe I can send Vic out shopping with you."

"Cut it out. I'm too tired."

"Maybe you can pick up an armful of fashion magazines at a newspaper stand, and then make a stop at the mall and ask one of those sixteen-year-old clerks to walk you through—"

"Stop it, Ellie."

His irritation only made her smile. "Well, I guess you know what to do. We should start showing you around first thing in the morning."

"I can't. I'm talking to Chris."

"After that, then. I'll be back in the shop after lunch. Put yourself together and drop by...say, about one. We'll see if you can pass the Desposito exam."

Nate grimaced. "I'm almost afraid to ask."

"Don't worry, it's not an internal exam," she said, grinning. "Vic claims to be an expert at recognizing 'P and Ps' on sight."

"What's a 'P and P'?"

"You know, Prince and the Pauper. A fake."

"Naturally."

"When you come in tomorrow, I'll introduce you as Nate Moffet. We'll go from there."

"A straight Nate Moffet," he warned.

"Vic would say that just means you haven't met the right man." She put her feet up on the seat he had vacated earlier.

Nate rubbed the back of his neck. "You're stressing me out, and we haven't even started this cover. Why the heck do I even need to face your assistant at all?"

She shook her head from side to side in disappointment. "Agent Murtaugh, you don't need me to tell you that to get this job done, we can leave no stone unturned. We don't want to miss making a crucial contact. I might own that shop, but Vic is the one who is on the phone and behind the desk most of the time. He talks to everyone. You convince my man that you're Mr. Millionaire Moffet, and the East Coast will know it in a day."

Nate nodded in resignation. "I'm on my way back to my hotel. Do you need a ride home, Miss Littlefield?"

"No thanks." She crossed her arms and tried to get more comfortable in her straight chair. "I don't believe I'd feel safe getting inside a car alone with you, Agent Murtaugh."

Twelve

Sanford Hawes tried unsuccessfully to rub smooth the headache that was pounding in his temples as he listened to Nate. There was no point in yelling and screaming about him taking Christopher Weaver to Philadelphia; Nate appeared to have covered all the bases. He had a statement from the kid. When he didn't hear from Hawes last night, Nate contacted the family services people and the local police in Ticonderoga first thing this morning.

"I faxed them the report a couple of minutes ago."

"What is it exactly that the kid knows?" Sanford growled into the phone.

"Nothing about the fire," Nate answered. "He first heard about it from McGill when the cop was trying to get him to come out of hiding at the body shop Sunday night. His story is that he came out of the bathroom and went into the room with the flag and one of the guards grabbed him."

"That's bullshit. No guard said anything. Can the kid identify him?"

"No. Chris says he never looked up into his face.

He just thought the guy was a guard from the color of his uniform.''

There was a light tap at Hawes's office door. He looked up as Cheri poked her head in.

"Do you have a minute?" she whispered.

He shook his head and spun around in his chair, turning his back to her. "Okay. What happened next?"

"Chris said he knew the museum was already closed, so when the guy started radioing something in, he broke away and escaped through the back door into the parking lot."

"And this supposed guard didn't pursue a kid wandering alone in the museum? Doesn't sound too likely."

"That's Chris's story."

"Did the kid say if this guard had a Middle Eastern accent?"

"I doubt an eight-year-old would know what that means," Nate replied. "Look, he didn't get a good look at the guy who grabbed him. And I don't think Chris could give us anything that would help identify him, either."

"So then, why the hell did he run? What was the disappearing act all about?"

"Chris is eight. He has no parents that he could rely on. And he was scared."

Sanford snorted. Looking around, he was relieved to see Cheri gone. He picked up a pen and started jotting down some notes. "What does he know about the McGill thing?"

"He took off through the junkyard and into the woods when he saw a muddy car—a sedan—race into the parking lot. He didn't actually see McGill get hit, either. He said it happened too fast. Then he just ran."

"He's got his disappearing act down pat, doesn't he?" Hawes grumbled. "What was he running away from this time?"

"He told me that he saw this same car before. They drove to his father's trailer in the woods. He says these two guys got out and looked for him." Nate's tone turned doubtful. "But of course, the ones at Weaver's place could have been local cops or someone from the social services. He has no proof for this. No license plate. Not even a description of the car—except that both cars were muddy."

"And that's it?"

"Pretty much…except that the cops up there are going to check for matching tire tracks out at the trailer."

"I'll have them send those results to me." Hawes methodically tapped his pen on the paper. "Does he know anything about the flag being destroyed?"

"No," Nate answered. "I made sure he only knows what went into the papers, about a trash can catching fire. He'd heard about McGill, though, from a classmate who brought him to us. That's the big news up there now."

"Okay, so it's like I told you. Going after the kid was a waste of time." Hawes leaned back in his chair and stared at the wall displaying his diplomas and pictures and citations and medals. "What's your next move?"

"The New York family services people have agreed—since he's still technically in my custody—to leave him with Sister Helen for a little while until they figure what would be best to do with him. The Ticonderoga police might want to question Chris themselves, but if they do, Buckley said they'll send someone to Philadelphia to do it."

"Is this kid going to slow you down any more than he already has?"

"I'm not baby-sitting him. After today, I won't have much to do with him, at all."

"How about Ellie? She started all of this, didn't she?"

"She's doing what she needs to do. I don't think having the kid around is putting a strain on her time." There was a pause on the line. "By the way, I was on the phone with Wilcox this morning about an idea that Louis Littlefield came up with."

Hawes tipped back his chair. "I was wondering when he'd crawl out of Helen's basement and put his two cents in. So what did he have to say?"

"He had an idea about coming up with a forgery."

It was like a Philadelphia Christmas at the end of June. Even though it was midweek, the sidewalks were jammed with people. Traffic on Walnut Street was crawling, and Chestnut Street was a madhouse. Everywhere Ellie looked, people had that half-harried, half-delighted look about them that you only saw on holiday shoppers.

Clutching several shopping bags of all sizes, she waited for a young couple to step out of her shop and a group of four women to go inside before going in herself. Brian was writing up a sale at the counter, and Vic immediately appeared at her side to take the bags.

"You're late," he scolded under his breath. "I thought you were coming back at noon."

"I thought so, too. But I didn't get out of Sister Helen's until half past. Then I had to make a couple of stops and pick up some donations for next Thursday's auction. Then I had another stop to buy a few things for this boy who's staying at the convent.'' She peeled the last bag from around her wrist. "What time is it, anyway?"

"Two-fifteen."

"I didn't realize it was so late."

"Good thing your date is an angel."

Vic rushed off with the packages before she could say anything more. Ellie looked around the shop but saw no sign of Nate. She walked to the counter where Brian had just finished writing up a customer. He turned and put both hands up to stop her from coming behind the counter.

"Listen, hon. You don't keep someone like this one waiting. Run up those stairs and change." Brian shooed her toward the steps. "Go! Go! We have everything under control."

Her curiosity was now totally piqued. Vic and Brian did not usually behave so...so motherly. She went toward the back of the store where Vic had disappeared seconds earlier. Aside from the four women, there was another older couple, and a man Ellie vaguely recognized as another dealer. Still no sign of Nate. Vic came out of the back storage room, his hands empty.

"What did you do to him?" she asked.

"Not what I would have liked to do."

"Don't pout, Vic."

"Easy for you to say. Some people seem to have all the luck." He touched the sleeve of her band-collar cotton shirt and looked down at the knee-length skirt. "You can't go out dressed like this. Do you own any leather?"

"Excuse me?"

"Leather? The skin of an animal?" He looked at her critically. "You know, that Olivia Newton-John thing from *Grease* could really knock his socks off. Have you got anything like that?''

"I'll have to look," she said sarcastically.

"Then look. You'll definitely need to think about styling a little if you want to have him hang around here a couple more weeks.''

"So you got the whole scoop?" She poked her head into the back room, still looking for Nate.

"Of course. And you owe me big time on this one.''

"How's that?''

"If I hadn't opened the door and let him in Sunday morning—over your objections, I might add—you would never have landed an opportunity like this in a hundred years.''

"So he told you about the flag he's looking for?''

"Of course. Nothing escapes Victor." Vic's voice turned low and confidential. "And it's good to see you're playing it smart for a change.''

She raised a brow.

"Good commission aside, babe, men like him don't come knocking too often. He told me you invited him to go sightseeing around Philly this afternoon.''

"Yeah." Ellie poured herself a cup of coffee. "But after being out all day yesterday and seeing how busy we are today, I think he'll take a rain check.''

"Don't even think about it." Vic wiped the counter, cleaning the coffee ring she'd left behind. "He told us what a great time the two of you had yesterday. Let me tell you, this is the best way to land them. Yesterday, New York. Today, you show him Philadelphia. Tomorrow, maybe you go to Baltimore or D.C. By the weekend, who knows…Bermuda?''

"Why not keep going, Vic. By next week, if I play

my cards right, I might just reel him in, close the shop and retire to Palm Beach.''

"At least you know this time, with his kind of money, you'll be able to afford to.''

The dirty snake had clearly put it over on Vic, Ellie thought. She'd issued a challenge to Murtaugh... Moffet...whatever name he was going by today, and he'd risen to it.

"I give up. Where is he?''

"I took him up to your apartment.''

"What for?'' she exploded.

"Because he was a distraction down here. And I didn't think he'd be up for doing any nude modeling on the second floor.''

"You know I don't take anyone up to my apartment.'' She dumped her coffee in the wastebasket and started for the stairs.

"Brian and I come up all the time,'' he said, trailing after her.

"You know what I mean. I'm talking about strangers.''

"You never take any of your boyfriends up there, and I told him that, too. Men are vain like that. They like that first-time business. So I told him how you date, but that you don't generally sleep around.''

"You've got to be kidding.'' She started up the steps, two at a time.

"No. And I also told him how this past year, you've had a real dry spell.''

"Great! Is there anything you didn't tell him?''

"I didn't mention your bra size,'' he said. "I figured it was too insignificant to mention.''

Ellie whirled around on the second-floor landing and punched Vic squarely in the arm. "At least I *have* tits.''

"So? Everybody has tits."

"I can't believe I'm discussing this with you."

"I get it. Some tits are more equal than others."

"Vic—"

"Well, that was my point to start with." He took her by the shoulders and turned her around. "What do *you* think of them, Mr. Moffet?"

If a gaping hole had opened on the stairwell and swallowed her up entirely, that would have suited Ellie just fine. Nate was sitting on the top step. His long legs were encased in well-worn jeans, and he was wearing a pair of handsome boots. A black T-shirt stretched across his broad chest and flat stomach. He was appraising her breasts with the attitude of a connoisseur.

"Perfect, I'd say," Nate said, his blue eyes twinkling.

Ellie felt like her face was sporting a third-degree burn. She brushed off Vic's hands and growled at Nate. "You're blocking my way."

Jeez, he looked even better standing up.

"Can you handle it from here, boss?"

She turned to answer, only to realize Vic's question was addressed to the man standing on the top step. A dozen different threats—starting with firing him—ran through her mind, but Ellie knew she couldn't go through with any of them. Maybe she'd just kill him.

"Thanks for everything, Vic." Nate came down to them and looped an arm around her waist. Maybe she'd just kill them both. She peeled his hand off her hip as they started up the steps and shot a warning look at him.

As they went past the second-floor studio, Ellie continued to hold her tongue, though her mind was racing. A couple of the regulars were painting by the windows, and a new sculptor was working with clay at the far end of the studio. They continued up to the third floor, and as soon as they stepped through the door to her apartment, she whirled on him.

"I thought I explained everything to you yesterday. I don't like you. You don't like me. There is no us, and there never will be. So there's no point in pretending that we're anything else in front of—"

"How do I look?"

She gaped at him as if he had two heads. "Did you hear what I just said?"

"You told me I had to change my look. So what do you think?"

She'd seen him briefly this morning at Sister Helen's while he'd been questioning Christopher. He'd been wearing one of his suits from the G-Man Boutique.

"Great. The stuff actually fits." She eyed the boots, the jeans—which fit too well—and the T-shirt. She noticed even his hair was different; it had kind of a wind-blown, finger-combed look. It was the look of a rich man who was very comfortable with himself. "Clothes alone wouldn't fool Vic. What did you say to him?"

He only gave her a smug look.

"Vic is pretty shrewd when it comes to this kind of stuff, but you've obviously pulled the wool over his eyes. Come on," she pressed. "Out with it."

"I don't ask you to hand over your trade secrets. Do you really think you should ask me to divulge mine?"

Ellie considered this for a moment while continuing to study every little detail of his rich, bad-boy look. All he was missing was a tattoo on that sculpted biceps. Feeling the room growing warmer, she tore her gaze from him.

"Suit yourself," she said, her voice sounding a little

hoarse. "Vic bought the whole package. A good first step. We'll let it go at that for now."

She walked away, not feeling too good about the fluttering sensation in her stomach or about the way he seemed to dominate the space in her apartment. Of course, it *was* a small apartment, she told herself.

"Good. Why don't you change into something more comfortable before we go?"

"Go where?" She lifted the strap of her purse from her shoulder, dropping the bag on the love seat. "I am not your personal tour guide. You weren't serious about me showing you around Philadelphia, were you?"

"Thanks for the offer, but some other time." He glanced at his watch. "How long does it take to get to the northeast section of the city?"

"Depends on the address. Why?"

"Your father gave me a name this morning. He said he already called this guy, who is interested in hearing the details of what we're looking for."

Ellie was mildly irked that Lou had made no mention of it to her. "What's his name?"

"Theo Atwood."

Ellie couldn't put a face to the name. "Do you have an address?"

He took a folded piece of paper out of his pocket and handed it to her. She recognized Lou's handwriting. "Depending on the traffic, it could take us twenty minutes or two hours to get there. When exactly is he expecting us?"

"Apparently, he does some tailoring at a little tuxedo shop he owns. That's the address. Lou said it'd be best if we showed up about four."

All of this fit. Many of Lou's friends who were in

the business also worked part-time as sign painters and in framing stores and even as college art teachers. This gave them a respectable front, even though their true vocations as forgers, fences and middlemen paid much better.

Ellie looked up at the clock on the wall. "If we leave now, we'll be early, but we'll at least be ahead of the rush-hour traffic."

He walked in and sprawled on her love seat. "You should still change before we go."

She looked down at her casual but stylish outfit. "You're the third person who has told me that in the past five minutes. What's wrong with what I have on?"

"Nothing." His gaze wandered appreciatively over her. "You have very nice legs. In fact, that little slit on the side of your skirt is a real tease. I'll just have to make sure I sit across from you where I can get the best view. And I really like the shirt, too. Especially the way it molds to your breasts. Did you know that whenever you turn, the buttons pull, and I get this peek of—?"

"Don't touch anything," Ellie croaked. "I'll be right back."

Thirteen

Ellie took a step back from the motorcycle standing in the narrow alleyway next to her building. "You don't really expect me to ride on this thing, do you?"

"Don't embarrass me, Ellie," Vic cut in before Nate could answer. "This is not a *thing*. This is a limited edition Hundredth Anniversary Ultra Classic Electra Glide Harley-Davidson."

"Oh. How could I not have known?"

"I'd give my left nut to take this bike out for a ride."

Ellie raised an eyebrow. "Well, that would still leave you two, wouldn't it?"

"You don't have to mutilate yourself, chief." Nate laughed. "Why don't you take it out when we get back?"

"That's a deal." Victor beamed from ear to ear.

"Here, I even brought a helmet for you." Nate trapped Ellie against the fence and removed her sunglasses, lowering the shiny black helmet onto her head instead. She put up a struggle for a second when he tried to take her purse, but eventually gave up. He tucked it into a rear saddlebag compartment.

She'd changed into a shapeless linen blouse, loose, ankle-length pants and a pair of sandals. "You look real cute like this, though you should have worn better shoes.''

"I hate cute." Her eyes were shooting darts of fire.

"Sorry. You look beautiful like this." Nate took her by the helmet and kissed her directly on her lips. She tasted even better than he'd imagined. He quickly lowered the visor before she could spit in his face. "Climb on, babe."

Vic opened the small gate for them. Nate grunted under his breath when Ellie climbed on and poked him sharply under the ribs. He rolled the bike onto the street and then fired it up. With a nod at Vic, he revved the engine and they roared down Pine Street. At the first red light, she pushed the visor up.

"You found out about Victor's weakness for Harleys, didn't you, you dirty cheat. That's how you fooled him."

He half turned to her. "Wanting to have sex with anything that walks is a weakness. Drinking soda in the morning is a weakness. Talking baby-talk to puppies might even be a weakness. But the feel of this much motorcycle between your legs is a religious experience."

Ellie leaned close to his car. "You can be pretty darn scary."

Nate didn't know what it was about her that brought out the daredevil in him. He raced through the next two lights. The layout of the city was fairly familiar to him, and while she'd been changing, he'd looked up the address they were going to on the map.

Instead of shooting up through town, he went out Kelly Drive. The smooth, winding road, with the Schuylkill River on one side and the branches of trees intertwined overhead, gave him ample opportunity to

test the power and handling of the bike. As he sped
along the road, her light grip changed to a firm hold
around his waist. Then, cutting away from the river,
they flew up through Fairmount Park. When he didn't
slow down for some speed bumps, her little screams
made him smile. After that, it was a blur of city
streets…and a few sidewalks…until they reached the
Northeast section. When he pulled into a parking space
across the street from the tuxedo shop, her grip was
slow to loosen.

"You're a maniac. And a jerk. And I'm taking a cab
home."

Nate swung his leg over and climbed off the bike.
Stifling a grin, he tried to help her with the helmet. She
waved him away as if he were an annoying insect and
started removing it by herself.

"Coming here should have been a straight shot up
Broad Street, but you had to take the scenic route
around the city and show off all your adolescent
tricks."

When she yanked the helmet off, her face was
flushed, and her dark hair was sticking straight out in
all directions. He reached up to smooth it, but she batted his hand away again.

"Let me help. You look like a porcupine."

"Thanks to you. And you, by the way, look like
something off the cover of some cheesy biker magazine."

"Seriously," he said. "Let me just smooth it down
a little."

She let him, and Nate was shocked by the softness
of the short tresses. They molded like fine silk around
his fingers.

"Much better." He pulled back, trying to ignore the

image of how her head would look on his pillow. Ellie took out her purse and lifted Nate's hand to glance at his watch. "We're still a half hour early."

Nate looked across the wide street, past a line of parked cars, at the row of run-down shops. Retractable steel doors covered with graffiti hid several of the storefronts. An older man walking a scrawny dog passed by the tuxedo shop, which was sandwiched between an ancient-looking pizza parlor and a mom-and-pop convenience store that had Checks Cashed banners running across the top of dirty plate-glass windows. There was very little traffic on the street, though there were a number of kids and adults on a patch of grass a half block away. As he watched a skateboarder hop the sidewalk, it occurred to him that the crowds of people gathering in Center City for the July 4 celebration would not be seeing this part of town.

Nate looked back at the tuxedo shop. A dark green awning shaded a nonexistent window display. The tinted glass on the door hid whoever was inside.

"By the way, which hat should I be wearing when we walk in there?"

"Your first name is enough. We're a referral. Other than how much you're willing to pay, and how we go about exchanging cash for the flag, he won't need to know anything else."

"I got Wilcox to agree to overnight us some specifics about the material and the weave and wear of the Schuyler flag. He's sending copies of recent pictures taken of it, too. Of course, we'll only give Atwood that stuff after we make a deal here."

"I'm surprised Wilcox agreed to anything. People like Atwood are a thorn in historians' sides."

"Never mind thorns. I believe Dr. Wilcox would

welcome any degree of pain so long as he can salvage his job after this whole fiasco is over.''

A couple of teenagers walking by nodded admiringly at the Harley as they passed.

''Are you sure it's safe to leave this thing here?''

''Absolutely.'' He touched her arm. ''But why don't you wait here while I go inside and check the place out first.''

''No way. I'm not letting you mess this thing up. We're going in together.'' Helmet in one hand, she slung her purse over her shoulder. Taking hold of his arm, she pulled him into the street. ''By the way, is the bike yours?''

''No questions, remember?''

''Come on, Agent.''

As a small delivery truck with restaurant supplies for the pizza shop pulled up and double-parked in front of the tuxedo shop, Nate saw the black Suburban with smoked glass in his peripheral vision. The SUV came out of nowhere but was bearing down on them with increasing speed.

Grabbing Ellie around the waist, Nate yanked her back out of the vehicle's path as the Suburban blew by. He fell backward over the hood of a parked car, and she came with him.

Fury ripped through him. Before he could get to his feet, though, Nate felt the blast rock the street. Rolling with her on the pavement as shards of glass and rubble rained down on them, he pulled Ellie beneath him just as a second explosion tore through the air.

Chris crouched by an open window in the convent's sitting room, watching a group of kids outside argue and curse as they picked their teams for a baseball game. He'd watched this same group open the fire hydrant across the street earlier and run barefoot under the spray of water for more than an hour before a city worker showed up and shut it off.

Most of them seemed older than him. All of them had foul mouths that would put Chris's mom to shame. He imagined himself growing up here. It would be good not to be a freak. It was comforting to look around and see that these kids had holes in their shirts and shorts and wore raggedy old baseball caps, and a couple of them had duct tape on their sneakers. They even played baseball with what looked like a piece of a broomstick and cheap rubber ball. Nobody cried and ran home when they got pushed from behind or somebody slapped them in an argument. It occurred to him that maybe they didn't have homes or parents to run to. They all seemed to be having a good time, even if they were constantly yelling and teasing and squabbling.

Chris wondered how long they would let him stay here. He'd been smart in answering the questions. He knew the less he said the better, so he'd said nothing about funny gadgets or about what anybody looked liked or about the name he'd heard. They had no reason to take him back to ask more questions.

Allison was the only person he was sorry to leave behind, but she had her family and friends and a nice house in town. And it would've only been a matter of time before she started listening to everyone else. It wouldn't be long before she realized that she was hanging around with a loser.

The loud cheering of the kids outside drew Chris's attention. Somebody they knew and obviously liked was coming up the street. Chris leaned out the open window. Peeking around the corner of the brick wall, he saw a couple of the younger boys hanging from the neck of some guy in a T-shirt, jeans and baseball cap, just getting out of a station wagon. The arguing between the two boys who were picking the teams got louder. From what he could hear, they both wanted the man on their team.

"Can you see okay from there?"

Chris jumped, bumping his head on the window in his hurry to pull back in.

"Yes, I'm sorry." He rubbed his head.

"Nothing to be sorry about, Christopher."

It was clear Sister Helen was the one in charge around here. Everybody minded what she said—and that included Mr. Lou, the handyman, and even Miss Ellie's friend, Agent Murtaugh. The nun was nice to him, though. Last night, she'd come in to check on him a couple of times during the night, and this morning he found a new box of Lucky Charms on the breakfast table in the kitchen. She said she always wanted to try them, but she didn't eat much when the two of them sat down together.

"You can go out and play with them if you want."

"No, that's okay."

She had a bundle of mail under one arm, and she sat down on the wing chair near the fan. "Never mind me, go on and watch the game."

He hesitantly sat down on the corner of a chair by the window and looked out again. They were done picking the teams, and they were using one boy's shirt and some rusty hubcaps for bases. The guy in the baseball cap was pitching, and he was as loud as the kids, busting on the batter, a tall teenager who must have just showed up, too. There was a foul ball off the

Dumpster across the street, and two of the younger kids ran over to the pitcher to give him a high five and run back.

"Is he one of the dads?"

Chris heard Sister Helen move behind him. "No, Ted is just a good friend."

"Does he live around here?"

"No." She pulled a chair up and sat down by the window, too, watching the game. "Ted comes around two or three days a week, sometimes more. He likes playing baseball or basketball with the kids in the neighborhood. He's the best thing that has happened to some of these children."

The pitcher threw the ball to first and had the first baseman throw it back.

"Too many of these kids never had a good father figure until Ted started coming around. Do you know what a father figure is, Chris?"

Chris nodded. He was pretty sure he knew. He had a father. He didn't need his fingers, though, to count the number of times his dad tried to do something fun with him. It was zero. He looked from the older woman's thoughtful face to the ongoing game on the street. The teenager hit a grounder; the shortstop caught it and threw to first in time.

"Have you ever been to a baseball game, Chris?"

"You mean like the Yankees?"

She nodded.

"I've seen it on TV."

"Ted—" she motioned to the pitcher "—is taking the kids to the Philadelphia Phillies game this Friday night. I know he'd be thrilled to have one more customer."

Chris tucked his hands between his knees and looked

out. "I don't have no money...and I know it's wrong to want something that expensive."

She smiled. "None of us has to pay to go. A few years ago, Ted arranged it with the Phillies. They invite the inner-city kids to come and watch the game."

"For free?"

She nodded. "In fact, I can take you out right now and introduce you to him and some of the kids. That way you'll know some of their names by the time Friday comes around."

Chris felt a tingle of excitement, but he was afraid to show it. What happened if this Ted guy had no extra tickets? What if those men in suits came from New York and took him?

"So what do you say?" The nun was already on her feet and had her hand stretched toward him. Chris hesitantly reached up and took it.

"What should I call him?" he asked on the way out of the house.

"These hooligans call him Ted, but since you're such a polite young man, you can start with Mr. Hardy."

People were screaming and running in every direction. In minutes, a roaring fire had swept through the block of stores from the point where the initial explosion had happened. The sound of sirens filled the streets, growing louder by the second.

Ellie's gaze was riveted on Nate's bloody back as he ran down the block, dragging her behind him. At the first intersection, he shoved his badge in the face of a cabdriver who had slowed down. Vaguely, she could hear Nate shouting the address of her shop at the driver.

The back door of the cab opened, and Ellie felt herself slung inside.

"You're hurt," she cried, holding on to him.

"I'm fine," he said, handing Ellie her purse. "I'll call you later."

The door slammed in her face, and the cab sped away. Ellie turned around and looked through the back window at Nate, who was running back down the block toward the fire. The images she'd seen of New York since September 11, 2001, rushed back. But two blocks away, people were walking on the streets and—with the exception of police cars, ambulances and fire trucks racing toward the scene of the explosion—there was no indication that anyone was even aware of the chaos she'd just left.

The cabdriver was talking excitedly to his dispatcher, then turned on his radio. The local all-news station came up, but there was nothing about the explosion yet.

He turned down the radio when they went to a commercial and glanced at her in the rearview mirror. "They got us all peeing in our pants whenever a car backfires these days. Yous was right there when it happened, huh, lady?"

Ellie could only nod. The feeling of the ground dropping from under her while objects flew in every direction wouldn't leave her. Nate had shielded her body with his—he could be bleeding to death now for trying to save her life. She batted at a tear that escaped. They'd probably both be dead if it weren't for that delivery truck...and that black SUV that almost ran them down.

"Didja see any airplanes or anything crash?"

She shook her head and looked out the window. The

streets were backing up with traffic. Impatient drivers honked their horns, unaware that anything had happened.

"Maybe it was a gas line. Or something in a restaurant," the driver suggested. "So your husband's an FBI guy, huh?"

Ellie didn't have the strength to explain. She just continued to stare out at the stores flashing by. He'd covered her with his own body. Nobody had ever done something like that for her.

"It's good he was right there. With all their fancy equipment and everything else, I bet by the six o'clock news they'll announce what was it that happened exactly."

Another tear trickled down her face. There had to be other people inside those buildings. She tried to recall if there were any apartments above the shops, or if the old guy with the dog had had enough time to get away from the explosion. The driver of the delivery truck couldn't have escaped. Traffic came to a standstill just past Temple University. Ellie reached into her purse, took out a ten dollar bill and stuffed it through the sliding window separating her from the driver.

"I'll get out here."

"Are you sure? Your husband said—"

She didn't wait for change, and she was on the sidewalk in a moment. The warm sun and the pavement beneath her shoes made her feel alive again. Nate would be okay, she told herself. Unconsciously, she reached inside her purse, took out her cell phone and started dialing his number to check. But she realized her own stupidity and disconnected.

Anger replaced worry three blocks down. Mad at herself and Helen and Nate and Hawes and the world for getting her involved in this sordid business, she lengthened her strides. She was happy with her life. Finally, she had the things she'd always wanted. Financial security. Status. Connections with important people. She was no longer the hungry little girl on the sidewalk, gawking at the beautiful people inside the stores, restaurants and clubs. Ellie was now on the inside, and these people had no right to shake up her life like this. They had no right to make her care about things that she had no control over.

Homeless Jack was sitting in his wheelchair on the shady side of Pine Street when Ellie went by. Seeing her, he called and asked if she was okay. She waved her answer and noticed for the first time that her clothes were covered with dust and debris. Again, the image of Nate and his bloody shirt flashed before her eyes. She was complaining about the disturbance to her lifestyle, while Nate was putting *his* life on the line by going back to those burning buildings to save lives. By the time she reached the shop, Ellie had worked herself into a knot of worry and guilt.

"What happened to you?" Brian asked, rushing to her as she entered. There were no customers in the shop.

Vic was on the phone, and as he turned around, his eyes rounded with worry.

"She just walked in," he said into the receiver. "But let me see if she can talk to you right now or not." He pulled the phone down. "My God! Did you have an accident?"

"Who's on the phone?" she asked, hoping for some news of Nate.

"I don't know. He wouldn't give me his name, but

he said it has something to do with one of your clients...."

She took the phone. "Hi, may I help you?"

"Ms. Littlefield?" There was a pause in the line.

Ellie didn't recognize the voice. The accent was vaguely British. "This is she. Who is this?"

"That's not important. But I should very much like to verify that you have a *bona fide* client who is interested in an original Betsy Ross flag."

"I might." She plopped down on the stool next to the register, suddenly feeling very, very tired. The weight of everything that had happened in the past hour sat directly on her shoulders. She couldn't shake off the image of Nate, hurt.

"'Might' is not exactly the answer we are looking for, Ms. Littlefield."

"Well, I've had a very tough day. Do you have the flag?"

"There will be an auction for the item I referred to very soon. I should tell you, however, that the list of those invited to bid will be quite exclusive."

"Are *you* conducting the auction?"

"If you would confine yourself to answering my queries..." The man's tone reflected a growing impatience.

"I do have a client...a *bona fide* client...who's interested. But how can I even attempt to prequalify him when I am not told the terms, conditions or time of this auction?"

"The terms will be the usual ten percent, the starting bid will be thirty million U.S., and we shall need verification that twice that amount is available in your client's bank account prior to the actual day of the auction. Of course, you do understand that the hammer price could easily be twice or thrice that.''

"Having that much cash sitting idle in a bank is stupid. The time frame will be critical to my client.''

"That is understandable. I can tell you that we hope to conduct the event prior to the month's end. But again, there will be no guarantees.''

"Where would the auction be held?''

"That is not necessary for you to know at this point.''

"But it is. My client is planning to depart—''

"I can tell you it will be somewhere on the East Coast,'' the man interrupted. "Now, I suggest you contact your client and pass on these terms and conditions. If he is interested, then we shall see about adding his name to the list.''

"How do I reach you with the answer?''

"We shall contact you, Ms. Littlefield.''

Ron Kent stood by the window of the Oval Office, looking out at the beautiful Washington afternoon. His chief of staff stood by the president's desk.

"What do we want out of this meeting, George?''

"We want to withhold any indication of your position, Mr. President. We want to keep it informational.''

"And our strategy going in?'' He glanced over his shoulder at the younger man.

"Our best strategy would be to keep the discussion from becoming personal, sir.''

"That's impossible. Graham Hunt's favored technique is to get down and dirty, make it personal, to bully and blackmail if need be, but win at all costs.''

"That's true, sir. Which is exactly why we insisted on inviting the Vice President, Senators Kennedy and

Schumer, Congressman Fattah, the Agriculture Secretary, and the Interior Secretary and Undersecretary.''

"Even knowing that, Hunt is still coming in.'' Kent chewed on that for a moment. "What's going on, George? Graham isn't one to waste his time or mine. What exactly does he have that he thinks will keep me onboard?''

Street paged through his notes. "The meeting agenda that I included in your packet, sir, indicates only a clarifying discussion of the Water for America project, but my sources tell me that they'd like to push an additional bill through the Appropriations Committees to expand the scope of the project.''

Kent turned and glared at Street. "Expand it how?''

"Hunt and his cartel want to make it a national project versus regional. I believe he thinks an expansion will give it broader appeal. In fact, I know Hunt has two New York advertising execs standing by, in case you'd care to see their new ad campaign.''

"How are they going to make this a national project?'' Kent planted both hands on either side of the packet of information that Street had prepared for him. "I have no time to read through all of this, so just give it to me straight. No smooth ad slogans or fancy graphic presentations. Just tell me what the hell they want to do.''

"They're proposing the creation of enormous underground water-storage basins in different parts of the country. Different states could be allocated federal money to fund the pipelines from these locations to their own potential drought regions or to recommended industrial development areas.''

"Let me get this straight. Basically, they're just expanding the size of the original project.''

"Yes."

"Originally, we were planning only to pipe…say, Colorado River water and water from the National Forest lands to where we wanted it. Now, we have basins."

"Underground basins."

"Who owns the basins?" Kent asked, walking to the center of his office.

"Hunt and his cartel. In the new project, we now pay these companies to store it, keep it safe and pump it out when it's needed."

"And they make a hell of a lot more money."

"That's the idea." George nodded. "But they also make it look better for the American people…and you."

"How is it better for me?"

"It allows you to undercut the opposition's argument. You can sign the original bill, get elected on the merits of expanding it, and if the opposition party doesn't pass the expansion bill, they're the ones who look bad. That's what the New York PR guys are here for. They'll sell the idea that in going this route, no one in the country worries about drought or economic favoritism."

"Okay, what are the negatives…other than the costs and the fact that Hunt and his friends are the chief profit-takers?"

There was a knock on the door, and the President's personal assistant poked her head in. "They're ready for you in the Cabinet Room, Mr. President."

"Thank you," Kent said, not taking his eyes off of his chief of staff.

Street tucked his own folder under one arm, waiting for the door to close. "Well, there certainly could be dangers to the desert ecosystems, since that's where most of these basins need to be built. Then you have the danger of controls for overpumping. There is no guarantee that we won't deplete the underground springs and kill off wildlife in those regions. Should I go on?''

"No," Kent replied, starting for the door. "I understand what's going on now.''

Fourteen

The explosion and the fire received Section C coverage in the *Inquirer* newspaper account. The six o'clock news had a twenty-five-second report on the incident, saying that several people were injured in a fire in the city's Northeast section. By eleven o'clock, it was confirmed that two were dead and seven more injured. The dead were identified and the next of kin notified.

With potentially record-breaking numbers of visitors supposedly en route to Philadelphia for the opening ceremonies of the Spirit of America celebration, no one wanted to throw a wet blanket on the planned festivities.

Nate tried not to think too much about the strange coincidence of Theo Atwood being one of the dead.

After the fire was contained, Nate had worked all afternoon and through the night with the investigators on the scene and later at the station. So far, they were going on the assumption that a faulty gas line inside the tuxedo shop was the cause.

Nate didn't believe in coincidences, though.

It was a little before five in the morning when he

finally left the fire commissioner's office downtown. The predawn air was damp, and the smells of the city hung heavy in the streets. His body ached. They'd had to dig a shard of flying glass from his back, and the stitches the ER doctor had used to close the cut felt like they were standing out two inches. The stiffness in his knee was as bad as the early days after his surgery. He looked up and down the deserted street, hoping for a cab.

A sleek black BMW turned the corner and raced down the street, pulling up smartly at the curb. He took a step cautiously toward the rear of the vehicle as the passenger window slid downward. Then he relaxed, seeing Ellie in the driver's seat.

"Climb in."

Baseball hat, no makeup, a sleeveless T-shirt, a pair of old jeans. She was a sight for sore eyes.

"What are you doing here?"

"I said climb in," she said again. There was tension in her voice.

Nate forgot about all his aches and pains, and opened the door. He remembered the stitches, though, when he leaned back against the seat. She took off as he was still fumbling with his seat belt.

"You are the most irresponsible, selfish jerk I've ever met," she exploded, sailing through a yellow light. "I couldn't sit still. I couldn't eat. I couldn't sleep. I had to cancel my meeting with Augusta Biddle last night for this fund-raiser I'm doing because I was incapable of thinking of anything other than how badly you were hurt."

Nate watched her profile as she drove like a madwoman through the city streets. Her cheeks were glowing. Her knuckles were white on the steering wheel.

"What did I do?"

She slammed on the brakes at a red light. "You think you can tell people you're going to do something and then just forget it?"

"What did I forget?"

She burned a stretch of rubber twenty feet long when the light turned green. "You were supposed to call me, to let me know you were okay, dammit!"

"I was working."

"You said you would call."

Nate reached for the phone at his belt and started dialing. Three seconds later the cell phone in Ellie's purse started to ring.

She slammed on the brakes at the next light and snatched his phone away. Without uttering a word, she threw it on the floor at his feet. She gunned it again when the light turned green.

Her phone kept ringing. Nate's gaze fixed on her flushed face and parted lips. Ellie was mumbling curses under her breath. When she slammed on the brakes at the next intersection, he reached over, slipped a hand behind her neck and pulled her face toward him. Before she could form the next complaint, he sealed her lips with his own. She remained rigid in his arms for only a second. He felt her press a hand to his chest, and he wondered fleetingly if she intended to push him away, but then those same fingers clutched at his shirt as her lips moved beneath his.

Nate pushed the hat off her head and kissed her deeply. His fingers delved into her hair, his mouth taking and giving to the play of their mouths. He lost himself in her intoxicating taste. He hadn't even known how much he wanted to kiss her.

The loud horn of a truck behind their car tore them

apart. The light was green. Ellie pressed her foot on the gas and accelerated through the intersection.

"Have I told you today how annoying you can be?" she asked under her breath.

"No, but you just showed me."

The blush on her cheeks had deepened and stretched down her neck. He reached up and traced the delicate lines of her ear with the tip of his finger.

"Don't," she snapped.

Nate stopped, but he couldn't tear his gaze away. Maybe it was the lack of sleep or the post-traumatic stress, but he couldn't remember the last time, if ever, a kiss had stirred him so much.

The car pulled up in front of his hotel.

Nate didn't ask how she knew where he was staying for the same reason that he hadn't asked how she knew where to find him this morning. She had her ways.

"He was in there, wasn't he?" She didn't look at him. "Dead."

"Yes. The investigation is still ongoing, but it appears that Atwood was in there."

"Great."

She was silent for a moment. Nate waited until she was ready to talk.

"Yesterday afternoon," Ellie said finally, looking straight ahead, "when I got back from the northeast, I got a call from someone about the flag. I assume it was the auctioneer organizing the sale. No specific details, but I got what we need to do for you to be qualified as a bidder. Through Sister Helen, I passed on the information to Hawes. He called me back to say they didn't see any problem with following their directions."

"Which is?"

"Verification of a minimum of sixty million in a bank account in Nate Moffet's name."

"Even if he said there was no problem, Hawes must have choked on that amount. When is the auction?"

"I don't know. And I don't have a name. And I even did a star sixty-nine check to get the last incoming number, but no good."

"We can get that, but it probably won't help. He could have used somebody else's line." He thought a moment. "Did you give all of this to Hawes, too?"

"Yeah." Ellie sent him a side glance. "There's no way I can say that this guy was legit or not. But I have a phone call in to Ray to see if he's heard anything in the past couple of days."

Nate had talked to Hawes a couple of times last night, but each phone conversation had been brief and only pertinent to the explosion at the tux shop.

"How is your father taking it...about Theo Atwood?"

"I assume he's okay. I haven't seen him. Sister Helen gave him the news."

"I'd like to go over there and talk to him some more about other possible contacts. Also, it would be good if he could tell me anything he can about Atwood. Like who might have wanted to see him dead."

"I thought it was an accident."

"Maybe. Maybe not." He undid his seat belt. "But first I need to shower and get out of these clothes."

Ellie's gaze moved down to take in the front of the navy-blue T-shirt he'd changed into. The words Fire Police were emblazoned across the chest. "I don't know, you look so much in character wearing this."

He was happy to see the twinkle of mischief back

in her eyes. He also couldn't stop himself from thinking about how good she'd tasted. "Want to come up?"

"What for?"

"Breakfast. I'll order room service."

"No thanks. I can get my own."

"I'll show you the stitches in my back. They're pretty ugly."

"You needed stitches?" she asked, worried.

"Yeah, but they said I'll live."

"I'm sorry that you were hurt." Her expression softened.

"Sorry enough to come up?"

She shook her head. "I'll pass."

"How about a couple of hours' sleep? We could both use it."

"We could both use a lot of things, but we're not going to let ourselves be tempted." She picked up her baseball cap and pulled it on low.

"Not even when it comes to sex?"

The blush was back. "Not too romantic, are you?"

"Just asking a hypothetical question," Nate replied, feigning innocence.

"Is that right?"

"Absolutely. Temptation and doing something about it are two different things. I am honest enough…no, maybe tired enough…to say what is running through my head. Of course, if you were hopping out of this car and running ahead of me toward my hotel room, then my sanity might have returned, and I'd be trying to talk you out of it."

She gave him a narrow stare. "So if I say no, you say come on. And if I say yes, you say slow down."

"Right."

"That fills me with confidence," she concluded.

"So, you want to come up?"

"It's a good thing that one of us has her head screwed on." Ellie leaned over him and opened his door. For a brief second their bodies were in contact, and Nate was tempted to kiss her again, but he restrained himself. "I assume you'll be coming around to the shop when you've gotten yourself together, Agent Murtaugh."

Nate picked up his phone and climbed out. "Count on it."

"By the way, what can I tell Vic about what happened to your motorcycle?"

"What did you tell him happened yesterday?" He stood on the sidewalk, leaning on the open door.

"That we got caught in traffic near the explosion, and you took a rain check."

"I had the Philadelphia cops take it back for now. The Harley is a drug-confiscation item. It's supposed to go on auction in a couple of weeks." Nate thought about the logistics for a moment. "When would be the best night to bring it around? You know, when could I let Vic borrow it for a few hours? I want to get the biggest bang for the buck."

"He'd become your slave for life if you let him use it on a Friday night."

"Good...I mean about Friday. Talk him out of the slave thing, and I'll bring it Friday."

"I'll see what I can do." She gave him a two-fingered salute, and Nate shut the door of her car and watched Ellie drive away.

For the first time in his career, he was straying from regulations when it came to personal involvement. For years, he had toed the company line, but things were changing in him and he knew it. He even knew where his ambivalence originated. A year ago, when he looked at that gun pointed at his chest, he realized that he'd done his duty and it was time for a change.

On Nate's last assignment in the field, the shooter who'd missed blowing a hole in him had only hit him in the knee. That kid was supposed to be an FBI informant. A reliable source, Joey Sullen had been providing the when and where and who for the group Nate had just joined, in exchange for small perks. What Nate had not known until after the fact was that this young man, despite his size and his tough look, was only fourteen. And what he also didn't know until it was too late was that the boy would do anything for his pregnant, sixteen-year-old girlfriend—including spoiling a sting because she liked the protection of the bad guys much better.

The reports had praised Nate for heroically saving four other agents' lives. The fact remained that Nate had killed Joey that day, and his career goals had never felt quite the same since.

People were not as one-dimensional as they showed up in reports. Profiling was not a science but an art. Special agents were not machines, but humans. Not that knowing these things made him feel better. He'd still killed a kid. A kid who was never given a chance in his entire life.

Something had changed inside of Nate. He knew now that there was another side of life that needed to be explored. He was ready to move in a different direction. Set down roots. And not only to serve and protect, but to cherish and nurture. That was what he wanted now. He stared at the taillights of the BMW as Ellie turned the corner and disappeared.

* * *

Hawes almost cursed out loud when he stepped inside the elevator and found Cheri there. The only thing that saved him was the six other people that were waiting for the doors to slide shut, too. She was wearing a black miniskirt, and her blue eyes glanced meaningfully at his crotch before looking up. She had her "come and play" look on, but Sanford immediately turned around and stared at the lighted buttons over the door.

He'd left work a couple of hours early last night and taken Martha and three of their grandsons to an Orioles game in Baltimore. It had been ages since he'd done something that stupid and fun. Sitting in a ballpark with three rambunctious boys between them, Sanford had looked at his wife's smile and had felt his priorities somehow aligning themselves again. In that moment, the meaninglessness of getting screwed in sixteen different ways by a woman less than half his age dawned on him. Instead, he realized that what he wanted was to make just one woman happy, and that woman was Martha, who had put up with him for all these years despite all his flaws.

Sitting in Camden Yards and looking at that smile that he'd loved for almost forty years, he knew that he could make things right with her again. He had to.

The door opened at his floor, and Hawes practically raced out of the elevator. Cheri's perfume stayed with him. The *click-click* of her high heels followed close as he headed toward his office. It was still early. Very few people had arrived for the day. He was disappointed to see that his secretary wasn't in yet, either. He hurried into his office and closed the door.

From the very few tiffs he'd had with Cheri over the past few months, Hawes knew that she was temperamental and explosive. Telling her straight out that it was time to call it quits was not an advisable approach. He had to think it through, plan it carefully, and then make the break with her as gently as possible. Of course, it would be better if she'd just get tired of him not being available as her old stud boy and find someone else.

No sooner had he taken off his jacket and sat down behind his desk when the office door opened and Cheri slipped in.

"I brought you some coffee." She leaned back against the door, still holding the mug in one hand, and started unbuttoning her blouse. "You have to get your own milk and sugar from here."

"Stop," Hawes ordered. "Cheri, I'm expecting a conference call from the White House in five minutes. I have to be ready for it."

She pouted. "You didn't come over last night. Take me out for lunch."

"I can't," he said shortly, shuffling paperwork around and turning on his computers. "There's something already on my calendar."

"After work, then. We'll go back to the house and order in."

He shook his head. "Sorry, I'm watching a couple of my grandkids. Martha and my oldest daughter are going to some class." Hawes was proud of himself for making this latest thing up. Wife, daughter, grandchildren—he was hoping the mention of all these things would make Cheri realize how much older he was than her. "Look, my life has become very hectic with my family commitments. I don't have a minute to spare."

He turned his chair and buzzed one of the agents downstairs, asking him to bring up a file. It was a meaningless case, but it started the clock ticking for Cheri to get out.

"So when is *my* time?" Disappointment and anger added a sharp edge to her tone.

"I don't know. I'll let you know."

She put the coffee cup on the bookcase nearest to the door and buttoned up her blouse. "You weren't such a doting husband and grandfather two nights ago when I had my mouth around your—"

The hard slap of his hand on the desk shut her up. "That's enough."

She angrily reached for the door. "I don't think so."

"Cheri, this workplace has always been, and always will be, off limits for this shit. So never again try to pull something like this in here or you'll find your ass on the street."

"We'll just see about that, you old bastard."

She slammed the door hard enough on her way out to spill the coffee on the bookcase.

So much for the gentle, carefully planned approach, he thought.

Fifteen

Ellie sat in her car by the Dumpster for quite a while, content to watch the ball game in progress. Her windows were rolled down, and the ripe aroma of the six-day-old garbage mingled with the smell of baked asphalt. She hardly noticed it, though, watching the bounce in Chris's step as he ran to third base. She could hear his mouth running at least thirty miles an hour.

A child's resilience is the most amazing thing, and although Ellie had been there herself once, she thought it almost a miracle to see how quickly the eight-year-old had come out of his shell. It *was* a miracle.

She could have used a little of that youthful toughness today. Nate had managed to throw her system completely off kilter first thing this morning. After that, her entire day had gone downhill. Back at her apartment, she'd been too wound up to sleep. In the shop, she'd been too tired to be productive. When Vic had come in later to open up, she'd been too grouchy to face customers. So she'd been sent upstairs to lie down—only to toss and turn for an hour and a half and think ridiculous things about an arrogant FBI agent who sure knew how to kiss. She'd finally fallen asleep, thank God, even though it had only been for a couple of hours.

Ellie watched Chris score and was surprised to see him run over to someone sitting on the steps of one of the row houses beyond home plate. She had no view of them from here. Closing the windows, she took her purse and a cooler from the back seat, and then stepped out of her car as a young black kid from the neighborhood limped over.

"Wash your car, Miss Ellie?"

"The usual three bucks, Toni?"

The twelve-year-old kicked her dusty hubcaps and took a quick look around at the back bumpers. "I guess that'd be okay."

"First, help yourself to some juice packs and fruit." She put the cooler down and opened it.

He reached inside and took a juice pack and tucked it under one arm before taking a fistful of grapes. "Fer cryin' out loud, Miss Ellie! Couldn't you bring over some cold beer and Tastykakes? Or something good, at least?"

"No chance, pal." Ellie took out five dollars and paid him in advance, telling him to keep the rest as a tip. Toni—born with one leg shorter than the other, missing an arm and subject to all kinds of medical conditions—was the hardest-working kid and the loudest mouth on the street, in addition to being one of the smartest. He didn't play baseball during the summer months like the other kids, but worked any odd job he could hustle. And during the school year, he studied.

"Are you guys ready for a break?" she asked, carrying the cooler to the curb near home plate and leaving it open. Ellie got out of the way just in time to avoid being stampeded. Chris high-fived her on his way to the cooler.

Ellie looked over at the steps of the row house where

Chris had been. There in the shade sat the grandmother of one of the ballplayers, two girls who had decided that they were the official cheerleaders, Ted Hardy and Nate. Trying to give herself a moment to get over the kick-start her heart was feeling at the sight of him, Ellie grabbed a handful of water bottles out of the cooler before heading over to them.

Nate was dressed in a navy-blue polo shirt, khaki shorts and sneakers. And it was her tough luck that he had to have muscular thighs—just another reason to lie awake and lose sleep. His left knee was a route map of white scars. He was listening to something Ted was saying, but his gaze never wavered from her face as she approached.

"I hear this is the happening place in the city," she joked, returning the welcoming smile of the older woman and distributing the water bottles.

"It is now," Ted answered, tipping up his baseball hat to look into her face. "What kind of crap are you feeding my kids today, broccoli and tofu freeze pops?"

Ellie knocked his hat off. "And what are you doing playing hooky? I want the name of your boss. I'm going to call and complain."

"I know you wouldn't betray the one true love of your life." Ted grabbed her hand and tugged until she lost her balance and fell against him. As the others laughed, she delivered a solid punch to his arm and stepped on his hat before sitting down on the step next to him.

"Care for a pretzel?" the grandmother asked.

"Thanks." Ellie took the bag being offered to her as a phone started ringing inside.

"Oh, that'd be my boy," added the older woman, going in to answer.

"So how's the game going?" Ellie asked.

Ted picked up his hat and dusted it off. "It was going great until you showed up and ruined it."

She stole his hat away again and this time threw it on the street. "Watch what you say. People might think you don't like me."

"Nobody would think that." He reached over and messed up her hair. "You're too cute."

"I hate cute." Ellie moved the bag of pretzels out of Ted's reach when he tried to take a couple. She turned and offered it to Nate. "When did you get here?"

There was a mildly puzzled look on his face. When Ted looped an arm casually around her shoulder and wrestled the pretzels from her, she couldn't miss the frown that creased his forehead.

"Hey, you guys," Ted shouted to the kids. "Don't leave that trash around."

"About an hour ago," Nate answered coolly.

It was clear that Nate assumed there was something going on between her and Ted. As surprising as that was, the possibility of letting him continue to believe that lasted for less than a second. She would never use Ted like that—not after everything that he'd been through.

"Have you been inside?"

"Briefly. Sister Helen was busy, and your father wasn't back from the hardware store."

Ellie needed to know who Ted thought Nate was. "So how did you guys happen to meet?"

"Helen introduced us," Ted explained. "With the kind of free time this guy has on his hands, I'm figuring we can get him involved with some coaching. A little football starting at the end of August. Basketball after that. Baseball—''

"No scheduling anything for the next two weeks," she ordered, cutting Ted short. "After that, you're welcome to do whatever you want with him."

"What are you going to do to him that takes two weeks?" Ted's tone was teasing.

"Ted, get your mind out of the gutter," she ordered, pretending to be insulted and pushing his arm off her shoulder. Hearing Nate's chuckle, she swung the pretzel bag at him. "I don't know what you're laughing about."

"Think you could give him a few hours off on Friday night?" Ted asked.

"What for?"

"We're all going to a Phillies game. You can come, too, if you want."

She thought about Ray Claiborne's party Friday night—an important affair in the world of Philadelphia area collectors. There was a possibility that whoever was running the Morris flag auction might have someone there. And having been Ray's apprentice for years, Ellie would be expected to bring along her rich client.

"No time off. I'm taking him out for dinner Friday night."

"You mean, as in a dinner *date?*" Nate asked with interest, leaning over her shoulder. His breath tickled her ear.

"No. As in a 'feeding you and putting you back on the street' dinner."

Ted turned to Nate. "Then maybe you can still catch the ball game. I can leave you a ticket at the box office."

"Good idea."

"Bad idea," she corrected. "Okay. As in a dinner date."

Ellie was relieved to see her father's car pull onto the street. The combination of these two men was lethal. She stood up. "I'm going in."

"I need to find out more about this dinner date." Nate got up, too, following her.

Chris, waiting for his turn to bat, gave Ellie and Nate a big smile as they went by. She greeted Lou through the open window of his car, but he grunted something unintelligible.

"Do you need a hand carrying this stuff in?" Nate asked just as Lou was getting out of the station wagon.

Ellie stood on the sidewalk and watched her father go into a long story about the cost of things and how they were making it impossible to repair anything anymore and how you had to replace everything these days. All the while, he was loading Nate up with odds and ends that he'd bought. A pang of envy stung her a little at the level of comfort that already existed between the two men. And they were barely more than strangers.

There was never any small talk between Lou and Ellie. The extent of their conversations was usually limited to her asking questions and her father answering with a yes or no. She had to be fair, though. Sometimes he did extend himself to an "I don't know."

Initially, she'd blamed his dour silence on the years he'd spent behind bars. But he had no trouble communicating with Sister Helen, the other nuns, Ted or now even Nate. The problem obviously lay with her. Ellie couldn't figure it out at all. She was the one who'd been wronged when Louis Littlefield had been sent to jail, but he appeared to be angry with her about it.

"There are some bags of groceries in the car. Do you want to get them?"

Nate's question jarred Ellie out of her trance. Lou had already started for the convent door. She went to the open back door of the station wagon and stared inside. The smell of mold attacked her sinuses. The seats were worn and splitting from age. Rust had eaten away at the floorboards, and there were gaping holes through which she could see the pavement. She didn't know how Lou could possibly get this junk heap past inspection every year. Ellie glanced at her own two-month-old BMW across the street. It was shining, thanks to Toni, and guilt slid coldly along her spine.

She tried to give her father things, she told herself, but he never accepted. She made enough money that he didn't have to live in a basement, and that there was no need for him to work.

Ellie felt herself growing angry. They didn't have to be strangers. She wanted to make up for the years they'd missed, but he had no interest. There were times when she wondered if he wanted to forget that she existed. If he wanted to put her behind him as he would any other bad memory. Like her mother. Maybe he expected Ellie to leave him, too, and never look back.

"Taking a nap?"

She frowned into Nate's smiling face. Her temper reshaped and refocused on him. "Yes. I was having this wonderful dream. I had my fingers around your throat. Sort of a dream date."

"Were we doing anything kinky?"

"Depends on your view of murder."

Smiling, he picked up the bags and closed the back

of the car. "Now, if you had taken my suggestion of coming upstairs and taking a nap with me before, right about now you'd be having a totally different type of dream."

"Does it involve stabbing? Shooting? Guillotining?"

He shook his head, moved the bags onto one arm and placed the other around her shoulder, pushing her up the walk.

"Nothing quite so violent," he whispered in her ear. "Think hot and sweaty...and maybe a little noisy."

"Hot, sweaty and noisy." She thought for a second. "Let's see. In this dream, I must be working in a fast-food place. Of course, I'd be firing your butt because I'm your boss."

His laughter was contagious. Ellie bit her lip to hide it.

"Vic wasn't joking, was he?" Nate said, still chuckling.

She immediately bristled. "Joking about what?"

He immediately put on his innocent face. "Uh... about that great collection of antique maps you have in the shop. How come I didn't see them?"

"That's *not* what you were talking about."

"Really?"

She fired a cross look at him and went ahead of him into the convent. They took the packages to the kitchen. There was no one there, and he put the bags on the counter.

"Come on. Confess. What was it exactly that Vic told you about me?"

"You don't really expect me to get him in trouble now, do you?"

"No." She pushed him out of the way and started

emptying the bags. She was trying to keep it light and joking, but in truth Ellie was frustrated with her father and with Nate, but mostly with herself for encouraging him. She knew she was sending him mixed signals, but she was being a coward about following through one way or another.

"What do you want me to do?" he asked, standing right behind her.

Ellie's body was already in overdrive. "Say something that will make me really lose it. You know, give me a chance to take it out on you. Let me punch you or something."

He had a surprised look on his face when she turned around and faced him. "Go ahead. Do it."

"Don't," Sister Helen said, coming into the kitchen at that moment. Nate immediately moved away. "Never strike a federal agent, Elizabeth, unless you want to spend your youth behind bars. I speak from personal experience."

The nun moved to the counter and took a quick inventory of the items purchased.

"So," she said brightly, looking at Ellie. "Did you hear anything more?"

There was no need to ask what the nun was referring to. "No, he hasn't called back yet."

"Was Ray any help?"

"Not yet." Ellie started putting the groceries away. "The clock is definitely ticking."

"I need to get Lou to look into other possible contacts," Nate said from a corner of the kitchen. "Real or replacement, having something flying up there behind the President is a safety net I would personally like to pursue."

Ellie leaned against the counter. "If that's the way

you feel about it, I can check with some people I know, too. This whole business works by word of mouth. I think I might be able come up with some names of people who could do the work, too.''

He didn't do a very good job of hiding his surprise. Though she had kept herself clear of items with a questionable pedigree, Ellie was irked by the idea of Nate relying on Lou for all the answers. Childish, immature, selfish—Ellie could think of a hundred names for herself that might fit right now. But what had originally started as a race against time now also felt like a race against her father. After all, she knew people who restored tapestries and antique clothing, people who were experts with both fabric and period stitching.

Lou appeared in the doorway to the kitchen and looked only at Nate. ''You wanted to talk? Now's the time.''

A heaviness welled up in Ellie as she watched Nate disappear with her father down the steps. A life that appeared so perfect just a few days ago now seemed incomplete and full of flaws. She had things—money, security, a house, a career—but not a single relationship in her life that was working. She was alone. As she always had been.

And she was tired of it.

''Are you okay?'' Helen asked with concern.

''Really tired,'' she said softly, picking up her purse and going out of the house.

Chris didn't whine when one of the nuns called out to say they were eating dinner in half an hour. Instead, he left the baseball game despite being next to bat. He ran down the alley to the back of the convent and fetched a broom, quickly sweeping the sidewalk out

front. Putting the broom back, he took his shoes off
before going in. He washed his hands and face, ran
into the sisters' living room and stacked up the newspapers and the books. From there, he ran to the kitchen
and, without being asked, started setting the table.

He was happy, safe, thankful for being here, and he
wanted to show it. Agent Murtaugh had said they'd still
made no plans to take him back to New York. Miss
Ellie and Sister Helen had both told him not to say
anything to anyone about Nate being an FBI guy, and
Chris had given his word on that one. It was a special
thing to be trusted with secrets—especially when the
people were cool like these people.

"What a good boy!" Sister Helen said, coming into
the kitchen and catching him putting the last plate on
the table. She went to the oven and checked the lasagna
one of the other sisters had made. "We've got plenty
here, if you want to ask Ted to stay for dinner. Would
you like to go and see if he's still around and if he'd
like to join us?"

Christopher dashed for the front door. Most of the
kids had disappeared. A group of the younger ones was
playing four square on the sidewalk down the street.
Three women were sitting on the steps of the house
two doors down. Chris searched the line of parked cars,
looking for Ted's.

He stopped looking when he saw the black car. It
was parked at the end of the block, facing the convent.
There were two men sitting inside.

The thin bubble of security popped. They were here
for him.

Chris turned and ran inside the convent, quickly
closing and locking the front door before running back
into the kitchen.

Sixteen

Thursday, June 24

Nate sat back on his hotel bed with the phone in the crook of his neck as Victor read off Ellie's appointments for the day.

"Let's see. Mrs. Harriman of the Havertown Harriman's at ten-thirty. The original purple-haired dowager, complete with poodle. Wait a second." Vic's voice became muffled. "Good afternoon, ladies. If you have any questions, I'm here for you."

Nate heard the potential customers return the greeting. Vic came back on the line, his voice low. "Tourists. Professional shoppers, but not buyers. Their clothes came off the clearance rack at an outlet two weeks ago. The bags are Gucci knockoffs, probably got them on the street from a vendor. The husbands are sitting in the bar at the Striped Bass, hoping to see Jennifer Aniston, but they'll take Bruce Willis. The old goats are also praying these two don't find anything they'll have to come and look at." Vic paused. "My guess, from the way their hair's been done, is they want to look like Lower East Side Manhattanites, but they're really from Yonkers."

"That's pretty good, Vic."

"It's a gift." He paused and Nate heard the pages of the calendar rustle again. "After Mrs. Harriman, lunch with Augusta Biddle. Smart move, considering the celebrity auction is next week and Ellie's already canceled the first two meetings with her this week."

Nate had seen a write-up in today's paper about the auction. Biddle definitely seemed to get top billing with her picture pasted in at the top of the article. But even to the socially savvy reporter who did the article, Ellie was clearly the one who had done the bulk of the work putting the auction together.

"Back massage at Pierre and Carlo's at four," Vic continued. "Things must not be going well. She hasn't done that for a long while. Let's see, dinner with…oh, Christ. Not him!"

"*Who* is she going out to dinner with?" Nate asked, sitting up.

"With the jackass."

Nate shifted the phone from one ear to the other. "Is that a first name or a last name?"

"Both. I just can't believe she is going out with him again."

When Nate called first thing this morning about getting together, Ellie had brushed him off completely. She'd reminded him about dinner at Ray's tomorrow night and said she didn't need to see him until then—unless something came up. There was no need to read between the lines. She'd told him repeatedly that there was not going to be any personal involvement between them.

"Who is this guy, Vic?"

"The jackass. Aka Donald Shore, Philadelphia lawyer, old Main Line family, comes from money, has money, thinks he can buy anything with money.

Armani suits, expensive hair weave, works with a personal trainer at the Rittenhouse Athletic Club. Likes to hear himself talk, has an opinion on everything. Met Ellie through the Biddles. Thinks our girl is very cute and has been putting the squeeze on her for a while. She keeps putting him off. He had his decorator buy a shitload of stuff from us. He wouldn't dare say it to Ellie, but I know he's homophobic. I hate him.''

"Ellie hates cute," Nate offered.

"You're right. That's why I can't figure what the hell she is doing going out with this guy. I thought things were going good with you two."

"They were. They are. Everything's cool." Nate got up from the hotel bed and limped around the room. Never in a million years would he have thought that there would come a day when his confidante would be a muscled gay antique dealer who had a crush on him.

"Then it must be a sex thing."

"What sex thing?"

"I shouldn't talk about it. Hold on." Vic greeted another customer and asked the two New Yorkers if they were okay. He was back on the line in a minute. "But what the hell, I might have started this whole mess yesterday afternoon."

"What happened yesterday afternoon?"

"She was pretty upset. No. Wound-up, I guess, when she got back from Sister Helen's. So, innocently, I asked her how things were and if she'd seen you…just small talk, you know?" There was the grinding sound of a chair being moved. Nate visualized Vic moving one of the stools and sitting on it. His tone dropped low. "Then, out of nowhere, she explodes on me. And I'm not talking about a PMS bad mood or a temper tantrum. I mean, she really lost it. She accuses

me of meddling in her life. She reminds me that you're
only a client. Says she's no baby-sitter, and she's no
girlfriend, either. Then she keeps going…complaining
about Sister Helen and her father and the business and
before I know it, she's in tears. So I hug her and tell
her everything will work out, yadda yadda.''

Nate sat down on the bed and thought about how
Ellie's mood had turned sour yesterday. It was when
she and Louis had faced each other—or hadn't. She
was fine until he arrived at the convent in his car.
Whenever Ellie and Lou were in the same room, there
might as well be a ten-foot-high stone wall between
them, with barbed wire on the top and a moat alongside. They never talked directly. There was rarely any
acknowledgement of any sort.

''Now, when it comes to Ellie, I love her like family.
Hell, I love her better than my family. And she's not
one to fall apart like that, so it broke my heart to see
it. Wait a minute, I need to write up a sale. So you
found something. Lovely…'' Vic's voice became muffled.

Nate decided he should hang up. This was absolutely
ridiculous. He could imagine Hawes's reaction if he
knew that Nate was spending the day like this, lying
around a hotel room and having a heart-to-heart with
Vic. He'd have a coronary.

In his own defense, Nate *was* working. He reached
for the folders on the bedside table and started taking
notes. He'd been on the phone with Wilcox for more
than an hour this morning, going over the package he'd
received from the museum director. Now he had in his
possession all the pertinent information about the
weave and texture and condition of the Schuyler flag

prior to the fire. Pretty quickly, he needed to locate a person who could produce a duplicate.

"I'm back. Where was I?"

"The sex thing."

"Yeah, family. Anyway, I pull her into my arms and start giving her all this advice. Now, at this point I don't care if she's listening or not. The important thing with women is just to hold them when they're like this. Are you listening, Nate?"

"I'm listening."

"Good. So I give her this speech about the importance of having a well-rounded lifestyle. This means eating right, which she doesn't do, sleeping enough, which she appears to be skipping lately, and having family and friends around, like me and Brian and Helen but not grouchy old Lou. And then I talk about sex, and how important it is for a thirty-year-old woman...I did tell you that she turned thirty this year, didn't I?"

"Yes, you did."

"Anyway, I give her this speech about relationships—and different facets of it, including sex. Now we're talking, and I couldn't remember the name of her last boyfriend. But she couldn't, either. That tells you how long it's been. Anyway, he was just another one of those rich Main Line boys who isn't worth remembering. So I bad-mouth him for a minute or so, and she laughs a little, and I can see she's coming around. But I have this lousy habit I got from my mother. I tend to end these kinds of tearful sessions with a general 'one size fits all' piece of advice. My mother says, 'Find a nice girl, have some kids and help yourself to another manicotti.'"

"What advice do you give?"

"A hot dose of sex gives perspective to any problem."

"Very profound."

"It's a gift. Hold on. Goodbye, ladies. Stop back again." Vic sighed heavily. "But I think Attorney Shore can thank me for his hot date tonight."

"Do you know where they're going for dinner?"

"No...but now you're talking."

Sister Lisa, the youngest nun in the convent, was tall and athletic, and the talk among the boys outside was that she was strong enough to wrestle three of them to the ground at a time. Christopher needed protection right now, so he cheerfully volunteered to help with all kinds of chores, and he had not left Sister Lisa's side all day.

"Hey, I hear another ball game heating up outside." For the first time since lunch, the nun sat down with a book in her lap. "Why don't you go out? You have enough time to play a couple of innings before dinner."

Chris shook his head and went back to lining up his opposing lines of Crazy Bones, those little molded statuelike pieces of colorful plastic that he could use like army men or like marbles. Ellie had given them to him yesterday, and he loved them. His favorite, an inch-high blue one he'd named Ziggy, was at the center of three lines of defense.

This morning, he'd peeked out of the upstairs window. The car was still there, though he could only see one man in it. Later, helping Sister Lisa take some bags of used clothes to Lou's car, he'd seen them again. The car was still parked at the end of the block, and both guys were sitting in it. They weren't coming in. They weren't going. They were just watching. Waiting.

Chris remembered the Disney movie *The Hunchback of Notre Dame.* The ugly Quasi-guy had wanted sanctuary in the church. Maybe convents worked that way, too. Maybe it was that sanctuary thing that was keeping him safe. Or maybe, just like in the movies, they were waiting to see if he squawked. Then they'd get him and put a bullet in him for ratting on them.

Whatever, he wasn't going to jinx anything.

"Maybe you should go and check to see if Mr. Hardy is playing with the kids out there."

Chris was tempted, but the idea of going on the street where anyone could grab him was too scary. He really liked Ted. As far as grown-ups went, he was the coolest Chris had ever met. He was one of those dads you saw in the playground, throwing the ball or wrestling and having fun with their kids. Or the ones who were always waiting at school at the end of the day to pick their kids up. Or the ones who went on all the field trips. Chris just knew that Ted was the kind of dad who would always be around and never forget a birthday.

He leaned on one elbow and rolled one of Ziggy's soldiers at the opposing army, knocking two of them down. Ted would even be a dad who would play Crazy Bones with him.

"Does Mr. Hardy have any kids?"

Sister Lisa held the book against her chest and looked up at Chris. She opened her mouth to say something, but then closed it. Suddenly, she seemed sort of sad. "Mr. Hardy...well, he did have kids once. Two little girls."

"What do you mean? Doesn't he have them no more?"

She shook her head. "No, they're both in heaven now."

Chris stared down at the orderly lines of little statues. Ted had a way of staring into space every now and then—especially when a couple of the younger girls on the street would squeal or laugh. "What happened to them?"

"It was a...a while ago. They died in a fire." Sister Lisa touched the cross that hung from a chain around her neck and opened the book in her lap.

"Where was the fire?" Chris asked softly.

"At the house they lived in."

"Was Mr. Hardy there?"

"No." She shook her head when Chris opened his mouth to ask his next question. "No more questions now, Christopher. And I think it would be best if you didn't bring up any of this with Mr. Hardy, either. He had a very difficult time recovering from that loss, and it's only been this past six months or so that he's gotten back to being more like his old self."

Chris thought of his own parents. Neither of them knew or cared where he'd gone. They didn't care if he was ever coming back. Something was messed up when a nice guy like Ted loses his children, while a kid like him can walk around with nobody caring about him at all.

It was the kind of elegance that seemed to envelop you, shaping itself to the contours of your consciousness the way silk molds to the lines of your body. It was a sense of comfort that moved with you. It made

MIRA ®

AN IMPORTANT MESSAGE
FROM
THE EDITORS

Dear Reader,

Because you've chosen to read one of our fine books, we'd like to say "thank you"! And, as a **special** way to thank you, we're offering you a choice of <u>two more</u> of the books you love so well, **and** a surprise gift to send you—absolutely **FREE**!

Please enjoy them with our compliments...

Editor,
The Best of the Best™

P.S. And <u>because</u> we value our customers, we've attached something extra inside ...

Peel off seal and Place inside...

EDITOR'S
FREE
GIFTS
SEAL
THANK YOU

glanced down at her watch. She'd lost count of how many times today she'd wanted to walk away from these people. Mrs. Harriman's rambling account of her upcoming dinner party for Senator Santorum, all the while feeding broiled chicken livers to her spoiled little poodle, nearly turned Ellie's stomach. In the discussion of finding a last-minute replacement for the celebrity host of the Children's Hospital Auction next week, Augusta Biddle had been insistent on paying an exorbitant amount for a has-been television hunk to come in. It didn't matter that his fee for appearing would cut deeply into the money Ellie hoped to raise for the hospital. It didn't matter that this guy was not going to bring any added luster to the event. It didn't even matter that Augusta had told Ellie months earlier that she'd had the hots for the former star for years. She wanted him here, they would pay his ridiculously expensive fee, and he'd stay at the Biddle's Main Line mansion.

Ellie took another sip of the champagne. Donald was still talking about his world. She was finding it more and more difficult to communicate with these people. They had a different concept of reality, and she was getting tired of trying to explain this. People just didn't listen to one another, particularly in some elevated group. She'd worked so hard to be included in this exclusive circle. She'd worked hard to belong, but suddenly she couldn't stand them. She'd met a number of wonderful people who were a part of that world, people who really cared about other people. But they were a rare commodity.

Ellie was beginning to realize the Harriman-Biddle world would never be her world. She knew it when her fifty-dollar reflexology session at Pierre and Carlo's you feel secure, welcome. It left you intellectually and sensually satisfied.

The frescoed ceiling, the ornate moldings, the beveled mirrors, the marble busts, the dazzling crystal and chandeliers...all beautiful. The impeccably attired service staff—mostly men, but a few women, too—gliding between the tables and welcoming guests in soft tones, even translating the French menu for the unprepared, was charming. The meal consisted of six courses, each a creative wonder. Ellie didn't think she had ever been treated to such a dining experience. Le Bec-Fin was the best restaurant in town, and the recent renovations to the decor only enhanced the occasion. There was a time in Ellie's life—not so long ago, either—when she would have been in awe of Donald for bringing her here to dine. But not tonight.

Ellie hoped she was being successful at hiding her boredom as she sipped the Dom Pérignon that Donald had insisted on ordering. The attorney continued with his endless story regarding the bloodletting that had accompanied the merger of his Center City law firm with another. Meanwhile, her mind wandered. Today had been a day like dozens of others she'd lived through this past year. Days spent with important and influential people. Hours spent being noticed by the elite in the city. She was building her network of contacts, getting referrals and growing her business while extending her personal connections. And now even a date with one of the most prominent bachelors in the city. A successful day.

Everything was going as she'd always hoped and planned for herself in life, except that Ellie wasn't feeling any joy in it.

Pretending to adjust the napkin on her lap, she

THE EDITOR'S "THANK YOU" FREE GIFTS INCLUDE:

- ▶ 2 Romance OR 2 Suspense books
- ▶ An exciting surprise gift

YES! I have placed my Editor's "thank you" Free Gifts seal in the space provided above. Please send me the 2 FREE books which I have selected, and my FREE Mystery Gift. I understand that I am under no obligation to purchase anything further, as explained on the back and opposite page.

PLACE
FREE GIFTS
SEAL
HERE

check one:

☐ ROMANCE
193 MDL DRUR
393 MDL DRUS

☐ SUSPENSE
192 MDL DRSS
392 MDL DRSW

FIRST NAME	LAST NAME

ADDRESS

APT.#	CITY

STATE/PROV.	ZIP/POSTAL CODE

▼ DETACH AND MAIL CARD TODAY! ▶

The Reader Service — Here's How it Works:

Accepting your 2 free books and gift places you under no obligation to buy anything. You may keep the books and gift and return the shipping statement marked "cancel." If you do not cancel, about a month later we'll send you 3 additional books and bill you just $4.74 each in the U.S., or $5.24 each in Canada, plus 25¢ shipping & handling per book and applicable taxes if any.* That's the complete price and — compared to cover prices starting from $5.99 each in the U.S. and $6.99 each in Canada — it's quite a bargain! You may cancel at any time, but if you choose to continue, every month we'll send you 3 more books, which you may either purchase at the discount price or return to us and cancel your subscription.

*Terms and prices subject to change without notice. Sales tax applicable in N.Y. Canadian residents will be charged applicable provincial taxes and GST.

If offer card is missing write to: The Reader Service, 3010 Walden Ave., P.O. Box 1867, Buffalo, NY 14240-1867

BUSINESS REPLY MAIL

FIRST-CLASS MAIL   PERMIT NO. 717-003   BUFFALO, NY

POSTAGE WILL BE PAID BY ADDRESSEE

THE READER SERVICE
3010 WALDEN AVE
PO BOX 1341
BUFFALO NY 14240-8571

NO POSTAGE
NECESSARY
IF MAILED
IN THE
UNITED STATES

had been a total failure; she couldn't stop feeling guilty about the extravagance.

Ellie looked up, surprised to find Donald quiet for the first time tonight. In fact, he was waiting.

"I'm sorry, did you ask me something?"

He leaned toward her. "You have this way of turning your left ear toward me when you ask a question— as if you can hear better from that side. I think it's an absolutely charming habit." He reached over, cupped her chin and angled her face a little more. His thumb caressed her cheek. "Everyone has a better side. I think your profile from the left is very cute—especially this tiny mole under your earlobe."

Ellie pulled out of his reach. "You had a question, Donald?"

"Oh, yes. You haven't touched the duck. Is it satisfactory?"

She looked down at slices of duck breast fanned beneath a rich sauce and sprinkled with herbs and green peppercorns. The plate was a work of art. The smell was heavenly. But she had no appetite.

"It's delicious. I had some." She moved the food on her plate with her fork, and then sat back.

"I hope you saved some room for dessert."

Donald started on a long-winded explanation of the restaurant's famous cheese cart, which would soon be making its appearance at their table, and Ellie felt her frustration beginning to boil up inside of her. She'd wanted this date to work. She'd convinced herself it was time to have a relationship with a man. And Donald Shore was a great candidate. He was rich, smart, very interested in her. And as far as looks...well, if he was on the short side, that suited her own height. He was in very good condition, muscular but not unnaturally developed. His hair did have that look of perfection that surgery had obviously restored, but there were many balding men who were going that route. He was even considered handsome by many in town.

Handsome. Vic and Brian and everyone else seemed to believe Nate was handsome, too. Even Sister Helen sometimes looked at him in an odd way for a nun. As far as Ellie was concerned, though, he was too tall. He made her feel like a dwarf next to him. Another problem was that he was too muscular. He had a rawboned power in his body that made him...unmanageable. And he was obviously a flirt. What happened to the boring, ultramacho G-man image she always clung to? With Nate, she would never know if he was practicing one of his everyday lines on her or if he was really paying her a compliment.

A vision of Nate's devilish smile flashed in her mind. Those eyes that were too blue. Those hard planes that came together at curious angles, making a tough face irresistible when he came close enough to kiss her. Her stomach tightened and she felt the tingling of delicate places at the mere thought of him kissing her.

She asked for her dinner to be boxed when the table was being cleared. She didn't remember ever taking a duck dinner to Jack.

She'd turned off her cell phone when Donald picked her up at the shop. Now she found herself worrying whether or not there were any important messages that she'd missed.

"Will you please excuse me?" Ellie announced abruptly. "I'll be back in a minute." She grabbed her purse and escaped to the ladies' room.

Inside, Ellie felt that she could finally breathe. There were three messages that she'd missed. The first one was from Ray. Nothing urgent, but he wanted her to know that another collector who was interested in purchasing the same flag as Ellie's client had come out of the woodwork. Ray was inviting the woman to his dinner party tomorrow night, so she could check out the competition.

The second message was from her dealer friend John Dubin in Ticonderoga. She'd put the bug in his ear yesterday about finding the name of someone who'd be interested in making a duplicate of the old flag. John had connections in some unconventional circles, just as her father did, though John refused to buy or sell stolen or forged properties himself. And in his message, John said he had a name for her.

The last message was from Nate, and Ellie unconsciously leaned against the wall at the sound of his voice. He had nothing new to report. He'd been at Sister Helen's this afternoon, and Lou still had not been able to find anyone else who might be interested in the job. He wanted her to give him a call about tomorrow night.

The victory of coming up with a name before her father was a minor one, but Ellie was thrilled. She was ready to dial Nate's number when she realized the matronly attendant in the rest room was looking at her curiously. Suddenly, it dawned on Ellie that she'd been away from Donald for too long. She tucked the phone inside her purse and left the rest room.

When Ellie sat down at the table, she told her dinner companion that she had to leave. Donald did a fairly good job of masking his annoyance with words of concern, though he could not seem to understand her need to leave before the cheese cart and the dessert cart made their appearance.

"But I want you to stay. Finish your meal," she pressed. Thoughts ran through her head of the complication of him driving her back to her place. He certainly would expect to be invited up to her apartment. In his voice she had heard an obvious anticipation of sex from the moment she had called him and accepted his invitation.

"No, Ellie. Absolutely not. I'm taking you home."

"Please don't." She was fighting the urge to run. Suddenly the formality of the restaurant began to feel restrictive. "I already asked for a cab to be called."

"Then they can just send him on his way."

"Listen, Donald." She took his hand when he was ready to wave at one of the waiters. "I'm sorry. I appreciate your effort and the expense of tonight. But I'm afraid I'm way too distracted with other things right now to be good company."

"The auction for the Children's Hospital," he said with a condescending nod. "It's a lot of responsibility."

"That's only part of it."

He entwined his fingers with hers. "I like you, Ellie. I like you very much. You're so easy to talk to. So beautiful to look at. I don't want to wait another two months before you call me back." His tone softened. He caressed her palm. "I know I talked shop too much tonight. Probably just nerves on my part. Why don't you let me take you home? If you give me a chance, I promise I'll make it up to you in ways you've only dreamed of."

Ellie shook her head. "That's quite an offer, but no. Maybe some other time."

She blew him a kiss and stood up, ignoring the curious glances around them. Their waiter, carrying the boxed dinner, caught up with her by the door, and Ellie quickly left the restaurant.

On the sidewalk outside, she wanted nothing more than to disappear before Donald came after her. She had a feeling he would not give up, though the cheese and dessert carts had an obvious allure for him. A brisk power walk down Walnut Street would clear her head and get her away from the restaurant, but the tight, mid-thigh dress and high heels were not very well suited for that.

A homeless woman pushing a grocery cart piled high with trash inched along the sidewalk. Ellie approached her and offered her the boxed dinner. The woman took it gladly, thanking her and glancing back at the name of the restaurant before moving on.

Ellie stepped off the curb and raised her hand for a cab, but a motorcycle pulled up in front of her instead. She looked in disbelief into Nate Murtaugh's face. Jeans, boots, T-shirt, powerful arms, blue eyes that set her body on fire with that once-over look.

"I dare you to climb on."

Seventeen

Without a moment's hesitation, Ellie looped her purse around her neck and sat sidesaddle on the seat behind him.

"I dare you to get some wind in my hair."

"Just hold on tight."

There were gaping stares as the Harley sped down the block. Nate could only imagine what a sight she presented. The black dress was too tight and too short. Her legs were strong and beautiful. Ellie was truly stunning in the sleeveless, open-neckline dress. He took the fastest route from the fifteen-hundred block of Walnut Street to her house on Pine.

"Wait a minute," she complained as soon as Nate shut off the engine in front of her building. "What happened to getting some wind in my hair?"

"Not looking like that." He turned and arched an eyebrow meaningfully at the skin showing below the rising hem of the dress. "You go and change into something loose and ugly, and I'll take you for the ride of your life."

"Promises, promises." She grumbled under her breath, climbing off and searching inside her purse for her keys.

Her hair was windblown. The dress, twisted and hitched up from the ride, was slow to drop back into position, and Nate couldn't help enjoying the view. The pleasure he'd felt when he'd seen her come out of that restaurant by herself was inexplicable.

He still didn't know why he'd gone there tonight, anyway. After talking to Vic, he'd done some serious thinking. What Ellie had been telling him all along was right. And in thinking about it, Nate had added a few of his own arguments that supported the conclusion that they didn't belong together. As she said, they were different people. Their paths were crossing for a very short time. Work and play didn't mix. It wouldn't be fair or intelligent to muddle their lives with complications like this.

And so Nate had been there, thinking maybe if he saw her go home with this lawyer, then he could put an end to whatever sexual fantasies he'd started having about her.

She'd sure blown that idea to hell.

"Coming up?" she asked from the open door.

He was speechless for a second.

"I have to return a call and get more information, but I think we might have the name of someone else who's handy with a needle."

Nate breathed a sigh of relief, glad for the clarification. It would have been embarrassing as hell if he ripped that dress off her before they reached the staircase. He took the key out of the bike ignition and climbed off.

The store downstairs was dark, and she didn't bother to turn on any lights. Her perfume wafted in the air. Nate closed the door behind him, locked it and leaned against the glass for a few seconds. The light from the street cast shadows around the room and on her. Her white skin, contrasted against the black dress, was lu-

minous. He watched Ellie take off her shoes and walk
barefoot through the store—checking the messages on
the phone and thumbing through the mail. Even the
way she walked teased and seduced him.

She looked up and their gazes locked. "How did you
know where I was tonight?"

"I can't betray my sources."

"Vic will be happy to hear that."

"What did your friend—your dinner date—do to
make you leave without him?"

"Nothing," she said casually, heading for the stairs.

Nate followed her, admiring the fit of the dress on
her body and the slim, silky legs.

"You didn't meet John Dubin," she said. "He's an
antique dealer in Ticonderoga and a good friend. He's
the one who left a message on my cell phone tonight
about a possible contact."

"Are you sure you want me to cross this threshold?"
Nate paused with one foot on the top step.

Ellie looked over her shoulder at him. "You've been
in my apartment before."

"True, but the last time I was there you weren't
wearing a dress designed to drive me crazy."

A smile touched the corner of her lips. "And I always thought they took you FBI guys apart and rebuilt
you as million-dollar machines during your training."

"They do. In my case, though, they ran out of
money, and I was left with a few human parts."

Ellie's once-over look made Nate's clothes go tight
in certain places.

"I can see I'm sailing in dangerous waters." Her
dark eyes were full of mischief. "Even so, you can
come in."

In her apartment, Ellie tried to eliminate the tension

between them by turning on every light and opening the windows and the doors onto the balcony. She started some coffee and then told him about what she'd heard from Ray about another potential buyer. Though he was concerned, Ellie told him that it was to be expected, and it actually gave more credibility to the rumor that there would soon be an auction for the flag.

Nate walked around her apartment when Ellie got on the phone with John Dubin. It had been a surprise to see that the decor of the place where she lived was so different from her shop. He guessed it was different from the stylish apartments of the people she socialized with, too. Though individual furnishings were tastefully arranged and obviously comfortable, the chairs and tables in the living room did not match one another. Nor were they antiques. They looked more like the hand-me-downs that people keep to make a place feel like home.

Nate remembered what Vic had told him the first time he'd brought him up here to wait for Ellie. This was sacred ground. She didn't allow customers, boyfriends or even casual friends to cross the threshold. This was the place where Ellie could drop the mask of who she should be. This was the place where she could be herself.

Nate thought of his own apartment in New York. For all his time with the Bureau, years that amounted to a whirlwind of assignments and travel, he'd never given more thought to the place he lived than he'd give to a hotel room. Comfortable. Impersonal. Definitely not a home.

Until a year ago. The impersonality of the arrangement, though, had hit him when he'd been pushed behind a desk after his injury. With more time on his hands than he'd ever cared for, Nate had walked into his place every night wondering what the hell he was doing there. And why he wasn't getting out.

Bookcases covered one wall, and Nate moved closer to look at the dozens of framed photos that shared the shelves with the books. Ellie as a leggy preteen, cuddled against Lou on the steps of the art museum. Another picture of a young Lou on a beach with a beautiful woman with long dark hair flying in the wind. The woman had a strong resemblance to Ellie. On the shelf below, there was one of Sister Helen and the nuns. And another of Ellie, Ted Hardy and three other people. Most of the others were people he didn't know with the exception of a glimpse of Ellie here and there among other families. He heard her hang up the phone.

"His name is Hank Teasdale, and he lives near Saratoga Springs." He looked over his shoulder and saw Ellie disappearing into her bedroom. "John said I should call Mr. Teasdale in the morning and square away the details of when we can meet with him. He's an odd duck, apparently, kind of a recluse. He restores old tapestries and reupholsters furniture with antique fabrics. He's one of the best, apparently. Works out of his house."

From this angle, Nate had a partial view of her bed through the double French doors. "That's my neck of the woods."

"What do you mean? I thought you worked in New York City."

"The Saratoga area is where I was raised. My family still lives there."

The sound of drawers opening and closing came from the bedroom. The black dress sailed through the air and landed on the foot of the bed. Nate turned around and faced the bookcase again as his body responded to the sight with a healthy natural reaction that he didn't want to deal with right now.

"Do you know him?"

"No. Never heard of him. But the place has changed and grown a lot since I left."

He found himself staring at the picture of Ellie with Ted again.

He didn't hear her behind him. "That's Ted's sister Léa and her husband, Mick, in the picture with us. And that gorgeous blonde is Heather, Mick's daughter from his first marriage. She's turning out to be a real knockout."

"Yes, I can see that."

She grabbed a picture of a tiny infant being held by Ted from the shelf above it. "This is Troy. He's Léa and Mick's son. Born this past March. The cutest little thing."

"I read the files on Ted," Nate admitted quietly. He'd liked Ted from the moment they'd been introduced, though he seemed familiar. Curiosity—and caution—had made him run a quick check through his guys in New York. They'd faxed Nate the files on Ted's arrest, conviction and ultimate exoneration for the murder of his wife and daughters. "He's had a tough road."

Ellie ran her finger gently over the glass. "I met Léa a few years back, when she was living in Philly and taking care of her aunt during the day and going to school at nights. We took a couple of classes together. I met Ted and his wife and daughters through her. It was a shocker when they arrested him."

"Ted's refusal to say anything in his own defense didn't help things."

"That was his way of dealing with his grief. It was a good thing that Léa was such a fighter."

"It seems like he's come a long way."

"He has. His life is slowly improving now." She put the frame back on the shelf. "Mick and Léa and their family live right in Bucks County, an hour north of here. Ted is back to work and has gotten himself involved in dozens of projects for children. I think as long as he doesn't have any free time to think back and brood over things, he'll be okay."

Nate scanned the shelves and found the picture he was looking for. He pointed to the photo of Lou and the young woman on the beach. "Your mother?"

Ellie nodded. "I don't remember her at all. She left when I was still a toddler."

"You've never heard anything from her?"

She shook her head and started toward the kitchen. "I think the coffee is ready."

Nate watched her go. Ellie had never known her mother, and almost never talked to her father now. She had no siblings. No aunts or uncles or cousins, as far as he knew. He glanced over the shelves of pictures again. But she cherished other people's family moments.

He followed her into the kitchen. She stood, pouring two mugs, with her back to him. She had changed into an old, thin T-shirt that ended at her midriff and a pair of old sweats. The band of ivory skin at the waist was sexy as hell.

"You know, I just realized that I don't know what you take in your coffee."

"Nothing. Just the way you made it."

"That's good." She turned and handed him the mug. "Because I don't trust the stuff I've got in my fridge."

He took the mug, and his gaze wandered over her. He could tell she was wearing no bra beneath the T-shirt, and he admired her long, delicate neck. She had a beautiful chin, and he stared at her mouth for a couple of seconds before looking into her dark eyes. He took a sip.

"Good coffee."

"You should be outlawed."

"Me?"

Ellie put her cup on the counter and planted a hand at her hip. "Yes, you and your bad-boy attitude. You and your eyes, you and your 'I want to tear your clothes off' expression, you and your 'let's think hot, sweaty, maybe noisy—'"

Nate kissed her hard, and this time there were no sparks. This time it was full-fledged fireworks. His coffee somehow made it to the counter, spilling over, but neither of them noticed. Her fingers threaded into his hair. She rose up on tiptoes while Nate tasted and explored her mouth. She was soft, delicious, hot, and he couldn't get enough of her. His hand moved beneath the shirt on her back. She was as soft as silk. They turned and he lifted her up, sitting her on the counter. He stepped between her legs, and she wrapped herself around him, deepening the kiss.

Nate's hands were all over her. He touched her back, her neck, her throat, her breasts. They were absolutely perfect. She moaned softly, and her body leaned into the touch. He tore his mouth away and kissed her throat. He pulled up the T-shirt, and his lips closed on Ellie's nipple.

She whispered his name, cradling his head for a few seconds before dragging Nate's mouth up to hers.

"This is what I meant." She pressed her forehead

against his. Both of them were breathing heavily. "You're too hot—too much for my system to handle."

He gathered her closer in his arms. "You are so beautiful. You just know how to drive me crazy. I want to make love to you, Ellie."

"We can't. You and I…no."

"Why?"

"Because…" She closed her eyes and let out a frustrated breath. "Because I just know making love to you would be…shattering for me."

"What's wrong with that?"

"I don't think I could walk away from something like that so easily."

"Maybe neither of us can. But that's part of life, isn't it? Experiencing what it offers. Taking risks."

She shook her head. "I've lost too many pieces of my heart along the way. I don't think I can handle this risk. At least, not right now." She placed feather-light kisses on his face. "Please understand."

"Coward," he growled into her ear, holding her so close that their hearts seemed to beat as one. Nate wanted her. His body ached whenever he was in the same room with her. But he understood what she was telling him. Still, he knew that if they had met under other circumstances, things would be much different. "Maybe we could spend some time together after we're done with this assignment?"

Ellie's doubts still lingered in her eyes when she looked into his face. "You'd want to do that?"

"I want the chance to change your mind."

"Stubborn, aren't you?" She smiled, her fingers playing with his hair.

"Dogged."

Nate kissed her again, but this time did his best to

keep it light. He helped her down from the counter and immediately saw the spilled coffee. He went to the sink for a sponge and paper towel to clean the mess.

"By the way, what's the dress code for tomorrow night?"

She moved the mugs out of his way. "Ray likes to dress up. Most of his parties are flashy, but black-tie. Do you think you can handle it?"

"You haven't seen nothing of what I can handle, sweetheart."

From his private study, Graham Hunt knew the moment when the car cleared the estate's front gate. His security system was the best money could buy.

The single visitor, arriving in an unremarkable car that was chauffeured by Graham Hunt's personal driver, was driven around the hillside mansion to the rear entrance. There, Hunt's personal assistant escorted him to an elevator that took him two levels down to the private study. No one else in the household had seen the man come. No one would see him go. This was the way Hunt conducted business. Here, deep within the earth, the air was cool, the walls were thick, and the affairs remained private.

"I had to make personal guarantees of the success of this program today. I'm talking about six different discussions with six different investors. There will be at least that many phone calls tomorrow, too, and over the weekend. They're rightly concerned about the money we're spending. I'm talking about bucks we need to dole out to keep the press coverage positive, never mind the advertising slots we've already paid for. Our new campaign is ready to air, despite the White House's clay feet. We have *got* to proceed on schedule." Hunt stopped pacing across the antique Persian carpet and stood over his visitor. "Are all *your* plans on schedule?"

The visitor nodded. "They are, sir."

"Any complications?"

"None that we can't handle."

"That's what you say." Hunt walked to his desk. "I'm not happy that the kid just walked away like that."

"He didn't see anything."

"But I was told that he did," Hunt barked.

"I believe you've been misinformed, sir. But if he did see something, he isn't talking. Though he's only eight years old, the boy is street-smart. A kid like that—"

"Are you listening to yourself? This kid is eight years old. *Eight years old.*" Hunt's voice dropped low. "Tell me something. Do you think I'm willing to put everything in the shitter for an eight-year-old?"

"We're watching the kid. At the same time, he's being watched practically around the clock by those nuns and Murtaugh."

"You listen to me. If we need to, we're going to assassinate the President of the United States to make this deal go through. I'm *not* going to risk billions on a scrawny punk." Hunt sat down and glared across his desk. "Take care of him. And make it look like an accident."

Eighteen

The dry eighty-degree temperature was a rarity for Philadelphia in June, and it was only nine in the morning. Ellie, still in her pajamas, sat cross-legged on the cushion of a cast-iron lounge chair on her rooftop balcony. A notepad was balanced on her lap, and she almost dropped the handset when she leaned down to put her empty glass of iced coffee next to the chair.

"What's that? Yes, I'll have the package overnighted to you with a Saturday delivery. Yes, Mr. Teasdale, I already wrote the address down," Ellie said reassuringly. "Back door. They already know to leave it by the back door, but I'll make a special note, as well." She paused. "Monday morning at eleven. Got it. We'll be there."

She looked down at her notes with the phone dangling from one ear as Hank Teasdale started summarizing for the third time everything they'd agreed upon. The price, the artwork, the importance of having the specs in his hands tomorrow. He reiterated the time of their meeting on Monday again, too. He was planning to have some relevant samples to show them.

Delivery of the actual duplicate was to be by next

Friday—only two days before the ceremony. They were cutting it close, but she'd already dickered about the time frame, getting him to cut it down from ten days to a week. He couldn't or wouldn't do any better than that.

Hank Teasdale obviously liked to dot every *i* and cross every *t*. This suited Ellie fine. John Dubin had also praised the older man's almost obsessive perfectionism.

"So we're clear on everything, Ms. Littlefield?"

"Yes, we are. So if you'd like to give me an account number, we could arrange a wire transfer for half the amount today."

"That won't be necessary," Hank replied. "I'm from the old school. Before I take anything from your client, I want him to see what I'm capable of."

Ellie wasn't going to complain. This was the same way Lou used to do business. Sometimes he got paid, sometimes he didn't, but he wouldn't do it any other way.

If for nothing else but for the conversation, she suspected, Hank began summarizing everything once more. Ellie stood up and stretched her back. She lifted her face to the sun, knowing this was perhaps the only time today she would get outside. Vic had been doing the lion's share of the work around the shop this week, but doing paperwork was not his forte.

And it wasn't only this week's sales and orders and shipping records that she needed to catch up on. There was also the pile of donations for the Children's Hospital auction next week that she had to appraise and number. She didn't even want to think of the thankyou letters and charitable-deduction vouchers she had to send.

Finally, Teasdale appeared satisfied, said goodbye and hung up. Ellie immediately dialed Nate's cell phone number. After a few seconds' delay, she heard the faint sound of ringing from inside.

"What the heck?" She'd been using her home phone. Her cell was off and charging in the bedroom. She opened the screen door and marched in. Nate was standing in the middle of her living room.

"Do you want me to answer that?" he asked, an overnight hanging bag in one hand, his phone in the other.

Polo shirt and khakis. Ellie had to admit he looked great in the morning. And at night. And in jeans. And shorts. Even in his G-man suits. She was definitely losing it, she thought.

"Who let you in?"

"I have a carefully placed mole in your operation."

Vic was always in early, drat him. "What are you doing here? And what's all that?"

"My tux and a change of clothes. Where should I put them?" Without waiting, he headed for her bedroom.

"Why did you bring them here?"

"I had to loan somebody's shop assistant the Harley tonight. I thought I'd change here after I bring Vic the bike. You can drive us to the dinner."

"So you don't think a tux and a Harley go together?" She tied the belt of her robe tightly in front and leaned against the doorjamb, watching him hang his bag on the molding above her bathroom door. "You had me sitting on the back of that bike with barely a dress on last night. Remember?"

"Sure do. And I had a rough night sleeping because of it." He glanced at her bed. The sheets and blankets were a tangle, and half of them were on the floor. The pillows were scattered everywhere. It looked like a tornado had touched down in it. "And how did *you* sleep?"

"Like a rock."

"You could have fooled me."

"I'm just an energetic sleeper. I move around a lot." Ellie backed out of the room quickly.

He followed her. "Well, if you ever need someone to hold you down..."

"Thanks, but no." Ellie found the pad of paper she'd stuffed in her robe pocket with all the information Teasdale had given her. She tore off the top sheet and handed him the paper, escaping behind the kitchen counter. While making fresh coffee, she told him about their entire conversation. "Can you get the information he needs to him by tomorrow?"

Nate nodded, serious now. "Of course. Wilcox sent me everything right before we were to meet with Atwood."

"How about Hawes? Do you have to get approval for using this guy?"

"No. Can I keep this?"

"That's yours. Just remember the address for Monday morning."

"Why couldn't he see us sooner?"

She took two clean mugs out of the cabinet. "He doesn't take cold calls. And in this case, even though he was told most of the specifics by John and me, he says he needs a couple of days to play with it."

"What's your confidence level that he can do the job?"

Ellie was gratified that he thought enough of her opinion to ask. "Based on a few calls I made this

morning, Hank Teasdale is a master at what he does—
but at the same time, he's known to be pretty finicky.
He turns away many of the referrals he gets.'' She
filled up the cups. "But he sounded excited about getting the package and meeting us. How do you like that
for an evasive answer?"

"Better than most of the politicians I know." Nate
picked up the cup she slid in front of him.

"I think he can do the job."

"Good enough for me. Who knows that we're going
to see Teasdale?"

"With the exception of John Dubin, who found him
for us, I guess no one."

"How about the other people you called this morning?" He sat on a stool. She saw him rub his left knee.

"That thing is really bothering you, isn't it?"

He followed the direction of her gaze and immediately withdrew his hand. "It's nothing."

"What happened to your knee?"

"You were telling me about the other people you
called."

Ellie was curious and concerned for him, but she
also understood his desire for privacy.

"I talked to Ray. But I just asked some general questions about Hank's reputation. I never mentioned anything about the flag or that we were going up to see
him. I talked to Sister Helen, too, but that was before
I'd spoken to Hank, so I had no idea when and where
or if we were going to see him." She cupped the mug
with both hands. "What's going on?"

"Nothing. I just want to play it safe. Let's keep this
one to ourselves."

Ellie saw the lines of concentration on his brow. He
made a couple of notes on the paper with Teasdale's ad-

dress on it. "Does this have something to do with the explosion that killed Theo Atwood?"

"No."

"Then what is it?"

"We're taking a pretty unorthodox approach, having a duplicate made. I just want to keep it quiet."

She sipped her coffee and came around the counter. "Mum's the word."

"I have a few things to check on this morning. What time were you planning to leave for Claiborne's party?"

"Six o'clock. You should plan to get here about five fifty-five. That should give you plenty of time to get ready."

No guides. No sticky strips. She had very steady hands.

"I like the square look better than the rounded one, don't you?" Cheri asked loudly. She finished the last nail by painting a straight line across the tip.

She could hear drawers being yanked out and dumped upstairs. She held out her hands, waiting for her nails to dry. A closet door squeaked open and slammed shut a moment later.

"I hope you appreciate how much money I'm saving you by doing my own French manicure." She chose a bottle of translucent shell-pink polish from her collection and shook it. At the top of the stairs, the bathroom door practically came off its hinges from the force of being pulled open. "Becky said she tried this Chinese nail place last week. You know, one of those places in the strip malls where you don't need appointments. You just walk in. It cost her only forty bucks, and they actually did a great job. But the joint was in Alexandria, and there's no way I'm driving all the way down there twice a week to touch up my nails.''

The footsteps of the man coming downstairs sounded like thunder. Cheri laid one hand flat on the table and began applying the translucent polish over each nail.

"I love this smell, don't you?"

Hawes charged into the kitchen and yanked open the medicine drawer under the liquor cabinet. From where she was sitting, Cheri could see him over the island separating the kitchen from the dining area and living room. With one sweep, he emptied half of a dozen prescription bottles into an open overnight bag.

He came out of the kitchen and looked around. "Where's your purse?"

"Looking for money? Do I have to pay to have sex with you now?" She laughed at her own joke and carefully tightened the top on the bottle of polish.

"I want the goddamn car keys." He rumbled past her into the living room like an angry bear. He looked behind the chairs, threw the pillows off the sofa. Nothing.

Cheri sat back and put her feet up on the dining table, admiring her own legs. "You know, I'm tired of this shaving business. I think I'll go to one of those health spas and start waxing."

She tried not to flinch as her chair was jerked back roughly and swung around. She looked up into Sanford's murderous eyes.

"Stop pretending that nothing is happening."

"Don't mess up my nails or you'll pay."

"I'll pay? I'll *pay?*" he shouted into her face. "Why don't we just add it to the sixty-seven thousand dollars you charged to my credit card last month?"

"Good idea."

Hawes looked at her, speechless for a moment. "Sixty-seven thousand dollars! And that's on top of paying for this house and your sports car and your goddamn food! What the hell do you think you're worth?"

"You tell me. Do you want some now?" She raised her leg and rubbed her instep against his genitals.

He slapped her foot down and backed away. "We're done, Cheri. Finished. Do you hear me? I don't shit golden eggs. I can't afford you. This ride is over. The house goes on the market in two weeks. You have that long to move your sorry ass out of here and find a new sucker to pay your bills. I canceled that fucking credit card this morning, and I'm taking back the car."

She looked at her nails. "Sorry, I need at least ten minutes for this to dry. And after that, I still have to apply a clear, glossy topcoat. And another—"

Cheri winced when he took a fistful of hair and dragged her out of the chair and forced her onto her knees. His face had gone white with fury, and she prayed he'd drop dead on the spot.

His voice, though, was low and dangerous. "You have five seconds to come up with those car keys, or you'll need a lot more than nail polish to patch up your looks."

Cheri considered calling his bluff. He would never beat her and chance having her press charges. At the same time, she didn't want to get marked up.

"Four."

Besides, he was shitting in his pants to get the car back, which meant the old prick was in a serious financial bind.

"Three."

He couldn't possibly explain all this to his wife or

the director or anyone else. He was in a shitload of trouble and he knew it.

"Two."

She thought for a second about all the stuff she'd charged to his credit card this month. And then there was the damage to the passenger side of the car from an accident yesterday that he didn't even know about.

"One."

Cheri reached inside her back pocket and took out the key ring. She threw it at his feet. Pulling her hair out of his hand, she jumped to her feet.

"Asshole!" she hissed, marching out of the room.

Nate arrived at Pine Street at precisely five fifty-five.

"You don't have to take everything she says so literally," Vic told him as he walked through the door into the shop. "You definitely have to allow some play in whatever schedule Ellie gives you. Believe me, she would never think of it herself."

Nate tossed him the key to the motorcycle. "Is she upstairs?"

"Yeah, getting dolled up, as we speak." Vic turned the Closed sign outward in the window and grabbed his shoulder bag.

"You mean she's not ready?"

"She just got back from Sister Helen's about five minutes ago."

Nate took the steps three at a time. The door to her apartment was open, as always. He heard the shower running when he went inside. In her bedroom, a sheer, silky red dress and a pair of high heels were on the bed. He took a quick look at the dress. It had cleverly placed bits of lining that covered key areas. He always wondered how that worked. Ellie was still in the shower, so Nate tortured himself for a few seconds, staring at the dress from different angles, imagining where the see-through parts would fit on her body.

His tuxedo and shirt and shoes had been taken out of the bag and were lying on the bed, too. As he peeled off his shirt and kicked off his boots, the water stopped running. He grabbed his shaving bag and knocked on the bathroom door.

"Go away," she answered.

"I can't. I have to shave and dress in under three minutes."

She opened the door, and he was assaulted by a burst of steam and perfume. And then he saw Ellie. Her hair was wet and combed back. Her shoulders were bare and droplets of water glistened on her skin. A big white towel was tucked around her breasts, covering her to below her knees.

She stared at his bare chest for a second before looking up. "Good luck making it."

"My thoughts exactly." He leaned down for a quick kiss, but Ellie kissed him back with an unexpected heat that changed all of his plans.

Before he knew what he was doing, Nate was pushing her back against the doorjamb and pressing against her with his body. He couldn't get enough of her. The way she tasted, the way they fit together was like nothing he'd ever experienced with another woman. Her fingers delved into his hair, and she returned his passion every step of the way.

The friction between their bodies loosened the towel, and Ellie broke off the kiss and caught the wrap before it slid down.

"Your three minutes are up, Agent Murtaugh," she whispered. She bit on his earlobe and slipped out of his arms. He watched her walk away. The towel dipped dangerously low on her back. He would have liked nothing better than to tackle her onto that bed and give her a lesson or two about the consequences of teasing him.

"And you might want to add a cold shower to your routine," Ellie suggested, directing a meaningful glance at the front of his jeans. The moment he took a step toward her, though, she ran off into the living room.

"An hour," he growled at her, turning toward the bathroom. "And I'm planning on spending every minute of it in that shower."

The subway platform was noisy and swarming with people. Everyone was still celebrating the tenth-inning victory. It had been a pitcher's duel until the top of the ninth, when the Phillies pitcher had given up two runs. The home team then came back to tie it in their own at bat. Then, in the tenth, a two-out homer had given them the win.

"Stay together," Ted shouted to his rambunctious group of eleven.

Chris didn't know the names of the Philadelphia Phillies players. He wasn't sure who'd pitched or who came in as reliever. He had no clue what slugging percentages meant or what the batting averages were of any of these players. Other than street ball, he'd never been part of a baseball league. He never played T-ball when he was little. The only thing he knew about the sport was from what other kids talked about. But tonight, eating hot dogs and soda and cotton candy as they watched the game from the upper deck, Chris had had the best time of his life.

He saw Ted waving the whole group closer to the tracks. Eager to please, he was the first one standing by the yellow line.

"We're taking the next train," Ted announced over the voices. Their group crowded closer behind Chris. "Stay together. Toni, why don't you come up next to me?"

The twelve-year-old weaved through till he was next to Chris. "How did you like it tonight?"

"It was awesome."

"Yeah. It always is." Toni jabbed Ted in the chest. "Guess we'll keep this old guy. He's pretty cool."

The whistle of the train could be heard down the dark tunnel. Chris was momentarily pushed past the yellow line by the throng behind him, and he scrambled back quickly.

"Be careful," Ted warned.

"We don't want to peel your ass off the tracks, Chris baby," one of the boys behind him taunted.

"Let me fix that hat." Another boy pulled the baseball hat off Chris's head and started shaping the brim. Chris never took his eyes off it. The hat was a present from Ellie. She'd brought it over this afternoon, right before they'd left for the ballpark.

"I want everyone to turn to the right when they get on the train. Hear me?" Ted called to the whole group. "I want all of you together."

Chris watched his hat shaped and rolled and punched. He wanted it back, but he didn't want to sound like a whiner. The whistle from the train was getting louder.

"Here it is." The boy stretched it out to him, and

Chris reached out. The concrete platform was shaking with the arrival of the train. The screeching noise of the brakes drew Chris's eyes toward the tunnel.

And then he felt the hard shove from behind.

Nineteen

The sumptuous dinner had been served promptly at eight o'clock. Ellie had been told in advance that there would be nine courses in all, and each one seemed to complement the one before. Of course, that nine didn't include the hors d'oeuvres carried on gold trays by a legion of waiters and waitresses. Lobster bites and caviar, Scottish salmon dumplings, Oriental-spiced duck liver and a variety of exotic foods only set the stage for the feast Ray was happy to present to his guests.

As with all of Ray's dinner parties, the attention to detail was unbelievable. Even in the selection and preparation of dishes, the individual tastes of the guests had been considered. Ellie knew the menu had been designed to please everyone.

There were thirty-two guests in all. More than half were new faces for Ellie. The others were Ray's friends and long-time acquaintances whom she'd met on other occasions. Everyone was dressed to the nines, and Nate looked dashing in his black tux. As they sat together at a small table on the terrace listening to the band play, they watched a number of the guests dancing. Two waiters appeared with coffee and yet another dessert.

There had been a point in Ellie's life, not too long ago, when this lifestyle of extravagance had been her ideal. She'd learned it from Ray himself, whose credo had always been that to live and be happy, you had to live the life of the rich. She had believed it, too. Up to now, it had been the guiding factor in her life.

Tonight, though, looking at the behavior of these guests from an outsider's perspective—specifically Nate's—Ellie could see not just the fraying edges, but the gaping holes in that philosophy. Earlier, as she'd mingled among the different groups chatting by the rock garden or by the fountain, she heard whispered criticisms of Ray's "gaudy flamboyance," jokes about his "deviant" sexual preferences and his "sordid criminal connections." All this while sipping his champagne and eating his food. One couple was even complaining about the wine.

This collection of people included some of the shallowest members of Philadelphia's Main Line set, and Ellie had early on become conscious of it. As a result, she had been trying hard ever since dinner to keep Nate away from their host. She made a mistake in portraying him as a spoiled trust baby to Ray. He just didn't come across as self-absorbed or superficial. In this crowd, he stood out like a gold medallion among brass, and even though he'd had no difficulty convincing Vic, fooling Ray would be impossible.

"What do you think my chances are against the competition?" Nate gestured vaguely with his cup before putting it down beside his dessert plate.

Ellie followed the direction of Nate's gaze. The blond woman who had been manipulating everyone's attention, including Ray's, had been holding court on the far side of the terrace since dinner. Kathleen Rivers was in her forties—give or take a tuck or two—and striking to the point of being glamorous. When Ellie had been introduced soon after their arrival, she had not realized that this was their opponent. But then, just before dinner, the blonde had approached Nate, asking about his hobbies and collections and explaining her own fascination with Early Americana. As his potential client, Ray had alerted the woman about Nate. Ellie was certain of it.

"It's not so much what *your* chances are against her, but what *my* chances are against Ray." Ellie watched her former mentor laugh at something the blonde said, while motioning for more wine to be served to her. "Ray saves this kind of personal attention for important clients. Kathleen Rivers has money and is willing to spend it to win the flag. Otherwise, he wouldn't waste his time."

"Would he do that to you? Take food from his protégée's mouth?"

In a minute, she thought. But Ellie didn't like to think about the calculating coldheartedness of the people around her—those whom she thought of as family. Ray, in particular.

"It's not personal, Nate. Just business."

"I think I heard that in a movie."

"It's true."

He nodded toward Ray. "That's how cutthroats try to justify their actions."

"I can be as ruthless as he can."

"I doubt it."

She frowned at him. "Do you really think I'm not tough enough?"

"Tough? Yes. Stubborn? Plenty. Tenacious? Absolutely. Sexy? Hell, yes. But ruthless?" He leaned over and whispered in her ear. "You have no teeth, baby."

Ellie caught his smile. "Did you just call me a toothless baby?"

He nodded and put an arm around her. His hand caressed her upper arm. "And I meant it, too. But what are you going to do about it?"

"Nothing at present, Mr. Moffet. But you won't be so safe later on."

"I'm going to hold you to that." His hand moved down to her waist where the sheer fabric hugged the line of her hip. "And you have to leave this thing on while you're doing whatever it is you're going to do to me."

"Do you like the dress?"

"Too much." His gaze moved slowly down the front of it. "By the way, are you wearing anything under it?"

"I'm not telling." She smiled, putting her hand on his knee.

Ellie had dressed and escaped from her apartment while Nate had been in the shower. By the time he'd come down, she was wearing a jacket over her dress. She hadn't shed that until they arrived at Ray's. After that, there was safety in numbers.

"I *thought* you looked like a man with an appreciation for the finer things in life." Ray placed one hand on Ellie's shoulder, the other on Nate's. Neither of them had seen him approach. "Hope you're enjoying the party, Mr. Moffet."

"Very much."

"Glad to hear it." Ray gazed down the dress of his former protégée. "Well, babycakes, this is quite a little nothing you have on. What do you think, Mr. Moffet?"

Ellie felt her temper begin to rise at Ray's rudeness. Before she could respond, though, Nate picked up his dessert fork and gently cut through the concoction on his plate.

"I like it. Dense chocolate in pastry with some kind of sorbet underneath." He moved aside a stack of cookies. "Very clever, chocolate mousse beneath these. I also love these miniature balloons, painted with stars and an American flag. Very patriotic. What are they made out of? Brown sugar?"

"Yes, as a matter of fact, they are," their host answered, laughing heartily. Ray's hand stayed on his shoulder. Ellie was forgotten. "Mr. Moffet…may I call you Nate?"

"Absolutely."

"I'm sorry I haven't had a chance to spend any time with you tonight. But I was thinking, if you're available tomorrow, I'd love to take you out on my yacht and show you—"

"I'm afraid I can't."

"Oh, too bad. What about Sunday, then?"

"Not good, either." Nate reached across the table and took Ellie's hand. "You've ruined my surprise, Ray, but it was time I told her, anyway." He brought her hand to his lips. "I'm taking Ellie away for the weekend."

"You are?" she asked, genuinely surprised.

"That's too bad," Ray growled, shooting an annoyed look at Ellie.

Nate placed a kiss on the palm of her hand and looked into her eyes. "I should have told you earlier, but I wanted it to be a surprise."

"Sure. Whatever." She'd just have to think of an explanation in case she ran into Ray this weekend.

The older man straightened up, taking his hands off their shoulders. "You're a quick worker, Mr. Moffet."

"Not usually. But I do have a taste for the finer things in life."

* * *

A hand had shot out, grabbing a fistful of Chris's shirt before he hit the gleaming tracks. Chris could feel the train bearing down on him.

He twisted in the air, suspended as the headlights blinded him. His stomach heaved as he felt himself yanked upward. Then, just as the shrill whistle screamed by, his body landed with a bang on the concrete platform, his arms and feet flying clear of the train.

The wind from the slowing subway train forced his eyes shut, but the breeze soon died away as the train came abruptly to a halt. Chris opened his eyes. The steel was only inches from his face. Ted pulled him against his chest, and they were enveloped by voices and hands and arms.

Minutes later, Chris still couldn't loosen his grip around Ted's neck. He couldn't open his eyes. He also couldn't stop shaking.

Like something from a scary movie, the whole thing was playing again in his head. The ground was shaking. The train was coming. Somebody shoving him from behind, and him going over the edge. Then he was falling into the deep pit where the rails were shining and the train was about to smash him like a bug.

"Is he going to be okay?" one kid asked.

"Yeah. That was a close call," Ted answered.

Everyone had gotten so quiet from the moment they'd followed Ted's lead and gotten on the train. All of them were sitting around Chris and Ted. No jokes, no talk of the game. He could feel them just watching him.

"I was behind him, but I didn't push him," one of the older boys blurted out a few minutes later.

''There were some drunk guys behind us,'' one of the girls added.

''My nana says there's too much boozing at the ballpark and everywhere else. She says to me if she ever catches me with a bottle, then I can just start looking for someplace else to live.''

''You can come and live with me and my dad,'' another boy chirped.

There were other offers, too, but Chris couldn't bring himself to look up. He was terrified of what would happen if Ted put him down.

''We're the next station,'' Ted announced quietly to the kids. He gently rubbed Chris's back. ''How are you doing, buddy?''

He couldn't answer. The shaking was making his teeth clatter.

''If it's okay with you, I'd just as soon carry you back to Sister Helen's house,'' he said.

He was too big to be carried around like a baby. But nobody made fun of him, and Chris kept his eyes shut when Ted and the group left the train and walked down to their block.

There were a few pats on his back. One of the boys put Chris's hat back on his head.

''I fixed it all up for you.''

There were whispers of thanks and goodbyes by others. He continued to shiver, even when Sister Helen opened the door. Ted made a quick explanation about the subway, the close call and Chris getting the scare of his life. He carried Chris up the stairs behind the nun.

''How about a bowl of Lucky Charms before we tuck you into bed?'' Sister Helen asked, rubbing his back gently.

They were in the room at the top of the stairs. Ted sat down on the edge of the bed.

"Christopher?" she asked again, taking his hat off and pushing the hair out of his face.

He was nestled against Ted's chest. He could hear the man's strong heartbeat. He would be safe here.

"Is he feverish?" Ted asked.

Chris felt the cool hands of the nun on his forehead. "I don't think so. But it might not hurt to call a doctor."

Twice when he'd been sick, his mother had taken him to the emergency room. Everybody was loud there, and lots of strangers sat around bleeding and watching the televisions that were hung on the walls. Chris hated the place, and the thought of leaving this room, this house, was terrifying.

"No," he croaked, slowly opening his eyes. Sister Helen crouched in front of him.

"I'm sorry for what happened," Ted whispered.

The nun took Chris's shoes and socks off. "Do you want to eat or drink something?"

He shook his head.

"Do you have to use the bathroom?"

He shook his head again. "I'm cold."

Ted pulled the covers off the bed and carefully placed him on the sheets. Chris was reluctant to let him go, but he had to.

"Whenever something scary happens, or I have a bad dream, or see something that bothers me, I try to read something happy to get my mind off of it." Ted tucked the blankets around him.

"I'm still cold," Chris whispered, glancing at the open window.

Sister Helen went over and closed it tight, locking it.

"So how about if I read you a book?"

"Elizabeth brought these over for Chris this afternoon." The nun handed a stack of books to Ted.

He thumbed through them. "Huh, what do you know! One of my favorites. Chris, have you read anything by Roald Dahl?"

The door to the room was still open. He didn't think Sister Helen had locked the front door when they'd come in. She sometimes forgot to lock the kitchen door, too.

"No," he whispered, still shivering.

"Then I have just the book for you." Ted sat down on the floor next to the bed, stretching his legs out. "Now, it doesn't matter what it says in the book, I don't allow any laughing or giggling. Got it? No body noises of any kind while I'm reading. Understood?"

Chris nodded. He was going to like this book, no matter what. He'd be safe as long as Ted stayed here with him.

Stars were faintly visible above the lights of the city, and Nate breathed in the balmy air. Traffic on the Vine Street Expressway was fairly heavy, in spite of the late hour, but the BMW sped along the fast lane.

"Take the next exit. I'm coming back to your place."

"You are?" Ellie asked, a tinge of apprehension thinning her voice.

"Vic has my Harley."

"I can have him drop it off at your hotel."

"No. Too complicated." Nate turned to her. Ellie's fingers were wrapped tightly around the steering wheel.

Even in the darkness of the car, he could tell her breathing was unsteady. To convince Ray that theirs was more than just a dealer-client relationship, they'd put on a little show of not being able to keep their hands off each other before leaving. Whoever was watching them would have been more than convinced that they'd be heading off to a weekend of hot sex.

Even Nate had felt the line between truth and fiction begin to blur. Luckily, she'd put her jacket on when they got into the car to drive back into Center City.

"I know Ray. He won't give up until you meet with him." She made the turn.

"I have no problem with that. So long as you're there to protect me."

She smiled. "He'd give me a one-way ticket to another continent, if he could, to get some time alone with you."

"Why, you don't think he bought our sex-starved-lovers routine?"

She bit her lip. "I don't think so."

"Then he must be blind." He ran the tip of his finger down the side of her throat. "I have to be honest with you. I'm getting so hot for you that swimming naked in the Arctic Ocean wouldn't cool me off."

"That's pretty hot," she replied quietly, making another turn.

Nate couldn't tear his gaze away from her. She was beautiful, compassionate, sexy, intelligent, and he knew she was attracted to him. A relationship with her would not be simple, though. The more time he spent with her, the more he realized how afraid she was of what was happening between them. For his part, Nate knew he was past denial. He was thirty-six years old, and after coming face-to-face with his own mortality last year, he didn't want to play any games. What he was feeling for Ellie was a first for him. But he was also determined to be patient and try to understand her without scaring her away.

"The problem wasn't you back there," she said after a stretch of silence. "Ray's known me all of my life. He knows that I keep my emotions under lock and key. I don't show affection. I don't kiss in public. I'm very discreet about the few boyfriends I've had. In fact, what Vic said about going through a dry spell is true, but it's been my own choosing. I don't get into relationships too often…and I never jump into affairs."

"Then I guess making love at the top of the art museum stairs is out of the question?"

"Be serious," she said, giving him a backhand to the chest. "Now that Ray seems to have landed a client for the Morris flag, he'll hear the details of the auction way before I do. He's much better connected. We'll need him to believe who you say you are so he'll share the info."

"Or maybe he won't say anything. That way his client can walk away with the flag."

"Not likely. He takes a commission based on whatever the final hammer price is. He'll want to win it, but his style is to push the price up every penny that he can. He has no loyalties to anyone but himself." She pulled her car into the parking lot a block away from her building. "We want him buying your cover, but the problem is that Ray doesn't think that I'm capable of landing someone like you. And he's right."

She wasn't talking about the job, and this made his temper flare up.

"Just because you think Ray or your father might not appreciate you, that doesn't mean you should trust their judgment. I mean it, Ellie. Look at who you are and what you're accomplishing with your life."

Ellie shut off the engine, undid her seat belt and sat back, staring straight ahead. "Helen told me everything she knows about you. You're an FBI special agent, a man with an Ivy League education and a law degree, a man with medals for bravery." She turned to him. "As much as I like to sweep the truth about my past under fancy carpets, I don't kid myself. I'm the daughter of a crook, a forger. My mother was a club dancer who couldn't get away fast enough when I was born. I didn't go to college. I didn't even finish high school. I only got my GED when I was twenty-five. I was a thief, Nate. I stole, I lied, I cheated as a teenager to survive. I've only recently realized that my biggest accomplishment in life has been my ability to make an honest living. But these days, I even question that, because Ray was the one who helped me to get started. He bought that house for me. He helped me stock my antique shop to get started. He introduced me around. You don't build an honest life on dishonest foundations."

She leaned her head back and stared up at the dark ceiling. "I have no guilt about dealing with the rich people in this town. They can be whatever they want. They can spend their money however they want. I don't have to get emotionally involved. Even with men like Donald, the guy I went out with the other night. I don't have to put any of myself into a relationship with someone like him." Tears were rimming the edges of her lashes when she turned to him. "But with you…I'm scared…because I know I don't match up."

"I can't believe you." He cupped her chin. "Ellie, all of us have a history. All of us have stuff that we're not too proud of. Stuff that haunts us, even. We all make mistakes. But the smart ones...the strong ones...learn from them and go on. Our lives are not carved out of stone. Our lives are putty that we shape every day.''

"Easy for you to say. Your life is perfect.''

"Is it?'' Nate wiped away the tear that trickled down her cheek. "In spite of what I said, I understand how you feel, because feeling guilty is part of my life, too. And that one happens to be *my* hang-up.''

"What do you have to feel guilty about?'' she asked brokenly.

"Shooting and killing a fourteen-year-old.'' He waited for her to retreat, but instead she cupped his hand against her cheek.

"That must have been horrible.''

"It was part of the job. It was either kill him, or five other people would have died...me included. But it still hurt like hell when I found out afterward that he was a kid. That was when I was promoted to a desk job. Because of that, and my knee.''

"Did the fourteen-year-old do that to you?'' She touched his knee.

"Yeah. I was lucky that he was a bad shot. He was aiming for my heart.''

"Nate, even as a card-carrying antiauthority radical, I can see that you had to do what you did. He was in the wrong, and you had to protect yourself and those others. So there's nothing for you to feel guilty about.''

"But I do,'' he responded earnestly.

"Then you have to stop. You did what the situation required. Isn't your motto something like Fidelity, Bravery and Integrity?''

"Very impressive. How do you know that?''

She smiled. "I read everything I could put my hands on about your organization in the years after my father was arrested and sent to prison. To hate something really well, I've always felt I had to understand it first."

"And do you? Hate the FBI?"

"I thought I did—or at least I made myself believe I did. But since you've come into my life, my prejudices keep crumbling away beneath me."

"We're two of a kind." He kissed her hand and then pulled her into his arms. She lay her face against his chest and let out a little sigh. Nate loved holding her. He was amazed by the way his thoughts and plans shifted and refocused whenever he was with her. She had the ability to make him step away from the past and look into the future. He hadn't done enough of that in the past. "About our weekend getaway...?"

She moved out of his arms. "I'll stay in and have Vic take all the calls. Ray doesn't have to know that we didn't leave town."

"But we are going away."

"No, we're not."

"Yes, we are," he said more firmly. "I've planned it out. This is all part of the job."

She turned fully to him. "Nate, there's too much going on right now for us to complicate our lives with...well, with..."

"Sex?"

"Yes," she said. "Or any relationship beyond what we—"

"I agree wholeheartedly. This is a work weekend. I have to go up to Ticonderoga for half a day. I had a call today that McGill is showing signs of improvement."

The lines of tension disappeared from her brow. "I'm glad."

"At the same time, I want to do a little background checking on Teasdale, and I'll need you for that."

"No, you don't. You know everything I know about the guy."

"More reason for you to be there, because I don't remember everything that you told me."

"Liar." She couldn't hold back her smile.

"Besides, tomorrow is my father's birthday, and there'll be hell to pay if I drive past Saratoga without stopping at the house. And since my mother would never approve of us having sex under her roof, I figured it was safer all the way around staying with them for the weekend."

Ellie stared at him without saying anything for several seconds. "You...you want me...to..."

"Stay with my family. They're a well-behaved bunch, for the most part. My father is not all there, and spends a lot of time in the basement. My mother loves her animals better than my two younger brothers, who happen to be deadbeat bums. The three dogs and two cats run the house. We're just an average all-American family."

"No sex?" she asked shyly.

"When we were teenagers, my mother threatened us with bodily harm."

"But there's so much to do here," she argued. "The shop—"

"Victor can handle it. We'll come back after talking to Teasdale on Monday."

"I can't believe I'm even considering this," she whispered to herself. "Okay. What time are you going to pick me up?"

Twenty

Saturday, June 26

"From day one, Graham," Kent said adamantly into the phone, "I've always demanded that my people give me their best analysis of the facts, even if it's different from how others in the administration might see those facts. But I've also insisted that the members of my team stand together when it comes to public displays."

"I'm not part of your administration, Mr. President." The voice from the other end was cool.

"I know that. But we've been in the same camp for years. If we have a disagreement, we need to fight it out inside the house. We don't want to carry our debate to the court of public opinion. That's not our way."

"For the past six years, I have been doing my damnedest to give you good advice, but lately you've been looking pretty indifferent to anything I've had to say."

"It's the timing, Graham. The corporate scandals have hurt this country bad. These days, most Americans are tightening their belts. They're not sure about their jobs—their future. Retirees have seen their pensions shrink to a fraction of what they should be. And we haven't done shit about universal healthcare, even though it's long overdue." Kent swirled the Scotch around in his glass and placed it carefully on the coaster bearing the Presidential Seal. "In good conscience, I'm having a hard time allocating billions of dollars to a specific project simply out of loyalty to friends. But this doesn't mean we have to drag it through the mud in front of the TV cameras."

"I have not spoken to the press."

"But the advertisement you had released last night spoke directly to American people and made it sound like I was supporting it."

"You're not?"

Kent ignored the sarcastic tone and charged on. "And never mind the initial project. Now you're going even further. The scope of this one is much bigger. The cost will be far higher than we'd originally planned."

"The polls say the American people are in favor of it."

"I know how polls work, damn it. The twenty-five people they called are in favor of it. But did you have to air it on every major network? And during prime-time slots? Jesus, you didn't spend that much money on my campaign."

"We spent enough to have you elected, Mr. President. And I'm afraid to say, some of those campaign contributors are concerned that those expenditures on your behalf were a bad investment."

Kent paused for a moment. He wanted to make sure he got through to this guy and all his cronies. He, Ron Kent, was calling the shots. Nobody else.

"Listen to this good, Graham. I have a solemn responsibility to the people of this nation. The future rests on the choices I make. I'm not worrying about any short-term investments.'' He pushed away from his desk and stood up. ''You can tell those friends of yours that I've kept their fat asses out of trouble every chance I've had during my first term. I've always believed that a strong business climate means a strong America. My opponent in November is not so sympathetic to your cartel's interests. So that means, I'm the man. Whatever course I decide on will be the course this country takes. If I say we're not doing that Water for America project until I'm ready, then that's the way it's going to be. Your choices are simple, Hunt—stand in line or find yourself another boy. But stop trying to railroad me with this public relations campaign. Got it?''

The silence at the other end was profound. Kent waited, knowing Graham Hunt was not a man who was accustomed to being slapped down.

''It's clear to me that you've chosen your course of action, Mr. President. Now we'll have to choose ours.''

Nate's mother, Karen, was a veterinarian. His father, Bill, was some big-shot engineering manager at an area Fortune 500 company. And as far as the two ''deadbeat bums,'' Nate's younger brothers, Neil was a security expert working for the U.S. government, and Milt was finishing his law degree at Harvard. Not exactly what Ellie had been told.

This was the first time in a year that everyone was home at the same time, so the Murtaughs had another reason to celebrate.

With the exception of Karen, who was average in height, the rest of them were over six feet tall. They argued more than talked, and they were merciless in giving each other a hard time. But they were all polite and especially welcoming to Ellie for the first hour.

Then, as if it were the most natural thing in the world, the line between them evaporated, and she found herself in the middle of the verbal free-for-all that constituted life in the Murtaugh household.

By eight o'clock, Ellie had eaten more in one day than she would normally eat in a week, had drunk more than she would normally drink in a month, and had laughed more than she would laugh in a year.

At nine o'clock, the two women retired to the porch that wrapped around the side of the house. The night was comfortably cool, and two citronella candles were the only source of light. Karen talked about her veterinary practice and how she and Bill both wanted to slow down a little and have more time to play. Ellie talked about her antique shop and about living in Philadelphia. Nate's mother listened with interest as Ellie talked about what she liked and disliked about her routines. Karen told her about a program a few of the vets in the area had been trying to start that would provide trained animals as pets to senior citizens for free. Though Ellie really didn't know anything about animals, she found herself sharing ideas about funding and logistics. She told Karen about the celebrity auction to raise money for the Children's Hospital.

With the family's dogs and cats curled up all around them, Ellie couldn't remember a day in her life when she'd felt such a sense of belonging. She could only imagine how comforting it would have been to grow up here with these people. Meeting them, she understood Nate and the confidence that was an integral part of him.

Ellie thought of Chris and how her little gifts could never fill the void the eight-year-old must be feeling in his life. She remembered how homeless and alone she'd always felt as a child, even after Ray had taken her under his wing.

Karen Murtaugh was a woman with ideas, and she managed to pull Ellie back from the mists of her past with more talk of a fund-raiser.

"You know how they open the track here in Saratoga for a month in August for horse races. How about if I have a huge cookout in August on the day of the week when they're not racing? Maybe even two or three of them, depending on how things go? You and I can get the boys to set up a huge tent in the backyard. Whoever wants to can bring their antiques to see what they're worth, and we can ask for a ten-dollar donation to our Animals for Seniors program."

"Plus they get fed," Ellie added. "And I'm sure you could get a number of the antique dealers from the area to serve as experts."

"It'll be like one of those antique road shows on TV," Karen continued enthusiastically. "But even better, because they'd be dealing with you."

Ellie didn't have the heart to mention that she wouldn't have any reason to be here with Nate in August. By then, his life would have taken him back to New York, and he might not want her to have anything to do with his family.

"Another solid fund-raiser is also an auction, as long as you can get enough donations," Ellie suggested.

"That would be great." Karen nodded. "You know, we could plan something for every weekend. And the best part of it will be getting you two up here often."

Karen went on to tell her how peculiar she found it that the local charities mostly ran fund-raisers that involved some kind of sports tournament. What she was really looking for was a way to get entire families involved. Did Ellie think the barbecue-antique tent idea would bring in families?

Ellie was a little slow on the uptake, but she eventually recognized the matchmaking tone—or at least the assumption that she and Nate were already an item. She was looking for a way to clarify things when Nate walked out on the porch with a plate full of cupcakes and three beers.

"Your gift went over better than mine." He smiled at her. "A military-and-political history book. And here I thought Dad couldn't read anything other than technical manuals and magazines. He hasn't moved from his chair since he opened your present."

"Yes, he loves the book you gave him." Karen looked at Ellie. "He told me it's dated 1879 and showed me all those engravings. It must have cost you a fortune."

Ellie shook her head. "It was nothing."

Not knowing anything about Bill Murtaugh, and with no time to go out and shop, she was relieved she'd chosen the right gift.

Nate plopped himself down on the porch swing next to Ellie. She tried to slide over to give him room, but there was nowhere to go. He balanced the plate of cupcakes on her lap and handed her and his mother one of the beers.

"I don't think I could eat or drink again for at least a week."

"Yes, you can." He put an arm around her shoulder and started the seat swinging gently. "Sunday brunch at the Murtaugh Inn is when we *really* eat."

"Bill is famous for his French toast." Karen smiled.

"And Mom is famous for her cinnamon rolls…right out of the container."

"Don't forget my doughnuts, either. I get up every Sunday to go buy doughnuts."

"She sure does." Nate rubbed his hand up and down Ellie's arm and drew her closer to his side. Too conscious of Karen's interest in the extent of their relationship, Ellie had the intense desire to run and hide.

"What are your no-good brothers up to?"

"Arguing over some TV commentary about this year's election and plowing down cupcakes."

Karen got to her feet. "Then I think I'll go and sit on the birthday boy's lap for a few minutes and look through his book with him."

"That should make his birthday."

Ellie smiled as Karen winked at her son and went inside.

"She's a wonderful person."

"She has to be. She's my mother."

Ellie poked him in the stomach. "You are a spoiled brat."

Nate grinned. "Only if I can get the same thing from you on *my* birthday."

"Be sure to put it on your list." His blue eyes looked almost black in the flickering candlelight. "When is your birthday?"

"December."

"And what do you want?"

"You, on my lap." He leaned down and brushed his lips against hers. "But you can start now." He deepened the kiss.

"I can't," she whispered breathlessly a minute later. She clutched the beer bottle tightly as his lips trailed kisses on her face and her neck.

"Why not?" He pushed the collar of her shirt down and tasted her sensitive skin beneath it.

"I don't think I can sit on your lap without...us...you know. And you told me yourself about your mother's no-sex rule under her roof...how she used to threaten you?"

"I don't think she really meant it."

"She strikes me as a very serious person."

Nate took his arm from around her and began peeling the paper off a cupcake. "She is, most of the time. But threatening to neuter her own sons?"

Ellie laughed. "I have a hard time believing she would really say that to you three."

"Well, all of us were hellions as teenagers, and with parents who both worked more than a full-time schedule, some serious threatening was required."

Ellie was still smiling when she looked into his face. "You—the solid citizen, the decorated FBI special agent—a teenage hell-raiser. I can't wait to hear *those* stories."

"Well, you're not going to." He ate half of the cupcake in one bite. "I'm not talking."

"I bet with the right kind of bribe, either Neil or Milt will talk."

"Honey, you don't need to bribe those two. In fact, you won't even need to ask. They just didn't want to scare you off today. The next time we come up here, even my parents will be telling you horror stories about me."

The next time. The words made Ellie's pulse jump. Although she tried to hide it, there was no lying to herself. She'd fallen hard and fast for Nate. To hear him say that caused her throat to knot up with emotion.

Ellie put what was left of the cupcakes and her beer on the table next to the swing and cuddled up against him.

His arm was around her again in an instant, drawing her closer. "You don't have to be afraid. None of them are true. They make those stories up as they go."

Ellie shook her head and pressed her face against his chest. This was becoming her favorite place in the world. He rubbed his chin lightly in her hair. His hand caressed her back. He placed a kiss against her forehead.

"Did you have a good time today?"

She nodded, still not trusting her voice.

"Unfortunately, I'll have to go up to Ticonderoga after brunch tomorrow. I should be back in time for dinner."

"I want to go with you," she said softly.

He caressed her arm. "I'd like that."

"Did you find out anything about Teasdale?" she asked. Nate had been on the phone with the local police a number of times today.

"He's clean, apparently. Bought the house and moved up here about six years ago. Quiet—lives alone. As far as the IRS is concerned, he's retired and his only income is from social security. The only thing that doesn't jive is that he paid cash for the house to start with."

"Maybe he clips coupons."

"That must be it." He smiled. "He has no police record. He doesn't have any friends or enemies, as far as anyone knows. And that's pretty much it."

"You sent him the package."

Nate nodded. "I checked the tracking. It was delivered today."

"So he should be working on whatever it is that he's trying to impress you with."

They sat quietly for a couple of minutes, listening to

the sounds of the night and the voices of the Murtaugh brothers drifting out from the kitchen.

''Before we left, you didn't tell anyone else about us meeting Teasdale, did you?''

She shook her head.

''Me, neither.''

Nate took a sip from the bottle, kicked the swing into action and stared into the darkness at the country road leading up to his parents' house. He hadn't said anything, but she sensed the change in him. His muscles had become tense. The concentration and intensity were back, even in the way he was supposedly relaxing on the porch swing.

''What's wrong?'' she asked quietly.

''Want to go for a ride?''

Ten minutes ago, she would have given him a hard time for the suggestion, convinced that he had an ulterior motive. But right now, she knew something much more serious was on his mind. ''Where are we going?''

He got to his feet and pulled Ellie with him. ''We're going to ride by Mr. Teasdale's place.''

''He was pretty definite about not wanting to see us until Monday.''

''I know. We're not going to drop in for dessert.'' He gathered up the bottles and the plate from the table. ''I'm just going to tell the guys inside we're going off to neck by the lake.''

''Don't you dare.''

He kissed her and disappeared inside.

Ellie grabbed her sweatshirt off the railing and put it on. She understood how Nate felt. To start with, this job should have been a simple one. No matter how valuable an offered artifact was, whether stolen or legitimately owned, the auctions were generally hyped with more bells and whistles than this one. The secrecy about the whole thing was getting on her nerves. And since they'd started looking for someone to duplicate the flag, there was a feeling of doom hanging over them.

She thought back to when she'd felt this first. It all started with the SUV heading right for them in front of Atwood's shop. In all the years of her life, living in the city, Ellie had never had a car come that close to running her over.

"Are you ready?"

Nate had pulled a light jacket on over his T-shirt. She didn't try to make small talk, or ask any more questions. He needed to concentrate, and she understood. They'd driven up to Saratoga in Nate's sedan— what he called the company car—but they took Karen's new Explorer tonight since it had a global-positioning device in it.

The address they had for Teasdale put his house northwest of the town, in a wooded area and far off the beaten track from the regular summer tourists. Ellie watched the map display as Nate drove. Soon, the houses became farther apart. After another half a mile, occasional bright lights down a long driveway were the only sign of anyone living in the area.

A few more miles along the rolling, pine-covered countryside, and Nate stopped the car by the mailbox across from a gravel driveway. The number matched the address. Ellie looked down the dark drive. Other than a small, carefully painted No Trespassing sign nailed to a tree, there was no sign of life down the drive. The destination matched what was on the vehicle's map display.

A newspaper carrier route box was next to the mailbox. Ellie noticed the paper inside at the same time as Nate. He pulled the car up to it, and she took out the paper. He turned on the overhead light.

"Today's paper."

"Maybe he didn't want to walk out and get it," she suggested.

They sat in silence for a few seconds, Nate looking out at the still countryside. She rolled up the paper and put it back in the box.

"Didn't he say the overnight package should be dropped by the back door of the house?"

"That's right," she answered.

"If this road is okay for delivery trucks, then it should handle us." Nate turned down the private road.

"What do we tell him if he comes out with a shotgun?" she asked apprehensively.

"We arrived in town early and were double-checking the way to his house for Monday."

Ellie still couldn't get rid of the hot ember of worry that had nestled in the pit of her stomach. As a teenager, she'd had nerves of steel. She didn't allow fear when she was about to do a job. Concentration, speed, remembering verbatim and following the instructions she was given—these were the things that had guided her on occasions like this. It was far too time-consuming to let her mind dwell on anxious thoughts.

That had been the life she left behind a dozen years ago. For more reasons than one, she was glad of it now.

The single-story, ranch-style house came into view after a sharp bend along a creek. Not a single light was on. The door to the attached garage was closed. As Nate approached the house, two sets of floodlights mounted on the house came on.

"Did we wake him up?" Ellie asked.

"Motion sensors, I think."

They sat for a couple of minutes, waiting for other lights inside the house to go on. But nothing happened.

"It could be that he's not home," Ellie offered. "I think we should go."

"I'm going to take a look around first." Nate turned off the engine and shut off the lights. "You sit right here and wait for me."

Ellie's instincts were telling her that they should get out of here, but she clamped her mouth shut. Nate was a professional. He knew what he was doing. If *his* instincts told him that he needed to check the place out, then she needed to trust him. Besides, she was certain nothing she said was going to change his mind.

"I'll leave the key in. You lock the door as soon as I get out. Just toot the horn if any cars come down the driveway."

He grabbed a large flashlight from under the seat. As soon as he opened the door to get out, though, Ellie climbed across the seat after him.

"I'm coming with you."

He considered that for a moment, nodded and took the keys. "Let's try the front door."

As they moved toward the house, Ellie gazed at the dark woods surrounding them. The screech of an owl and the buzzing of summer bugs around the floodlights were the only sounds. She remembered what she'd once read in a Sherlock Holmes story about the safety of the city versus that of the country. Holmes preferred the city, where neighbors could hear the cries for help of victims. In the country, nobody heard you scream. She shivered and hurried to keep up.

Nate rang the doorbell and waited. There was no

answer. After ringing it a second time, he walked over to the garage door and shined the flashlight in one of the small windows.

"There's a car inside."

"Somebody could have picked him up," Ellie whispered hopefully.

A graveled walkway with meticulously kept flower beds on either side led toward the back of the house.

"Are you sure you don't want to wait in the car?"

Ellie shook her head and grabbed on to the back of Nate's jacket as they started in that direction. No floodlight came on to light the backyard, and Ellie was glad they had the flashlight.

A number of raised-bed vegetable gardens sat on the southerly slope by the house, but Ellie didn't feel a need to take inventory of anything in the dark. She just wanted to get out of here. The yard in the back dipped sharply, with a wooden deck coming off the main floor. There was a sliding glass door underneath the deck that she imagined led to a basement. There was a welcome mat by the door, and a table and a couple of chairs close by.

Nate pointed the flashlight at the glass door. She stepped closer and saw a workshop with benches and tools beyond the glass. As she did, she kicked something on the ground.

"What's this?"

Nate pointed the light on it.

"It's the package I overnighted to him yesterday." He picked it up and looked at the unbroken seal of the envelope before handing it to Ellie. "Hold on to it."

The sick feeling in her stomach got worse. Teasdale had insisted on having everything there on time. Nate pointed the light at the welcome mat they were standing on. He ran it slowly up along the edge of the door and looked closely at the lock. He flashed it again inside the workshop, specifically on the floor. Carefully, he used his sleeve to open the door. It was unlocked and slid open a crack.

When he took a gun out of a shoulder holster inside his jacket, Ellie's heart almost stopped. He was an FBI agent, it was natural that he would be armed, but before tonight she'd never noticed that he carried a weapon.

"What...what are we doing?" she asked in a whisper.

"It appears that Teasdale might have had some unwelcome company today."

"Are we going to call the police?" Ellie realized how stupid that sounded as soon as she said it. "For help, I mean."

He took his cell phone from his belt and handed it to her. He also handed her the car keys.

"Stand on the walkway over there and call the police. Give them my name and tell them who I am. Give them the address and tell them I suspect a possible burglary. I'm going inside to check for possible victims."

She didn't want to be left out there alone. Still, though, she moved to where he told her and pressed her back against the house. The back door slid open easily, and Nate called out, identifying himself before disappearing inside.

Her hands were shaking when she dialed 911. Her voice sounded even worse. But she managed to pass on the information Nate had given her to a dispatcher.

A light went on inside, and Ellie felt a little better, as it illuminated the area around her somewhat. What she could see of the backyard was well kept and carefully landscaped. But beyond that, the dark woods were too close. She glanced toward the partially open door, wishing Nate would come out.

Ellie let out a small scream when a black cat landed right at her feet. Her heart almost stopped, and she glared at the animal. She turned her gaze upward, realizing he must have been perched on the deck above. The cat rubbed up against her legs and meowed loudly. As she reached down to pet it, though, the complaining animal spotted the partially open door and ran inside the house.

Unable to stay outside any longer, she followed the cat in. The basement had been set up as a workshop. Two rows of benches stood at angles off the walls. Wooden shelves housed an array of tools and served as a bookcase. One section had a compartment with dozens of small drawers. Rolls of material were set up on a pipe rack. A door in the back of the room led to the rest of the basement, and the cat disappeared through it.

Ellie was going to follow the animal when something on her right caught her attention. On a board above a workbench, an array of Betsy Ross flag sketches had been pinned up. Looking closer, she saw that Teasdale had small pieces of fabric, and even a couple of square inches of what looked to be a faded old flag. She double-checked the package under her arm. It had definitely not been opened. A drawer right above the bench had been left partially open, and Ellie noticed a piece of paper with a phone number scribbled on it. Surprised, she started to open the drawer.

''Don't touch anything.''

She turned and breathed a sigh of relief at the sight

of Nate standing in the doorway. ''Did you find anything?''

''Yeah, I did. Teasdale's sitting at the kitchen table with his throat cut. I'm going to need my cell to let them know we'll need the coron—''

The bile rose up quickly in her throat. Ellie ran out the back door and doubled over at the edge of the grass. Even as she retched, she was conscious of the sound of approaching sirens.

Twenty-One

Sunday, June 27

The police report, with its usual flair for elegant prose, identified the victim as Henry Teasdale, aka Hank Teasdale. Male. White. Sixty-seven years old. No known relatives. Found sitting facedown at the kitchen table. Clothing at the time of death: blue shirt, gray pants, no shoes. Preliminary judgment for cause of death: five-inch incision severing the left-side carotid artery and the windpipe. Preliminary judgment regarding instrument of death: victim's own kitchen knife. Instrument recovered on scene.

Milt drove over and took Ellie back to the Murtaugh house sometime before midnight. As much as Nate wanted to keep her totally out of it, standard procedure had dictated that the detective in charge take down some basic information from her. After she was gone, Nate participated fully in the homicide investigation.

The crime scene was secured, and the work inside the house proceeded, even though the outside search had to be postponed until daylight. Nate requested that the locals extend the boundary of the investigation to include the entire length of the gravel drive.

Other than the murder itself, there was no evidence

of a struggle. It was obvious that someone had gone through the dresser drawers and closets and taken whatever he'd found there, as well as all the cash from Teasdale's wallet. Despite the fact that there was evidence of forced entry, Nate was not ready to let this murder go down in the books as a random burglary gone bad. Though the policeman's rule was to go with the obvious, the fact that Teasdale was killed two days before his meeting with Nate was just too coincidental. It was also the policeman's rule to go with your gut feeling, and looking around the place, Nate sensed that this was a first-class job done by a true professional.

At around four in the morning, Nate called Hawes at home and brought him up to date on everything that had happened. The assistant director didn't raise his voice once, listening without argument to Nate's reasons for quietly going about finding someone else to duplicate the flag. The only thing Hawes insisted on was having the agents from the FBI field office in Albany take over the investigation, in cooperation with the Saratoga Springs Police Department, thereby freeing Nate to stay on-course with his assignment.

To stay on-course was to play a waiting game, though, something that Nate was not too good at.

Dawn was just breaking across the eastern sky when he headed back to his parents' house. His mind continued to race as he drove. Next week at this time, everything had to be in place. A flag had to hang proudly behind the podium at Independence Hall, where the President was announcing the start of his Spirit of America celebration. But the casualties were adding up. Two men who excelled in forgeries, men he had only gotten as close to as a phone call through Ellie, were dead. McGill had come close to being killed. Chris was still scared, but at least he was safe in Philadelphia. Three others had died as a result of the explosion, as well.

Crime scenes, reports, eyewitnesses, backgrounds— Nate's mind reeled as he tried to connect all of these people and events.

The moment Nate turned into the driveway, he felt the sense of peace that imbued this house wash over him. This was the place where he and his brothers had grown up. This was the rock on which he'd built his world. His family represented the ideal that he hoped someday to emulate. He parked behind the line of his brothers' cars, knowing his mother would be leaving in a few hours on her Sunday morning doughnut quest.

He got out of the car and looked at the stretches of stone walls they used to hide behind during snowball fights every winter. He saw the old oak tree and the special limb they would hang a rope from to crash-test their Tonka trucks. At the far end of the field, he could see the brook that disappeared into the woods. Down the path a hundred yards was their swimming hole, where the stream dropped in a series of falls, eventually carving a slide in the rock that ended in a shallow pool before continuing down into the gorge. While growing up, Nate and his brothers and their friends spent hours swimming there.

As a kid, this had been a great place to grow up. In his late teens, he'd been naturally restless and ready to move away. Except for August, when the horse races ran, there was little action here and less excitement. Now that he was a thirty-six-year-old workaholic with increasingly jaded views of the world, this was becoming the place that he enjoyed returning to. This was the place where he could leave the problems of the world behind.

He looked up at the windows of the guest room above the garage and imagined coming back here with Ellie. The image of her snuggled up in his arms on the porch swing last night came into his mind. The way she looked wrapped in a towel as she stepped out of the bathroom in her apartment. He was becoming addicted to her smiles—to the quick wit with which she cut him no slack. He was looking forward to having sex with her. She was right about that, too. It was going to be an experience. He'd make sure it was.

There was so much that they didn't know about each other, but still everything felt right.

Of course, she was slow to warm up and accept him. Look at what she'd had growing up. He glanced around at the fields. She didn't have anything like this. She was slow to trust. He thought of his family. Who had she ever been able to trust growing up? She was slow to open her heart, but Nate already knew that when she did, it would be forever.

"Are you going to stand there all morning?"

The quiet voice came from the porch. Nate went up the steps, surprised to see Ellie cuddled up on one of the wicker chairs.

She pushed the throw blanket aside. "Good morning."

"Have you been waiting there all night?"

"Not all night. I couldn't sleep."

One of the dogs was jumping about excitedly behind the screen door. Ellie got up and let him out. She was barefoot and wearing jeans and a T-shirt. Nate watched the vulnerability play across her face, and he pulled her into his embrace. She wrapped her arms around him and pressed her head tightly against his chest. They stood silently wrapped in each other's arms like that for a few minutes.

Nate spoke first. "I'm sorry that I took you there last night."

"I'm sorry I embarrassed you by getting sick. I was just so scared and confused. Then I just hit overload, I guess." She pulled away and tugged on her sneakers.

"You didn't embarrass me." He caught her hand when she started folding the blanket. "Are you okay now?"

She nodded.

"And you're not mad at me this time for not calling you?"

She shook her head and smiled. One of the cats meowed at the window, and the golden retriever Ellie let out came back up on the porch. He sat at the door smiling at them, waiting to get back in.

"Do you think we should go in and feed them?"

Nate glanced at his watch. "It's only five-fifteen. We don't want to throw their schedule off, or there'll be hell to pay with Dr. Murtaugh." He opened the door and the other two dogs ran out. "Let's take them out for a walk. Mom usually feeds them about eight on Sundays. They should last that long."

"The air is cool." She rubbed her hands up and down her arms. "Let me run in and get a jacket."

He grabbed the blanket and draped it over her shoulders. "The sun will be heating things up pretty quick now. And between me and this thing, we should keep you warm."

They started down the steps and across the field. His knee was stiff, so he set a casual pace. The grass was still wet with dew. Nate watched Ellie's profile when she lifted her face to the sun and filled her lungs with the fresh morning air.

"Is this a routine I should get used to?" He pushed the loose tendrils of hair out of her face. "Anytime if I have to skip a night of sleep because of work, you don't sleep, either?"

She stared at the path that was leading into the woods. The two springer spaniels ran ahead, and the golden retriever walked beside her. "I guess...I guess that's true as long as we're partners on this assignment."

Nate took her hand and stopped. He lifted her chin until he could look into her dark eyes. "Is that what we are? Partners on an assignment?"

"I guess...I thought so. Or at least, that's what I wanted us to be when we started," she explained softly. "But somehow, over these past few days, you've managed to confuse me about so much."

"And how have I done that?"

"By bringing me here. By introducing me to your family. Even by taking me with you last night to check on Teasdale."

"I'm sorry. I shouldn't have done that."

Ellie shook her head. "No. I'm glad you did. Being there, experiencing firsthand the danger you face in doing your job, made your world more real to me. It made me realize how artificial this perfect little world is that I've been trying to create for myself."

"Don't romanticize what I do, Ellie. It's just a job."

"I don't," she quickly answered. "It's just the opposite. Now I know why we have to cherish every moment that we have together. Every moment that we're alive."

She started walking again. He stayed beside her.

"I'm mad at myself because for so long, I've been solely focused on putting together the kind of life that I didn't have as a kid."

"I think we all try—consciously or unconsciously—to do better than what we think our parents did."

"It's more than that. In my case, it's been close to an obsession. I had to have the perfect, successful business. I had to have important friends. Fancy cars. Belong to the right clubs. I even had to have the right boyfriends." She let out a frustrated breath. "For me, it's been more than compensating for not having a mother, or for seeing my father go to jail at the time in my life when I needed him most, or for having a pretty unconventional childhood. This thing just... became a monster. I needed perfection at the expense of losing the opportunities that could fix my... my psyche. I forgot about me, the real person. Instead, I've focused on how others should perceive me. Somewhere along the line, I even forgot about, or lost interest, in what always mattered most to me." She pulled the blanket tighter around her. "I've flat-out avoided sitting down with my father and trying to thrash out whatever we're both so wound up about."

A couple of times during this past week, Nate had been ready to make a comment to Lou or Ellie about this ignoring game the two of them played so well with each other.

"Don't put that one off. Sit down with Lou this week, tomorrow. Force him to get it all off his chest—and do the same thing yourself. Life is too short. It'd be very sad to have regrets about that years down the road...after he's gone."

Ellie turned to him. "This is the big difference between us. Rather than tossing and turning and losing sleep, you do something about whatever it is that's bothering you. Rather than having the same argument eighteen different ways with yourself—without ever solving the problem—you know what to say."

"And I say it," he admitted. They were walking alongside the brook, and the water was running clear and strong.

"And you say it." She nodded. "No beating around the bush. You want something? You ask for it. You have a problem? You fix it."

"You're making me look pretty darn good. Maybe I could get this all on tape and play it back to you the next time you think I'm a pain in the ass."

Ellie lifted her face to him. "The reason I'm saying all this is to let you know that *I'm* going to work at not being a pain myself. Spending time with you has changed my perspective, Agent Murtaugh. From now on, I'm going to do my best to be Miss Congeniality."

"This could change Bureau policy, you know."

"What do you mean?"

"We may have to institute a 'Take an agent home with you' program to change everyone's attitude toward the FBI."

"I'm serious." She bumped him with her shoulder. "And this has nothing to do with the FBI, really."

"Don't tell me you're going to be nice to everybody."

"Not everybody. Just people I should care about. You know, the riffraff like you." She smiled.

Nate pulled her against him. His head bent over hers. "How nice?"

"It all depends," she drawled.

There was a splash right next to them. They both turned and found the two spaniels chasing after a family of ducks across the water hole. The retriever was standing on the edge, looking back at them expectantly.

"Nice enough to go swimming with me?"

"When?"

"Right now." He motioned with his head to the water. "You and me and the dogs and the ducks."

She smiled and shook her head. "You're crazy."

"So?" He pulled the blanket off her shoulders and threw it on a flat rock that extended out over the water. He took off his shoes and socks. "You told me yourself—I want something, I go for it. Right now, I want to go swimming."

"That water is probably freezing." She took a step back. "And I don't have a bathing suit, and your family will be getting up any minute."

"The water is warmer than you think." He peeled his shirt off. "And I promise not to stare if you take all your clothes off. And those guys won't get up for at least another couple of hours." Nate unbuckled his belt.

"You wouldn't."

He unbuttoned his pants and lowered the zipper. "Come on, city girl."

She turned around, her cheeks burning. "What about your mother's rule about—"

"We're not under her roof." Nate tossed his pants and boxers over on the rock. Moving up behind Ellie, he pulled her against his chest and kissed the silky skin of her neck. "And who said anything about sex? This is considered morning exercise."

To prove his point, he let her go and stepped off the stony ledge into the shallow section of the pool. The water was freezing. Nate bit back a curse and walked a few steps in until he was waist deep.

"It's like bathwater."

The golden retriever standing next to Ellie barked, calling his lie. So much for man's best friend.

"How many stitches did you get on your back?" she asked gently.

"Twelve."

She'd turned around and was watching him. "When do they come out?"

"In another week or so."

"Do they hurt?"

"Like hell," he lied, "especially when they get wet."

Before his teeth started chattering, he dived headfirst into the deeper section of the pool. The water was much more bearable once he was completely wet. When he came up, she was standing on the stones near the shallow end and was reaching down to put a hand in.

"Over here," he called, swimming to the deepest end. "There's a warm spring right under here. You can jump in from these rocks."

Ellie straightened up and gave him a doubtful look. Then she stepped back and took off her shoes.

"You said you wouldn't look," she scolded.

"I said I wouldn't *stare*." He turned his back and took a stick from one of the spaniels that was swimming around him. He threw it and both of the smaller dogs swam after it. From the shore, the retriever leaped into the water in pursuit, too. Nate took a quick glance behind him, and his mouth watered. Ellie, wearing nothing but a lacy white bra and panties, was walking to where he'd told her the water was warmer.

He swam closer, admiring the perfect curves and the contrast of her dark hair against her pale skin. She was breaking out in goose bumps, and Nate couldn't wait to warm her up.

"How deep is it?"

Nate touched the bottom with his feet and came back up. "Maybe eight feet."

"And you promised it's warm."

"Like a bathtub."

She dived in head first and came up sputtering and cursing. "You liar! This water is ice cold."

Nate swam to her. "What are you, a baby?"

"You lied," she accused, pushing him away. "You tricked me. I'm getting out."

Ellie turned to leave, and Nate reached out and grabbed her by the waist, pulling her under with him. She turned in his arms, and they both kicked to the surface.

"Move around a little. You'll warm up in no time."

She splashed water in his face. "You're such a liar." She pushed his head down.

The view below was superb. The bra became nearly translucent underwater. He brushed his thumbs over the dark nipples showing through. He caressed her slender waist. He ran his fingers along the elastic of her panties and then traced a path on the inside of her leg to where the triangle of dark hair showed through the sheer fabric.

Ellie tried to pull his head out of the water. When he came up, she looked flushed and was no longer shivering. Her body slid against his, and he pulled her against him. There was no way Nate could hide the evidence of his arousal against her legs.

"Warmer now?"

She didn't answer. Instead, her arms twined around his neck and she kissed him deeply. Nate wrapped her in his arms and backpedaled to a shallower section beneath a rock overhang.

"You're so beautiful." Nate pushed a shoulder strap of her bra down her arm. His mouth closed around her nipple. She moaned and impatiently tore the bra away from her body.

"I want you, Ellie." His hand moved inside her panties and curved around her perfect bottom. "I'll go crazy if you don't let me make love to you."

She continued to kiss his face, his neck, taking small bites of his shoulder. Her naked breasts slid against his chest.

"I can't let you go crazy," she said breathlessly.

"Say it." His other hand cupped her. His fingers played against her folds. "Tell me what you like, Ellie."

When she started moving against his touch, he felt his control begin to slip. She reached down and wrapped her hand around him, and he knew he was finished. "Make love to me, Nate."

They were both starved for each other—for the joining of their bodies. Nothing was a hindrance now. The temperature of the water. The danger of someone coming upon them. Nothing. Nate carried her to a very shallow end where the stone was as smooth as polished marble. He quickly stripped off the little that Ellie had left on.

When he entered her, he knew that they had always been intended for each other. When they came together in the shallows, with the dappled sunlight shimmering on the surface of the pool, he knew that this was the woman he had been made for.

Afterward, they stretched out and dried themselves

in the sun, wrapped in each other's arms. And then they made love again. And when they had recovered a little, they swam once more with the dogs and the ducks and the shared desire to live this day to its fullest.

Twenty-Two

Ellie took Nate's suggestion and waited in the lobby of the hospital, instead of in his car, when he went up to the critical-care unit to see Tom McGill. Settling into a surprisingly comfortable upholstered chair, she held the innumerable sections of the *Sunday New York Times* on her lap.

She needed this. She needed time to take control of her high-flying emotions and settle her thoughts.

This entire morning had been a whirlwind of sensations in so many ways. She was feeling more fulfilled as a woman than she'd ever felt. Nate had not only made love to her, he'd made her feel whole. He'd brought out in her a sense of confidence that Ellie hadn't even known she lacked.

At the water's edge, he'd made her cry his name out loud, and she in turn had driven him out of his mind.

Later, at the breakfast table, she'd noticed other changes in herself. No longer did she cringe at subtle comments by his family about her and Nate being an item. Suddenly, she was perfectly comfortable arguing politics with Harvard-law-trained Milt. At some point in talking to Karen, Ellie had even realized that she was no longer embarrassed to speak openly about her troubled youth. Doughnut in hand, she'd even talked about her father, his painting and his time in prison.

The family's response had been one of surprise at first, but they all had moved easily past it. In fact, Karen was very interested in the types of things Lou liked to paint. They were an amazing group, and she had felt Nate's supportive presence beside her throughout the entire brunch.

They hadn't left Saratoga until midafternoon, and en route to the hospital Nate had suggested that since neither of them had gotten much sleep, perhaps it would be best if they'd stayed someplace overnight on their way back to Philadelphia. Ellie agreed and made the necessary calls as they drove.

Victor was already set to open the shop on Monday, though he had to relay the dozen or so stories of the tourists who were invading Philadelphia and the store. Sister Helen told her of the scare that Chris had after the ball game Friday night, but she didn't want Ellie to be concerned. He wasn't sick or running a fever. In fact, Chris was eating and drinking as he should and was just lying low for the weekend. Ellie had thought to ask about Lou, too. After a slight pause, Helen told her that he was as ornery as ever.

One more phone call that she had to make was to her friend John Dubin in Ticonderoga. At Nate's suggestion, she hadn't said anything about finding Teasdale's dead body at his house. Instead, they'd just talked over the news that local TV stations had already broadcast.

Nate's call to Ticonderoga had informed them that Tom McGill was still in the ICU in critical condition. There had been some slight improvement over the day before, however. He was off pressure-support medications, his neurological functions continued to improve, he was alert and responding to yes and no questions by moving his head. On the discouraging side, Tom had fluid in his lungs, remained on the ventilator, and the prognosis was still uncertain.

The sensation of being watched made Ellie very aware of her surroundings and the people in the lobby. She tried not to look up, shuffling some of the newspapers on her lap to look as if she was actually reading as she sat there.

She glanced up casually at the groups of people coming in or leaving the main entrance. The last time she'd been here, Chris's friend Allison had easily found her. The lobby was more crowded today than it had been last Monday. Families, more so than the individuals, were obviously taking advantage of the pleasant Sunday afternoon to visit their loved ones.

Again, that uncomfortable feeling that someone was watching came over her. Ellie folded the newspapers and put them in a neat pile on her lap. She took her dark sunglasses out of her purse and put them on. Settling into the chair, she rested her head against the back and pretended that she was getting ready to take a snooze.

She scanned the waiting room. There were very few individuals, and even fewer people who weren't obviously on their way in or out. A young man paced back and forth right near the main entrance, talking on his cell beneath the Turn Your Cell Phone Off sign. An old lady sat in a wheelchair with an attendant, obviously waiting for her ride to arrive. Two volunteers were changing shifts by the information desk.

Ellie saw him standing against the wall near the registration windows. Black, considerably shorter than Nate, he was wearing khaki pants and a sport jacket. He was squarely built, like a club bouncer. His gaze flickered toward her and then back to the flyer he was pretending to read. Her sixth sense kicked into gear. He was a cop. No doubt about it. But she couldn't figure why he'd zeroed in on her.

Last night, while being questioned by the detectives in Saratoga, Ellie almost froze up several times. As irrational as it was, the old fears were quick to come back. Inwardly, she expected them all to point fingers at her and assume she must be guilty of the murder of Teasdale. For all the years that she'd been trying to change her life and her image, the one feeling that continued to nag her was that people never forget. A criminal is always a criminal, no matter what the offense. No matter how many years might pass, old prejudices lingered. Nate's presence, though, had been Ellie's salvation. More protective than she could ever have imagined, he had not left her side until his brother had come to take her home.

The man across the waiting room was being discreet, but he was still watching her. Ellie wondered if his surveillance had something to do with last night.

"Taking a nap?"

She almost purred when Nate's fingers gently combed through her hair before pushing up her sunglasses. Ellie smiled at him. "How's McGill?"

"I'll tell you when we get to the car. Let's get out of here."

She let him pull her to her feet. "Do you know the guy who's hanging around the registration window?"

He frowned and fired a look in the direction she said. "What guy?"

Ellie turned around. The cop was gone. She shook her head.

"I must be more tired than I thought. I thought someone was watching me, and I got nervous."

"Whoever was there was probably looking at you because you're very beautiful and very sexy." He pulled her against him as they walked out of the building together. "But I'm afraid I'll just have to find the bastard and take his eyes out for ogling my woman."

"I like the word *ogling*. And I like it when *you* ogle me." She put her arm around his waist and smiled up at him. "You don't mind being my ogler?"

"I'll be whatever you want me to be." He leaned down and whispered in her ear. "And that's in and out of bed."

He knew exactly how to melt her heart. Ellie couldn't wait until they were locked up in some hotel room, so she could show him how she would be whatever he wanted her to be, as well.

Nate held the car door open, and Ellie climbed in.

"So how is McGill?" she asked as soon as he closed his door.

"Healthwise, not too good." Nate started the engine. "But there is nothing wrong with his mind."

"Did he talk to you?"

"Not in the usual sense of the word. Nodding a yes or a no is still the extent of it." He pulled out of the hospital parking lot. "From what his parents told me, the doctors are keeping him pretty doped up most of the time. When he's conscious, he gets irritated pretty easily. Of course, with those tubes and all that machinery, who could blame him."

"How was he with you?"

"He was actually pretty glad to see me."

Nate fell silent, but Ellie sensed there was something else that he wasn't saying. He glanced in the mirror a couple of times, and she turned around and looked behind them at the line of traffic.

"What's wrong?"

"Nothing. Do you mind if we find a place in town to stay? I could really use a good night's sleep before we head back to Philly."

"No, not at all."

"Good." At the next intersection, he did a quick U-turn.

"You want to see McGill again tomorrow before we leave town, don't you."

He looked at her curiously. "How did you know?"

She shrugged. "You don't seem satisfied with whatever took place up there."

"Chief Buckley was there, too."

"In McGill's room?"

"Yeah."

"You called ahead. They knew you were coming. Maybe Buckley was trying to impress you with his devotedness to his men by being there on a Sunday," she suggested.

"Whatever he was trying to do, I wasn't impressed." He looked in the mirror again. "But he did tell me that they've been showing Tom mug shots of possible perpetrators, hoping he'd be able to identify the drivers of the car that hit him. So far, no luck."

Following his gaze, Ellie looked out the back window again, but there was no one behind them. "Do you think McGill might have something to tell you that he can't say with his chief there?"

"I got that feeling, but I won't know for sure until I talk to him again tomorrow…without anyone else there."

Ellie could just imagine how happy Sanford Hawes

would be if he knew what Nate was doing. But he wasn't going to know.

"I think we should order takeout for dinner and stay in the room until you're ready to go back to the hospital tomorrow."

"You're reading my mind." Nate flashed her a devilish smile.

He pulled into the driveway of a decent-looking motor lodge that they'd passed coming into Ticonderoga. The parking lot was less than half full.

"I don't think we'll have any trouble finding a room," Ellie said. Already the excitement of spending the night with him was giving her butterflies.

He checked in and then parked in the back parking lot, where the car wouldn't be visible from the main road. He turned to her. "It's not the Four Seasons or the Ritz."

Ellie looped her arms around his neck and kissed him with enough passion to set both of their bodies on fire. She pulled back and gazed into his eyes. "I'll take a flat rock anytime over those places. I'll even take the back seat of the company car."

"You don't say?" He glanced over the seat to see how much room there was back there. "Well, maybe we should try it before we go in."

Ellie scrambled out of the car, smiling broadly. "You're incorrigible, Agent Murtaugh."

"And you're a tease, Ms. Littlefield," he replied, taking their bags out of the trunk.

She looped an arm through his as they headed for the building. "By the way, some of these rooms have a balcony. I wonder what it would be like to make love on one of those. You know what an outdoorsy kind of girl I am."

Nate dropped a bag and swept her up into his arms, growling fiercely against her throat. "The way you're going, baby, we'll be lucky to make it to the room."

Gently, he put her back down, and she pressed her body against his.

"I see an elevator." She smiled, feeling his arousal hard against her. "Do you know how to stop one of those between floors?"

Sister Helen opened the door and motioned Ted to follow her into the front living room. Once inside, she closed the double French doors behind her.

She turned to him. "Thank you so much for coming over on such short notice so late at night."

"No problem." He didn't bother to sit down. "What's wrong?"

"I need some guidance."

Ted wasn't able to hide his surprise. "You, Sister?"

"Yes, me." She walked to the center of the room. "Recently, I read an interview where a nun was telling the story of getting sick and going to the doctor. The doctor's first question to her was 'Nuns get sick?' She told him, 'We're real people. We get sick. We have fun. We have fears and we sin. Like everybody. Our lives can be stressful, so we celebrate life when we can.'"

"And you sometimes need help from your friends."

She nodded and turned to him. "I called you because of Chris. To tell the truth, I don't know if anything is wrong with him at all. Maybe I'm just overreacting. I was never a parent, so I don't honestly know if this behavior is normal for a boy his age. I just don't know if I'm being concerned for nothing."

Ted felt his insides tighten. It happened every time

someone reminded him of how he'd been a parent once. It was as if he was a damp rag and being twisted. At times in the past, when this would happen, it felt like the pain would go on until every drop of feeling was wrung out of him. Not this time, though. He forced himself not to let that happen.

"What's going on? What's he doing?"

"Nothing! And that's what scares me most." She sat down on the edge of a chair. "You stayed in his room until Chris fell asleep Friday night. When he didn't leave the room on Saturday, except to run to the bathroom and back, I didn't think too much about it. Sister Lisa spent some time with him and took up his meals. I just assumed he was recovering from his experience the day before."

Helen rose to her feet again. "But he did the same thing today. All day. He wouldn't leave the room to go to church with us or come down for any meals. And then he told me he's sick, so I got Lou to sit with him."

"How do you know he isn't really sick?"

"He told me he thinks he's got the measles." She gave him an incredulous look. "Of course, this was right after reading one of the books Elizabeth gave him that had a kid in it who contracted measles."

Ted remembered the summer his daughter Emily had decided that it was cool to have a broken arm. She didn't believe her doctors and actual X-rays showing that there was nothing wrong. She wanted a cast.

"Tonight, another thing happened that made me more concerned about what's going on." Helen started pacing the room. "When I went up to check on him about eight o'clock, I couldn't get the door open at first. And then Chris moved a chair from behind it to let me in. Now, you know how small that bedroom is at the top of the stairs, and there's no air-conditioning in this house. Inside, I found he's got the window shut and locked. It was at least a hundred degrees in that room. And I had a feeling he wasn't sleeping in the bed, either.''

"Where was he sleeping?"

"Under the bed."

"He must be scared of something."

"I think you're right," Helen agreed. "I came downstairs and talked to Sister Lisa, and she said all day yesterday she was fighting to keep that window open in his room. And Lou said today, when all of us were at church, Chris had been asking questions about secret passageways and if there were any good places where someone could hide in this house."

"This seems like a strange reaction to the scare in the subway."

"I'm no psychologist, Ted, but I agree."

"He hasn't watched any TV or scary movies this past couple of days," Ted said, thinking aloud.

"And he hasn't been talking to any of the kids since the ball game you all went to," Helen added. "By the way, Elizabeth called this morning and I held off telling her all this. I didn't want to get her wound up while she's out of town. But after tonight, I started getting a little nervous. There's definitely a change in Chris, and I don't know what to do about it."

Ted looked down at his watch. "It's nine-thirty. Do you think he's asleep?"

"I doubt it. I've been up and down the stairs at least a half dozen times this past hour. He hasn't tried to block the door with his chair again, but the last time I peeked in, he was crouched in the corner of the room, trying to read with no lights on."

"Can I talk to him?"

"I was hoping you'd say that." Helen opened the door and started leading the way.

"If you don't mind, maybe it would be better if just the two of us had a chat. Maybe he'll feel more comfortable telling me what's wrong."

"You're right," she agreed good-naturedly. "That's a much better approach than 'Tell us what's wrong this minute so Sister Helen can get a good night's sleep.' You know the way. I'll be right here if you need me."

Ted didn't remember any extreme nervousness in Christopher before the near tragedy in the subway station on Friday night. He climbed the steps to the room at the top of the stairs. He wished he knew more about the boy's background, about his parents, about whatever he'd been doing that weekend that Ellie mentioned he'd disappeared.

The light in the hallway was on, and the door ajar. He knocked and gently pushed open the door a little. Inside, the room was completely dark.

"Chris?" he called softly, not wanting to wake the boy up if he was asleep.

"Right here."

Ted opened the door all the way. The light from the hallway poured into the room.

"There you are." Crouched down in the corner farthest from the window, Chris had a book open in his lap. "Can I turn on the light?"

"Uh...could you please...not turn it on?"

"Sure thing." There was no doubt in Ted's mind that this boy was scared. "Can I come in?"

"Yeah. That'd be great."

Ted walked into the room. Everything was just as Helen had described it—including how stuffy and warm it was. He sat down on the foot of the bed. "What are you reading?"

Chris closed the book and handed it to him. Ted looked at the title and then held it up to the light from the hallway to see the blurb on the back.

"My eyes aren't what they used to be. Is it a good book?"

He nodded.

"Scary?"

"No."

"Funny."

"Kind of."

Ted decided to change the topic. "How did you like the baseball game Friday night?"

"It was awesome," the boy said, obviously meaning it.

"We could go again next weekend."

Silence.

"We don't have to take the subway."

There was still silence.

Ted planted his elbows on his thighs and looked closer at Chris. He was still crouched in the corner with his knees up. "I bought a new bat yesterday, and I was thinking about bringing it around tomorrow. Would you like to be the first one who tries it out?"

He shook his head.

Ted noticed for the first time how the boy kept glancing in the direction of the window. He got up from the bed and walked casually to it. "Hot in here. Do you mind if I crack this?"

"I kind of like it closed. I'm really cold." His voice was edged with panic. As if to prove his point, he dragged a quilt off the bed and pulled it on top of himself.

"I'm sorry. I won't open it." He looked out the window. Nothing seemed out of place. The Dumpster beneath the street lamp, the cars parked along the street. With its mix of abandoned and inhabited houses, it was an all too typical South Philly neighborhood.

Ted walked back, and instead of sitting on the bed, he plunked himself down on the floor next to Chris. He pointed to the quilt.

"You don't really need this, do you?"

Chris shook his head and pushed back the heavy cover.

Helen was definitely not imagining things. There was something wrong. But to get to the root of it was another story. Ted wondered how his sister Léa would feel if he called her now, looking for her professional expertise.

Nine-thirty on Sunday night. The baby was probably asleep. Since school was finished, Heather would be out with her friends. That left Mick and Léa a couple of hours for each other. He decided against it.

Anyway, Ted knew from experience what Léa would say in a situation like this. Keep talking. Keep listening.

"Can I tell you something about myself?"

Chris gave him a hesitant glance. "If you want to."

"I'm scared."

The boy's eyes rounded instantly. His gaze went from Ted to the window and back.

"Can I tell you what I'm scared of?"

Chris nodded.

"To be honest with you, a lot of things scare me," he started. "I think the thing that scares me the most, though, is losing people that I love."

"I know you lost your girls."

Ted wasn't surprised that Chris knew. Still, though, he had to take a couple of seconds to control his emotions before he could go on.

"Did you know I also lost both my parents when I was a teenager? And then I lost my aunt. She took care of us after my parents died. After I...after I lost my girls...I got so sad...and scared. I got so scared that I wanted to just shut out the world. I didn't want to feel anything. Because of that, I almost lost my sister, the only person I had left in this whole world."

"How did that happen?"

Ted leaned his head against the wall, contemplating how to explain being found guilty of killing his own family. How could he explain the time he'd spent on death row? How does an adult explain a two-year bout of depression so severe that life itself, for a time, became meaningless? How could he put all that into a few simple words that an eight-year-old could understand?

"You know how sometimes we do things that are wrong? And other times, we blame ourselves when something goes wrong. Then, there are times when somebody else does a bad thing to us, but we choose to ignore it, hoping it'll just go away." Ted looked at Chris. He still had the eight-year-old's attention. "For me, it was a combination of all those things. The worst thing is that often those bad things don't go away on their own. I had to face them and *make* them go away."

"What did you do wrong to your girls?"

Ted hadn't expected the direct question. "I...the night I lost them, I had an argument with their mother. I lost my temper. That was wrong. If I hadn't let my anger at her boil over, maybe she'd have paid more attention. Maybe she'd have let our girls come home with me. Maybe then the terrible things wouldn't have happened.''

"This is the blaming part."

He nodded. "You're right."

"Was it the bad people who hurt your kids?"

Ted nodded again.

"What did you do to those people?"

"At first, nothing. I was so sad about my family being gone that I couldn't think of anything else. I never thought it was my responsibility to make sure those people were caught so that they couldn't do the same thing to someone else."

"Could they hurt you, too?"

"I didn't care about me. But my sister was the one who was in real danger."

"How did you fix things?"

Ted stretched his legs out. "I got the right people's help. There were some real good people around me, and I had to tell them the truth and let them do their jobs."

"And the bad guys got caught?"

"Absolutely."

"Was your sister okay?"

"She's great now." Ted sidestepped the question, not wanting to say anything about Léa's final scare. He noticed, though, that Chris had not looked at the window for at least a couple of minutes. "Maybe sometime I could take you to her house for a family dinner."

The trace of a smile broke across the eight-year-old's face. "When?"

Twenty-Three

Monday, June 28

It was still dark outside the window of the motor lodge. Ellie heard the shower running. She rolled, stretched out across the bed and turned the alarm clock around. It was 4:07. Nate wanted to visit McGill at the hospital around dawn. He'd also told her she should sleep and that he would wake her up when he got back.

Ellie sat up in bed, reached onto the floor and put on the first piece of clothing she found. It was Nate's T-shirt. When she stood up, it covered her practically to her knees. Barely eaten containers of take-out food cluttered the top of a small table in the corner. Ellie swept them all into the trash can and wiped off the table before plugging in the small coffeemaker.

The shower was still running when she got into the bathroom. She used the toilet, brushed her teeth and washed her face, and perched herself on the vanity, waiting for him to finish.

Ellie once told Nate that sex with him would be a life-changing experience—shattering, she recalled saying—and it was scary to think how correct she'd been. Yesterday, they'd been all over each other in the elevator. Once in their room, the only thing either of them had worried about for the next couple of hours was getting enough air. Their dinner came in about nine, but even that had only been a temporary distraction.

What had transpired in the past twenty-four hours was like nothing she'd ever experienced in her life. With Nate, it wasn't only the act of physically making love. He saw her for who she was. He understood her. He challenged her mind even while teasing her body. He made her talk to him and branded himself in her heart and mind.

The water shut off. When he pulled the plastic shower curtain open, all she could do was stare for a moment and think of what she'd like to do to this wet human lollipop next. And she'd *never* felt like that before.

"What are you doing up?" he asked with great surprise.

"I wanted to see you before you left." She tossed him his towel.

He looked at her with such tenderness that Ellie felt herself go soft. "You're constantly sacrificing your sleep for me. If we keep this up, we'll both be suffering from sleep deprivation."

She smiled. "I started some coffee. I don't think there's any room service this early for breakfast."

"I don't think there's any room service, at all." Wet and dripping, he stepped out of the tub and kissed her long and hard. She was light-headed when he pulled back. "But you're the only breakfast I want right now."

"I didn't want to be a distraction. I know you have to leave." She took a hand towel off the rack and started patting the wet drops on his chest and neck.

"I'll be right here waiting, though, when you get back."

"Right here, sitting on the edge of the sink?" he asked with a smile.

"If this is where you want me."

"Wearing my T-shirt?"

"Okay." Ellie loved the twinkle of mischief in his blue eyes.

Nate took his razor and shaving cream out of a bag.

"Can I watch you shave?"

"Are you accustomed to watching ritual bloodletting ceremonies?"

"Of course. Philadelphia is famous for them." She watched closely every step of the process. Being with Nate filled gaps in so many experiences she'd missed in her life. Swimming in a clear running brook. Making love in the open air under a blue sky. Having Sunday morning brunch with a real family. Feeling personally as well as intellectually valued. Having sex more than once in twenty-four hours. And now, watching a man shave. Spending time with him also made her heart ache, as she was quickly finding out how it felt to fall for someone without having a clue what the future might bring.

Ellie's gaze followed the contours of the muscles in his arm, the wide powerful chest, the strong neck, the handsome face that was quickly disappearing under white foam, and she knew her infatuation ran much deeper than mere physical attraction. She liked his flaws just as much. He had a bum knee. He snored when he slept on his back. And the last time they made love last night—or was it this morning?—he'd even whispered to her that he would love to see her pregnant with their child. Never in her entire life had Ellie heard a man say such a thing to her. She knew it came from his heart. And she'd learned early in life that honesty that deep and uninhibited had to be a flaw.

In just a few minutes, Nate successfully scraped away a day's growth of whiskers and a substantial amount of skin.

"What do you think?"

Ellie was shocked at the number of nicks he'd given himself while shaving.

"If the Red Cross sent a truck over every morning, they could have a steady supply for their blood banks." She stood up, moistened the corner of a wash towel and started dabbing the bloody spots.

"How can you look so good this early?" His fingers delved into her hair, and he brought her face to his.

"Are you sure you don't wear contacts, because I'm told that in the morning I look like a twelve-year-old having a bad hair day."

"And who told you that?" His lips brushed against hers and moved down to her neck.

"Vic."

"Ah...the last person you should listen to." His hand caressed her breast through the T-shirt. "Look at that beautiful woman."

Ellie followed his gaze and saw their reflection in the mirrored bathroom door. She looked tousled and sleepy, but he was magnificent—naked and fully aroused beneath the towel that was tied loosely around his waist.

"There's going to have to be a little change of plans about when I get back."

Ellie leaned into his touch, dropping the wash towel on the floor. "What do you mean?"

He put a dry towel on the vanity and lifted her easily

onto it. Her legs were dangling over the edge, and he stepped between them. "I still want you sitting on this sink, but I want my shirt back."

Ellie shivered as he peeled the shirt over her head.

"Look at you now."

Heat rushed into her face when she looked over and saw how her nipples were extended. Her body was straining for his touch.

"Don't take your eyes off those two in the mirror," he whispered to her when she reached for him.

The towel around his waist dropped down to the floor. Still watching him in the mirror, Ellie slid forward a little, expectant. Instead, Nate pushed back her arms until her breasts were fully exposed to his face, and gently opened her legs. And then, she watched as he began a slow, torturous journey down her body— kissing, tasting, tormenting her in the most exquisite ways.

The reflection was wickedly arousing, and Ellie shivered as waves of ecstasy rippled through her. Wanting to give in to the feelings and yet wanting to hold on to them, she fought the pressures building rapidly within her. Finally, when she thought she could take no more, Nate drove himself fully into her, and she exploded in a dazzling kaleidoscope of sensations.

Lost in the waves of rapture even as she answered his thrusts, Ellie recalled Nate's last flaw and found herself wishing for the same thing.

There'd been a significant improvement in McGill during the night. Although he was still in the intensive care unit, late last night he'd been taken off the ventilator.

Tom's parents had been keeping their vigil around

the clock, taking turns staying at the hospital every night.

Nate met Tom's father in the long corridor when he arrived at six.

"He was hoping that you'd stop back, Agent Murtaugh," the older man said. Weariness did little to dampen his enthusiasm. "With the ventilator off, Tom has even spoken to us. There were moments when I wondered if I'd ever hear him say another word."

The officer's father choked for a moment with emotion, and Nate put a hand on his shoulder.

In a minute, the man took a deep breath and composed himself. "He even asked me if there was a way I could get hold of you today."

"Has Chief Buckley been told of Tom's progress?"

"No. It was too late to call anyone last night."

Nate was relieved about that. After a word with the staff member in charge, he was led to the police officer's bedside. Despite the remarkable improvements, Tom was still terribly weak.

"Take your time," Nate told him after some initial small talk. He put a pen and a pad of paper on the hospital bed, not knowing what would be easier. He pulled a chair close and sat down. Rather than asking specific questions, Nate wanted to hear what McGill had to say…about anything.

"The boy. Chris," Tom said. His throat was obviously hoarse, and Nate knew it was painful for the officer to speak.

Nate gave him a complete rundown, finishing up by telling him that Chris was in Philadelphia where he was staying with some nuns.

"They were after him," Tom said.

"The people who ran you down?"

The officer nodded. "Two."

"There were two of them," Nate repeated, taking notes. "Would you be able to identify them?"

He glanced toward the door first. "Never seen them. Shirt-and-tie look. Headlights were bright. But I might be able to."

Tom's gaze flicked toward the door again. Nate turned and thought he saw a shadow of someone passing. He got off the chair, but his knee was slow to respond, and he limped to the doorway. Other than a gray-haired custodian swabbing the floor, there was no one else.

He walked back inside. "How do you know they were after Chris?"

"Passenger saw Chris. Pointed. Driver came at me. No robbery."

"How about the car?" Nate asked, pulling the chair under him again. "Do you remember anything about the car?"

"Crown Victoria. Late model. Muddy. No front plate."

Nate jotted down the information. Two men coming after an eight-year-old. But this was the same story Chris had given him. Two men in a muddy car. Nate had checked, and the boy's father was still in jail. The mother hadn't moved from the trailer she'd set up house in. Nate recalled he hadn't heard anything about the report that was supposedly being done comparing the tire tracks from McGill's accident to Weaver's trailer.

"Another thing." Tom's hand lifted weakly and dropped back onto the sheets. "Tapes."

"Surveillance tapes? From the Fort Ticonderoga Museum?"

He nodded. "Looked at them…again. Last weekend. Some missing."

Nate had looked at them, too. But now that he thought back, he'd only seen the tapes with Chris and Ellie on them. The view from the hallway. "Do you think someone tampered with them?"

"Don't know. But there're…segments of the hallway tapes…missing."

"Are you saying they've been cut and spliced?"

Tom nodded. "Maybe. No time to check. There are time segments missing…unless they stopped…and started camera…without us knowing… Check time notations on pictures."

The hallway shots Nate had seen showed the groups of kids on field trips. Later, the security cameras had captured Chris and Ellie. Then Chris coming out of the bathroom and walking to the flag room. There were also shots of him running out, and then the cameras were shut down.

The face of the guard that Chris claimed had been in the room was not on any tape Nate had seen. And the hallway was the only way for the man to get in there.

"Who knew that you were suspicious about the tapes?"

"Didn't figure it…till Sunday. Only told…the chief."

Ellie packed their bags, checked out at the office and waited downstairs in the lobby for Nate to pick her up.

He'd called from the hospital about thirty minutes ago and hadn't given any information other than saying that she should be ready. They were leaving for Philadelphia as soon as he got back. Something must have happened, but Ellie knew better than to ask. She trusted him to tell her what he could when he was ready.

Her cell phone rang for the second time in an hour, and Ellie answered. This time it was Ray.

"You're awake!"

"Good morning," she said pleasantly, checking the clock on the wall.

"Are you out of bed already?"

"Of course. You know I'm an early riser. It's eight o'clock."

"And here I thought this was going to be your hot weekend away."

Ellie recognized the tone. The spoiled 'I had a bad day, so I have to ruin everybody else's day' tone. A specialty of her old mentor.

"What do you want, Ray?"

"All weekend, I kept having this recurring vision of a pair of muscular biceps planted on either side of your head and a very muscular ass pointed up toward the ceiling, with our young man pumping away. So is he as good as he looks?"

"Let's not go there, okay?" she said sharply.

"Why not?"

"You can be so crude sometimes." She tried to keep the hurt that she felt out of her voice.

"I'm jealous." He laughed. "For the first time in your life, looks like you've landed a man with a cock bigger than the pinheads of those guys you're used to dating. I want to hear all the details, babycakes. All the wet, delicious details."

"Goodbye, Ray." Ellie disconnected the phone and stepped out of the lobby. She needed the fresh morning air to cool her temper.

Ray made what she and Nate were sharing sound

cheap and dirty, and Ellie didn't like it. Over the years, she had generally been spared Ray's sporadic bursts of coarse vulgarity. Ever since she was little, she knew that he had an insensitive streak. Usually, it only emerged when he was unhappy or drunk. But Ellie always felt that her mentor directed his venomous blasts at people he despised—at his personal and professional enemies. It hurt her to think that he now considered her an enemy.

The phone started ringing again. Instead of answering, she looked at the caller ID. It was Ray again. She let her voice mail pick it up.

Nate's car turned into the lot, and Ellie felt a sense of relief wash through her. She walked out and was waiting before he could pull up to the door.

"Are you okay?" he asked as soon as she opened the door.

She gave a small nod and put their bags into the back seat before getting in.

"What's wrong?" he asked more gently, reaching across the seat to her and touching her face.

Her phone rang again. Ellie's anger bubbled over when she saw Ray's name flash on the display again.

"Please excuse me for a minute, I have a personal problem that needs to be settled."

She got out of the car and walked a few steps away before turning on the phone.

"Listen to me, Ray," she blasted as a greeting. "I don't know what the hell got you going on this, but as an old friend—as someone who has been looking up to you all her life—I deserve to be treated better."

"Babycakes, I was joking."

"No, you weren't," she snapped. "But I want to tell you something. Just as I've respected your desire for privacy all these years, I expect you to respect mine. I find it wrong and hurtful to make fun of something that is private and intimate. And I would appreciate it if you'd stop harassing me just for your own entertainment.''

"Wow." There was a long pause. "I apologize, baby."

Ellie shoved her fingers into her hair and looked up at the sky in frustration. Ray continued with his apologies, and she felt tears well up in her eyes. This was so much like him—hurt you and then try to lick the wound.

"I have to go," she said in a more controlled voice, not willing to let him off the hook so soon. "We can talk about this later."

"Wait," he said before she disconnected. "You'll want to hear this."

Ellie listened to what he had to say, clicked off the phone and walked back to the car.

"You told him off. Way to go," Nate said proudly. "Feel better?"

She nodded.

"So what was Ray's problem this morning?"

"He got the call. He thinks one might be waiting for us, too."

"The auction?"

Ellie nodded. "This coming Friday. But there's a preview on Wednesday. In Newport."

The two men came through the stairwell door and quietly stood watching as a heart-attack victim was wheeled out of the elevator. All of the staff present jumped into the fray as they worked together hooking the man up to the life-support machines.

One of the two visitors, a black man wearing a sport jacket and tie, nodded toward the end of the critical-care unit where Tom McGill lay sleeping. Wordlessly, they moved into the unit and approached the "on duty" desk.

One of the nurses at the far end hurried toward them. "Can I help you?"

The black man took a badge from his jacket pocket and showed it to her. As she looked from the man's weathered face to his square build and then back at the picture ID, he produced some paperwork that he handed her, as well.

After scanning it, she picked up the phone. "I'll get help immediately."

The phone conversation was brief, and she could feel the man's eyes boring into her. When she hung up, the two men moved a few paces down the glass partition.

She stuffed the paperwork into her side pocket and looked back at the patient, surprised that anyone had authorized moving Tom McGill so soon.

Twenty-Four

The traffic had been heavy all along the way, a situation that only added to Nate's growing sense of frustration. A few times, when everything had come to a standstill, he was sorry that he hadn't arranged for a chopper to take them back from Ticonderoga. It was almost three in the afternoon when the skyline of Philadelphia came into view.

He wanted to go directly to Sister Helen's convent. After talking to McGill, he was concerned about Christopher's safety, and he had a bad feeling that there were some crucial pieces of the story that the eight-year-old might have left out. Ellie had called Sister Helen, and she assured both of them that there was not even a remote possibility that Chris would be stepping out of the house. In fact, he wouldn't even leave his room. She had also said that Christopher had something to tell Nate when they arrived.

Ray had been correct about the auction. After talking to him this morning, Ellie called her answering machine in Philadelphia and, sure enough, a message had been left only minutes before by the mysterious connection with the British accent. And this time the information was much more specific. If Ellie's client was still interested in the previously discussed property, then they should check into the hotel on Goat Island in Newport, Rhode Island, this coming Wednesday. More information regarding a preview of the property and the specific time of the auction would be communicated to them in the hotel on that day.

Nate decided not to call Hawes with the news until he was done talking to Chris again. Apparently, the waiting game was over.

Nate remembered Ellie's charity event. "What about your celebrity auction Thursday night? Do you think we'll be done by then?"

"I don't know. It all depends if they have the preview of the Morris flag right before the auction or the night before the actual event." She shrugged. "But it's no big deal. If I have to miss it, then I'll miss it."

"But you're co-chairing the event."

"I know. But it would actually be a relief if I ended up not being there for it." Her tone was sincere.

"Why?"

"I believe in the fund-raising aspect of the event. Augusta Biddle is hung up on the celebrity end of it. I want to give a huge check to the hospital. She wants to throw a marvelous party. Our goals make a difference. And we've already had a couple of minor tiffs." She stretched and stifled a yawn. "My work on the auction is pretty much done. There are only last-minute details about the appraisals and the follow-up letters to donors that I'll take care of. And as much as she'll complain loudly to anyone who will listen, I don't believe Augusta would mind at all if I canceled my appearance at the actual event."

"I'm sorry." Nate took her hand and brought it to his lips. "I'm totally messing things up for you."

She entwined her fingers with his. "You have my permission to keep messing."

Nate glanced at her and felt the hard tug on his heart. She was under his skin. Ellie and all that was happening between them was forcing him to rethink his life, his career and where he was going. Everything was changing now, even his old loyalties.

He turned his attention back on the road, forcing himself to focus. There was still a lot left to do.

When they arrived in South Philly, a ball game was in the team-picking stage in the street in front of the convent. As they'd been told, Christopher was not among the kids outside.

Sister Helen quickly told them everything that had happened with Chris since Friday night. She also said that since the eight-year-old had spoken to Ted Hardy the night before, he was visibly less agitated. But he'd also asked at least a dozen times today when Nate would be coming back.

He went up and found Chris sprawled on his stomach in the small bedroom at the top of the stairs. He was doing a puzzle. As Helen had told them, Chris's window was closed. But the door to the hallway had been left open.

"Can I come in?"

Chris's brown eyes flicked up at him with an expression of recognition and then relief. The little boy nodded and scrambled quickly to a sitting position. It was easy to forget how young he was and how frightening everything must be, having no one. Nate sat on the floor and stretched his legs out in front of him. The hours in the car had left his knee aching.

He took a look at the partially finished dinosaur puzzle. "This thing is one complicated monster. How many pieces is it, anyway?"

"Two hundred."

"Two hundred?" he drawled. "I never graduated past those wooden puzzles with the little handles that you fit inside the shapes."

Chris bit his lip, but Nate saw the trace of a smile. "Now, who would get you something like this?"

"Miss Ellie. She bought me those books, too." He pointed to the neatly stacked pile on the shelf beside the bed.

"I hope they have lots of pictures in them."

Chris took one down. "Some. Most of them are chapter books." He leafed through one to show him.

"Any big words?"

He gave a big nod. "Lots."

"That's it." Nate leaned on his elbow and grabbed one of the puzzle pieces. "I'm not sending *her* my Christmas list." He connected a corner piece to a middle one.

"You're pretty funny," Chris said, giggling and taking out the piece Nate had put in incorrectly.

"And you're pretty smart." He looked at the puzzle. "Will you show me how you do this thing?"

Chris leaned over the puzzle, grabbed a few pieces and explained with a grave face about corner and edge pieces. He showed Nate how trying to do those first made the rest easier.

Nate followed the eight-year-old's step-by-step directions and put a piece in correctly.

"You learn fast," Chris said encouragingly.

"I have an excellent teacher." Nate put another piece in and got a high five for his effort.

Although he knew Chris had specifically asked to talk to him, he let their conversation circle around the puzzle for now. When there were only half a dozen pieces left, Nate hid one in his hand. When that was the only piece remaining, he watched Chris search under and over everything. Then he triumphantly revealed the puzzle piece.

There was a mad wrestle for it, and of course Christopher was the victor.

"I won!" the boy said gleefully, fitting in the final piece.

They both sat cross-legged and stared at the fierce teeth of the *Tyrannosaurus rex* for a while. At the predator's feet, there was a young herbivore of some kind, freshly killed.

"It would have been tough putting one of those babies in jail," Nate commented.

"Do you think if they lived today, they'd be the bad guys?"

"Only some of them." Nate stood the puzzle box up next to their completed project. "I imagine we would have found as many bad brontosauruses and stegosauruses. You can't always tell the bad guy by his sharp teeth."

"Are you saying that some of the people who everyone thinks should be good guys, are bad?"

"Maybe a very small 'some.' But that's certainly a possibility." Nate had to tread lightly here. He didn't want to destroy Chris's future trust in the "good guys."

"But if they're the good guys and everyone believes they are...and they do something bad...and a kid knows...then there's no way anyone would believe the kid's word over theirs."

"There are people who take an eight-year-old's word very seriously."

"Like you?" Chris asked quietly.

"Like me. Would you tell me what you saw at the museum?"

Chris started taking the puzzle apart piece by piece. "They'll hurt me."

"I'll stop them. I'll put them behind bars, and they'll never touch you."

The brown eyes turned huge. "Can you really do that?"

Nate nodded.

Chris cast a worried look in the direction of the closed window. Without saying anything, he crawled on all fours past Nate and pushed the bedroom door until it was only open a crack. He came back, sat cross-legged next to Nate and started to talk.

Ellie saw the basement door was open. She hesitated a moment, took a deep breath and headed for it. She didn't know if Lou was downstairs or not. She was resolved, though, to take the first step. Let the chips fall where they will.

Her stomach was doing somersaults as she started down the stairs. She paused and took a deep breath. The bottom step was as far as she'd allowed herself to go in the past. But she was determined. Still, as she descended each stair, another page in their life flickered through her memory.

She was the only kid in the first grade who always made her own lunch. She walked to school alone and went home alone. Her father couldn't show up for parents' nights or the teacher conferences, and Ellie scribbled his initials on the report cards herself.

Not that any of that upset her. He loved her. He was proud of her. He always came home before she went to bed at night, and she was his precious little girl.

She went down a step.

She had five A's on her report card in fifth grade and zero friends her age. She'd changed schools three times since first grade. She was small, awkward and didn't know what it was like to be a kid. She was in charge of everything at their apartment and understood that what Lou did for a living was illegal. She had no dreams or expectations of the future, and she was content with her father's love.

Another step.

She was twelve years old and still as flat-chested as a boy. Getting A's was a breeze. Finding friends was impossible. A social outcast among the seventh-graders, her favorite hobby was sitting next to Home-less Jack on Rittenhouse Square and watching people.

She took another step.

That same year, they came and took Lou away to jail. She was angry, scared, but she managed by herself with no problem. It took them a couple of months to catch up to her, but eventually she was placed in a home. She ran away. They caught her and put her in another home. Ellie ran away again. She dropped out of school and shoplifted groceries to feed herself. Lived out of a gym bag and camped out a night here and a night there on the floors of Lou's old friends, but it was scary that she had no real roof over her head.

She went down another step.

Ray Claiborne was Lou's fence. He was a deal maker. He knew everyone. He had a steady business going in the art and antique world, and he was gener-ous. He had always been nice to Ellie, so she went to him begging.

Ray had no use for a twelve-year-old girl. He was not a pimp, and he had little interest in charity work.

Ellie talked him into giving her a room in exchange for doing work for him. She was smart, hardworking, loyal and a quick learner. He agreed, if only because he knew he owed her father for keeping quiet about him.

Ellie descended to the next step.

She started stealing for him—small jobs at first, but then larger ones. Ray was the middleman, and he took no personal risks. Sometimes he made the contacts; other times he'd give her a heads-up on a solo job. Either way, he was protected. Then he'd liquidate the property himself afterward.

She was arrested only once. She was sixteen. She shut her mouth and they gave her two years in the juvenile detention center. Two years.

Ellie stood on the landing halfway down and blinked back the tears that were blurring her vision. Those were her two years in hell.

When she got out of the can, she went to see Lou in jail. He treated her as if she was the biggest disappointment of his life—like she'd had a choice in becoming a thief.

Ellie went down another step.

Ray Claiborne was happy to take her back, but she didn't want to steal anymore. He started her on other jobs. Learning the business of dealing antiques. Working in auction houses. She learned fast, focused on the job and became good at it. Later on, Ray started Ellie in her own business.

She took another step.

She was financially secure by the time Lou came out of jail. She'd wanted him to come and live with her— to be part of her life—but he wouldn't have anything

to do with her. He told her once point-blank that he
didn't have a daughter.

By the time Ellie reached the bottom step, she had
to scramble in her pocket for a tissue. Her cheeks were
wet with tears.

Lou's basement apartment was empty. Ellie told herself she was here to mend things, not to stir up a pot
full of hurt. Sometime this year, thanks to Sister
Helen's intervention, they'd started talking a little.
They would tolerate each other in the same room. It
wasn't enough, Ellie told herself again. She was here
because she wanted more.

Ray had done a lot for her, but he'd always stressed
that their relationship was business. Lou, on the other
hand, was the only father—the only family—she had
ever had.

There were a number of frames high in the bookcases that drew her into the apartment. She'd spotted
them the last time she was here, when she'd been sitting on the steps and talking about forgeries with Nate,
Sister Helen and her father. But from that far away,
she couldn't tell who was in the pictures.

She was surprised to find they were pictures of her
as a kid. There was about an inch of dust on each
frame. Ellie scanned the bookcases and then moved to
the canvas on the easel in the corner. She walked
around it and smiled. He'd been painting this room,
but he'd made the walls into endless vistas of field and
forest and the ceiling into a blue, cloud-dotted sky.

A thick photo album was sitting on a table next to
his ratty old easy chair. Ellie was always fascinated by
photo albums. They occasionally came her way
through estate sales and auctions. She'd never known

enough people to put together one herself. She sat on her father's chair and opened it on her lap.

The first page was startlingly empty, except for a tiny newspaper clipping of a hospital birth notice.

This was a vision from a dream. Lou didn't want to make a noise. Ellie was bent over the one possession he truly valued—the scrapbook of her.

He'd gone through it so many times that he knew exactly what was pasted on each page. The funny sketches from the time when she'd been little more than a toddler. The report cards from elementary school. The handmade birthday and Christmas cards that Ellie had given him when she'd been little. He hadn't stopped adding to his collection. He also had recent clippings of her giving a class at some school, or being one of the organizers for one project or another. His latest addition had been a copy of an interview a local magazine had done with Ellie about her business. Lou had been damned proud the way she'd come across—smart, savvy, involved in the community, compassionate. Damned proud.

When she was a child, Lou had considered her a gift from heaven. She was smart as a whip, never complained, took care of herself and him. And God knows, he didn't deserve her. He was no father. How badly he'd let her down as a child and then even worse later on, when she'd just been released from the detention center.

He tried to swallow around the lump caused by his lifelong failure with her. He would have been content to stand on the stairs all night and just watch her cuddled up on that bench in his room. But the moment he saw her wipe the tears off her face, he couldn't take it anymore. He descended the rest of the steps.

Ellie lifted her head from the album, and she quickly closed it and jumped to her feet. "I hope you don't mind."

He shook his head.

She put the album back on the bench and wiped her palms on the seat of her pants. "We just got back a little while ago."

"How was your weekend?"

His question seemed to throw her off a minute. "It was...nice. Very nice. I met Nate's family."

"Are they anything like him?"

"Very much." She smiled.

"That's good. I like him." He opened his fridge and looked inside. "I have beer and chocolate milk. Do you still drink the stuff?"

"Sure. I love chocolate milk."

"I didn't know if you still did or not." Lou felt his heart growing warm. "But I've been buying these for a while—in case you happened to come down." He tossed her a carton.

She caught it and looked at the bottom. "They do have an expiration date on these things."

"I throw them away every couple of weeks and buy new ones." He took a glass out of the cabinet next to the fridge and offered it to her. "I would never do anything to hurt you again, Ellie."

She put the glass down and walked into his arms.

"I know, Dad."

"Are you serious about putting the kid into the witness protection program?" Hawes's tone was doubtful at best.

"There's been an attempt on his life. That's a good enough reason for me," Nate said into the phone.

"But there's no proof of that. You said yourself that nobody else saw anyone push him. Another kid could have bumped him from behind. There are hundreds of ways to explain—"

"Listen to me, Sanford," Nate said more forcefully. "The boy says he saw a gadget of some kind on the frame that held the Schuyler flag. That was the same incendiary device that our people found remnants of later. There's no way he could lie about that. More important, Chris believes he can identify the security guard who was in there. He even thinks he might be able to narrow down what the two guys who'd been chasing after him looked like. Don't you think that's reason enough to protect him?"

"Of course it is," Hawes barked. "If it's true. But he's changed his story from a week ago, and I just have a feeling he might be pulling our legs."

"But you'll start the ball rolling on it," Nate pressed.

"Okay, goddammit. I'll start the paperwork. But *you* have got to focus on bringing that fucking flag back this week."

"Wednesday. I told you before, we're going up there this Wednesday."

"Good. I'll arrange to have the kid picked up in a couple of hours."

"By the way…" Nate grimaced before continuing. "Chris won't be alone."

"What do you mean?"

"One of the nuns—her name is Sister Lisa—she's agreed to go and stay with Chris for a while until we get him settled."

After a moment of dead silence, a stream of obscenities exploded from the receiver.

"Sister Lisa goes with him," Nate insisted a few seconds later.

"I can't!" Hawes blasted again. "I can't drag any more civilians into this. I'll send a goddamn female agent, if I have to. I'll drag that drugged-out slut of a mother of his out of that trailer and bring her along. But no fucking nuns."

Nate walked to the door of the living room and glanced up the stairs. Chris was sitting on the top step, his baseball hat on, a zippered gym bag on his lap. An unopened box of Lucky Charms was tucked under his arm. Ellie appeared at the top of the stairs and sat down next to the boy.

Nate was not going to lose this one.

"No, Hawes. Forget that I made the suggestion. I'll take care of it." Nate backed into the room before talking into the phone again.

"You have an assignment that takes precedence over any—"

"I'll get him local protection until the flag is in our hands. Chris can lie low here in Philly until I'm done with the assignment. We can run the pictures and suspects and everything else by the kid afterward."

"Nate!"

"I'm doing my job, Sanford. We'll get the flag and handle the details of this later."

"Nate!"

"Forget it. We'll talk about this next week," Nate said, disconnecting the phone.

Twenty-Five

Wednesday, June 30

The limo sped along the ribbon of highway from the train station in Kingston toward Newport. The trip to Rhode Island had been uneventful, and Ellie stared out at the towers of the Newport Bridge, rising far above the white-fringed waters of the Narragansett Bay.

She hadn't seen Nate since he took Chris from Sister Helen's on Monday night. He'd called her three times since then, but the conversations each time had been short and to the point. Nate was not offering any specifics about Chris, and Ellie understood why. She'd seen enough movies to know how the witness protection program worked.

As upset as she was to see Chris go, she understood the danger he was in. The night at Teasdale's house was still fresh in her memory. Nate believed Theo Atwood's death might be related, too…and no accident. Ellie asked no questions when he called.

On the train ride from Philly, she spent a lot of time thinking about Nate's conspiracy theory. He believed the same group of people who had destroyed the flag were trying to stop them from replacing it now with a forgery. This gave her a lot to think about.

In the collector's world, one remaining artifact of this magnitude was much better than two. The value of the remaining item generally rocketed upward, and its owner profited by the destruction of the other. But if that was what was going on here, then Nate's theory didn't make sense to her. Ellie couldn't imagine the owner of the remaining Betsy Ross flag being the culprit, because the value would only go up if the interested collectors *knew* that the other artifact had been destroyed. In this case, there hadn't even been whispers in the wind about the loss of the Schuyler flag. That meant someone else had to be benefiting. But who? It didn't make sense.

There was very little traffic on the bridge, and it was about three when the limo crossed the causeway leading out to Goat Island and pulled up in front of the hotel. The suite Ellie had booked for them was ready, but Nate had yet to appear.

Kathleen Rivers, the blond collector she'd met at Ray's party, arrived right behind her, sweeping into the lobby with three bellhops in tow. Unable to avoid her, Ellie had to make some small talk before peeling the woman off.

There were no messages waiting for her in the suite. Ellie turned off the air-conditioning, opened all the windows in the two-story unit and let the ocean breeze rush in. The blue of the sky with its puffs of clouds scudding by reminded her of Lou's painting. For the first time ever, her father had dropped by the shop yesterday morning. The two of them still had a long road ahead, but now Ellie felt they had a chance. She blinked back tears and moved about the spacious bedroom, putting her luggage away.

Ten minutes later she was standing by the open window again, watching the sailboats and yachts on the bay. She went back inside. She couldn't sit still. She knew a large part of her restlessness had to do with not seeing Nate. They'd become so close in such a short time. She'd been a loner all her life, and yet now she craved his company around the clock.

She explored the suite—a single king-size bed, a spacious bathroom easily accommodating two, a spiral staircase leading to a generous sitting area with a wet bar. Ellie couldn't wait for him to get here.

There was a knock, and Ellie practically ran to open the door. A valet delivered an envelope. Inside, there was an invitation for seven o'clock at a private address in Newport for the preview of the property to be auctioned. She glanced at her watch and hoped Nate was on schedule.

It was preposterous to have him go to Newport, but then stay in a hotel like some tourist. Ray glanced with distaste at the run-of-the-mill furniture. Whoever designed these places should be shot. Sipping his drink, he walked to the window overlooking the pool. No wonder these hotels changed hands every few years. It was insulting.

The boring affair was to be at seven. He looked across the causeway leading from town. The harbor was filled with yachts and sailboats, and the town of Newport, with its steeples and clapboard and redbrick, lay beyond. He considered calling an old friend or two and setting something up after the preview.

From experience he knew, though, that he would just be opening the waterworks. After that, there'd be no end to the calls and invitations and parties. Bad idea, he decided. His client wouldn't like that at all. Kathleen would feel deserted for the three days that they were stuck in this place.

Ray's attitude improved a little when he saw Ellie walk into the pool area and sit down on a lounge chair. There wasn't another soul by the pool, and she dumped a pile of newspapers onto the chair beside her. He waited for Nate to follow her in, but there was no sign of him.

"Where there's honey, boys and girls," he said out loud, "the bee is never far off."

Refilling his drink, he started down to the pool.

The "city by the sea" had too much to offer on such a beautiful day for the tourists to be hanging around the pool. The beaches, the shops, the restaurants were all prepared for the holiday weekend onslaught, and the early birds were no doubt reaping the rewards. Although Ellie certainly had no interest in going into town or going to the beach, she was too wound up— and worried about Nate—to sit in their room.

She almost groaned aloud when she saw Ray amble into the pool area. She resigned herself to being civil, however, and moved the papers for him as he came over.

"Am I forgiven?"

Dressed fashionably for the occasion as always, he stood in front of her with his head bent to the side. Ellie would have loved to rip into him good for his inappropriate comments the other day, but she was well accustomed to the older man's fleeting moods. There was really no point in it.

"Are you going swimming?" she asked, evading the question.

"What for?" He put his drink on a table and sat

down on the lounge chair next to hers. "I'm sure the water is freezing, and I have no audience to show off the cut of my new swim trunks."

"No audience?" she asked good-naturedly. "What am I?"

"Unfortunately, a woman." He gave a dramatic sigh and stretched his legs on the chair. "So where's your *man?*"

Ellie forced herself to count, breathe, and then answer. He hadn't said anything demeaning...yet. "He hasn't arrived. But I expect him any minute."

"My client, Kathleen Rivers, is here." He sipped his drink.

"I saw her in the lobby."

"Yes, she's impossible to miss. Quite eye-catching and very much the shrewd businesswoman, I'm finding."

"You certainly can't hold that against her." She glanced at Ray's pensive expression. "She picked you, Ray. That certainly gains her a few points."

"Yes, but she is also pushing up my expenses. Giving me last-minute headaches. She's being very difficult."

"Maybe you should just tell her to forget it. You know, forget about the flag."

"Nice try, babycakes." He saluted her and took another sip of his drink. "I wouldn't be too quick to wish her away, if I were you. What she wants to do would serve your client well, too. And all the other rich amateurs who'll be there tonight and haven't a clue what they're bidding on."

Ellie guessed he was talking about a way to confirm that the flag was genuine. Though she really didn't think it appropriate to share the information with Ray or his client, she'd talked to Nate in Philadelphia about getting Dr. Wilcox from the Smithsonian flown in to Newport to verify the flag's authenticity on the day of the auction. Of course, she first needed to get the seller's approval, which she intended to do tonight. Nate was going to check with Wilcox.

"Mrs. Rivers wants to bring an expert in?"

Ray nodded. "Some dusty old Ph.D. from Penn. Two or three years ago he apparently published an article on the possibility of this flag still being around. Kathleen says that reading his article was what interested her in the first place. Anyway, she's having me bring this guy up. If the creeps running the auction let us, our old boy gives it his stamp of approval or something."

"I can't see why they'd be against it."

Ray shrugged. "We'll find out tonight."

Ellie's pulse bumped up a few beats when she saw Nate walk into the pool area. He was wearing khaki pants and a hunter-green polo shirt, and she guessed he'd just arrived.

Ray followed the direction of her gaze. "Well, well, well. Isn't he the sight for sore eyes?"

At least they agreed on something.

Ray stood up and shook Nate's hand. "Speak of the devil. Ellie was just saying she hoped you'd be a no-show tonight."

"Did she, now?" Nate smiled at Ellie as she shook her head from side to side. "Maybe there's enough time for me to change her mind."

He leaned down and kissed her slowly and thoroughly. By the time he pulled back, every inch of her body was tingling.

"So what time is this affair?"

Ray answered. "Seven. Plenty of time to do fifty or sixty laps to burn off all that extra energy you kids obviously have. We could have cocktails at six and leave here at forty-five minutes past. Fifteen minutes should be plenty of time to get there."

Nate pulled Ellie to her feet. She gathered up her key, cell phone and the newspapers.

"We'll see you at the preview at seven," he said cheerfully to Ray. Putting a hand on Ellie's waist, Nate strolled with her toward the hotel doors.

A family of four and a half shared the elevator with them. When Ellie and Nate entered, the boy and girl— who both looked to be about six—were wrestling to see who would press the button for their floor. In the end, the twins pressed them all, and as their father tried to quietly control the pair of wild things, the elevator door opened and closed at each floor. The woman's maternity dress was stretched to the max, but she looked quite happy and relaxed in the midst of the chaos.

Nate stood behind Ellie and placed his hand over her flat stomach. Her face turned upward to his, and she smiled. At that moment, Nate knew he'd never wanted anything in life more than this woman.

As luck would have it, the family was staying on the same floor, two doors down from them. Ellie handed him the key card, and as he started to swipe it, she put her hand over his. "Chris?"

"He's doing okay."

She smiled and nodded. He opened the door, and Ellie went in ahead of him. She dropped the newspapers and her phone on the nearest table and then turned to him.

"The place is beautiful. You have to see the view."

Nate locked the door and leaned against it. He tossed the key on the same table. "I'm seeing it now."

She walked toward him, and then his mouth was fused with hers, his hands molding her body against his. It was madness, this urgent need in both of them. It felt like a first time. Their hunger for each other should have been satiated after their weekend. But it had only become more intense.

"God, I missed you," he said hoarsely.

Ellie's mouth, soft, desiring, invited him in. She tugged his shirt free of his pants. Her hands swept over his back, his belly.

"I was going crazy waiting for you." Her fingers slid downward. "I don't know what you've done to me, Murtaugh. But I was lost without you."

His lips brushed over her face and down to the soft lines of her throat. "Where's the bed?" he asked.

She pointed him toward the stairs, and they somehow managed to climb to the next floor without any mishaps. In the bedroom, all the windows were open. The sheer curtains danced to the rhythmic whispers of the ocean breeze. Nate stood Ellie next to the bed and peeled the silky sundress from her body.

"I was stopped twice for speeding today."

The white bathing suit was the only thing that separated his hands and mouth from her body.

"Did they give you a ticket?" She pulled off his shirt, her lips caressing his chest and neck.

"Not a chance."

He lowered the straps of her bathing suit and it slid down her legs. Ellie unzipped his pants and helped him as he shed the rest of his clothes.

"They must have been intimidated by your...by your badge."

Nate's lips twitched. They fell onto the bed, and their naked bodies entwined. "No. But they were impressed by my story."

Gathering her hands on top of her head, he pressed his body against hers. A moment later, their bodies joined, and Ellie's dark eyes clouded with passion.

"What was your story?" she whispered huskily.

"I told them I was impatient to get here..."

"That's no story."

"Because I had to tell someone that I love her."

The preview was not held at some prestigious Bellevue Avenue or Ocean Drive address. The sprawling French château-style home by the country club, however, with its cone-topped towers and rolling lawns, expressed elegance of a more private nature. The location suited the occasion perfectly.

This was far from a social gathering. No food or drinks were served, and there was almost no interaction between the competing parties. Nate and Ellie were the last of the invitees to arrive. In all, it appeared that there were about a dozen and a half guests, three servants and Robert Philips in attendance. Philips, a fiftyish gray-haired, pleasant-faced man whose British accent was quite familiar to Ellie, introduced himself to everyone in the library, making it clear that he was not the owner of the artifact, but only serving as the agent and auctioneer for the owner. He went on to explain in detail the rules of the sale.

"The flag is presently in a protective frame in the dining room. I shall personally escort each one of you and your agent, if you have one present, to inspect the artifact.'' Philips glanced about the room. ''In the dining room, you are welcome to take as much time as is reasonable to study the item. I'll be more than happy to answer any questions you might have. Afterward, one of the attendants will escort you out. I ask that you return to your hotel and wait there for further instructions from me.''

''How long do you expect us to wait, for Chrissakes?'' one of the guests asked irritably.

''I'm afraid that all depends on how much time the other interested parties here take. In the spirit of fairness, we've arranged it so you will be taken to the dining room in the same order that you arrived here.''

''That means you and I will be last,'' Ellie whispered to Nate.

''Maybe Philips will be worn out by the time we go in and just give us the flag.''

''Forever hopeful.''

''That optimism has already paid off for me, hasn't it?''

Ellie didn't miss his meaningful look. She herself was still suspended halfway between reality and dream. Nate's declaration of love hung like some ethereal presence before her. She just wasn't sure if what he'd told her was the truth. After all, they'd been joking about his ''story'' for the police officers. Then again, she didn't know if he'd even really been pulled over. She was too afraid to ask. She was too afraid to put her heart out there and have it stepped on.

The fact that their lovemaking had stretched into the evening had curtailed her opportunity to talk to Nate about what was happening between them. Not that Ellie was a very good communicator when it came to sensitive matters like that, anyway. It had only taken her eighteen years to start a positive dialogue with her father.

The preview began promptly with Philips ushering an Asian-American gentleman and a colleague from the room. As a group, those left in the library glanced at their watches. Ellie checked the time on the large grandfather clock standing between two long windows.

"Did you talk to Wilcox? Ray said his client was bringing someone in."

With a hand on the small of her back, Nate ushered Ellie toward the French doors overlooking some meticulously manicured rose gardens.

"Yeah. Unfortunately, with everything that he already has on his plate for Sunday, there's no way he or anybody on his payroll can get out here. He said he feels confident that this is the real McCoy, though. Apparently, word of the flag is out and the academic types he's connected with have their boxers in a knot about it. Bottom line is he thinks with such a buzz going and all this money gathered here, we should go for it."

"I wish I could be so trusting."

"You don't trust this Philips?"

"I can't help myself. Don't forget that I was raised by thieves and crooks." She brushed a speck of lint off Nate's jacket collar. "Kathleen Rivers, though, is taking a more conservative approach." She told him what Ray had said about the University of Pennsylvania professor coming in to look at the flag.

"Well, now we know who put the word out to the mortarboard circuit." He gathered her closer to his side. "And speak of the devil."

She turned and watched the two people who were weaving their way toward them. Kathleen Rivers appeared agitated. Ellie wasn't sure if the possessiveness that Nate showed whenever Ray was near was for her sake or his own. But she loved it, anyway.

"Somewhat uncivilized, I'd say, that this crowd couldn't even serve drinks," she said, looking over her shoulder.

"When are you going in?" Ellie asked Ray.

"A couple of groups before yours."

"What do you think of the competition?" Nate asked the older man.

"What competition? The only two who have a chance at it are right here." He looked at Nate, then patted his client's hand gently. He turned to Ellie next. "It's between you and me, babycakes. Fist to fist. Bare knuckles."

Ellie gave a small nod, accepting the challenge. She wasn't cowed. What Ray didn't know about Nate was that there was practically no limit on how much he was authorized to pay for the flag. On the other hand, Ellie had been able to gather through her Augusta Biddle connections that Kathleen Rivers was in the middle of a discreet and yet expensive divorce—her third. The way the rumors went, a settlement was nearly finalized and a very large sum would be transferred from Kathleen to her previously penniless artist husband with the signing of the final divorce papers. To Ellie's way of thinking, this had to create a ceiling to Rivers's available funds.

"I need some fresh air." Mrs. Rivers took Ray's arm. "Show me the gardens."

She was obviously accustomed to having her way. Ellie and Nate watched them walk outside onto the terrace and down the steps into the gardens. They made a very striking pair.

"If Ray doesn't watch out, he might end up being a prime candidate for slot number four."

"A fourth marriage?" Nate asked.

Ellie nodded and smiled. "And Ray would jump at the opportunity. He'll do anything for her kind of money."

Everyone's gaze was drawn to the door as Philips returned to the room and left a moment later with the second interested party. There was no way to tell how the first potential buyer had responded to seeing the flag.

Nate's fingers pushed a strand of her hair behind her ear. She turned to him.

"I have a question for you," he said in a low voice. "I was wondering what made you decide to go to the Fort Ticonderoga Museum. The Friday that the flag was destroyed."

She looked up, surprised. His expression was unreadable. "I told you before. I was meeting with John Dubin, and he was taking me to a—"

"No, not that. I mean why that date and not all the other times that you might have gone up there?"

Ellie didn't know where he was going with this, but she trusted him to have a good reason. "Ray called me. He'd read about the Schuyler flag being handed over to the Department of the Interior brass that day for the Spirit of America thing, so he thought since I was up there, I should go see it."

She watched Nate look at the faces of the people around the room. "Why do you ask?"

"I don't know. I was just curious."

"Come on," she prodded gently. "You can do better than that."

He looked around again. Everyone appeared preoccupied within their own individual groups. "I don't believe in coincidences."

"Do you think the fact that I was up there was orchestrated?" Ellie lowered her voice. "Is Ray a suspect?"

"At this point, everyone is a suspect." He took her hand. His eyes were filled with tenderness when they met hers. "No matter how this whole thing turns out, meeting you has been by far the best part of this assignment. So if Ray ends up being one of the guilty parties, I suppose I'll just have to let him live."

Twenty-Six

Thursday, July 1

Kathleen Rivers asked her accountant to stay on the line until the wait staff finished arranging the breakfast on the table beside the window. She tipped the two young men and waited for them to leave before continuing.

"I'm back." She poured herself a cup of coffee. "Where were we?"

"You wanted to transfer another thirty million dollars to your antiques account before 10:00 a.m. tomorrow morning," the man said wearily from the other end.

"Now that I think of it, make it an additional forty. Yes, I want a total of a hundred million in that account."

No negotiations. Kathleen was not about to give her long-time financial adviser a chance to talk her out of it, so she immediately changed the topic to a private yacht that was moored at Goat Island and how she suspected the owners might be a friend of a friend. A knock on the door gave her a reason to cut the conversation short, though, and she hung up.

"Thank you for joining me here. You're absolutely

precious, Ray." She brushed her cheek against his and held the door open for him to come in.

Kathleen assessed him from behind with the eye of a connoisseur. For a man his age, he was quite fit. Still had his hair. Good shoulders. Trim waist. And a very nice butt, which was a requirement for her with regard to men. Kathleen knew from experience that you can't drive a spike with a tack hammer.

"Breakfast." He glanced at the large spread of food. "How did you know I was starving?"

"You are a dear and a sweet liar." She tightened the belt of her robe and led the way to the food. "I know you're an early riser. And I also know that you already had your breakfast around seven downstairs."

He glanced at his watch. "It's ten-thirty. I'm ready for the next course."

"That's what I was hoping." With a flourish, she removed the covers from the eggs, the waffles, the fruits, and tipped the basket of pastries for his inspection. "There's tea and coffee and orange juice. Make a plate for yourself and come and join me on the sofa. We have some work ahead of us this morning."

Kathleen took her own plate and a napkin to the sofa and settled herself with her legs tucked beneath her. "What time is the appraisal being done today?"

"I was hoping it would be done this morning. But I still haven't seen your professor friend." Ray made himself a cup of tea. "When I spoke to him last night, he mentioned that he was planning to leave very early and drive up. But traffic is always heavy around a long weekend like this and—"

"Don't worry about it." She popped a piece of melon in her mouth and waved her fork at him. "If he gets here, he gets here. If he doesn't, he doesn't."

Ray started fixing a plate.

"Actually, after seeing that flag last night," she continued, "I don't think I need the opinion of any expert to tell me if that's the *real* thing or not."

"Oh?" he asked, coming and joining her on the sofa as she slid her plate onto the coffee table.

"Do you ever get that feeling in your gut that you *have* to have something?"

He put his plate on the coffee table, as well. "Occasionally...and if the price is right."

She sipped her coffee and shook her head. "No, no, no. I'm talking about the feeling that some antiques communicate to someone sensitive enough to feel it. It's an experience like no other. Do you know what I'm talking about?"

"Yes, I do. There's an energy source that accompanies some artifacts. I've heard of people who have a gift for experiencing it."

"I'm one of those people, Ray." She put her cup down.

"I'm not surprised."

"I remember the first time it happened to me. I was at an auction in Boston. I held in my hands a prayer book that Abigail Adams had held in her hands two hundred years ago, and I felt her spirit rush into me...just *rush* into me. In that instant, I knew her thoughts, her emotions. I saw her life in a moment. I *became* her."

"That must have been quite an experience."

"Yes, it was," she said fervently. "And that wasn't the only time. The same thing happened to me with a needlework sampler that Martha Washington did as a child. It was like electricity in my veins. I don't know how to explain it. When I touched that material, I could feel her in me. I could see her past, her future. I saw her life at Mount Vernon. She was alone quite a lot. Did you know that? She had her companions, of course, but she was alone. I felt that pain in her. In me.''

She paused as her vision blurred because of tears. She dabbed at them with the starched napkin. In a few seconds she continued.

"I have a rare gift within me. I connect with these women. I become the inheritor of their lives. Their protector.''

"You must be a very sensitive woman, Kathleen.''

"I felt it again last night.'' She reached for his hand and squeezed it. "The moment I touched the glass that held the flag, my spirit flew from my body.''

"I noticed that you seemed preoccupied.''

"My spirit transcended the moment. I traveled in an instant across centuries. Then, suddenly, I was with her. Elizabeth Ross. She, too, was alone. I could hear her children playing in the street outside. She was sewing. She was doing what she could to keep her life together. This flag was on her lap. She looked at me as if she were looking in a mirror. And then she held it out to me....''

Kathleen Rivers sat back against the cushions. Her outstretched hand dropped into her lap. Abruptly, she sat upright and turned to Ray. "That flag is mine. I must have it. It is my duty to have it. To protect it.''

"Kathleen,'' Ray started, his tea untouched in his hand.

"I want to hear your strategy,'' she said calmly. "I must own that flag, no matter what it costs.''

The secluded stretch of grass on the cliffs overlooked the narrow passage where the Narragansett Bay met the Atlantic Ocean. Located just south of Fort Adams Park, the place was like a secret hideaway. Just the top of the empty Eisenhower House was visible up the hill from the bluffs. The stone walls of the fort stretched out to guard the harbor's mouth to their right, and the water forty feet below them sparkled in the afternoon sunlight. Across the narrow passage, the rugged shoreline of Conanicut Island rose up, providing a lush green backdrop of pine for the occasional sailboat racing by. Together, Ellie and Nate lay on a blanket, the remains of their lunch on the grass.

The place seemed to belong just to them. Theirs was the only car on the gravel drive. And with the exception of the tour boat's horn as the vessel passed close to the cliffs on its way back and forth to Hammersmith Farm, the only other noises were the constant whoosh of the surf and the cries of the gulls floating above them on the fresh ocean breeze.

Nate, shirtless, lay on his back on the blanket. The sun warmed his skin. The light breeze kept him cool. Ellie, dressed in a white tank top and matching shorts, sat cross-legged on the blanket next to him. Occasionally, she would read aloud the clues from the crossword she was doing and torment him by giving the answer just as he was ready to tell her. Other times, she was looking after him—brushing off an ant or putting more sunscreen on his chest and face. Nate was being spoiled and he loved it. He couldn't remember the last time that he felt this relaxed and content.

All the same, he knew this time would be brief.

"Turned to the right," Ellie said. "It's a four-letter word. The second one is an *E*."

"Let me see it this time." He reached for the puzzle.

"No." She held it back out of his reach as if they were both six years old.

"I just want to look at it."

"No. You'll pretend you're taking one look and then do the rest of it on your own."

Nate grinned at her. He loved it when she got that stubborn look in her eyes. "Just because you play that way, that doesn't mean I'll do the same."

"It's *my* puzzle." She balanced the folded newspaper on her lap and wrote down some letters. "Never mind, I got it, anyway. The word is *geed.*"

"Give me another one."

She inched away on the blanket. "No, you're getting too cranky."

Nate grabbed her by the waist and wrestled her down onto the blanket until she was lying flat on her stomach, her body trapped by half of his weight. She'd somehow managed to stuff the newspaper under them.

"Can I please do the puzzle with you?" he whispered in her ear.

"This isn't a nice way to behave."

"You haven't seen anything yet."

He kissed the soft skin beneath her earlobe. Her face turned to him and he had to taste her lips. But he couldn't stop there. Ellie had the most arousing effect on him. The kiss deepened. His arm and leg gathered her more closely under him until there was no hiding the evidence of his hardening body as it pressed against her.

"This is a dangerous place to be doing this," she said teasingly as he broke the kiss.

"Let me help you with that puzzle or the people on that tour boat will be taking home some very explicit three-by-five mementos of their weekend in Newport."

"You're not scaring me."

She slid her hand along the front of his pants. Nate's head dropped on the blanket in defeat when she caressed him.

"But for the sake of not making a public scene, thereby avoiding arrest..." She pulled the newspaper out. "I'll let you look over my shoulder."

There was nothing Nate would have liked more at that moment than to drag Ellie behind one of the large boulders or into the back seat of the car and show her just how dangerous things had become.

She leaned on her elbows, found the pen and put the crumpled newspaper where he could see it, too. "Common expression. Five letters, the first letter is an *I*."

Nate's hand reached beneath her where her bare stomach was resting on the blanket. Her skin was smooth and warm, and he was becoming obsessed with the feel of it.

"Idiom," he said vacantly as his hand slid up under the tank top and cupped her breast.

This time, she was the one who took an unsteady breath.

"How come you're not writing it down?"

"You're the devil, Nate Murtaugh." She offered him the pen. "You write it down. I need to see where your hands are."

He took the pen, but his body remained draped over hers. His leg moved along the backs of her smooth thighs. He wrote down the letters.

She read the next block. "Chatter."

"Gab," they both answered at the same time.

They went through a few more clues, and each time it was a race to come up with the answer first. Nate drew up a little block in the corner and started keeping score. She tried to cheat by covering the questions with her hand for an extra few seconds to have a little head start. When the puzzle was done, Nate tallied up the score and wrote it down. They were close enough to call it a tie.

When Ellie stared at the final scores, he thought she was double-checking his math.

"Your fours and sevens…"

"What about them?"

"The way you write them." All traces of humor were gone from her face. She continued to stare at his handwriting. "Write down your cell phone number."

She knew his number; she'd called him on it several times. Nate didn't ask why, though, and wrote it down. There were two fours and one seven in the phone number.

She picked up the paper and frowned. Nate sat up. "What's the matter?"

"I can't believe I didn't recognize it."

"What?"

"At Teasdale's house, when I came in after you. There were things on one of his workbenches. Scraps of materials. Flag sketches. Other things, too."

"What about it?" Nate had only glanced at the stuff on his way through. He really hadn't had a chance to look at it closely, though, because the police had bagged and tagged it all while he was with Ellie during her questioning.

Ellie sat up, too. "I stood there with the envelope you'd given me under my arm, still sealed, but there were all these sketches and fabrics on that bench…like he already had the information."

"He might have done a little research up front. But

what does that have to do with the way I form the numbers?''

"In a partially open drawer right above that stuff, there was a torn piece of paper with a phone number on it. I was not too with it then. I looked at it, but I didn't think much of it. But now I remember, Nate. It was your cell phone number.'' She held the newspaper out so they could both see. "In *your* handwriting.''

Nate's mind raced. "That's impossible. I'd never met Teasdale before.''

"And I was the contact with him. He didn't know your undercover name or your real name, so he couldn't have known your cell phone number.'' She stared at the paper again. "Could he have known you from one of your other assignments?''

He shook his head. "Are you a hundred percent sure that it was my handwriting and my number?''

"I'm no handwriting expert, but I'm as certain as I can be.''

"If it was, then somehow that piece of paper was planted there.''

"Why?''

"To make it look as if I'd already been in contact with him.''

She nodded. "And they put it in a partially open drawer above the flag sketches.''

"Cops don't believe in coincidences, and I guarantee you they already know whose phone number that is, even if they haven't realized yet that it shouldn't have been there.''

"But why would someone bother?'' she asked thoughtfully. "After all, Teasdale was expecting us. We were planning to do business with him. There's no saying that I might not have given him your cell number instead of mine.''

''There's still the question of the handwriting being mine…and how it got there in the first place.''

They stood under one of the quaint gas lamps that lit the corner of Third and Bridge Street in Newport's Point Section. A fog had descended on the old seaport town, cloaking the colonial neighborhood with an atmosphere that was positively mysterious.

''Come downtown with me,'' Ray said.

Kathleen shook her blond head and pulled her Falchi purse onto her shoulder. ''No. The dinner, this place, everything was lovely.''

The little restaurant had given her the perfect opportunity to get Ray Claiborne away and observe and talk to him as they dined alone. And she knew now that he wouldn't be her next husband. She'd had enough of the artsy type. Perhaps what she needed now was a younger man. Perhaps an athlete.

''Let me call a cab for you, then,'' Ray persisted. He pointed off through the fog toward the brassierelike tents that stood beside the visitor's center. ''They are all right there.''

''No. Thank you, though.'' She looked down the deserted street. ''If it were clearer, we'd be able to see the hotel from here. It's just over the causeway.''

''I know, but…well, you're a big girl, Kathleen,'' he said, giving her a kiss on the cheek. ''I'm off to meet my friends at the White Horse, so if you need to reach me…''

She turned with a jaunty wave and started down the sidewalk toward the harbor, breathing in the scent of roses that were trailing over the tops of the garden walls lining the street.

It took only a few minutes to reach Washington Street and the little park by the harbor. Crossing it, she started up onto the causeway that traversed the narrow stretch of water separating the town of Newport from Goat Island. She could hear the sound of the bell buoys, muffled by the fog, but she couldn't see the light on Rose Island, a deserted pile of rocks in the middle of the bay.

The water was washing up against the piers beneath the causeway. When she and Ray had strolled down to the restaurant earlier, there had been a dozen or so Asian-looking people fishing over the side, but there were none now.

A sudden chill raised the gooseflesh on Kathleen's arm, and she looked about her. The fact that the bridge was deserted was no reason for alarm. Newport was perfectly safe for strolling at night.

It was just the wine...or that story Ray told her earlier. Yes, that was it. About the pirates that had been captured by a British naval vessel, back in the 1700s. The men had been carried back here to Newport, where they had been tried and found guilty. All but one of them was convicted, Ray said.

The townspeople had hanged the pirates in the typical gruesome fashion of the period and transported the bodies out to Goat Island, which was common grazing land at the time. Then the cutthroats had been buried on the island's beach, between the high- and low-tide marks...so that their souls would never rest.

Rubbing her arms to ward off the persistent chill, Kathleen reached the top of the causeway. The hotel was right at the end of the bridge, and she could see the shape of the building and the lights of the rooms beginning to appear dimly through the fog.

She saw the man suddenly emerge, walking toward her along the sidewalk from the Goat Island side. A moment of panic swept through her, but she quickly controlled herself. This is Newport, she told herself.

As he came closer, his features became clearer to her. He was tall and athletic-looking. He smiled in a friendly way, no doubt to reassure her. Actually, he was very handsome. In a dangerous way, she thought. He had the look of a pirate.

Perhaps she'd forgo the athlete and have a pirate.

As he passed her, she was considering saying something to him when she felt him grab hold of her purse.

"Hey!" was all she was able to get out as she spun around.

The blow to her head shocked her more than it hurt, and as Kathleen felt herself being toppled over the railing, she heard her silk shirt tear on something sharp as she fell.

She hit the black water with a loud slap, but she didn't feel anything. Kathleen's only sensations were the cold wetness closing over her, and the taste of salt in her mouth.

Twenty-Seven

Friday, July 2

They had plenty of time, so this morning they'd taken a circuitous route to reach the place. Coming south along Lower Thames Street with its trendy stores and restaurants and waterfront condos, they'd followed the harbor past the lighthouse and the Brown House, which had been kept by the New York Yacht Club as a place to party during the years when the America's Cup races had made Newport shine.

Out past Fort Adams and their little hideaway above the rocks. Out past the rolling horse farms and converted estates. Out past Hammersmith Farm, where Jackie Bouvier had spent her childhood summers, and where, as a young adult, the dashing war hero Jack Kennedy had come courting.

From there, they had turned toward the center of the island along winding country roads. They had seen the green fairways of the country club, but then the tall trees of the landscaped estates and the hills had obscured it. And then they had turned into the gated drive. The car had glided along the serpentine stretch of finely groomed gravel, past a grotto carefully designed to recall a shrine to some minor woodland god, past a gazebo adorned with roses just coming into bloom. Finally, they'd seen the house beyond the stretch of emerald lawns and the fountain. The turrets and spires rose high above the grounds, and the diamond-shaped panes of glass in the windows sparkled in the light of the bright midday sun.

There was so much more to see and appreciate, coming back to this place a second time.

A few minutes later, they were back in the same library. The Robert Morris flag—perhaps the oldest existing flag of the nation—sat propped up in its frame on a table beside a portable podium. Two dozen chairs, arranged in equal rows, filled the open space in the middle of the library. By the time the grandfather clock between the windows struck noon, everyone had arrived except Kathleen and Ray.

Ellie saw the auctioneer, Mr. Philips, glance with annoyance at his watch, and she forced herself to stay calm. She took Nate's arm and led him to the back row of chairs, where they sat.

"Tell me what the exact arrangements are, once we get the flag," she asked quietly.

"You and I drive it back to the hotel."

"No police? No FBI escort for security?"

"I'm it."

The government was willing to pay sixty million dollars or more for this flag, and not protect it? Ellie had no doubt about Nate's abilities, but what if some nutcase decided to...

She forced her mind to stop thinking the worst. This was their line of business—it was what they were experts at. She glanced at the door again. Still no Kathleen Rivers or Ray.

"And after that?" she asked him.

"Two paths diverged in a yellow wood..."

"We split up."

"I'm afraid so. A limo will take you back to the station in Kingston, where you catch the train to Philadelphia."

"How about you?"

"I connect with my people."

"Where?"

He took her hand and brought it to his lips. "Don't ask."

She hadn't asked about Chris. Now she couldn't ask about Nate. Ellie's mood took a nosedive. This meant that she didn't know when she'd see him again.

Robert Philips asked everyone to take their seats. They could wait no longer.

"I'll call you," Nate whispered into her ear.

Ellie wanted to believe it. She told herself she *would* believe it. She nodded.

The door of the library opened, and Ray entered. One look at him and Ellie knew something was wrong. He had not shaved, and she thought he looked as if he'd slept in the clothes he had on last night. Ellie and Nate had seen Ray and his client leaving the hotel for dinner.

His gaze darted about the room. When he saw them, he came and sat down next to Ellie.

"Have you seen Kathleen?" he asked tensely.

"No," Ellie whispered. "Not since last night. She was with you. Why?"

"She's missing."

She looked at Ray a second time, and Nate leaned forward. "What do you mean by missing?"

"Missing, gone, like I can't find her. Her own people can't contact her." A few heads turned to them. Ray lowered his voice. "Nobody knows where she is."

"Start from the beginning," Nate ordered.

"We went out for dinner last night. Afterward, I went to meet some friends at another restaurant, and she told me she was going back to the hotel."

"Did she take a cab?" Nate asked.

"No. She walked."

"Did she arrive at the hotel? Did anyone see her get back?"

Ellie thought Nate might be revealing too much by asking his questions, but Ray was too frazzled to pay any attention. The auctioneer was standing near the podium, talking to one of the potential buyers.

"I don't know. She had her key, so there was no reason for her to check in at the front desk."

"When did *you* realize she was missing?"

"I had a call waiting from her secretary when I got back to the hotel around midnight. They were trying to get hold of her, but she wasn't answering the phone in her room, or her cell phone. They assumed she'd be out with me."

The auctioneer stepped up to the podium and made a final request for people to sit down.

"I went back to her door and knocked. She didn't answer. I called her, nothing. I even walked back along the route she would have taken coming back to the hotel, but there was no sign of her."

"Did anybody check inside her room?"

"This morning. Housekeeping told me they didn't have to make her bed."

"Did you tell hotel security, or call the police?"

"Of course I did," Ray said. "Hotel security says she's not in her room. The police say they'll check around, but it's too soon to get worried. They said she's an adult, and that with no sign of foul play.''

Ray had said himself that Kathleen Rivers would be their only other real competition. That meant he'd checked the credentials of the other parties. Ellie stared at the flag on display. Wednesday night, Robert Philips had opened the glass case so that she and Nate could take a close look. To the naked eye, the weave, color, texture, stitching, the cut of the stars and fifty other things that she'd researched about this period flag looked to be correct. But this was where forgers made their living. She remembered the patches she'd seen on Teasdale's bench.

The human eye just couldn't distinguish the fake from the original. And she was no expert. No expert.

She realized that the bidding had started.

Ellie turned to Nate. ''Why me? Why did you want to work with me?''

He looked at her. ''You were in the museum that day. Your face was captured on the security camera. That was *my* reason.''

Ray got up and walked to the back of the room, running his hands anxiously through his hair. Ellie turned and watched him. His shoulders were sagging, and he looked much older.

''Another reason,'' Nate continued. ''Wilcox came up with Sister Helen's name, and she came up with yours.''

The bidding was already at twenty-five million. Ellie had not raised her hand or nodded once. She tried to stand up, but Nate put a hand on her arm.

''Where are you going?''

''I need to ask Ray if the flag's authenticity was verified yesterday.''

The bidding was at thirty million.

"Bid on it, Ellie."

She met Nate's gaze. "This flag could be a forgery."

"If it is, then someone has gone to a lot of trouble for us to have it."

"If it is, we could make no bid, walk out of here and ruin their plans."

"Or you could win it for us and we'll see what it's all about."

She thought of all those who were dead, hurt and missing.

"Are you sure?" she asked, her heart suddenly in her throat.

"Do it, Ellie." He nodded confidently.

It all came down to this. Someone had orchestrated her life for the past two weeks, bringing her to this moment. She had a chance to put an end to all of it, or she could play the game. She looked again into Nate's blue eyes.

"Forty million," Ellie said, raising her hand.

The regulars were at their places along the causeway, with their buckets of water and bait and fishing poles, when the tide turned around midafternoon. The holiday had even brought out extra men, women and children, as well, who lined the bridge leading to Goat Island and were taking their share of flounder.

The traffic coming into town was heavy. Every hotel, inn and bed-and-breakfast was booked solid for the holiday weekend. Tourists jammed the streets and the shops. Kathleen Rivers's disappearance was still just a family affair.

Many things had been pulled out of the water from that bridge, but it was a rare catch when a ten-year-old boy hooked a very expensive red handbag. His Vietnamese-born mother had to help him bring it up, and a fisherman next to them used a long-handled net to land the water-filled prize.

Half a dozen people gathered to look over the fancy, fringed bag. None of them had heard of or cared a bit about designer Carlos Falchi. They had no clue that the material was deerskin or that the seams had been whipstitched by hand. They would have been stunned to know that this waterlogged bag was worth anywhere near the eight hundred dollars Kathleen Rivers had paid for it. The name of the blond-haired woman on the driver's license meant nothing to them, either. They all recognized the presidents and founding fathers that filled the wallet, though.

Without touching the cash, the boy's mother waved down a police car crawling across the bridge.

"Look, Graham, you're too damn smart—probably for your own good. But I should have known you'd be right about this." President Kent moved the phone to his other ear and picked up a paper from his desk. "I have it right here. The ads started airing a week ago today, and our polls show eighty-two percent rise in the approval rating on the project. That's pretty much across the board. How the hell did you know?"

There was a pregnant silence at the other end of the line.

"Come on, Graham. I can hear you smirking. I made a mistake and I'm man enough to admit it. The American people want this Water for America project. Obviously, the additions to the program appeal strongly to the East Coast, as well. These numbers tell us the more we spend, the better." He lowered his voice when there was still no response. "We go back a long way. We've been friends for almost our entire careers. We both know there's no way I'd be here without your help. Let's forget all the bullshit that went on last week."

Hunt finally spoke. "Certain things are difficult to forget...or undo."

"That's a crock, Graham. What do you want me to do, kiss your ass on national TV?"

"Nothing so dramatic, Mr. President."

"Good. Then let's talk some details. I'm flying to Philadelphia tomorrow night. We're kicking off the Spirit of America celebration at noon on Sunday. I speak at one and answer questions for the press at two. I'll make the announcement then. We'll connect your project to the day's events so that the American people know that as we're celebrating our past, we're also planning for our future independence. We'll even use that line in the kickoff speech. We'll let America know I'm one hundred percent behind the project. How does that sound?"

"That could work."

"Not could work. It *will* work," Kent said with enthusiasm. "You pushed the initial bill through Congress. That was a fine job. Now, with my signature, we'll start spending money on this before the summer's out. Once Congress reconvenes, we'll hammer those additions through...election or no election. So are we together on this or not?"

Hunt's voice sounded almost weary. "Yes, Mr. President. We are."

They finished their conversation, and Kent hung up the phone. He stared thoughtfully at the papers on his desk for a moment before turning to the small group sitting in his office.

"So how did I do, gentlemen?"

Ray sat on the edge of the bed, remote in hand, his eyes riveted to the TV screen. The newscaster read her script from the monitor with a phony earnestness that made him sick.

"The body of missing Philadelphia socialite Kathleen Rivers was found by divers earlier this evening in the waters of Newport's Point Section. Rivers, well known to the art world for her charitable contributions to numerous museums, had been missing since last night. Newport police are now treating the death as a homicide, and a spokesman for the Rivers family told Eyewitness News that her third husband, Ivan Fenwick, a noted artist, is offering a reward for any information about the tragic death of his wi—"

Ray clicked off the television and sat in stunned silence, staring at the empty screen.

After all their years of marriage, Martha was accustomed to calls in the middle of the night. She stopped minding the ones that were work-related years ago. It was the FBI life.

She saw Sanford swing his legs off the bed and sit up. She couldn't make anything of what he was saying, but she knew it wasn't that whore trying to milk her husband out of more money. The way his head hung down, she knew it had to be work.

Martha had her connections. She knew about Cheri. She knew about the ones that had preceded her. Cheri. The best part of it was that she also knew he'd dumped her. She glanced at the clock on her side of the bed. It was only eleven-thirty.

They'd already had an hour of sleep. If he didn't have to drive back into Washington or to Quantico tonight, she'd seduce him again before they went back to sleep.

Martha felt her body begin to tingle just thinking about it. How many years had it been since their love life had been so good? This past week had been about the best she could remember of all the years they'd been together. And she really thought this wasn't her imagination. He thought it, too. It was amazing how exciting he could be when he was focused only on her.

She propped herself up on one elbow and rubbed his back gently while he continued to listen to someone on the phone. She could feel the tension in his muscles. She knew a good way to help him release some of it.

She pushed off the covers, unbuttoned her satin pajama top and turned on the light. She wanted him to see her every time they made love now. She wanted him to know who he was with.

Interest flashed in his eyes when he finally hung up the phone and turned around to find her waiting.

"What's wrong?" she asked, sliding her hand along his thigh.

"Nothing, babe," he said, rolling toward her. "Just a slight change of plans."

Twenty-Eight

"Ellie, come here. Hurry or you'll miss it!"

At Vic's urgent call, Ellie hastily excused herself from the customer she was talking to and ran to the back of the store. Vic stood in front of the TV with a heaping spoonful of coffee grounds suspended in midair. On the screen, the reporter had just wrapped up her report. Behind her was a composite picture of a Betsy Ross flag and the Spirit of America logo.

"What's going on?"

"You missed it. What a mess-up!" He pointed to the TV, which was going to a commercial. "They said the Smithsonian announced that they're undecided about what flag will be used for the celebration kickoff tomorrow."

"Why?" She came closer and turned down the volume.

"They said they just discovered that the flag in their possession is a fake."

Ellie tried to keep her mind clear. "Did they say that they don't have the Schuyler flag?"

"He didn't say. All they're saying is that they have

a forgery, and they can't comment on any of the details because the FBI is investigating.''

Her nagging fears about the flag were all coming true. But why hadn't they used it, anyway? Their original plan of saying this Robert Morris flag—whether it was authentic or not—had turned up would have worked out fine for the celebration. Other than Wilcox, who would have gotten close enough even to guess? Why raise a ruckus now, the day before the event?

"And you said they haven't got a flag?"

"Undecided about what to use," Vic repeated. "The White House says the last-minute discovery doesn't change anything for tomorrow, and the President is coming into Philadelphia today as planned. And a decision will be made about the flag by the end of the day.''

The phone rang and Ellie reached for the wall unit.

"I deserted a customer," she said, gesturing toward the front of the shop. Vic gave her a reassuring nod and left the room.

Ray was on the line.

"Are you watching the news?" she asked accusingly.

"I just got home." His voice sounded weak. Ellie switched off the television set.

"Please tell me that you're not calling to gloat." She didn't give him a chance to answer. "You had that appraisal done the day before, didn't you, Ray? You knew it was a fake. That was just an act about your client disappearing, wasn't it? What did she do, pack her bags and head back to Philadelphia?"

"Ellie—"

"No honor among thieves, is there? What I don't understand is how you could go to that auction and watch me pay so much for a worthless rag. How could you do that to me, Ray?''

"Kathleen didn't show up because she was already dead.''

Ray's words knocked the wind out of her sails for a minute. Ellie leaned against the wall. "What did you say?''

"Kathleen Rivers is dead. Somebody whacked her on the head and threw her body off the bridge going out to Goat Island.''

Ellie took an unsteady breath. "How do you know this?''

"They found her body late last night. I was still in Newport. It was on the late night news there. Didn't it make the news here today?''

"I don't know," she said quietly. "I'm really sorry, Ray.''

"Forget about her. I'm worried about you, baby.''

Ellie jammed her fingers into her hair. She'd been railing at him about something he knew nothing about. He didn't know the original Schuyler flag had been destroyed. He didn't know that Nate worked for the government. He didn't have any idea that Nate and the Spirit of America celebration were even connected.

"You *should* worry about me," she replied, her frustration evident in her voice. "You must think I've lost my mind.''

"No, babycakes," Ray said gently. "I don't.''

"There's an explanation for all of this," she started. "There's a lot that you don't know. And I don't know if I can explain any of it yet.''

"There's more that *you* don't know. And I think it's time I explained all of it to you.''

A few seconds went by before Ray's words pene-

trated. And then panic seized her. Nate had suspected
Ray's involvement. And where was Nate now?

"I'm coming over," she said.

"No, don't. It might not be safe."

"What's going on, Ray?" she asked worriedly.

"The way these people are doing things, I might get
knocked off before you even get here."

Ellie saw the shadow of a customer browsing toward
the back of the store. She closed the door and leaned
against it. "What people? What do you mean?"

"The people who paid me to set you up."

Her mind went blank for a second. She was not sure
if she'd heard the words correctly. "Run that by me
again?"

"You were set up from the beginning, Ellie. The
whole thing was orchestrated. I was paid. I sent you to
that museum in Ticonderoga on that specific afternoon.
I suggested to them that they connect with you through
Sister Helen. Then, when the word of the auction was
released, I had to arrange it so everything looked be-
lievable enough to you—and that included finding and
bringing along credible competition with a name and
face you might recognize. Even claiming that I'd take
care of the appraisal. My job was to make sure your
client bought that flag and paid lots of money for it."

"The other people at the auction?"

"Their people. You weren't going to lose."

"Who paid you?" she asked brokenly.

"I don't know. There never was a face. Everything
was done over the phone. I got a portion of my money
delivered in cash beforehand."

"You used me." With her back still against the
door, Ellie slid down until she was sitting on the floor.

"I'm sorry, baby. It was just business."

"I've heard that before," she said bitterly. "Why are you telling me all of this now?"

"Because this has gone beyond business. These people are killers. When I first agreed to do this, I never thought people would die. Kathleen…she…" He cleared his throat. "She was interested in the flag, but I knew she couldn't afford to go as high up as your client could go. That was why I brought her along. But the fool changed her mind as soon as she saw the flag. I…I told that to my contact when he called on Thursday. I told him things might get a little complicated, but that I still had control over everything. But then they killed her. They just eliminated her. That simple. Gone. Dead."

"So you knew Nate was undercover?"

"Of course. But I don't know how involved he is. As far as I know, he could be the one who set this whole thing up. I told you…there were no faces. That's why I'm worried about you."

Sanford Hawes glanced down at the new information that an agent handed to him.

"No, Ellie. I'm glad you called me directly. There's no reason for Sister Helen to get in the middle of this mess right now."

"I've left at least five messages on Nate's cell phone," she said. "But he hasn't returned any of them. I'm getting worried."

"Frankly, I am, too." Hawes motioned to the agent to wait. "Do you have the address where they held the auction in Newport?"

He scribbled down the information. "Hold on, Ellie." He handed the paper to the agent. "Run this address. Give me everything we have on it and on the owners."

He swung around in his chair and looked out at the Justice Department building across the street. "I'm worried about Nate, too."

"Do you have any idea where he is?" she asked. "Has anyone seen him since yesterday?"

"Nate met with our agents and the Department of the Interior personnel at the arranged location in Newport. He gave them the flag and left. No one has seen him since."

"But isn't it strange that he'd just disappear? Maybe something happened to him."

Hawes tipped back his chair. He rubbed his fingers into the ache in his neck. "I don't know if you've been listening to any news reports this morning or not, but we think Nate may have gotten himself mixed up in some funny business."

Her voice turned low. "You're talking about the Morris flag being a forgery."

"I can't talk to you about it, but I'll just say you're in the right ballpark."

"Are you accusing him of defrauding the government out of that forty million?"

"There's an investigation going on, Ellie, and I can't say anything right now. But you could really help us out by staying close to home and giving us a call if you hear anything from him."

"Mr. Hawes, you were the one who gave this assignment to Nate. There's no way he could have—"

"Actually, he volunteered." Hawes swung around to his desk. "He's been stuck behind a desk for a year, and he's been miserable. There was no one out there more qualified for this assignment than him, and Nate knew it. Ellie, I know what you're going through. I've known him for eleven years. He's been like a son to me. I'm having a difficult time dealing with evidence that keeps popping up and pointing his way.'' He took his glasses off and threw them on his desk. ''I'm flying to Philadelphia in an hour. You have my cell phone number. Call me immediately if you hear anything. He needs to know that I'm on his side. Running away won't help anything.''

Despite the angry look of the sky and the forecast of severe thunderstorms, foot traffic along Pine Street remained brisk all day. All the estimates had been right. Thousands of tourists packed the hotels, restaurants and shops of Philadelphia's Center City. The merchants loved it, the politicians were crowing about it, and the residents were feeling like French Quarter residents during Mardi Gras. Almost everything in Philadelphia was staying open far into the evening.

Ellie, of course, was ready to kick everyone out and close the shop at five. Vic, however, almost had a coronary when she started to do just that. Aside from a variety of small items, they had sold half a dozen large pieces today alone, and Brian was on the verge of selling a pair of Thomas Affleck chairs. It was easily the best day they'd had in a very successful year. With reluctance, Ellie conceded to keep the place open for two more hours, but not a minute more.

She was too wound up to take Vic's suggestion and stay up in her apartment, but she was too much on edge to deal with these high-rolling customers. With Brian and Vic working, though, they weren't short on help. Ellie was allowed to walk around the shop, as long as she didn't bite anyone.

Anything remotely resembling a ring had Ellie diving for the phone. After the third phone call, Brian forced her to carry the handset. With her cell phone in her other hand, she looked like a gunslinger...and had an attitude to match.

There were several business-related calls. Each time, she was extremely brief and a hair short of rude. Vic kept the coffee brewing. To cheer her up, Brian even made a quick run to the nearest convenience store and came back with a six-pack of chocolate milk. But Ellie was beyond help—she was way past calm. And to add to her stress, the closer she got to the hour she threatened to close the shop, the more customers came in. It seemed like there wasn't a breath of air left inside.

It was exactly six forty-five when the store phone rang again. Ellie answered it on the first ring. There was so much noise around her that she could barely hear anything on the other end.

"Don't hang up," she said into the phone. "Please don't hang up."

She threaded her way through the people to the stairs and climbed quickly to the first landing. "Can you hear me?"

There was nothing but the sound of street noises on the other end. Cars honking, people were speaking. It sounded to Ellie as if the caller was at a busy intersection. She moved up a few more steps.

"Nate?" she called.

"No, it's Chris."

"Christopher!" she repeated.

"Miss Ellie."

His voice was weak. Ellie covered her other ear to block out the noise drifting up from downstairs. "What's wrong, Chris?"

"I ran away, Miss Ellie. I'm on the street. Everything is kind of scary."

"Sweetheart, where are you?" she asked urgently.

"I don't know."

"Are you in Philadelphia?"

"Yeah, I think so." He paused. "Yeah, I am."

She forced herself to stay calm. "Listen to me, Chris. City streets aren't the safest place for somebody your age. Look around you. I want you to tell me if you see any cops."

A long pause followed and all she could hear were the sounds of traffic.

"There's a police car parked on the next block."

"Chris, I want you to go to him and ask for help."

"No." His voice broke. "I don't want to go to any cops."

"Chris—"

"Miss Ellic, please. I want to see Agent Murtaugh again. I have to talk to him. Please," he begged. "It's really, really important. I told the people I was staying with that I needed to see him, but they wouldn't get him for me."

"What's wrong, sweetheart?" she asked softly.

"I remembered this other thing that I forgot to tell him. When I was at the museum, the guy who caught me, he called this other guy on his radio. He said his name. I remember it now."

"You know the name of one of the men from the museum?"

"Yeah. I think maybe that was why they tried to kill me…and I have to tell Agent Murtaugh. He said he'd catch the bad guys, and they wouldn't come after me no more."

"Listen to me, Chris." Ellie sat down on the steps. "Do you see any taxi cabs driving around?"

There was another pause. "Yeah, lots of them."

"This is what I want you to do," she said calmly. "After you hang up the phone, you go to the curb and raise your hand for one of the cabs. Now, don't get into any other cars except a taxi. You hear me?"

"I don't have any money."

"That's okay," she said reassuringly. "When you climb inside, give them my address and tell them your mother is paying for the ride when you get to your house."

"And they'll believe me?"

"Yes. They will." She rubbed the headache at her temple. "I'll wait for you at the door."

Ellie gave Chris the street address of the shop. Her mind was mush, and her limbs were Jell-O by the time she hung up. But she forced herself to concentrate. She had to kick everyone out. She had to close the shop. She had to be ready for Christopher to arrive.

Ellie prayed she was doing the right thing.

Twenty-Nine

Like thoroughbreds breaking out of a starting gate, the thunderstorms raced shoulder to shoulder across the sunless suburbs of Philadelphia. As the customers came out the shop door into Pine Street, the lightning strikes looked like fireworks over the city, and the sheets of rain fell hard enough to churn up the Schuylkill River.

Two men sat in a gray sedan three doors down. The black man's gaze never wavered from the shop door; the other listened through a headset and watched the thinning street traffic.

The lights inside the shop dimmed. An older man and a younger woman tried to go inside, but the door was locked.

A taxi passed the car and pulled up in front of the antique shop. The black man leaned forward and with one impatient sweep wiped the steam off the inside of the windshield. Ellie Littlefield ran out the front door, followed by the two men who worked the shop with her.

Large umbrellas opened. The woman leaned inside and handed some money to the driver. The back door opened and a small figure emerged. The four figures rushed back inside the store as a group.

The cab remained in front of the store, and the couple who had tried to get inside ran from another shop's overhang and jumped into it. A moment later, the two men came out of the shop again, looked at the cab disappearing up the street, and then set off at a brisk pace in the direction of Broad Street.

As the light inside the shop went out, the black man reached inside his jacket and clicked off the safety catch on his weapon.

The ringing of the bell was persistent. By the time Ellie made it down the three flights of stairs, loud knocking had been added.

She threw the hand towel she'd been using on her wet hair onto a bench and peered out through the glass. A large man wearing a gray trench coat was waiting outside. His collar was up, covering much of his face. When he spotted her, he stopped knocking.

She motioned to the little sign hung in the window. "We're closed."

"It's me, Ellie." The man pulled the collar slightly back. He had a large square jaw, a red nose that had been broken at least once. Rain streaked his glasses, but his dark eyes were riveted to her face. "Sanford Hawes. We talked on the phone."

She must have hesitated a second, for he immediately took out a badge from inside his coat and flattened it with a huge hand against the glass.

The picture and the name matched the face. Ellie turned on the inside light and unlatched the door.

He swept in on a gust of wind and rain. She quickly closed the door behind him.

"This weather is not being too hospitable for everything that's planned for tomorrow." He shook himself like a great dog.

"It's supposed to blow over before morning," she said in a small voice.

"I sure hope so." He gave her a glimpse of his big teeth. "We meet in person at last."

She didn't move away from the door. "I wasn't expecting you here."

"I know. But I had to be in Philadelphia, and I didn't feel right about the way we left it when you called this morning." He took another step into the shop, glancing around at the place. "I had six different people wanting something all at the same time. Just too many goddamn things happening all at once. You have a nice setup here."

"Thanks."

"Nice chair," he said, gesturing toward a Crosswicks chair on a pedestal toward the back of the shop.

When she only nodded, he walked back toward it, then went as far as poking his head into the darkened back room. He stopped at the foot of the stairway. "Do you live upstairs?"

"On the top floor."

"I remember the reports saying that you also rent work space to local artists."

"There's a studio on the second floor." Ellie picked up the towel she'd dropped on the bench earlier and held it against her chest. "I'm sorry about the panic call this morning. You have enough on your plate with everything else going on."

"Has Nate called you since this morning?"

"No. No, he hasn't." She went behind the counter and turned on a desk lamp.

"Has anybody else called you?"

Ellie tidied up, putting pens that were lying around

into a wooden cup and piling up the pads of sale slips. "I run a business here. My phone rings all day."

"You're not being accused of anything, Ellie."

"Not yet," she said in a tight voice.

"You don't get it." He walked toward her. "You're one of us. We came to you for help...specifically to you. You were paid to do something for your country, and you did an excellent job." His voice was gentle. "You've done *nothing* wrong."

"Nate was assigned to this, too."

Hawes nodded. "Yes, he was. Unfortunately, he's taken off. But you haven't. You're right here. You can understand why his actions and yours are being perceived very differently by the top brass."

Ellie used the towel to wipe a spot on the counter. "To tell you the truth, I don't understand what Nate is being accused of. His assignment was to bring back the Robert Morris flag. We did that. Now, because some crook pulled a fast one, you're going to crucify the messenger?"

"Things are more complicated than that."

"They don't have to be. Job assigned, job completed," she said stubbornly. "And as far as Nate running, you and your 'top brass' might just be jumping the gun, you know. To my thinking, the fact that he's not in touch with us could only mean that he's hurt." She cleared her voice, clamping down on her emotions. "Something might have happened to him."

Hawes leaned on the counter, his dark eyes burning into her. "Ellie, Nate is being accused of masterminding this whole thing."

"He's been working for you people practically forever. Why would he do that?"

"There was an incident about a year ago where he

killed a teenager. We had him in therapy with the Bureau shrinks and moved him to a less stressful position. The fact is, Nate was scarred by that shooting. Mentally, I mean. He's become cynical. Even talked about leaving the Bureau if we didn't move him back to what he sees as a better job.'' Hawes took a deep breath. ''When I phoned him about the Schuyler flag, he'd already heard about the fire. He knew he'd get the assignment. Now we have a trail of evidence at least a mile long that makes it look like Nate's responsible for everything from destroying the Schuyler flag to rigging the final auction to routing forty million dollars to a Swiss account.''

''I don't believe it.''

''He paid your friend Ray Claiborne to con you.''

She shook her head.

''The auctioneer Philips was a fake, too. We can't find any such person. The house where the auction was held is vacant; the owners are in Europe and don't know anything about it. Nate set you up all the way.''

''I don't believe any of it.''

''Neither do I.''

His words knocked the wind out of her. She looked at him suspiciously. ''You don't?''

''What I *do* believe is that someone is trying to set him up. And that's the reason for why I'm here. We need to move fast. Whoever these people are who are behind this are operating in a search-and-destruct mode.''

Ellie rubbed her cold arms. ''Why? What do they want?''

''I don't have all the answers. But think about it. If you wanted to hang this on Nate, what would you do? You need to eliminate the key witnesses who can clear

Nate. The ones who are still alive. If we can protect them, we might have a chance.''

"Who do you mean?"

Hawes glanced at the window when a car came to a stop in the middle of Pine Street. The rain was pounding on the roof and hood of the car. The couple inside pointed at something in Ellie's window display. "Goddamn tourists. Can you turn off the light?"

She was reluctant, but she turned off the desk lamp. Only the lights in the display window remained lit.

"Who could help Nate?" she pressed.

"One of them is this Ticonderoga cop, Tom McGill, who was in ICU until Monday…when he disappeared." He watched the car outside drive away.

"What do you mean, he disappeared?"

"The hospital claims there was a legit patient transfer to another facility, but now there is no sign of McGill. All the paperwork has since disappeared, too. The main thing is that we can't find McGill anywhere. He could be dead, but I'm hopeful that he's out there, alive."

"How can McGill help Nate?"

"Two people run the guy down. My hope is that maybe he can identify them. Maybe they are even the same ones who destroyed the flag. I know this is tenuous, but from the beginning that cop was keen on helping Nate and working with him. So I figure something might be going on there. There has to be a connection. Otherwise, he wouldn't be missing, too."

"That could be read another way," she said. "Somebody could insinuate that McGill might have been an accomplice rather than a bystander."

"Better reason to find him and clear the air," he challenged. "Then there's the kid."

"Christopher Weaver."

Hawes leaned over the counter toward Ellie. "The kid saw it happen. He can identify the inside man. He heard the nickname of the guy on the radio. He can totally clear Nate, which puts him totally at risk. Now no one but Murtaugh knows where Chris is hidden. Unless you know."

She shook her head. "If Nate is not hurt, and he thinks Christopher can help him, he'd bring him forward himself."

"But what if you're right? What if Nate *is* hurt? What happens if these other guys get to the kid first?" His giant paw trapped Ellie's hand on the counter. "You can help me find him, Ellie. I say this for both of their sakes. The people behind this conspiracy are dangerous. This is the time for you to help both of them."

Ellie took back her hand. "Nate didn't tell me where he was taking him."

"Chris trusts you. He's not going to stay with strangers for too long. He'll run away and come to you. But the guys behind the conspiracy know that, too. They'll be waiting for him right outside that door."

She stepped back from the counter.

"How are you going to stop them, Ellie? Who's going to protect you?" he asked, his voice hard. "One bullet will finish the kid. They don't even have to come inside. He'll step in front of a window, and he'll be dead before he hits the floor. Chris will be dead, and they'll be gone. Nate will never have a chance."

She shook her head and walked away from him. "You can't protect him any better."

"Of course I can, Ellie. We've got the organization

and the resources to do it. Chris will make it with me. He hasn't got a chance with you.''

Outside, the street lit up like midday for an instant, and a second later, the thunder exploded, shaking the building and rattling the glass. When the lights flickered momentarily, Ellie moved to the bottom of the stairs.

''Is he here?'' Hawes followed her.

Ellie turned around, blocking his path. ''Who?''

''We don't have time for games,'' he barked. ''If the kid's here, they could have seen him come in. They could come in here after him anytime. We have to get him out of this place.''

''He's here because he trusts me,'' Ellie replied, holding her ground. ''I can't and I won't hand him over unless he's willing to go.''

Another peal of thunder rolled through the building. The lights in the front of the shop flickered again.

''Take me up. Let me talk to him. I won't force him to do anything he doesn't want to do.''

The wind outside had picked up. Sheets of rain slapped at the front windows of the store. Ellie looked up the dark stairs. The lights in the studio on the second floor were off, and she hadn't turned on any coming down the stairs, either.

''I don't want you to scare him.''

''I won't. I have grandchildren Chris's age. I'll treat him like one of my own.''

She took the first step, and then slowly she took the second. He followed.

''Christopher isn't the only one who can help clear Nate,'' she said.

''Without knowing if McGill is still alive, the boy is the best witness in Nate's corner.''

"No. I am." She continued up the stairs. "I was with him every step of the way. I can be used as an alibi for each incident."

"When this whole thing goes to trial, I'm sure his lawyer would want you as a witness."

"I don't believe they have enough to even arrest Nate." Ellie glanced over her shoulder at him on the first landing.

"Unfortunately, there's enough."

"Let's start from the beginning. You said yourself, the day that the Schuyler flag was destroyed in Ticonderoga, Nate was in New York. Now, between the agents in his group and the arrangements that had to be made to get him up there, I don't believe it would be too difficult to prove that he was not in the museum at the time of the fire."

"You don't have to be at a particular place to commit a crime. Nobody thinks he did this single-handedly."

"My mistake. He had help." She started up again. "In that case, then Dr. Wilcox at the Smithsonian must be in on it, too, since he was the one who brought Sister Helen into it. And, of course, Sister Helen must be an accomplice, because she gave you my name. Of course, with my criminal record, I'd be a shoo-in. Which brings us to my father, since he was the first one to suggest coming up with a substitute to carry everyone through the Fourth of July date. It's so convenient to deal with a bunch of ex-criminals, isn't it?" She stopped on one of the steps and glared at him. "How am I doing?"

"You're talking a lot, but you haven't said one thing that proves Murtaugh's innocence."

"I'll try to do better, then." She turned her back and

started up the stairs again. "Nate, the criminal mastermind, wants to pocket forty million dollars of the government's money. So, rather than sitting tight and waiting for me to give him the date of this bogus auction—which he himself has arranged—he almost gets himself killed going to see the first forger."

"An accident. Totally coincidental."

"So you say." She shook her head. "Anyway, now we have a semiretired antique dealer in Saratoga who must be part of the conspiracy, too, since he's the one who comes up with the name of Teasdale. But again, we get there and the man is dead."

"Nate had to kill him. Teasdale had made up the phony Morris flag that was auctioned off in Newport. Covering his tracks."

"Very thorough of him." On the landing by her apartment, she turned to Hawes. "I just can't figure why Nate would be so careless as to leave such obvious evidence as his cell phone number on a piece of paper in Teasdale's shop...especially since he remembers giving the same piece of paper to McGill the first time he met him. And Tom McGill says he had it in his pocket the night he was run down. More strange, how exactly did Nate arrange to go to Teasdale's house and kill him Saturday morning while he was on the road with me from Philadelphia?"

"He had help."

"How could I forget? Accomplices, a forty-million-dollar motive, Swiss bank accounts and a disappearing act. Never mind the fact that he could have sold the flag to Kathleen Rivers for at least that much...oh, I forgot. Nate was so unbalanced from that shooting that he decided to kill the socialite instead of profiting from her desire to have the flag." She walked inside her apartment. The place was dark.

"Your flippant attempt at wit won't help him, El-lie."

"Well, I fell in with a bad crowd growing up." She stopped and looked at him standing in the apartment door. "But, you know, the part of it that makes no sense at all is, if this whole thing was about money, then why was there some kind of explosive woven into that phony flag? Some high-tech explosive that wouldn't get picked up in a routine security check?"

"So you *have* talked to Nate since he left you in Newport."

"That's not an answer to my question."

"I don't know. You tell me."

"They wanted to kill somebody else." She crossed the room to the kitchenette and turned on a light above the stove.

"Maybe Nate just wanted to destroy this flag the way he did the Schuyler flag. Covering his tracks again."

"No. The way Chris described the first one, he could see some gadget on the frame of the Schuyler flag. That was when that bogus museum guard grabbed him." She switched on the light next to a love seat. "And he said when the guy radioed in, he talked to somebody named Gatz. Now, how strange that you knew he heard the nickname of the second man...because Chris didn't tell that to anyone until he talked to me on the phone tonight."

When she turned, Hawes was standing six feet from her with his gun pointed at the center of her chest.

"Where's the kid?"

Thirty

"Tell him to come out."

Ellie stared at the man's stony face. "Did you really think you could get away with it? Killing the President?"

"Get away with it? That depends on Nate. If he stays out of sight much longer, we'll hang that on him for sure."

"Just who are the 'we' you're talking about, Hawes?" Nate stood in the doorway to her bedroom, his own weapon aimed at the other man.

"You know me, Nate. I never lost touch with this part of the job. You make a move, and she's dead."

"Let me guess," Nate continued. "That would be you, Wilcox and someone else. Someone with both money *and* power. Someone who thinks he's untouchable, whatever the outcome of this little charade."

"Call the kid out, Nate. I'm losing patience."

"And what are your plans for the evening, Hawes? A mass execution for some light entertainment? Or are we going for spectacle and blowing up the block with another gas leak?"

"You're blowing your chance of saving this kid's life."

"Christopher is only eight years old," Nate said calmly. "But he's got more good sense when it comes to who he should trust than I've ever had. That kid knows his life wouldn't last five minutes in your hands. He's also smart enough not to put all his eggs in one basket. Ellie and I aren't the only ones he told about the man called Gatz. But once I heard the name, it all came together. Those two guys who are gunning for the kid and running down cops knew you from the old days. There are still people around who call you Gatz. Short for Gatsby, wasn't it, Sanford? Well, the word is out now."

"You're lying."

"Believe what you want. But just so you know, the shit is running downhill, and you're standing at the bottom of it. In the past twelve hours, we've been digging through your finances, and we know that Martha's money ran out a long time ago. The big question is how you've been able to afford the life you've been living, on an assistant director's salary."

"That's enough."

"And to make matters worse for you, as soon as Wilcox found out that we discovered the explosives in the flag, he pointed his finger right at you."

Behind Hawes, a black man wearing a very wet sport coat moved into the doorway with his gun drawn. Ellie knew him now. Nate had introduced her this morning to Mark Carpenter, one of the agents from his own group in New York. Outside the glass door leading to her balcony, the rain had eased a little, though the thunder and lightning was continuing unabated.

"The first thing Wilcox said was that his only point of contact was you. And he's accusing you of blackmailing him and then recruiting him for this job. He even said you're the mastermind behind an assassination attempt. Of course, that guy is so scared right now, he'd say you were Vladimir Putin's twin brother if he thought it would help him.''

Hawes's weapon was still pointed at her heart. Ellie took strength from Nate's calm words and his confident stance, but she tried edging a little to the side, anyway.

"Don't move," Hawes growled. "This is bullshit, Murtaugh. If you know so much, why wasn't I arrested before coming in here?''

"We had to get you to show yourself, but we also wanted to give you a chance," Nate said quietly. "You're the only person who can incriminate the one behind it all. You weren't arrested earlier because we didn't want them to shut you up. You and I both know how it works. You would have been dead before we got you anywhere near a police station. We set this up, Sanford, to offer you a deal.''

After a moment, Hawes's gaze drifted away from Ellie for the first time. The muzzle of the pistol remained pointed at her chest. His other hand went under his coat, and she heard a single clicking sound. She realized that if it was a wire, then that meant there were others close by.

"What kind of a deal?"

"Help us take Graham Hunt down. Testify against him and you could walk away. I'm not just talking about a reduced sentence. I'm talking immunity. That's never even been considered in a situation like this.''

She moved slightly as Hawes lowered his gun a couple of inches, but suddenly the glass in the door behind her shattered.

Ellie felt as if she'd been hit hard with a red-hot poker, and the blow knocked her to the floor. Carpenter raced past her from the doorway with another agent on his heels. In spite of his bad knee, Nate was on the balcony ahead of the others.

Her arm was throbbing, and she knew that something had hit her, but Ellie's gaze didn't move from what she could see of Nate's back. She'd been losing her mind with worry during the hours following their separation in Newport. He'd hinted to her that different levels of investigation were in progress. After that, though, she hadn't heard from him at all until this morning, after she'd gotten off the phone with Hawes.

Her home and business phones were being monitored by Hawes's men, but instead of disturbing the unauthorized wiretap, Nate had called her through Vic's cell phone. They had met an hour later by the art museum. That was when she'd been introduced to Agent Carpenter. That was when Nate had told her about tonight's plan.

Hawes was down, and Ellie could see blood pooling quickly under him. Sirens erupted from the street, and the cry of the storm mixed with the sounds of shouting and bullhorns. The female agent who had arrived in the cab, impersonating Chris, came back from the balcony and ran across to Hawes, securing his weapon. Ellie managed to move to the side of the wounded man, as well.

There were shouts that the shots had come from the building across the backyard. The agent next to her was working frantically to slow the bleeding from Hawes's chest and back.

Ellie looked at the man's pale face. She removed the bent glasses that were sitting crooked across his nose. His lips moved, but he was having difficulty getting the words out.

The agent fired instructions into her radio set. "Get those EMTs up here *now,* or we're going to lose him."

Ellie watched his fingers tap helplessly on the wood floor. She reached out and took hold of his hand.

"Martha," he whispered, closing his eyes.

He knew how many square tiles covered the floor, and where the chrome-and-fabric chairs had chafed marks into the paint on the walls. Nate knew this waiting room better than he wanted to. He'd been here for more than two hours, and the news coming out of surgery was not too encouraging.

While they operated on Hawes, Mark Carpenter was Nate's only means of contact with the cleanup at the house. Lou had been keeping him informed about Ellie, who was being patched up down in the ER. One of the bullets intended for Hawes had cut through Ellie's upper arm. Nate had been down in the emergency room with her, but she'd sent him back here, promising to call as soon as the doctor was done with her.

The thought of how close she'd come to being seriously injured...or killed...was driving Nate crazy. He would always regret his lunacy in accepting her offer to help, in actually placing her life at risk. He'd knowingly put her at the killing end of Hawes's pistol.

But they'd come so close. They still were so close to nailing Graham Hunt. Sanford had to pull through, though.

It had been a winding road that led Nate from the Schuyler flag business to Hunt and the plan to kill the President. Even though no group was taking credit, laying the blame for the fire at Ticonderoga on terrorists was not completely unreasonable until the explosion took out Theo Atwood. After that, with each coincidence, Nate had become more certain that something was beginning to smell very bad. Then, after talking to Tom McGill last Monday, he became certain of a conspiracy. For what purpose, though, he still hadn't been able to guess.

He didn't think Chief Buckley was knowingly a part of it. He was too insignificant to be anything but a pawn. Wilcox, on the other hand, was a prime candidate for involvement. A background check into his past showed a few gray areas, where some questionable purchases and losses of Smithsonian artifacts had occurred during his watch. He lived beyond his means, and if he was involved with the loss of artifacts, then he was a candidate for blackmail. But he still wasn't strong enough or knowledgeable enough to organize such a large-scale operation.

But as the days passed, it was becoming apparent that this scheme had been laid out and arranged long before the fire in Ticonderoga.

Sanford Hawes had been the surprise, and a painful one for Nate. Christopher had been the one to link Hawes to the destruction of the flag. Last Monday, when Ellie and Nate returned from New York, Chris had told him about the man at the other end of the walkie-talkie…a man the fake security guard had called Gatz.

Nate had made the connection immediately, but accusing one's superior, based on an eight-year-old kid's statement, was a bumpy road. Nonetheless, keeping Chris tucked away and safe, and making sure that the lines of communication with Sanford stayed open, they'd started digging into Hawes's private life.

The assistant director's financial burdens offered the motive, and his decision to allow Wilcox to bring in former criminals to acquire the flag was questionable by Bureau standards. Going around Hawes to the Bureau's director with the plan to flush out the conspiracy, Nate had received full cooperation. From the very top, the shared goal had been to find out who was involved. The decision had been made to let the plot unfold with the hope of catching even bigger fish.

Prior to that, Nate had gotten Mark Carpenter and the other agents from his New York group involved. They'd moved Tom McGill to a safe hospital. They also were the ones who took Chris into safekeeping after he was moved from Sister Helen's convent. The murder of Kathleen Rivers could not have been anticipated, though Nate regretted it bitterly.

The moment Nate had the flag, the pieces of the puzzle had fallen into place. It was clear that Hawes and the others wanted this particular flag used in the Spirit of America celebration. Taking no chances as to what might be the reason, the Bureau lab people went over it with a fine-toothed comb.

An explosive material woven into the fabric to which the flag had been mounted within the frame was immediately detected by the munitions experts. The explosive would be detonated by laser and the glass frame would have provided the pressure to make the explosion deadly for anyone standing in front of the flag. Realizing that the President had been the target, the FBI had called the White House.

President Kent himself pointed to Graham Hunt as the most likely candidate for funding and masterminding the assassination plot. At Nate's suggestion, they'd even tried to throw a monkey wrench into Hunt's plans with a phone call from the President, notifying the businessman of his change of heart regarding the Water for America program. But there was still no proof.

They had to find someone who was willing to cooperate.

With the explosives neutralized, Nate had sent the flag on to Wilcox. When the artifacts director immediately "discovered" that the flag was a fake, they knew that Hawes and Wilcox had been advised by Graham Hunt of the change in plan. Now Hawes was directing an investigation that attempted to incriminate Nate for everything.

After taking Wilcox into custody and questioning him, it was clear that Hawes was the direct link to Graham Hunt. Ellie had suggested playing her part in the dangerous cat-and-mouse game. As they'd already guessed, her apartment and phone had been tapped by Hawes's people for some time.

This was when Christopher's role became critical. With agents accompanying him, the eight-year-old had called Ellie's shop from a pay phone. The boy had played his part flawlessly. From that point on, Chris had been taken to safety, and a female agent had taken his place in the cab going to Pine Street.

Nate would never have come even this close if it weren't for Ellie and Chris.

The elevator doors opened and Ellie stepped out. Her left arm was bandaged from her elbow to the shoulder, and she looked weary. He went to her.

"Anything?" she asked as he took her into his arms.

Nate shook his head, taking comfort in just holding her. "How's the arm?"

"They wanted to amputate, but I wouldn't let them."

"That's my girl." He walked her to a bench in a corner and they both sat down. "Where's your father?"

"He went to phone Sister Helen and Vic. Did you let Chris know that everything is okay?"

Nate smiled thinly. "The kid was really excited about being included like this. His only complaint was that we didn't bring him back to your place in the cab. With Hawes in custody, maybe we can move him back to Sister Helen's by the end of next week."

"I'm sure everyone would like that. What's the news from the shop?"

"Two people on the top floor of the building across from you. Empty because of renovations, I'm told. My guess is their instructions were to kill Hawes if it looked that he might fail. When he shut off his transmitter to talk about a deal, they decided to take him out."

She shivered. "Where are they now?"

"They made a run for it, but we had the neighborhood swarming with agents and cops. The two tried to shoot their way out, but they didn't make it." Nate rubbed Ellie's back and gathered her closer to his side. "Hawes is our last chance. If he doesn't live, this whole assignment was a failure."

"No, it wasn't," she quietly corrected him. "Think about it. You defused a triple threat. You saved Chris's life, preserved a moment of national unity and you stopped a presidential assassination. Besides, there's always Wilcox."

"Sanford was the only one Hunt ever dealt with. Wilcox can't help us." Nate rubbed his chin against her silky hair. He inhaled her scent. Life was just more bearable with Ellie at his side.

"Maybe I can get Ray to think a little harder. Maybe there's something else about his payoff that could somehow connect it to Graham Hunt."

"Sure. We've got to pursue every angle we have."

"Just tell me what to do, and I'll be right there with you."

"My fearless little detective." Nate looked into her upturned face and kissed her.

"What was that for?" she asked with a smile.

"Just a reminder of how much I love you."

Ellie wrapped her good arm around him, and she kissed him in return.

"And that?" he asked.

"A reminder of how much I love you back."

Nate looked into her dark eyes and felt himself overcome with a dozen different emotions. "I know what I was missing in my life. I also know what I want for always. That's you. Whatever I have to do, I'll do. We'll make it work for us, Ellie."

She blinked back tears and nestled her face against his neck. "We'll make it work."

Minutes later, Nate saw one of the doctors who'd been working on Hawes coming toward them. He stood up. From the bend of the shoulders and the look in the man's eyes, though, Nate didn't even need to hear the words.

Martha hated driving in the dark or in bad weather, but after Nate's call, she had to get to Philadelphia. So she drove her Lincoln up I-95 through occasional squalls, contending the whole way with the glare of the trucks and the black glaze of water on the road. It would have taken longer to catch a flight. The trains were stalled due to flooding on the tracks south of Philadelphia. But she had to get there.

"There has been a shooting, Martha. Sanford is in critical condition."

Critical. Sanford is in critical condition. The rest of Nate's words were a blur. In fact, an hour later, driving

like a madwoman, she had to call Nate on the cell
phone to ask again the hospital's name and address.

There had been a few years in their marriage, while
he'd been working in the field, that whenever the phone
rang she expected to get this call. There had been other
times, as recent as a few weeks ago, when his selfish-
ness and womanizing had made her wish she would
get this call.

But why now?

Weaving through traffic for three hours and fighting
the rain and tears, Martha wanted to think of their good
times, though even now it was difficult. At the beginning, he'd been a good husband whenever he'd been
forced, and a good father when his arm had been
twisted. But he'd been a doting grandfather without any
pressure, and now he was coming back to her.

After years of marriage, Martha felt that, as much as
he was trying to change, it was the change in her that
had made their relationship better. She'd learned to
fight for what she wanted. And all she wanted was
Sanford.

By the time she arrived in Philadelphia around midnight, the storm had passed. But between the narrow
one-way streets, the dark and the crowds of people still
milling around, she had a difficult time paying attention
to the car's navigation system.

She was somewhere in the proximity of Independence Hall when she finally pulled over to check the
directions. Her cell phone's ring made her break out
into a cold sweat. She remembered giving it to Nate
when they'd talked last.

"Where are you, Martha?"

"Philadelphia."

"Where? I'll come and get you."

"Philadelphia."

"Martha, we need to talk," he said gently.

Philadelphia! Philadelphia! The word echoed again and again in her head.

She knew what Nate wanted to say to her. She remembered Sanford telling her how difficult it was to relay bad news to families.

She was too late. She'd gotten here too late. A sob escaped her, and he must have heard it on the other end.

"Please, Martha. Let me come and get you."

"No," she said brokenly. "I'll see you there."

She disconnected the phone and stared straight ahead.

Sanford was dead.

Strangely, the knot grew large in her throat, but the tears stopped. She remembered something from this morning—the way Sanford had held her before he'd left. The pep talk about her intelligence and strength. About the importance of pulling the family together in hard times. She didn't know what he was talking about.

Martha yanked open her pocketbook and took out the sealed letter he'd stuffed there that morning.

"If something happens to me before I get back from Philadelphia, give this to Nate," he'd said. "He'll know what to do with it."

She stared at her husband's handwriting. *Nathaniel Murtaugh.*

Martha gunned the Lincoln into traffic like a woman possessed. Sanford knew something was going to happen to him today.

He'd planned his revenge.

Thirty-One

Ellie turned up the volume of the television set in her father's apartment as she sat down between Helen and Lou on the small sofa.

"Today, on this historic day, we as a country pause to remember the courage, the struggles, the sacrifices and the victories of our ancestors. On this day, however, we must also remember that when those thirteen unhappy colonies declared their independence, the nation that they began was not immediately formed without disagreement. No, indeed. Even as the battle raged in the cities and in the fields of America, each former colony did so with its own needs in mind. Each growing city had the interests of its own citizens in mind. Indeed, each citizen had his own ideas of what constituted these inalienable rights of life and liberty and pursuit of happiness. Nonetheless, they overcame tyranny from abroad, and they overcame division from within."

The long applause of the audience to the start of President Kent's speech offered another opportunity to the news anchor to refer to the smaller box in the lower corner of the screen. A news helicopter camera was capturing the scene of billionaire Graham Hunt—long-time supporter of the President and the driving force behind the Water for America project—being taken out of his mansion in handcuffs by scores of FBI agents and Justice Department officials.

"I saw that George Street fellow on a talk show this morning saying that the President would be signing the Water for America bill, after all," Lou said.

"Good-looking young man," Sister Helen commented, shushing them as the President continued.

"We have grown great in the last two centuries. We have grown rich, and we have grown strong. And now we face difficult times. And these *are* difficult times, make no mistake. But the demonstrations across the globe, the concerted effort of so many, in so many parts of the world, to show their discontent with our American policy of strength over terrorism, will not deter us. We believe in peace and prosperity. They are the hand-maidens of liberty. It is what America truly means. After all, how many of those who proclaim their hatred of us would not trade places with any of us today? Here in America, we are living the experiment that began in 1776. And as Jefferson said, 'the God who gave us life, gave us liberty at the same time.' And life and liberty are not the domain of America alone. Life and liberty belong to all who walk on this planet."

Another wave of applause erupted from the audience. To the loud complaints of the people gathered in the room, Ellie flipped through the channels on the TV to see if she could get more news of the arrest. But all the stations were covering the events in Philadelphia.

"Nate said he'd call you as soon as he's done there," Helen said, wrestling the remote out of Ellie's hand and changing the channel back.

"If you were so hot on hearing Kent talk," Lou grouched at the nun, siding with Ellie, "why didn't you use the tickets Nate gave us?"

"Because it's a lot more fun to stay here and torment you. Now shush!" she retorted, turning up the volume.

"From the tangled threads of contention two centuries ago, our ancestors wove the fabric of this nation. From partisan feuding, our ancestors wove a cloth representative of unity, of strength, of diversity. From the fraying knots of tyranny and slavery, our ancestors wove a flag that would wave over a society of tolerance, of democracy, of liberty. That flag has been a symbol of a national strength that has shaken the globe for more than two centuries."

"What the hell is going on?" Lou leaned forward toward the television screen. "That's an old Betsy Ross flag. Is that thing a fake?"

"No, that's the real Robert Morris flag," Ellie said with a smile. "With all the hoopla in the news the past couple of days, the true owner—who, by the way, has no desire to sell it and knew nothing of all the rumors of auction—decided to come forward and loan the flag to the government for the celebration."

Everyone quieted down again as President Kent continued.

"Now is the time for us to use the same creative, determined action that our ancestors used to weave this great nation. Our task, however, is to bring their dream to those who now envy us. We must show those who say they hate us that we do not hate them. We must see to the needs of poorer nations. We must improve the lot of those who lack a sound education. We must build a relationship with our global partners—and we must all be global partners—so that we might transcend our differences. And we, here in America, must show the world that we are unified in this effort.''

At the roar of applause, the news anchor reported that the Attorney General had just told reporters that the President would be making a statement regarding the arrest of Graham Hunt at the news conference this afternoon.

''For years, historians bickered and feuded over the legend of Betsy Ross and our first flag. As we *now* know, in Philadelphia in the year 1777, George Washington approached a widowed seamstress and asked her to sew a flag that he had helped to design. That flag flew over his troops when the British surrendered at Yorktown. That flag was given to Robert Morris after the revolution. Today, you see that same flag hanging proudly behind me.

''This flag, wrought by the hands of a humble Philadelphia seamstress, is the centerpiece for a month-long celebration of unity. What we are beginning today in Philadelphia, we shall carry across this nation and beyond the seas. This symbol of freedom, made of cloth woven so long ago from tangled threads of discontent, will mean something new to those citizens of countries all over the world. Those who see it will know that the life and the liberty and the pursuit of happiness that belong to every American can belong to them, as well.

''This is our promise. This is our vow. Let the celebrations begin. God bless you all.''

''Good speech,'' Helen commented.

Lou looked at his daughter. ''Who owns the flag?''

''Some Saudi prince living in L.A.,'' Ellie answered, getting up from the couch.

Epilogue

Saratoga Springs, New York
One month later

The huge tent provided shade, and a gentle breeze kept the air moving for the crowd of two hundred or so people who had gathered for the scaled-down Saratoga version of the *Antique Road Show*. The grassy area behind the Murtaugh homestead was the perfect setting for the Animals for Seniors fund-raiser, and Karen Murtaugh could hardly restrain her delight at the turnout. With the money they had taken in for admission into the tent, they'd already raised enough to make a good start toward providing pets for elderly members of the community. And the refreshment tables and raffles were expected to bring in double the admission money. The extra funds were targeted for a new seniors' center that was being built.

At one of the six tables reserved for the antique authorities, Ellie sat with the family golden retriever at her feet and a line of attendees stretching out in front of her. Her friend John Dubin sat at another table, and four other local antique experts manned the other tables. Above each table, a sign had been hung, indicating the areas of expertise of that particular professional.

The show had only been going for a couple of hours, but the place was positively buzzing with the voices of people who possessed treasures beyond their dreams and those who had surprises of the other kind. Overall, though, everyone was having a wonderful time.

Nate handed a cup of coffee to Ted, and both men watched as Bill Murtaugh introduced Lou around to friends.

"Thanks for bringing Lou up today. Ellie was really surprised and delighted to see all of you."

"Thanks for the invite. Chris and I both needed to get away from the city, too." Ted looked at the eight-year-old, busily refilling the dogs' water dishes at one end of the tent. "I just hope that he doesn't have too much of a good time. I don't want him to change his mind about adopting me."

Nate smiled. "I don't think there's any chance of that. How's the paperwork going?"

"*Going* and *slow* are the best words to describe it."

"You're way too polite."

"Actually, there are other words, but I can't use them in public. We're moving in the right direction, though. And because the parents have agreed to my offer, the lawyers tell me that Chris can live with me and go to school in Philadelphia this coming fall, even if all the paperwork isn't finalized yet."

"I'm glad."

In the end, Chris's testimony wouldn't be needed for the trial. Sanford had left behind enough specifics in his letter to bury Graham Hunt. Nate had waited until everything had been pulled together into an airtight package for the federal prosecutors before giving his notice. To celebrate the occasion and to help his mother set up, he and Ellie had come up three days ago.

"So how's the job search going for you?" Ted asked.

"I'm going to practice law in Philadelphia."

"No kidding?" He slapped him on the back.

"Heck, I figured I must have liked it at one time. That's why I went to school for it." Nate shrugged. "I thought I'd try it for a while. If I don't like it, then I can always become a handyman for Ellie."

"Vic would love it."

Nate punched Ted in the arm, causing a little of his coffee to spill on the grass. "And here I thought I liked you."

"But you do."

Ted's laughter followed Nate as he moved under the tent and threaded his way through the crowd toward the dark-haired beauty wearing the billowy white antique dress. With its laces, hooks and eyes and everything else, Nate was certain that those dresses were devised to drive an impatient man out of his mind.

And he was getting impatient. Three days of separate bedrooms. Three days of stealing kisses in the hallways. Three days of not even being able to steal her away to the swimming hole.

A few steps away from her, Nate leaned a hip against an antique table and watched Ellie as she patiently explained to their local priest, Father Bob, how to take care of his collection of rare books.

"You have to move the bookcase away from the radiator. Overheating dries out a book. It makes it shrink. The leather and cloth bindings crack, and the book literally falls apart. Direct light can...can..." Ellie saw Nate watching and smiled.

"Excuse me, fella." The priest frowned at him. "Are you bothering Ellie?"

Nate shook his head innocently but didn't move.

"Sunlight fades the dyes," she continued. "Cool basements, so long as they're dry, are the best places for your books."

The priest gathered his three volumes. "I have one other thing you should look at."

He started searching his pockets. Though only one item was to be appraised at a time, none of the people in line complained that the priest was not following the rules. Father Bob finally came up with a small box that he placed before Ellie. She opened it and stared for a few long seconds.

"A step-cut diamond. This is absolutely stunning." She had a hard time tearing her gaze away from it, but finally she looked up. "But I'm not the best person to appraise this ring, Father. At the end of this row, there's a lady who's an expert in nineteenth-century jewelry."

"Which row?"

"The same as this one." She pointed toward the table.

Father Bob shook his head. "I don't see her."

Ellie motioned to Nate, and he approached. "Can you please take Father Bob to the first table?"

"Where's the first table?"

She gaped at him. "You put up the numbers."

"Someone must have mixed them up."

"Rita. Her name is Rita," she said quietly to him. "She appraises jewelry, and she's sitting at the far end of the tent."

"I don't see her."

Ellie shook her head at him and made a polite excuse

to the people in line. "I'll be back in a minute, folks. Come with me, Father, I'll show you the way myself."

With the ring box in hand, she started across.

"Father Bob wants to know how you like the ring," Nate asked when they were not a dozen steps away from her table.

"It's elegant. Absolutely beautiful."

"Father Bob wants to know if it fits."

Ellie came to a dead stop and turned slowly around. Nate saw her beautiful face turn a shade of pink when she realized that the priest wasn't following them.

She smiled up into his face. "What are you doing, Nate Murtaugh?"

"Proposing?" He took her free hand and placed a kiss on her palm. "I love you, Ellie. Will you marry me?"

All activity in the tent stopped at once and, though Ellie was not even aware of them, two hundred people stood holding their breath, waiting.

Authors' Note

We hope you enjoyed *Triple Threat*.

One of the great joys of writing novels lies in creating fictional worlds that come alive for our readers. We love receiving letters and e-mails from people all over the world who ask us about the characters who "live" in our books. As we often do, we also love bringing back individuals from our earlier books. For those of you who read about Ted Hardy's trials in *Twice Burned,* and those of you who wanted to know if Ted was going to be okay, we hope you enjoyed the glimpse into his recovery that we provided in *Triple Threat*.

For anyone planning to visit Philadelphia anytime soon, don't forget to stop by and see Vic. The antique shops along Pine Street and on the adjoining streets are a delight...as are the restaurants throughout the city. Most important, though, be sure to stop by the Betsy Ross House on Arch Street.

As always, we are so grateful to those of you who continue to read our Jan Coffey and May McGoldrick books. We love you for your kindness and support.

And of course, we'd like to thank our sons for their

love, patience and sense of humor. We love you more than life itself.

Please feel free to write to us at:

Jan Coffey
c/o Nikoo & Jim McGoldrick
P.O. Box 665
Watertown, CT 06795
or
McGoldMay@aol.com
www.JanCoffey.com

Jan Coffey

66919	TWICE BURNED	___ $6.50 U.S.	___ $7.99 CAN.
66859	TRUST ME ONCE	___ $5.99 U.S.	___ $6.99 CAN.

(limited quantities available)

TOTAL AMOUNT	$_____
POSTAGE & HANDLING	$_____
($1.00 for one book; 50¢ for each additional)	
APPLICABLE TAXES*	$_____
TOTAL PAYABLE	$_____

(check or money order—please do not send cash)

To order, complete this form and send it, along with a check or money order for the total above, payable to MIRA Books®, to: **In the U.S.:** 3010 Walden Avenue, P.O. Box 9077, Buffalo, NY 14269-9077; **In Canada:** P.O. Box 636, Fort Erie, Ontario L2A 5X3.

Name:_____

Address:_____ City:_____

State/Prov.:_____ Zip/Postal Code:_____

Account Number (if applicable):_____

075 CSAS

*New York residents remit applicable sales taxes.
Canadian residents remit applicable GST and provincial taxes.

MIRA®

MJC0703BL